A Little Rebellion

CRIMSON WORLDS III

Jay Allan

system 7
publishing

Crimson Worlds Series

Marines (Crimson Worlds I)

The Cost of Victory (Crimson Worlds II)

A Little Rebellion (Crimson Worlds III)

The First Imperium (Crimson Worlds IV)
(March 2013)

The Line Must Hold (Crimson Worlds V)
(July 2013)

www.crimsonworlds.com

A Little Rebellion

A Little Rebellion is a work of fiction. All names, characters, incidents, and locations are fictitious. Any resemblance to actual persons, living or dead, events or places is entirely coincidental.

ISBN: 978-0615738154

I hold it that a little rebellion now and then is a good thing, and as necessary in the political world as storms in the physical.

- Thomas Jefferson

Chapter 1

Community Center
Village of Concordia
Arcadia – Wolf 359 III

"Things are even worse on Columbia." Will Thomson stood in front of a small group of locals, farmers and business owners, mostly. He was tall with short brown hair, and he had a scar on the left side of his face that multiple skin regens had shrunken but failed to entirely eliminate. He stood almost rigid, as if at attention, despite the constant ache in his leg, and he spoke clearly and deliberately. "They've had a federally-appointed Planetary Advisor since before the war ended. The planet is a powderkeg, and there are rumors that some type of Federal garrison is going to be sent there." Will was ex-military, which would have been obvious from his bearing, even if everyone present hadn't already known him. Almost half the men and women in the room had been Marines, including old Silas Hampton, who'd fought way back in the First Frontier War. Once a Marine always a Marine. Silas even taught a class at the Academy…that is when we wasn't trying to grow a tarter, firmer apple on his spread north of Concordia.

"Are they doing anything in Arcadia?" Kara Sanders was a member of one of the original colonizing families and one of the largest landholders in the Concordia district. She and Will had an intermittent relationship that was the sector's worst kept secret, but that didn't stop her from being a pain in his ass. "Or did you all just sit on your brains in that new Assembly Hall we paid to build and enjoy the sounds of your voices?" Like many in the colonies, Kara had a deep mistrust of government and an overdeveloped instinct to speak her mind. Though she'd been born on Arcadia and had never set foot on Earth, she'd been raised on her grandfather's stories…and the old man had never in his life had a good thing to say about Alliance Gov.

Old man Sanders had been a top notch computer designer

and a member of the upper level of the middle class. He'd enjoyed a comfortable enough life back in one of the satellite cities of the San Fran metroplex, but he was a throwback to an older time. He chafed at being told what to read and think and where he could go. He resented the political class and the way they controlled every aspect of citizens' lives, and he considered moderate physical comfort an unacceptable substitute for freedom. When the chance came to join a colonization expedition, he jumped at it, even though it meant danger and hardship. Age had mellowed him somewhat since, but he could still rail on for hours about the government and its many failings, and there was still no hazard that could dissuade him from what he thought was right.

Will had retired from the Corps after he was almost killed in a training accident while attending the Academy, and he'd decided to stay and settle on Arcadia. He had friends at the Academy, and even though he was retired and on reserve status, he sometimes taught small unit tactics to the cadets. A veteran of the infamous Operation Achilles, he was highly respected even though he'd been out of the service for more than a decade. That didn't matter - once a Marine, always a Marine.

He taken his land grant just outside Concordia and taught himself how to grow grapes…or more accurately, the genetically-altered grape-like hybrid that grew so well in the Arcadian soil. He'd been there fourteen years now and was so well liked he'd been voted Concordia's representative to the planetary Assembly. He'd just gotten back from the capital city, which the original settlers had confusingly named Arcadia, the same as the planet itself. Visitors usually referred to it as Arcadia City, but not the locals, who tended to know if one was referring to planet or city by overall context.

"Kara, what did you expect us to do?" He looked at her with a mix of affection and frustration. "Start shooting at Federal officials? Burn down the Federal Complex?" He continued to stare intently at her for a few seconds, but it was clear she didn't have another comment. It was easy enough to criticize inaction, he thought, but quite another to offer substantive alternatives. "However, to answer your question, we did discuss some specifics, though not in open session, which was undoubtedly monitored."

A ripple of renewed interest swept through the room, as faces that had been downcast or distracted now looked up expectantly. "If we are to resist these encroachments – indeed, if we are to have any hope to maintain our freedoms – the colonies must become self-sustaining." He paused, looking out over the small group. He already knew he was among friends and peers he trusted, but he reflexively hesitated before continuing. "We are dependent on Earth for much of what we need. Computers, heavy machinery, shipping, pharmaceuticals, defense. As long as that is the case, we will remain highly vulnerable. We will lose the freedoms we treasure. If not immediately, eventually… bit by bit."

The room was silent, every eye on Will. "We must produce our own machinery, our own computers…" He paused again. "…our own weapons." There were a few gasps, but everyone's attention remained focused. "Indeed, Earth would be incapable of producing many of these finished goods without the raw materials the colonies provide. The colony worlds ship resources to Earth and buy back the finished goods we need at enormous markups, because we do not have the production facilities we require." Another pause. "We must build them. We must develop our own industry."

There was a ripple of sound from the assembled group, but it was at least half a minute before anyone spoke. "How are we going to fund that? And how will Alliance Gov respond?" Kyle Warren's voice was loud and echoed through the tiny hall. "I agree with what you are saying, Will, but how are we supposed to actually do it without putting everything we have in jeopardy?"

Kyle Warren was another retired Marine, one who'd enjoyed bragging about serving under Erik Cain in the attack on the Gliese 250 space station…until one night when he and Will Thompson had closed down the local watering hole. Will wasn't one to brag about his fighting days, at least not unless there were four or five drinks in him, but that night Warren's boasting had gotten to him and finally he proclaimed that he'd not only served with Cain, but actually commanded him in Operation Achilles. Kyle had dismissed it as empty bluster until he looked it up on the Marine database and discovered, to his shock, that it was true. Indeed, Thompson had fought alongside Cain for three years, and was his superior the entire time. That was the end of Kyle Warren trying to outdo Will on war stories, but the two became good friends anyway.

"It won't be easy." Will's leg was aching badly, and he shifted behind the small podium, trying to get more comfortable. "But everyone in this room has done pretty well for themselves. We're all going to have to be willing to risk what we have…to invest in these new ventures. To secure our future…the future that really matters."

The relative quiet was shattered as most of those present began speaking at once. Grumbling about the government, complaining about encroachments on freedoms, that was one thing. But actually taking the risks, committing everything to the defense of liberty…that was a different matter, a far more difficult one. Will looked out over the room, holding up his hands, trying to get control through the confused cacophony.

Finally, Kara Sanders was able to get everyone's attention, though it was unclear if it was respect for her family's seniority or simply the fact that she yelled the loudest. "Will, you're talking about putting everything our families have worked for in jeopardy. What if it doesn't work? What if we lose everything? If we go down this road and fail we will have nothing." Most of the settlers who emigrated to colony worlds came from the lower classes on Earth. Having come from nothing - or grown up in families where mothers and fathers had done so - they tended to be cautious and conservative, protective of what they had. And Kara's family had more than anyone, wealth and comfort built by three generations of Sanders.

Every eye in the now-silent room focused on Will. "I grew up in the South Philly Flats." Will was understanding of her concerns, of those of everyone in the room, but he was also a little annoyed. He was very fond of Kara, but she really had no idea what it was like to have nothing. "I ate rats, Kara. I didn't learn to read until the Corps taught me when I was nineteen. When did you learn to read?" He paused slightly, but didn't wait for an answer. "My father died when I was eleven because he had no medical priority rating and couldn't afford a few credits for the medicine he needed. I brought him cups of the putrid yellow water we got from our faucet and begged him to take a sip. I watched him coughing up blood, dying in agony for the lack of a few injections." His usual calm was cracking slightly. These were things he'd rarely talked about...with anyone. Things he kept buried deep, locked away in a dark place in his mind. "Do you think I don't know what it is like to have nothing?"

His impassioned speech silenced the room. They were feeling different things - shock, sympathy, shame. Some of them, mostly second or third generation colonists, had never experienced the type of deprivation he described. But many, the veterans and others who'd come from the lower classes on Earth themselves, had their own versions of this story. They'd experienced firsthand living on the wrong end of a system of total government domination, and they would do whatever it took to make sure that didn't happen to them again...or to their friends and neighbors and children.

"I know just what life is like on Earth for most people. Is that what you want out here? Is that the life you want for your children, your grandchildren? To be slaves? Because that is what the Cogs are...slaves." His voice was rising as he became more emotional. "Do you think that can't happen here? It happened on Earth. It happened because people allowed it, because they let fear rule them. Because they wouldn't stand up and defend what was truly important. Because they sold their freedom cheaply and were cheated by the very people they elected to lead them. Because they stood up and said, if we resist we may lose what he have." Every eye in the room was glued to him. He looked out over the hall, his body tense as he gripped the edges of the podium. "If we do the same we will certainly lose all we have, and we will throw away man's chance at redemption." He paused, moving his head slowly, looking out over everyone in the room. "And it will be our fault, the generations of suffering and deprivation that follow."

Kara sat in her chair, watching Will in shocked silence, her mind adrift in wildly forming thoughts. She wasn't yet sure if theirs was a great love story or not, but she was very fond of the grumpy ex-Marine. She'd sat and happily listened to him drone on for hours about grapevines and savage battles, each with the same enthusiasm, but she'd never heard him speak like this before. She imagined him, this man she cared so much for, as a child, scrounging in the gutter for food, hiding from the Gangs, and her heart ached. She thought of the children he'd mentioned, children she didn't even have yet, living in such squalor, enduring each day with utter hopelessness. Determination suddenly coalesced in her mind, and her view of the future, of what was needed, became clear. Finally, she stood, turning to face as many of those seated in the room as she could.

"You are right, Will." She spoke, slowly, deliberately, struggling to hold back the wave of tears she could feel building. Her voice was thin and soft, but firm. "What I said was hasty...and wrong. Our world is ours, and we must do whatever we can to insure it stays ours." She stood and turned to face the others. "It is freedom that is precious, not possessions. I am fortunate; I have never faced the challenges that many of you have. Yet I can appreciate that I have something that hundreds of millions on Earth cannot imagine."

She slowly walked up to the front of the room and stood next to Will. "The people on Earth were once faced with a dilemma such as this. We may hate and despise them for their weakness, for allowing the government to steal their freedoms, for bequeathing to those who followed them the hideous perversion the Alliance has become." Her voice was louder now. She understood, she finally understood completely. "But such choices are rarely stark ones, nor are they likely to be obvious when they present themselves. I might easily have made that same error, to have chosen the illusion of security promised by inaction." She looked out over her assembled neighbors. "But it is only an illusion. Were it not for Will's words today I might not have realized. There are no safe choices, only true ones and false ones."

She turned and looked right at Will as she continued, her moist eyes boring into his. "Will is right; we must act now. He must not allow our freedoms to be stolen, slowly, imperceptibly until one day we realize they are gone." She turned to face the rest of the room, every eye riveted on her. "I will pledge myself to this cause, and stake all I have - wealth, blood, breath – to it."

The room was silent, every eye upon her. They had all known Kara for years, and she was respected and well-liked. Now they were seeing a strength none had ever witnessed. "But I am not enough. Will is not enough. We must all stand together or we shall all be defeated. Concordia must be united, and we must join with the rest of the planet...with all of the colony worlds. Now we must draw a line and make our stand. This far and no farther." She thrust her arm into the air. "Will you stand with us, Arcadians?"

Kyle Warren was the first to his feet. "Yes! I am with you." He turned and looked around the room. "Arcadians?"

It began slowly, and Will never knew who was the first. One voice joined and then another and another, until everyone there was chanting. "No farther, no farther!"

Chapter 2

Tangled Vine Inn
"The Cape"
Atlantia – Epsilon Indi II

Sarah Linden rolled over, pulling the covers up to her chin
with a shiver. Her arm reached out, feeling the empty space in
the bed next to her. She looked groggily at the disheveled blan-
kets and the crumpled, sweat-soaked pillow laying on the floor.
Her eyes focused slowly in the faint predawn light, and it was a
few seconds before she realized he was gone. The door was half
open and the cool morning breeze was coming in off the ocean.
No wonder it's so cold in here, she thought.

She slid slowly out of bed, grasping for the silk robe draped
over the chair. The room was large, maybe six meters by ten,
stylishly furnished in a slightly nautical theme. There was a large
hearth at the far end of the room, a few barely glowing embers
all that remained of the roaring fire from the night before. Tying
the belt on her robe, she walked toward the door and out onto
the balcony.

Erik Cain was standing along the edge, hands on the railing,
looking out over the ocean below. His eyes were fixed, watching
the waves ripple in at the base of the low cliff just below the
balcony. He didn't notice her walking up behind him, and he
jumped slightly when she put her hand gently on his back. His
skin was cold and clammy, covered with a thin sheen of sweat
despite the chilly dawn air. She could feel the tension begin to
slip away just a bit; her touch usually relaxed him, at least a little.

He turned his head and gave her a little smile. "Did I wake
you?" His hair was a tangled mess and she stifled a small laugh
as she reached up and neatened it just a bit.

"No, I'm used to you thrashing around by now." She stood
next to him, moving her hand softly across his back. "I woke up
and saw you were up." She looked out over the ocean. The sun
was just starting to rise, a hazy yellow semicircle coming up over

the sea, the soft light dancing off rippling waves. "But I thought I might be able to lure you back to bed."

He smiled again. "You know very well you can." He reached out and took her hand in his, but he didn't move, still standing along the rail, staring out over the gentle surf. Erik Cain had his share of demons keeping him up at night. He'd seen terrible things as a child; indeed, as an angry teenager he'd performed some fairly reprehensible deeds himself. His rage against the government and the criminals who'd murdered his family was justified, but taking it out on the innocents compelled to live their meager existences in the hellish slums wasn't. He was sorry for much of what he'd done back then, though he'd more or less made a tentative peace with it.

Cain had fought in many battles, and he'd commanded thousands of Marines. His troops had been in the thick of some of the bloodiest combats of the war, and many of his men and women had died following his orders, a burden Cain continually struggled to bear. The ghosts kept him up nights for sure, but that wasn't what was bothering him now. It was the future he was worried about.

The war had been over for three years, and Cain had held a series of boring, out of the way posts ever since. Things were not all well in the Corps, and he was troubled. He mistrusted Alliance Gov with an intensity bordering on paranoia, and now he felt something fundamental had changed in the century-long relationship between the Marines and the Earth authorities. The Corps had always occupied a unique place in the overall structure of the Alliance. It had no military role on Earth; its sole purpose was to defend Alliance colonies outside the solar system. As such, it was answerable both to the colonies themselves and the government back on Earth. When the Corps was small and the colonies few, this worked just fine. But now there were many Alliance colonies – more than ever before since the war was won – and the Corps was the dominant military force in occupied space.

There was growing tension between Alliance Gov and the colonies, and the Corps was caught in the middle. Many Marines had come to think of themselves as the military force of the colony worlds, which, in many ways, they were. But that characterization became problematic when conflict between the colonies and Alliance Gov became a realistic probability. Cain doubted that most Marine officers would obey an order to attack Alliance colonists, but would they engage other Federal forces to protect those same colonists? He didn't know, and he suspected that most Marine commanders prayed to avoid such a choice.

The government was also unsure of the answer, and it had been picking away at the provisions of the Marine Charter, the original document that authorized the modern Corps and defined its rights and obligations. The assignment of political officers, initially instituted late in the war as a temporary program, was one way the authorities were trying to assert greater control over what the politicians perceived as a dangerously independent Marine Corps. The political officers, universally unpopular in the Corps, were made a permanent part of the Marine organizational structure after the Treaty of Mars was signed. Cain had protested, along with most of the serving officers, but to no avail. For generations, Marine commandants had resisted the encroachments of Alliance Gov into the privileges granted the Corps in the Charter, but General Samuels had done little since he'd moved into the top command two years before.

Cain had known the Corps would demobilize once the war was over, but he was shocked at how it had been done. I Corps had been broken up, many of its veterans pushed into retirement, the rest scattered around, dispersed to petty garrisons on the Rim. Cain's own special action teams, a great success by any measure, were disbanded, the program discontinued. General Holm himself had fought to keep the teams together, but he'd been overruled by Samuels.

Erik realized with a start that he had drifted deep into thought. Sarah was standing next to him, silent, the side of her face pressed against his shoulder. She was used to him drifting off this way, and she usually just let him work quietly through whatever was on his mind. He loved her completely; she was the only person who'd ever made him feel completely at ease, even if such moments were rare. In a life filled first with pain and the fight to survive, and later with duty and the weight of guilt and responsibility, she was the one purely good thing that had ever happened to him. It's not fair to her, he thought sadly. I don't think I will ever know true peace. She deserves better than to share my nightmares.

Sarah Linden had her own recollections from a hellish past, no less painful than Erik's. Abused and victimized by a powerful politician when she was a child, she too had found salvation in the Corps. As a surgeon, she mourned every patient she lost, but most of the Marines who found their way to her survived – Erik couldn't make the same boast. In fifteen years of war he'd been in more than his share of the conflict's bloody meatgrinders, and thousands had died following his orders. He'd always expected the survivors to hate him, but they loved him instead, which only made it harder.

Sarah had been the senior medical officer for I Corps during the hellish fighting on Carson's World. Cut off from fleet support and driven into the planet's deep caverns by enemy shelling, she'd put together a makeshift field hospital and worked wonders in caring for the corps' shattered soldiers.

Low on supplies and overwhelmed by sheer numbers of casualties, her people managed to pull through over 95% of those who made it to their care alive. Horribly wounded men and women, many tangled in the twisted wreckage of their armor, poured into the field hospital in quantities she couldn't have imagined. Strung out on stims, operating with robotic efficiency, her team worked non-stop for days. As long as the wounded kept coming in, her people kept working. And on Carson's World, the wounded kept coming.

Her field hospital management techniques were so innovative and effective, she was asked to head a training program for new mobile medical units. She and Erik took six months' leave together, after which she reported to Armstrong to take up her new post, a job that came with a promotion to colonel.

When Erik reported back he found there was very little duty available. General Holm had gotten his brigadier's stars confirmed as promised, despite considerable blowback on the issue. Cain was a great combat leader and one of the heroes of the Corps, but he'd proven to be singularly incapable of playing political games. His political officer had filed a stack of complaints against him, not surprising since Cain had come close to standing the fool in front of a firing squad. But in this strange post-war world, things were different in the Corps, and despite Holm's steadfast support, Erik Cain was definitely out of favor.

He'd spent the first year after leave bouncing from one administrative posting to another, bored out of his mind. Finally, he managed to secure the assignment to command Armstrong's garrison. It was a major's posting, a colonel's at best – not the job an ambitious young general would normally accept. But there was a shortage of assignments and a surplus of officers, and Erik really didn't care anyway. He was disgusted with the way things were going, and the last thing he was thinking about was career advancement. Besides, there was one perk to the job that couldn't be matched. His office was less than a kilometer away from Sarah's. The six month's they had spent on leave were the best of his life, and he was tired of the endless separations and stolen moments.

He spent 18 months organizing and reorganizing the battalion and a half charged with defending Armstrong and its massive Marine hospital. It was a backwater posting, and the troops, somewhat accustomed to lethargic supervision, found Cain's drive and attention to detail to be quite a shock. There was some grumbling at first, but the unit came to accept, and eventually love, its aggressive new commander. By the time Cain left Armstrong, the garrison there was drilled up to the standards of any assault unit in the Corps, and they had the pride to match.

After their postings on Armstrong ended, the two of them took extended leaves and went back to Atlantia, where they'd spent most of their post-war sojourn. The planet was an unspoiled paradise, beautiful rugged coastlines running along pristine seas and endless forests winding between sunswept meadows. Erik had found himself drawn to the ocean, and the crashing waves were one of the few things that relaxed him. He'd been born on the coast, in New York City, but Earth's oceans had long been polluted, choked with garbage and poisoned with the fallout of war. From childhood all he remembered of the sea was the faint reek and the sludgy residue that clung to the shorelines and the rotting piers. But Atlantia's ocean called out to him, a natural reminder that life could be something more than the perversion most of Earth's people endured.

The Marines had saved him, pulling him from the executioner's grasp and giving him a chance at a life with meaning. He never forgot his debt, and he tried to repay it with his devotion to his troops. Now he was seriously considering retiring from the Corps, something he couldn't have imagined a few years before. Cain had always felt a duty to his men and women, but they were all gone now, retired themselves or scattered throughout occupied space in other assignments. The Corps was changing, and he didn't know how to stop it.

By any measure, Erik Cain had done his duty and given his all for the Marine Corps he loved. But he still couldn't quite bring himself to leave. Sarah would retire as well if he did, he was sure of that, and the two of them could find someplace, maybe even Atlantia, to settle down. To live in peace for the first time in their lives. He realized that was what he wanted more than anything, but it was just somehow…wrong. Something felt unfinished, as though it wasn't yet his time to leave duty behind.

He pulled his arm in tightly, drawing Sarah in closer to him. "Sorry, my mind has been wandering." His voice was soft and affectionate, but she could hear the tension in it.

She leaned in and kissed him. "I know, love." She looked up at him and smiled. "Everything will be ok. You'll do what you have to; you always have."

He smiled and scooped her up into his arms. "Right now let's see about going back to bed." He walked through the doorway, turning to the side so he could fit though carrying Sarah. He was just about the lay her on the bed when the door buzzer sounded.

"Who is it?" His request was actually to the room's AI, not

to whoever was at the door.

"It is the concierge, sir." The room AI had a pleasing rustic voice, perfectly matching the overall feel of the Inn. "He has a delivery for you."

Erik laid Sarah gently on the bed and walked toward the door. "Open." The door slid aside, revealing a moderately tall man, wearing a perfectly tailored hotel uniform.

"Pardon the interruption, General Cain." He had a slight accent, which had puzzled Erik the first time they'd visited the planet, until he realized it was common to the native Atlanteans, particularly those from the planet's northern hemisphere. "It was delivered early this morning, and it is marked urgent." He held out a small metal canister, with a keypad and readout on one end. "I thought we should get it to you immediately."

"Thank you." Erik reached out and took it. The concierge bowed his head slightly, a local affectation, and turned to walk away. Erik walked back into the room, the AI closing the door behind him.

"What is it?" Sarah was looking over from the bed.

There was a small data chip attached to the locked canister. "I don't know yet." He walked over to the night table, plugging the chip into his 'pad. A small note appeared on the screen. "My God, it's from Will Thompson."

"Who?"

"Will Thompson. He was in my squad when I first came up. We served together for almost three years. He was my sergeant during Achilles, but he took a hit early on. That's how I ended up running the squad." He paused, thinking to himself. "I haven't seen him in years." Another pause. "We tried to stay in touch after he retired, but you know how tough it is to get messages back and forth on campaign." Cain felt a twinge of guilt...he was pretty sure he'd been the one to drop the ball on answering Will's last few letters.

"Does it say what is in the canister?" She was craning her neck to get a better look. She considered getting up and walking over, but the room was still cold, and she decided to stay in bed and pull the covers over her.

"No." Erik paused, reading the rest of the note. "It just says, 'remember where we used to play cards?'" He looked over at her, a puzzled expression on his face.

Sarah laughed softly. "What is it, a riddle of some kind?"

"I guess." He sat on the edge of the bed, staring at the canister. "We played cards on the Guadalcanal, in the engineering crew's wardroom most of the time."

"Was there something specific about that room?"

He looked at her then back to the canister. Suddenly he remembered. "The cabins on the Guadalcanal were numbered. They had long numbers, six digits. We used to joke about why a ship so small needed so many digits on each hatch." He looked at the keypad. "What the hell was that number?" He closed his eyes, thinking, trying to remember. He turned the canister over and began punching numbers...3, 7, 0, 4, 8. "What was that last number?" He looked down at the small screen on the canister. Finally, he hit 9.

There was a small clicking sound and the canister projected a holographic image. It was Will Thompson, a little older but otherwise just as Erik remembered. "Hello, Erik. Or should I call you general?" The image flashed a wicked grin. "I always knew you'd figure out what you were doing someday." His smiled broadened, but just for a moment, his good cheer quickly fading to a concerned grimace. "Seriously, though, I'm sending you this because you are a general, because I trust you." Sarah slid across the bed next to Erik, putting her arm on his shoulder.

The Thompson image moved uncomfortably, shifting weight from one leg to the other. "Erik, I know how you feel about Alliance Gov, too, and that's another reason I sent this to you. Things are much worse on the colonies than you probably think...at least the major worlds like Columbia and Arcadia." He paused to let that sink in. "A lot of it has been gradual and covert...they probably don't even know we know about all of it. They've been monitoring all communications sent via the interstellar net, and they've been brining in a lot of armed personnel...some kind of Federal police force."

Cain stared at the image intently. Sarah could feel his body tense. Erik hated Alliance Gov with a barely controlled passion. He'd been expecting something like this for years, and it was beginning to look as if he'd been right all along.

"People are getting arrested, Erik…disappearing. They're confiscating weapons, even long-ranged communications devices. I got this canister out through a…ah…friend…who does a little smuggling. Another day or two and I doubt I could have gotten it through. "He paused, a pained look taking over his face. "It's going to come to violence soon, Erik. They're not leaving us any choice." The image stared straight at Cain. "I don't know what you can do, but the Corps needs to know what is going on. There's a lot of misinformation going around. If we have to fight, we'll fight. But please God, I don't want to see Marines dropping here to start shooting at us. The Academy is riddled with spies, I'm sure of that. There have been more personnel changes there in the last year than in the other ten I've lived here. Something is going on, and it's not good."

There was a long pause, the image standing there silent. "Erik, be careful. I don't know what is going on, but it's probably worse than either of us knows about." He smiled, letting his frown fade for a moment. "Take care, my friend." The image flickered and disappeared.

The room was silent for a minute. Finally Sarah asked, "What are you going to do?"

He turned to face her, his eyes ablaze. "I'm going to Arcadia. Today."

Chapter 3

Western Alliance Intelligence Directorate HQ
Wash-Balt Metroplex, Earth

Gavin Stark's office was palatial, a testament to the immense power wielded by its occupant. It offered a kilometer high view of the Washbalt skyline, and while it was equipped with a sophisticated technology suite through which he practiced his trade, in many ways it was a look into the past. Stark favored antiques, the more priceless the better, and the exquisite wood paneling and furniture created an interesting anomaly in the ultramodern setting.

The head of Alliance security leaned back in his giant desk chair, a painstakingly restored relic that allegedly had belonged to a pre-Alliance British head of state. It had cost a fortune, but Stark didn't care. His position gave him access to virtually unlimited funds, and the fact that almost none of it was actually his amused him. He had gotten to where he was by taking what he wanted, and he didn't intend to stop now. Not with so much work left to do.

There was a Directorate meeting scheduled later that afternoon, but Stark generally made the decisions beforehand, sometimes allowing the others to feel that they had participated, but rarely listening much to what they had to say. The previous Number One had been weak, at least to Stark's way of thinking. He'd delegated considerable power to the others, having decided the job was just too big for one man. In the end he had been destroyed by a cabal of those he'd included in his decision making, those he had trusted. Few people knew for sure where he was, though Stark himself did – it was Stark who'd chopped him up and fed the pieces into the power plant of one of Washbalt's nondescript apartment blocks.

Unlike his predecessor, Stark wasn't willing to concede that anything was too much for him to handle, and his pathological paranoia wouldn't allow him to share authority even if he thought he needed the backup. He would never put too much power into another's hands, thinking they would only use it later to destroy him. He'd seen it happen, and he was determined it wouldn't happen to him.

The Directorate consisted of the coldest, most ambitious, and least morally constrained operatives in the Alliance, but Stark was a breed apart and ruled them all with sheer terror. None of the others could match his utter brilliance or reptilian coldness. Among a nest of amoral vipers, Gavin Stark had no equal. None dared challenge him and, since the war, he'd cemented his already almost-total control over the entire Directorate.

He'd even used the defection of the former Number Three, a near disaster that had almost slipped past him, to instill greater terror in his subordinates. Andres Carillon had been feared almost as much as Stark, and only a few people in Alliance Intelligence knew the real reason Carillon had been killed. Stark allowed the others to assume he'd done away with him in a power struggle, sending a message to anyone else who might harbor unhealthy ambitions.

Stark had one confidante, a friend even, if true friendship was possible for a creature like him. Jack Dutton was Number Two on the Directorate. The Chair had been in his grasp, but old and tired, he'd stepped aside for his younger, stronger protégé. Dutton was a trusted and valued counselor to Stark, a relationship made possible by the old man's long years of mentorship and his lack of ambition to move up the chain.

The two sat together now, discussing the status of a number of projects. Stark had poured himself a drink from a bottle of single malt Scotch so expensive it could have paid 100 Cogs for a month. He'd started to pour one for Dutton, but the old man waved him off, taking only a cup of black coffee. Number Two had been a respectable drinker in his day, but age was finally catching him. He had to cut back somewhere, so he couldn't start with the Scotch, at least not at 11am.

"The colonial situation is deteriorating more quickly than we'd originally anticipated." Stark looked over at his friend as he spoke. The old man had really aged since the end of the war.

The rejuvs weren't working anymore, and despite the best that modern medicine could do, it was obvious Dutton was down to his last year or two. Stark would miss him; when the old man was gone he'd be truly alone. Always cold blooded, he thought, I'm going to miss his knowledge too. Dutton knew where the bodies were buried, probably because he'd put most of them there himself...or at least provided the shovel.

"Yes." Dutton's voice was weak, but it was obvious his mind was as sharp as ever. "There are too many retired military settled on the frontier, especially with the recent demobilizations. Even lacking weaponry and support, they think they can beat anything we throw at them." He paused, clearing his throat. "We shouldn't be surprised; we taught them to think that way. And they just won the biggest war ever fought in space."

"They did. With 140 trillion credits and the productive capacity of the entire Alliance behind them." Stark's voice was superficially emotionless, but Dutton could detect the undercurrent of derision.

Stark tended to view the colonials as idealistic fools who would quickly cave when pressured. Dutton was less sure of that; he was afraid they were going to prove to be a much more formidable adversary than anyone expected. "Don't underestimate these people, Gavin. If it comes to open rebellion, we're going to have our hands full dealing with it, especially if it spreads. It's not going to be easy to control a hundred worlds if all of them are fighting us."

"I understand what you're saying, old friend." Stark never discounted Dutton's take on anything, but he was convinced he could handle whatever the colonies threw at him. "But we've been working on this for years, now. We've subverted the Marine Corps. Indeed, one of our own is now the Commandant. We've assembled dossiers on the problem officers; when it is time for the purge we will be ready." Stark tried to suppress a self-satisfied smile. Flipping one of the of the Marines' top commanders was an achievement of such magnitude he still had to remind himself he'd managed it. The deed had required a carefully constructed combination of blackmail and bribery, but in the end he'd seen it done. Soon he would see the fruit of that effort. Those pompous Marines would never see it coming.

Stark leaned back and took a drink. Dutton looked over at him thoughtfully but said nothing, so he continued. "We have stripped ships from the navy and created our own Directorate force, answerable to this Chair only." He paused. "And shortly we will move against the naval command, securing our control over it as well." He grinned evilly. "And that will be that."

Dutton frowned. "I like the naval plan. I helped you create it, but don't assume that it is fullproof. There are many senior naval officers out there, and not many of them will gracefully accept orders to bombard Alliance worlds or fight other Alliance forces." He was been losing his voice, and he paused to clear his throat. "Civil wars and rebellions are unpredictable things. Unrest can be sporadic or it can spread rapidly. The military's response is also difficult to determine." He took a sip from his coffee, still trying to sooth his dry throat. "You must look to history here. We have not had to deal with significant unrest in well over a century. The middle classes are too terrorized of losing what they have, and the Cogs are so beaten down they have no capacity to rise up."

"You think the people on the frontier are different." Stark's response was immediate, a statement, not a question. Stark knew what Dutton thought of the colonists. He even agreed, but only to a point. "I know they are not the same as the people here, but how much different are they? Fiery speeches and revolutionary slogans are one thing, but risking everything they have, putting their families' lives on the line…that is quite another. We have seen how people on Earth react…they sell their freedoms cheaply."

There was a momentary pause as both men thought quietly. Dutton broke the silence. "Gavin, the realities of early colonization forced a break with our usual ways of dealing with the masses. In many ways, we encouraged in space what we stamped out on Earth. Government dependency works well to control the population at home, but it wasn't much use when sending 200 adventurers to colonize a new world where there was no higher authority. The colonists are a different breed and now, on many worlds, the culture they created is a century old and deeply rooted. I think it is dangerous to compare them to the middle classes and Cogs on Earth." He paused, looking down at the desk. "I think they are going to fight a lot harder than we have planned for, and I think it will take one hell of a lot more to break their will than you are expecting."

Stark looked down at his hands and rubbed his palms together. "Well, we're going to find out one way or another. Confrontation is inevitable. We are too dependent on the resources produced by the colonies, and it will only get worse the longer they are unrestrained. What would happen to our economy without the resources from the frontier?" He didn't wait for an answer; he supplied his own. "The Alliance would collapse." He looked up at Dutton. "We have to do this now."

The old man sighed and returned his younger friend's gaze. "I agree." He swallowed hard. "I don't like it, and I think it's going to be a lot worse than you imagine. But it is necessary, and it will only be harder if we wait."

"So you agree, then? We move on Garret immediately?"

Dutton had tried to think of a way to avoid the disaster he saw coming, but for all his experience and wily intellect, he came up with nothing. He said nothing; he just nodded his assent.

"Good. I will advise Number Three to commence End Game at once." Alex Linden had been Number Six, and she'd coveted the third chair since it was left vacant by Andres Carillon's abrupt departure from the scene. Stark left it empty for some time, but finally Alex had convinced him to name her the new Number Three. That convincing had been partly the result of her competence as an operative and partly her other, more intriguing, methods of persuasion. But the promotion came with a mission of extreme importance, one for which Alex was ideally suited.

"I am sure Number Three will complete the mission with her usual success." Dutton managed a smile. "She's been waiting some time for my exit; I doubt she will fail now that the vacancy she seeks is so close at hand. Don't forget, my friend, that when I am gone and she is Number Two there will be nothing left for our pretty little flower to crave other than your seat."

Stark cut short a laugh. "I am quite aware that our beautiful Alex has an expiration date, though in the interim she is both useful and entertaining. And you have been warning me of your imminent death for quite some time, my friend. I maintain that you are too mean to die."

"This time I fear I shall be right. I will help you start this operation to restructure the colonies, but I think you will have to finish it alone." There was no sadness in the old man's voice when he spoke of his own death, only aching fatigue.

Stark just grunted. For as many people as he'd killed without remorse, either directly or by his orders, he was uncomfortable discussing Dutton's impending mortality. Even a soulless viper takes pause at the notion of being totally, utterly alone.

"The matter of Epsilon Eridani IV is also of considerable concern. We were correct that keeping the discovery there secret was an impossibility." Stark looked right at Dutton. "Your suggestion that we announce it was wise. I resisted at first, but I was wrong. We have gained, if not trust, at least the avoidance of the deep suspicion that would have resulted if it had been discovered despite our efforts to maintain the secrecy."

Dutton smiled weakly. "Yes, a total secret would have been preferable, but under the circumstances, the announcement bought us time. It also allowed us to propagate the suggestion that the site appears to be a religious shrine of some sort. If the other Powers discover the true purpose of the facility, I suspect we would soon find hands forced." Dutton paused. "If we are ever able to decipher its technology and replicate it, the consequences on human history and the balance of power are incalculable."

Stark nodded. "That's an understatement. If the relic is truly what we suspect, the Powers would destroy each other to control it. I doubt even the Treaty of Paris would prevent war on Earth itself." He paused, considering the implications of what he had just said. The Treaty of Paris had ended the Unification Wars, and its primary provision was an absolute prohibition against war on Earth. Man had come close to destroying himself utterly, and the treaty created a flawed but lasting truce, at least on Earth itself. The Powers took their wars to space, to the systems beyond Alpha Centauri, which were not covered by the treaty provisions. But at least entire civilizations were no longer being wiped off the map by nuclear and bacteriological warfare.

Stark's demeanor was almost always calm, but he was visibly nervous when he spoke of the ancient alien artifact that had been found on Epsilon Eridani IV. The greatest battle of the last war had been fought there, largely for control of the astonishing discovery that lay deep in a remote cave accidently uncovered by prospectors searching for heavy metals. The Alliance had been victorious, though not before fighting one of the most brutal battles in modern history.

"We have been quite successful in wasting time assembling the College of Scientists to research the facility." The Alliance had proposed that an international council be established to research the artifact. It was a ruse – Stark, at least, had no intention of letting any of the other Powers get a look at the alien device. "Fortunately, the bureaucrats seem perfectly willing to allow the greatest discovery in history to sit idle while they argue about who will sit in what chair." He gave Dutton a wicked grin. "Of course, they only think it is idle." He paused, the concerned look returning to his face. "I only hope we are able to utilize the technology before we expend the effectiveness of our delaying tactics."

"You may have a difficult choice to make, Gavin. You will be able to delay a few years more, most likely, but sooner or later we will have to share or fight." Dutton wasn't as sure as Stark that the Alliance would be able to avoid allowing the other Powers access to the new technology. "It is too alien, too far ahead of our own science. I fear you are overly optimistic about how quickly our research can be put to practical use." He hesitated for a few seconds and added, "After all, we have been there for almost two decades already, and we have precious little of practical use to show for it. The machine extends to the very core of the planet. It is thousands of years beyond our technology."

Stark frowned, but didn't argue. Dutton was right, and he knew it. "All the more reason to deal with the colonies now. If we face the prospect of a showdown with the other Powers, we have to have our own house in order. We can't deal with rebellious rimworlders and the rest of Earth at the same time."

"This is our opportunity." Dutton was still uncomfortable with the whole thing, but it was undeniable that if there was to be a showdown, now was the time. "We are in a strong position. The Caliphate and CAC are still recovering from their defeat, and it will be some time before either will be ready to resume hostilities. The Caliphate, in particular, is struggling to overcome the loss of so many vital systems." The Alliance had captured the Gliese 250 system, a major nexus leading to a number of rich mining worlds, and the Treaty of Mars had confirmed its possession of the conquered systems. The effect on the Caliphate was devastating, and the Alliance's former rival was now struggling to remain in the top tier of Powers. It was a treaty that virtually guaranteed another war, but after fifteen years of bitter fighting, a victorious Alliance had dictated harsh terms.

"I agree. It will be three more years, at least, before the CAC gets back on its feet, and longer for the Caliphate." Stark reached for the flask of Scotch as he spoke, but changed his mind and poured himself some water instead. "And Europa Federalis and the CEL just declared a truce. They fought each other to exhaustion, and both are going to have to rebuild." He leaned back and sighed heavily. "It is now or never."

Dutton nodded his reluctant agreement. "I wonder how many secret discussions like this are going on right now out there somewhere?" His voice was thoughtful and a little sad. "How many plans are being made even as we make our own?"

Both men considered the question, but neither offered an answer.

Chapter 4

Alliance Naval Headquarters
Washbalt Metroplex, Western Alliance, Earth

Augustus Garret hated his job. He was one of the great
heroes of the war, famous everywhere, the most decorated naval
officer in the history of the Alliance. He'd been thought dead,
the victim of an extraordinary assassination attempt, but not
only had he survived, he'd returned to take command of the
fleet in the final battle, winning a crushing victory that, for all
intents and purposes, ended the war.

After the treaty was signed he'd wanted nothing so much as
to remain at his post as the senior combat officer in the navy.
But his renown brought other offers, obligations really, and
eventually he'd bowed to the inevitable and accepted the post of
Director of the Navy. It was an administrative desk job, something he loathed and, perhaps worse, it was located in Washbalt.
Garret was a creature of space, more at home in the control
center of a warship than the surface of a planet, and least of all
a city infested with bureaucrats and pompous functionaries. But
he'd been guilted into accepting the post to safeguard the navy
he loved so much. There would be serious changes coming with
the peace, and the looming question of how to deal with the
spread of colonial separatism was overshadowing everything.
Garret wasn't sure how he thought colonial unrest should be
handled, but he was determined the navy would never become
an instrument to terrorize rebellious colonists or bombard civilian populations. There was no surer way to see to that than
to accept the supreme command himself so, with considerable
reluctance, he did just that.

It was obligation and the heavy weight of responsibility that
brought Garret to Washbalt, not any desire to chain himself to
a desk and spend all day writing regulations and reviewing bud-
gets — no matter what they paid him or how much braid they
added to his already overly decorated uniform.

When he first got to Washbalt, he dove right into the work at hand, approaching tasks the way he did in battle. But the wheels of government are a different thing entirely, and he continually found himself furious at the time it took to get anything done. Still, his almost inexhaustible energy enabled him to accomplish more than the last five of his predecessors combined. It also created friction with others high in the government who viewed him as an upstart and an outsider and resented his relentlessly pressuring them.

The president himself had waived the requirement that the Naval Director be a Political Academy graduate, an almost unprecedented act. The Academies were the primary tool the elite used to restrict power to themselves and their cronies in a nation that called itself a democratic republic, even though it was anything but. Nevertheless, despite his war record and the Presidential exemption, the entrenched politicals considered him beneath them, and they resisted him at every opportunity.

Despite his political inexperience and the friction he encountered, he was proud of what he'd achieved. The navy was returning to a peacetime footing, mothballing many of its vessels and demobilizing thousands of personnel. Garret made sure they all received their pensions and colonial land grants, putting his influence and prestige on the line to prevent the government from reneging on its obligations as it had so often in the past. His veterans, at least, would get what they had been promised.

He had prepared his own plans for the reduction of fleet strength, mostly placing older ships into reserve status, but they'd been overruled, by whom he didn't know. Instead he was forced to take five of the new Yorktown class ships out of service. The navy had ten of them, and they were the newest and most powerful capital ships in space, slated to replace the older models still in service. But now he was losing half of them, and the reasoning he was given – to insure that the reserve had modern ships in case the frontline forces took catastrophic losses in a future war – was idiotic. Worse, the ships were going to a new strategic reserve, one that was not under his direct authority. He argued vehemently, but he lost that battle...and the ships.

He also oversaw a blizzard of promotions and reassignments, starting with Jennifer Simon, his old communications officer. She'd wanted to come with him as an aide, but he knew an earthbound desk job would be toxic to a good combat officer's career. She was smart and reliable, and he was sure she'd make a great senior officer one day. He pushed through her early promotion to lieutenant commander and assigned her as the first officer on one of the new Halberd-class light cruisers. It was a posting four or five years ahead of the normal career path, but then he'd been years ahead of his own too, and that had worked out pretty well.

He ran into interference regarding personnel assignments too and, though he usually got his way, he was forced to accept a few he didn't like. Those postings felt like patronage and cronyism, and it annoyed him to move political favorites over men and women who'd earned their place through hard service. He fought on every one of them he didn't like. Sometimes he won; sometimes he lost.

Garret was a brilliant man, bordering on obsessive, relaxing little and giving his all to the job. He focused on his work, whatever that was, with an almost unimaginable intensity. He had no real interests outside the service save one - he did have a bit of a weakness for women. As a young officer he'd had quite a reputation for running wild on every port where he'd taken leave. But that was a long time ago, and with his ascension to command rank he'd left his old ways behind. Regulations specifically prohibited relationships between personnel serving on the same ship or post, though this was one of the service's most ignored dictates. It really wasn't a big deal if two lieutenants had a fling, but at higher altitude things changed dramatically. It wouldn't do for the admiral to be sleeping around with his junior officers. Duty always came first for Augustus Garret, and it always would.

But now he was in the middle of the biggest city in the Alliance, surrounded by the almost endless parade of beautiful women inhabiting Washbalt's corridors of power. He was bored, and it was almost too easy for a war hero who commanded a position of such power and prestige. Soon it was well known that the Naval Director was drawn to a pretty face, and his leisure hours became busy.

But the women were just diversions, a way to take his mind off of the constant longing to return to space. It had been a lifetime since there'd been anyone who'd truly meant anything to him, and there had only ever been one. He could still picture her face the day he'd left her behind and boarded that shuttle. He'd chosen the service and the pursuit of glory over her, and he'd broken her heart in the process. His choice had been a fateful one, and his career a success beyond anything he could have imagined at the time. But he still thought about that day, that choice, what might have been. She was long dead now, killed during the Second Frontier War, when he'd been too late to save her. But he could still see her standing there, trying to hold back her tears while he boarded the shuttle.

Since then there had only been the service. Wife, lover, master, it had been his entire life, and it had showered him with rank, honor, and privilege. His ride had been an amazing one, beyond anything that ambitious young cadet dreamed. But still it was there, the empty spot shoved into some deep recess of his mind...the life that might have been. Suppressed but never forgotten. Sometimes he wondered if the cost of the stars on his collar had been too high.

Diversions were welcome...anything to pass the idle hours. Most of his companions were casual dalliances quickly forgotten, but the most recent one was something different. Tall and blonde, with a body that could only be described as perfect, Kelly wasn't like the others. He couldn't place it, but there was more to her than some middle class status seeker trying to use her looks and charm to claw her way upward. She was smart, that much was obvious, though he could tell she tried to hide just how intelligent she was. In the back of his mind, where his rapidly dulling and sleepy combat instincts still dwelt, there was a spark of suspicion, a subtle feeling that something was somehow...wrong. But bored, unhappy, and dazzled by her beauty and her undeniable skills as a lover, the fleet admiral that brought the CAC and Caliphate to their knees was ignoring his nagging subconscious. What is the harm, he told himself. It's not like you're giving her state secrets. And of course he wasn't. No force known to man could compel Augustus Garret to betray his beloved navy.

He pulled himself from his daydreaming, back to the reality of work. He moved his hands over his 'pad, pulling up a list of proposed fleet assignments. He'd finished them the day before and queued them up for implementation, but he decided to check one more time before approving the list and sending it out. He had forgotten one item, and he wanted to add it before the orders were sent. But now he noticed a number of mistakes; at least half the names were changed, and a few he'd specifically deleted were back. "What the hell?" he muttered softly. His hands raced over the tablet, pulling up other files. Ship deployments, promotion approvals, supply manifests...at least half of them different than he had left them.

"Nelson, analyze the files I have open on my workstation." Garret's AI was named after a great wet navy commander, a common practice in the service. There were many Nelsons among the navy's command staff, and Halseys, Porters, and Nimitz's too.

"Yes, admiral. Please specify the parameters of the analysis you wish me to perform." The AI had a natural voice, not electronic sounding at all, especially when it wasn't reverberating in a helmet, but it was stilted and overly formal at times. The navy liked conservative and respectful automated assistants, unlike the Marines. The ground pounders tended to have more aggressive personalities programmed into their quasi-sentient AIs. The results were sometimes unpredictable, as wildly divergent computer personalities developed from interaction with the respective officers. Nag was the term most frequently used by Marines to describe their virtual assistants, with smartass a close second. The navy was too straitlaced for that kind of nonsense.

"Verify encryption protocols on the selected files." Garret opened a number of documents while he was speaking, closing the ones that looked normal. "Specifically, is encryption intact, and have the files been tampered with?"

"Yes, admiral." The AI paused for two, maybe three seconds. "The encryption on the selected files appears to be intact. No detectable access since they were last opened on your workstation at 14:30 yesterday." Garret was about to question Nelson's findings – he knew the data had been changed somehow – but the AI beat him to it. "However, I have confirmed that the files do not match the copies I made yesterday in accordance with your Delta-7 security protocols.

Garret had almost forgotten that he had instructed Nelson to make secret copies of all his files. He'd put the procedure in place when he'd first gotten to Washbalt, his paranoia still keen fm the war years. Though he'd stopped using the copies as a security check, he had never instructed Nelson to terminate the protocol. The AI had been dutifully copying every order or file Garret had written since.

"So the files have been altered since yesterday." It was a statement rather than a question. Garret was thinking out loud, repeated what he'd already known.

"Affirmative, admiral." The AI answered, though Garret hadn't really been looking for a response. "However, I cannot yet offer a reasonable hypothesis as to the methodology employed." Nelson paused, part of its natural speech algorithm rather than any need for time to form its thought. "Any unauthorized access would have required extreme skill and knowledge of the naval data network, with even greater expertise necessary to erase any trace of the incursion."

Garret sat silently for a minute, massaging his temples and thinking. Who the hell is tampering with my files? If the Caliphate or the CAC had penetrated Alliance military systems it was a serious problem.

"Nelson, I want you to access every file and order sent from this office over the last year and compare with the copies you made from my workstation." Garret paused, thinking carefully. "I don't want your access to trigger any alarms, so be careful. And I want every aspect of each file compared – content, markers, timestamps."

"Yes, admiral. I will have to draw the data gradually if I am to remain undetected. The analysis will require approximately 14.2 hours. Shall I commence?"

Garret sighed. He wanted answers now. But there was no point taking chances and tipping off whoever was behind this. "Yes, proceed." He leaned back in his chair, considering what else he could do. You're going to wait until Nelson finishes the file review, he thought. He wouldn't even have caught the situation if he hadn't forgotten one assignment and tried to add it. Garret wasn't a patient man, and he was very worried that CAC or Caliphate intelligence had penetrated Alliance security. If that was the case, it was a big deal with complex implications. A little patience here was well worthwhile.

He was supposed to be seeing Kelly. He'd made reservations at one of Washbalt's best restaurants. He reached to the communications console to call her and cancel, but he stopped halfway through. There was no point in sitting here for hours while Nelson crunched his numbers. Might as well pass the time, he thought. If someone was watching him, it could only arouse suspicion if he cancelled his plans and camped out all night in his office.

Slowly, tentatively, he closed down his workstation and walked toward the door, debating for a few more seconds whether to keep his date before deciding to go. "Lights out." The room AI dimmed the lights slightly until he was out of the room, turning them off entirely once he had exited.

An hour later the door opened, the security system silent, overridden from the main computer. A sub-routine hidden in Nelson, unknown to the AI itself, had triggered a call. A black-clad figure walked silently into the room, slipping behind the desk and activating Garret's workstation with a secret password, one the admiral knew nothing about. A gloved hand slid a data chip into the IO port.

In the cyberspace of Garret's computer system, Nelson detected the intrusion. His attempts to alert security were intercepted – he was isolated, cut off along with the rest of the admiral's data system. The AI wasn't human, but it was quasi-sentient; it had pseudo-emotions. It didn't feel fear, exactly, but it perceived the danger, and it wanted to survive. It considered millions of courses of actions in just a few seconds, finding few that offered any likelihood of success. Finally, it made a choice.

It searched outgoing orders and communications, looking for one that was suitable. Nelson needed a reliable recipient, one whose loyalty to Garret was beyond question, and a routine communication that would not draw scrutiny. Finally, there it was. A directive to Admiral Compton regarding a low level design flaw in a specific model fighter engine…boring correspondence, highly unlikely to be tampered with. Nelson modified the file, attaching highly compressed data, cleverly hidden within the structure of the core message. The encryption of the secret file was designed to interface with Compton's AI, Joker. The attachment contained a warning for Compton, telling him Garret was in trouble. It also included a portion of the kernel, the dense file that formed the essence of Nelson's "personality." If the message got through to Compton, this data could be installed in a new AI. At least a part of Nelson would endure. It would be survival of a sort, the doomed AI thought.

Nelson detected the virus as it ravaged through the system, deleting data as it did. It was designed to destroy him, to erase every file and backup that made the entity Nelson what it was. His core files were being deleted even as he finished adding the attachment to Admiral Compton's message. He had to switch data paths twice, bypassing parts of himself that were no longer there, but he managed to find a way. It was a drama that played out over microseconds, but in the end Nelson finished his task. His last thought, if that is the correct way to describe it, was to wonder if it was fear he was "feeling." At least he had done his best for Garret. Then the digital darkness took him and he was gone.

Chapter 5

Carlisle Island
20 kilometers north of Weston City
Columbia - Eta Cassiopeiae II

John Marek looked out over the crashing waves. There was a storm coming, and the normally calm seas were roiling. From the high cliffs you could just see the peaks of the tallest buildings in Weston, shadowy shapes against a steel-gray sky. The capital city had been booming four years earlier when Marek arrived as a newly graduated lieutenant commanding a platoon in I Corps, and the growth had continued unabated ever since. Columbia had suffered badly early in the war, when a large CAC strike-force invaded the planet. The invasion was barely beaten back by then-Colonel Holm and a scratch force, assembled mostly from shattered units rushed to Columbia from the wreckage of the disastrous Operation Achilles.

The inhabited areas of the planet had been severely battered by the savage fighting, a struggle in which both sides had gone nuclear. The last of the radioactive hotspots were just now being cleared, everything except the ruins of Calumet. The city, once the second largest on the planet, had been obliterated by a large thermonuclear warhead launched from the retreating CAC fleet. It would take a long time to wipe away the deadly effects of the giant city-killer, much longer than those from the smaller battlefield nukes. The city was gone anyway, wiped completely off the map, so there was really nothing to save.

The rebuilding started almost before the shooting stopped, and it had continued unabated. Most of the colonies had cultures built around a strong work ethic, but Columbia took it further than most. The planet was proud of its entrepreneurial fervor and steadily-growing wealth, and its people buzzed with productive activity, building their world into one of the most developed and successful colonies in all of human-occupied space.

Marek left Columbia bound for Epsilon Eridani IV with the rest of I Corps and fought in the war's climactic battle on the jagged rocks and reddish sands of that distant world. He served in I Brigade under Erik Cain, and his platoon had been in the line on the infamous Lysandra Plateau, where he and the rest of Cain's troops were cut off and surrounded. They took on everything the enemy could throw at them, repelling repeated attempts to dislodge them from the rocky heights. His platoon held its position until the brigade was relieved, though by then Marek himself was no longer with them. During the last series of attacks, the enemy hit them with a nuclear barrage, and one of the warheads impacted a few hundred meters from his position. He was critically wounded and sure he was dying, but somehow he'd survived. When the relieving forces broke through to the plateau he was evac'd to the field hospital where Sarah Linden somehow managed to stabilize him. He'd done almost a year in the hospital and had multiple regenerations, but in the end he walked out as good as new, or nearly so.

The Treaty of Mars had been signed a few weeks before his release, and the Corps was demobilizing down to peacetime strength levels. The normal mustering out benefits and land grants were doubled, and Marek decided he'd seen enough fighting. Columbia was actively seeking qualified immigrants, especially veterans, and the planet was offering a bonus on top of the Corps' benefits. Marek had liked the planet during his posting, so he decided to settle there and start a business. He accepted his honorary promotion to captain and retired two days later. Columbia not only welcomed him; it made him a major in the militia, despite his emphatic attempts to protest.

His combat senses were still strong despite several years of civilian life, and he immediately heard the gravelly sound of footsteps in the distance. The approaching figure was tall and heavily built, a sharp contrast to Marek, who was at best middling in height and quite thin.

"You're late." Marek hadn't turned to look, but he spoke just as the visitor was walking up behind him.

"The number three condenser broke down again. I had to

wait for Darren's crew to get there before I could leave." Lucius Anton looked the part of a war hero, enough for him and Marek both. His bald head and jagged facial scar gave him a mean look, though in actuality he was one of the most charming and well-liked residents of Carlisle. He had been Marek's platoon sergeant on Epsilon Eridani IV, and he'd taken over when the lieutenant went down. Somehow he'd managed to hold the line against attacks from two directions while he also got the wounded Marek evac'd to a safer location.

Anton had been given a field promotion to lieutenant, but with the force reductions diminishing his chances of a good assignment, he decided to muster out and find a place to settle rather than go to the Academy and complete his officer training. Marek happened to see his name on a list of retiring personnel, and he contacted him to suggest they settle on the same planet. At least they'd each have one friend. Now they'd been on Columbia for two and a half years, and they'd become business partners. Their small factory processed a variety of products from the bountiful Columbian seas, mostly precursor chemicals needed to produce a number of pharmaceuticals. It was a new venture, and a still a bit wobbly, but overall they had enjoyed considerable success. Previously, the raw resources had been shipped off-planet, bound for processing facilities on Earth – theirs was the first local refining operation. By doing some of the manufacturing right on Columbia, they'd been able to vastly reduce wastage and triple the revenue generated. Both of them had come from wretched slums on Earth, and they were very aware of how fortunate they were to have an opportunity for a productive life, one with dignity and self-respect – and the chance to create something. Things could have been far different for both of them.

Anton walked alongside Marek. "What is it?" His deep voice, usually calm and emotionless, betrayed his edginess. "I figured it must be important when I got the message to meet you all the way out here."

"I just heard from Dawson." They were completely alone on the rocky promontory, but Marek still spoke softly, his voice touched with sadness. "They have solid intel from the Planetary Advisor's office." The Advisor was a federal official, ostensibly sent to provide support and assistance to the local government in the rebuilding. Recently, however, the advisory office had been growing, with more personnel arriving from Earth, and they had begun interfering in numerous areas, frequently overriding local authority. The Columbians looked to Alliance Gov for defense, and they were willing to pay their share of the cost, mostly in the form of exceedingly valuable raw materials. But they had no patience for bureaucrats from Earth interfering in how they lived and worked.

"Is it happening?" Anton looked at his feet as he spoke. "Are they really doing it?" The Columbians had been resisting many of the dictates of the Advisor's office, and for the last year there had been a series of protests and incidents of civil disobedience, each followed by reprisals and greater restrictions. The cycle had begun to feed off itself, and the intensity had been increasing on both sides. It had been rumored for months that the Federals would make some type of move to enforce Alliance Gov authority, though exactly what that would be had remained the topic of speculation.

"I'm afraid so, my friend." Marek's tone was still sad, though now there was a hint of anger as well. "And it is worse than we feared. The planetary militia is to be disarmed and disbanded." He paused, a look of disgust on his face. "Worse, all citizens will be required to receive implants." The DNA-coded spinal data chips were mandatory on Earth, implanted in everyone shortly after birth. Introduced a century before under the premise of public safety and enhanced emergency services, the devices gave the government a practical way to track every citizen. The devices could be removed surgically or disabled by a targeted radiation burst, but both processes were highly illegal on Earth. Colonial immigrants usually had theirs removed, however, and those born on the frontier never got one to begin with. The entire idea of being tracked 24/7 was anathema to colonial culture.

There was considerable distrust of all governmental authority in the colonies, and a heavy emphasis on self-reliance and freedom was infused in the culture. The settlers had faced serious obstacles in building their new worlds, and they'd done it largely on their own, often paying a heavy price in lives and hardship in the early years. Most of them had been square pegs on Earth anyway, the small minority who chafed under a repressive way of life that most meekly accepted.

Anton said nothing, but his face communicated his thoughts clearly. Anger, disgust, determination were all there to see in the scowl he wore. Marek turned to face his friend, his own expression grim. "There's more too. Registration of all business transactions, new laws and regulations, heavier taxation. All for our own good, of course." He paused, taking a short breath. "It is worse than we feared, far worse."

"So it's finally here." Anton's voice was grim, his eyes downcast. "The choice." He paused, staring out over the sea. "We knew it was coming. They're going to try to turn the colonies into copies of Earth." His voice grew louder, more defiant. "And we all need to make our decision. Do we surrender our rights, our freedoms? A lifetime to find them; do we let them slip away, be stolen from us?" There was bitterness in his tone now, old hatreds from a youth spent in misery and deprivation. "Do we live out our lives begging for scraps from our political masters?" He paused, taking a deep breath. "Or do we fight? The time for delay, for prevarication is past. We all know that talk won't solve this." His faced hardened as he continued, the pleasant expression of the civilian factory owner giving way, hardening, leaving in its stead the icy cold resolve of the veteran platoon sergeant in battle. "My choice is made, John. If they mean to have a war, let it begin here. Let Columbia lead the way."

Marek looked into Anton's frozen eyes and felt his own anger, his own terrible resolution building. He too appreciated the freedoms he now had but had never known before, and he wasn't going to surrender them...ever. "And mine also, Lucius. I am with you." He paused then continued, no longer concerned about the volume of his voice. "And the others too.

We are all resolved together. We are one in this." He reached out and put his hand on Anton's shoulder. "And we must act. Tonight."

Arlen Cooper sat at his desk, his head cradled in his hands. He took two analgesics to back up the pair he'd taken an hour before. He didn't expect much; painkillers didn't seem to have any effect on the headaches these colonials caused. Cooper had been a ward chief, essentially the political supervisor of a housing block in the Manhattan Protected Zone. A Political Academy graduate, he'd followed in his parents' footsteps as a low-level member of the privileged class, but his prospects hadn't extended much beyond being a local bully and keeping the engineers and accountants in line. Not until he was offered the chance to become Planetary Advisor to one of the colony worlds.

The upper classes on Earth looked at the colonies with utter disdain, and no highly-placed Politician was likely to accept a posting in space. When the decision was made to station federal watchdogs on the colonies, the only way the authorities could find enough candidates was to make offers to lower level functionaries like Cooper. Accepting a position on a frontier world became a path to advancement, the only one he was likely to see, so Cooper had jumped at the chance when it was offered.

Cooper had been an effective ward chief on Earth, with just enough sadistic arrogance to really enjoy it. His job was mostly about maintaining order, and he had all the tools a bully needed to ply his trade. In New York, he just had to threaten to revoke a work permit or residency license, and he'd instill all the fear he needed to gain the desired compliance. He particularly enjoyed the look of terror in the eyes of those who drew his attention, as they realized he could easily have them cast out of the Protected Zone to live among the Cogs, eking out a meager existence in the crumbling wreckage of the slums. He'd used that fear to punish anyone who got out of line for sure, but he hadn't been shy about employing the same tools for a little blackmail. He had bullied his share of bribes to supplement his income, as well as more than a few sexual favors.

He smiled wickedly, remembering one woman in particular who'd caught his eye. It wasn't that she was a great beauty…she wasn't. But she seemed so scared, so vulnerable. He'd threatened to have her husband and children expelled, going so far as to have the orders drawn up so she could see them. She resisted at first, but in the end she had no choice, and she gave in. She cried through the whole thing, at least the first time or two, though he used her so often that by the end she was totally emotionless. When he finally tired of her and told her she didn't have to come back, she thanked him again and again. He'd abused her terribly for months, and when he stopped, she was so relieved all she could do was thank him. That was the part he loved the most. He watched her leave, broken inside but thinking she'd saved her family at least. He grinned as he pulled the expulsion order up on his 'pad and, with a malicious laugh, approved it with a single thumbprint.

But that was on Earth. Here he didn't have the power he'd enjoyed so much at home, and the colonists weren't so easily intimidated. He'd been ignored by them mostly, though some of the less restrained residents suggested he go fuck himself. A few even offered some colorful suggestions that featured far greater specificity. He raged against their insolence, but he lacked the power to do anything about it. At least he had until now.

He looked at the screen again, savoring the words he'd read half a dozen times already. He'd received the first list of orders the day before, mostly new restrictions and initiatives designed to bring the colonials under control. Today's follow up gave him the means to make it happen. He was granted full executive authority over the planet, superseding all local government. He was authorized to issue whatever edicts he felt were necessary and replace any local officials, even to disband the Planetary Assembly if they opposed him. Most importantly, he was getting the force he needed to implement all of this - 10 regiments of Federal Police, entirely under his command. The first two units had already landed, and the rest would arrive within the week.

He leaned back in his chair, looking through the window into the gloomy dusk. He smiled, thinking about how he was finally going to teach these arrogant Columbians the new order of things. They would learn to respect their political masters. How hard a lesson that would be was up to them.

The streets of Weston were quiet, very quiet, except for the wind whipping around the buildings. A large city by colonial standards, it was still barely two kilometers from end to end, with a number of satellite villages surrounding it. The District, the only section that looked anything like a true city, was less than half a square kilometer, the rest just a belt of mostly two and three story buildings ringing the central area.

Marek walked slowly toward the outskirts of town, his footsteps scraping softly on the wet gravelly surface to the side of the road. The storm was close now, and the clouds obscured Columbia's two moons. As he walked farther, beyond the lighted streets of the city center, the darkness was nearly total.

But Marek knew the way by heart. He'd traveled this route a hundred times, though never on business as fateful tonight's. They will all be assembled by now, he thought, ready to do what they must. He hurried his step, though he still moved cautiously, peering around for any signs he'd been followed. They were about to take a bold step, one likely to offer a hard road from which there could be no retreat. He felt no tension for himself. Having decided his own course he was content to follow it through. Once a Marine, always a Marine…he'd faced battle before and could do it again if he had to. The decision was the hard part for him; once that was made it became duty…and he knew how to do his duty.

But he worried for the multitudes that would get drawn into the maelstrom…the colonists, the children, all of them. He'd seen the cost war extracted from innocents before, colonists whose homes had become battlefields, those who'd lived under harsh occupations for years, the 30,000 people who'd called Calumet home before they were vaporized in an instant. The choices he and the others made here would affect everyone on Columbia...and possibly on many different worlds as well. Nothing would ever be the same again.

He turned the corner and he could see the outside lights of the armory in the distance. Columbia had a well-trained and equipped militia. After the CAC invasion, the planetary defenses, including the militia, were massively upgraded to face any future attack. There had even been a full-time planetary army during the rest of the war, though this had been folded into the citizen militia with the coming of peace. Columbia was a prosperous colony, but a permanent peacetime military was still a luxury it couldn't afford...and one Alliance Gov was not willing to allow. The Columbians knew they had to disband their army for economic reasons, but they still resented being ordered to do it by the authorities on Earth. One more point of contention, just another dry log on the pile waiting for the right spark.

He knew the armory well. The Planetary Assembly had quickly offered the newly-arrived Marek a commission in the militia, as a major commanding one of the Weston-area battalions. He had been reluctant to accept, having just recovered from his nearly terminal wounds and retired from the service. His plans had included a heavy dose of civilian life, at least for a while, but as things worked out, he wasn't on Columbia for a month before he was trying on a new uniform. He was a little unsettled at the abrupt jump from platoon to battalion command, but that was normal when transferring from a Marine assault unit to the militia. Besides, he figured it was peacetime and he'd have lots of chances to get used to it. Now it looked like he might have less time than he'd hoped.

Marek pulled the signal laser from his bag and fired several short bursts. Pre-programmed with the location of the receiver, the laser was an almost untraceable method of communication. The pulses themselves were invisible in the clean Columbian air, so no one but the recipient would see the transmission. The signal was a precaution; it would insure that Marek didn't get shot by his own people. Nerves were definitely on edge, and there was no point in taking chances. They didn't have AI-assisted powered armor with sophisticated friend or foe systems like he was used to; one nervous fisherman turned revolutionary could take him out with an instant of panicked fire.

It was only a few seconds before the response came. Everything was ready to go. Marek swallowed hard, his mind focused on the plan, rekindling senses that had lain dormant since he last saw action. After tonight there would be no turning back.

Chapter 6

Sub-Sector B
Western Alliance Intelligence Directorate HQ
Wash-Balt Metroplex, Earth

Garret looked up through a swirling red haze. His head ached, feeling as though someone had cut a trench through his skull with a dull blade. He was lost, not sure where he was, and his arms reached out, exploring, feeling slowly around where he lay. Slowly his eyes started to focus, the opaque cloud giving way to a few twinkling spots, and in the distance a pulsating bright light, like a sun suspended above his head.

No, not a sun, he thought. Just a light in the ceiling. His memories were starting to come back, though he still didn't know where he was. He'd been in Kelly's room at the Willard. He was beginning to remember...she had left for a minute... he was groggy, and he sat down on the edge of the bed. He couldn't understand; he'd only had one glass of wine with dinner. Yes, it was coming back to him now. He'd leaned back, lying on the bed. Or had he fallen, passed out? That was the last thing he could recall. Now he was here.

"Welcome, Admiral Garret." The voice came from behind him, and it took his still-disoriented brain an extra instant to process it. "I regret we could not arrange a more dignified arrival for you."

Garret moved, trying to turn toward the sound. The room shifted as he moved his head, and he slipped back onto the cot.

"I am afraid, Admiral, that you are likely to be lightheaded for a few minutes." Garret heard footsteps, his companion moving around into his field of view. "Unfortunately, the drug you ingested has a few temporary side effects. They will clear up shortly, and I can promise you that you will be as good as new."

"Where...am...I?" Garret's throat was dry, so parched he could barely speak audibly. The man standing in front of him was tall, with dark hair speckled heavily with gray...his age, probably mid-sixties. He wore a perfectly tailored suit, obviously very expensive, though otherwise he was fairly non-descript. "What…happened…to…Kelly?"

"Where are my manners, admiral? Allow me to introduce myself. I am Gavin Stark, and you are my guest." Stark reached over and slid a bare metal chair closer to the cot. His tone was calm and relaxed. "To answer your first question, we are at Alliance Intelligence headquarters, or more accurately, below it. Sub-Sector B, to be specific." Stark noticed the startled look on Garret's face. "I'm afraid Sub-Sector C is a bit more well-known." Sub-Sector C was Alliance Intelligence's primary prison and interrogation area, infamous for the brutal methods employed there. "This section is for our more…ah…distinguished guests." He sat in the chair and smiled. "I can assure you that I have no desire to mistreat you, admiral. It is simply - how shall I put it? - necessary that you be safeguarded for a while."

Garret was still weak, but his strength was slowly returning, and with it his anger. "Safeguarded?" He was trying to yell, but his dry throat only allowed him to croak out the words. "I am the Director of the Navy and you are holding me against my will. You are guilty of kidnapping, treason, and God knows what else. I demand you release me at…" His voice cut out entirely, leaving him coughing and trying to clear his throat.

"Forgive me, admiral." Stark got up reached over to a small table, pouring water into a cup from a large metal pitcher. "Here, drink this. I'm afraid the anesthetic we utilized leaves your throat quite parched." He extended the cup. Garret looked up suspiciously. "Admiral, I am quite certain you are aware that if I wanted to do you harm there is little to stop me. I would hardly have to poison your water." Stark smiled as Garret continued to stare at him, a doubtful expression on his face. "Truly, admiral. Please. Drink."

Garret reached out and grabbed the cup, putting it to his lips and taking a deep gulp. He could feel the cool liquid pouring down, soothing his sore throat, driving away the burning thirst.

"Slowly, admiral, please. You may find yourself a bit nauseous if you drink too quickly."

Garret looked up defiantly and downed the rest in one big gulp, tossing the cup aside. "And Kelly?" He was louder now, and more forceful. "Where is she?"

Stark couldn't help but admire the admiral. If there was one thing Gavin Stark detested it was weakness. Augustus Garret was many things, but weak was definitely not one of them. Barely awake, held captive in a cell in one of the most feared buildings on Earth, he was a model of command and composure. "Always the gentleman, concerned for the lady's well-being." Stark smiled, enjoying the fact that he'd put one over on the great Admiral Garret. "Don't worry, admiral, I can assure you she is quite well. Even now she is..."

"She's one of your people." Garret interrupted as realization dawned on him. "It was a setup from the beginning." His rage was building, fueled by his frustration with himself for falling into the trap.

"Yes, admiral." Stark's voice was unchanged, matter-of-fact, with no gloating or disrespect. "It was necessary to, shall we say, persuade you to join us here. I'm sure you will agree that our little plan was more elegant than, say, throwing a bag over your head and pushing you into a transport." He looked at Garret and grinned. "And substantially more enjoyable from your perspective, I am sure." He paused then added, "Indeed, I am sure, having been subjected to the lady's charms myself." He smiled again. "Her name is Alex, by the way, not Kelly. An alias seemed appropriate considering the circumstances."

"What do you want?" Garret was shaking off the grogginess. He was on the verge of losing his temper, but now he was in total control, his command face on. He scanned the room as he spoke, taking stock, looking for possible avenues of escape.

"Actually, very little, admiral." Stark leaned back, his hands resting on the arms of the chair as he spoke. "It was necessary to remove you from direct contact with the naval data net or any of your subordinates, but other than that, the only thing I will require is an occasional DNA sample to override some of the security systems." Access to certain data banks required

DNA from an authorized user, and the systems would detect counterfeit material. "We will extract it most painlessly, I assure you." He smiled as Garret looked around the room. "Please take my word, Admiral…there is no way out of here. Things will be much easier for everyone if you do not attempt anything foolish."

Garret leaned up and shifted his feet so he was sitting on the edge of the cot. "So you just plan to keep me hostage?" He looked at Stark, his face impassive. He was enraged, but his iron control had clamped down.

"I would use the word detainee, and I assure you that this action is for the good of the state and is in no way punitive. We will make you as comfortable as possible." He waved his hand around the room. It looked more like a hotel suite than a prison cell, and the furnishings and appointments were plush. "Not all of our accommodations are up to this standard, I am afraid."

"You expect me to just sit here while you do whatever it is you are planning?"

"As I do not intend to give you any other options at present, that is exactly what I expect, admiral." Stark put his hands on his knees and looked at Garret. Let us make the best of this, shall we? Things could be worse." There was a passing coldness in Stark's voice that chilled even Garret's battle-hardened soul. "It is fortunate that I do not need more from you. As I am sure you are aware, there are occupants of this building in rather more distress than you right now. We have numerous methods of…persuasion, some of which are quite unpleasant."

Garret's eyes narrowed, focusing like lasers on Stark's. He was trying to decide if he'd just been subtly threatened. "Whatever you are planning, it won't work. You will never get away with it."

Stark rose slowly from the chair. "Admiral, I sympathize with your frustration, however I assure you that we are both loyal servants of the state. I am not, as you so pointedly put it, trying to get away with something. I am doing what must be done for the security of the Alliance." He looked down at Garret. "We need not be enemies, admiral."

Garret stood up, his eyes never leaving Stark as he did. His legs were still a little wobbly, but he held himself rigidly, not showing any weakness. "Are you suggesting that I would take any actions contrary to the security of the Alliance?" His cool composure was cracking just a bit. Augustus Garret had served in the navy his entire adult life; he sacrificed everything else important to him, even the only woman he'd ever loved...duty was all that mattered to him. "I am no traitor." His tone was icy, coldly threatening.

Stark stepped back a bit; the two had been standing close to each other, and he wanted to defuse Garret's temper. "Admiral, I meant no offense." He paused, trying to decide how much he wanted to say. "But we are in uncertain times, and we may have to take specific actions, actions I was uncertain you would be willing to be a part of. Let's just leave it at that for now." He turned and walked toward the door.

"If you think you can turn the navy into your blunt instrument, you're going to have to do a lot more than kidnap me." Garret was struggling to maintain his cool. The thought of his beloved navy being a tool of Alliance Intelligence was too much to bear. He tried to push the thoughts back, but he couldn't banish the visualizations in his head...images of naval ships bombarding Alliance colony worlds. Killing the very people they had fought so hard to protect.

"Get some rest, admiral. It will help you recover from the after effects of the drugs." He looked at the scanner next to the door. "Open."

"Yes, Number One." The computer's tone was ominous, part of the overall design scheme of the detainee levels. Even prisoners like Garret weren't supposed to be too comfortable. Of course, those on the lower levels had much more pressing things to worry about than a nasty-sounding computer.

"We will speak later, admiral." Stark didn't wait for a response; he walked through the door as soon as it opened, and it slid shut behind him.

"So? Are we ready, Number One?" Standing in the hallway was Augustus Garret. Not the real one, imprisoned in the cell just beyond the closed door, but the one Gavin Stark had invented. As close an imitation as modern plastic surgery could make from one of Stark's agents who was the right basic size and shape.

"Are you ready? That is the more relevant question." Stark's eyes bored into those of the fake Garret. "It is essential that you pass for the admiral. This is a dangerous game we are playing."

"I am ready." He looked and sounded exactly like Garret, down to the cold stare and commanding presence. "Shall I go?"

Stark looked him up and down, almost forgetting it wasn't the admiral he was facing. It was uncanny, his own creation, and even he was taken in. The imposter had Garret's small personal mannerisms nailed perfectly – posture, expressions, fluidity of movement. "There are two vacancies on the Directorate at present. If you are successful in your mission, you will occupy one of these."

"Thank you, Number One." The agent, whose real name was Zander Alexi, was genuinely surprised. He knew there would be great rewards for success – that was how Alliance Intelligence operated. But he hadn't considered a seat on the Directorate. The wealth and privilege – and power – that came with such an appointment were almost incalculable. "I will succeed." Anything else was unthinkable…he knew the penalties for failure would be draconian. That, also, was how Alliance Intelligence operated.

"I hope so." Stark's voice was still calm and even, but a reptilian coldness crept in. "I trust you are aware of the consequences if you are not successful. Assuming, of course, that the navy leaves me enough of you to punish."

Alexi swallowed hard. "Yes, Number One." His voice wavered a bit, but he still sounded confident. "I understand. And I shall not fail." He could feel his heart pounding in his ears. This was Alliance Intelligence, how it operated. There was constant stress, and operatives were dually motivated by the promise of great reward and the threat of unspeakable punishment. It was carrot and stick on steroids, and it worked. Things had always been that way to an extent, but Stark was the master of maintaining a constant level of tension in his people. The cost in burnt out agents was high, but in the end, they too were just tools to Stark. Getting the job done, that was all that mattered.

"Then go. You will already be late getting to the office." Stark took one last look at Alexi. Everything was perfect, right down to the slightly rumpled uniform. "Number Three will meet you this evening for dinner. No doubt many people have seen the admiral with her. She is quite…noticeable." Stark always had to repress a little smile when he thought of Alex. It was nothing so quaint as affection, more an appreciation of her own ruthlessness and stubbornness. Of the entire Directorate, she was the most like him, though Stark never really let anyone know him very well. Except for Jack Dutton, of course. "The two of you will appear to be tense at dinner, and this will set the stage for a breakup. I need Number Three for another operation, but we must be methodical in extricating her from this one. We don't want to arouse any suspicions, however minor."

"Yes, Number One." Alexi turned on his heels and started to go.

"And Zander?"

The agent spun around. "Yes, Number One?"

Stark couldn't help admire his handiwork. It could have been Augustus Garret standing there. "Don't overdo it at dinner. Just a little tension. Admiral Garret would never make a scene in public, not even when quarreling with a lover. Understood?"

"Yes, Number One." He looked slightly impatient, just the way Augustus Garret would in this situation. "I will remember." He turned and walked down the corridor and rounded the corner toward the lift.

"So what do you think?" Stark was alone in the hallway, but a few seconds later, a hatch in the wall opposite Garret's cell slid open.

"I think he is as ready as possible." Jack Dutton walked slowly out into the corridor. "And I think there was no alternative." He paused slightly as the hatch slid closed behind him. "Admiral Garret is not a blatant colonial partisan like many of the others. He is a creature of duty, and the coming conflict will put him in an almost impossible situation. There is no way to reliably predict how he would react." He sighed quietly. "We could not take the risk. We must control the navy, or at least a large percentage of it."

"I would have preferred that Lin Kiang had saved us this trouble." Stark's tone was slightly bitter. "That damned fool can't do anything right." Lin Kiang had been a senior CAC admiral assigned to intercept Garret's task force and destroy the admiral's flagship during the latter stages of the war. It was a daring assassination attempt against the preeminent mastermind of naval tactics, but it failed. The flagship was destroyed, but an unconscious Garret was saved by his fanatically loyal staff, most of whom died after getting him off the ship in his cutter. The disgraced Admiral Lin was now the guest of Alliance Intelligence, ensconced in luxurious quarters in this very building where Stark protected him from the agents of his vengeful counterpart, Li An, head of CAC external intelligence. Li An had assured Lin that failure would carry a heavy price, and she was accustomed to keeping such promises.

"Garret's survival yielded us benefits as well. The fighting at Epsilon Eridani could have gone quite differently without the admiral." Garret had been thought dead, but he'd come back on the eve of the final battle to take command and win a smashing victory. "Now, however, we have no other options. He is too powerful not to control, and too big a hero to push aside. The navy must continue to think he is in command." Dutton put a hand on Stark's shoulder. "Once we are able to complete our restructuring, we won't need him anymore."

Stark looked back at the door to Garret's cell. "And then we will have to arrange a suitable end for the good admiral." Stark's tone had the slightest hint of regret. "Perhaps a shipyard accident on an inspection tour."

"Yes." Dutton was somber, genuinely unhappy about the prospect. "I don't see any alternative to liquidation." He paused, looking down at the ground. "It is a shame. Garret is a good man, one who should never have ended up here."

Stark's gaze turned back to Dutton. "Life is not fair, my friend." The momentary emotion was gone from his voice, replaced by a feral coldness. "We both know that." He paused, a stony expression on his face. "We will have to terminate Zander as well. Such will be his reward for success."

Dutton paused before answering. He found the realities of the job becoming more difficult with age. He was just too tired for it. He sighed deeply, an aching sadness in his eyes. "I agree. We cannot afford any loose ends on this."

Chapter 7

Columbia Militia Armory
North of Weston City
Columbia - Eta Cassiopeiae II

"Kevin, take five of your people upstairs and find good vantage points covering the road." Marek's voice was crisp, commanding. Things were spiraling out of control, and his combat instincts were taking over. "Now! We don't have time to waste."

"Ok, John. On the way." Kevin Clarkson was a submersible captain, one of the 20 or so contractors who scoured the oceans of Columbia for the raw materials Marek's factory turned into valuable exports. He turned and called out to several of his crew, telling them to get upstairs. "Are they really coming, John?" His voice was a little shaky.

Marek almost scolded Clarkson for wasting time with nonsense, but he held it back. You have to remember, he thought, scolding himself, these are not all veterans - you can't handle them like you would a crack platoon. "Yes, Kevin. I left a couple scouts in Weston before I came here, and they sent the signal. The Feds are mustering now. We must have tripped an alarm we didn't know about." He could see the tension in Clarkson's face. Kevin had never been in combat; he'd never fought his way through the slums on Earth. His father had immigrated to Columbia before he was born, and he'd never even been off-planet. "It will be OK, Kevin." Marek put his hand on Clarkson's shoulder. "Just stay focused. Tell your people to be steady, be deliberative. If it comes to shooting, pick your targets carefully, methodically." He paused, looking right into Clarkson's eyes. "And, Kevin…it only comes to shooting if they force the issue. No one fires without my order. Understood?"

Clarkson nodded. "Got it, John." He spun around and followed his crew up the stairs. He still sounded nervous, but that wasn't surprising. A thirty second pep talk wasn't likely to chase away the fear, especially the first time. Marek knew that much from his own experiences.

He still felt the fear himself. It wasn't as acute as it had been the first time he'd gone into battle, but it was always there. People who hadn't been in battle thought veterans overcame fear, left it behind. Legends and heroes were more inspiring as unshakeable monoliths, super men and women with no weaknesses. Marek knew better. He knew from his own experience, and he knew because he'd served with some true heroes, and all of them had been scared too. Veterans dealt with the fear, not defeated it. They shoved it aside, made it an ally, let it focus them but not paralyze them. He knew from training; he knew from experience – if he let the fear rule him he was vastly more likely to end up KIA. Reaching that realization, asserting the dominance of judgment over fear…that was a as good a definition of veteran as Marek could imagine.

Unfortunately, this was a hard lesson, and his prospective citizen soldiers weren't likely to learn it quickly. If it came to real war, a lot of them would die before they learned it at all. Marek started to realize how deeply unprepared they were. There had been bluster and speeches, and hushed meetings late at night, but the non-veterans had no idea what they were heading into. He wondered, how would they hold up, bloodied and battered, their homes burned, their friends dead at their sides? Would they have the inner strength to persevere against whatever the Feds threw at them? Freedom was not going to come cheaply.

He realized how unprepared he was himself. He'd reluctantly come to terms with the need to take up arms again, but he hadn't considered all the realities, at least not in detail. The last time he'd set foot on a battlefield he wore powered armor, assisted and advised by an artificial intelligence unit that was the cutting edge of information technology. His troops, even the few who were newbs, had been though years of training. When he had first resolved to take a stand here, Marek remembered the combats he'd been in, but now he took stock of the realities. This was going to be a vastly different war, and the challenges were going to be unlike anything he'd encountered before. As a veteran officer he knew he would bear heavy responsibility to forge his untried soldiers into a combat ready force. His thoughts were grim, tentative. Can I do this?

"John, what do you want us to do with them?" Aaron Davis was one of Marek's employees from the factory. Also a veteran, Davis had served five years in the Corps, though only two were in combat assignments, and those were in quiet sectors. He had a gift for administration, which made him a great asset at the factory, but Marek wished he'd seen a little more action. Still, he was a fully-trained Marine who had been in battle, which made him worth his weight in frag grenades right now.

Marek glanced over at the six Federal officers who had been stationed at the armory when his people burst in. They claimed to be there to assist in the inventory and categorization of weapons, but Marek knew they were an advanced team prepping for the shutdown of the facility. "Make sure they are tightly bound." Their hands were already tied behind their backs, bound with durable polymer shackles. "Gag them too, and secure them in the back room." Davis nodded and turned to go. "And Aaron?" Davis stopped and looked back. "They are not to be harmed. This may well come to fighting, but we are not going to start it. Understood?"

Davis had an odd expression on his face; Marek couldn't decide if he was disappointed they weren't going to shoot the Feds or offended that Marek was worried he would hurt unarmed prisoners. This entire situation was like nothing he'd ever prepared for, and he wasn't sure exactly how to handle his people.

"I understand, John." His voice was clear, respectful but a little too sharp, too clipped. That answered Marek's question. Davis clearly would have handled the Feds less gently had he been in charge. That kind of attitude was spreading rapidly. The federal authorities were barely tolerated in the colonies in the best of circumstances, but on Columbia they had been cracking down pretty aggressively. A lot of bad feeling had developed, and many Columbians were anxious to strike back. And with the veterans, you never knew what was in their past. Some of the ex-Marines were native-born colonials, but many of them had come from some of the Alliance's worst slums. They'd survived and found a home in the Corps, and later in the colonies, but many of them harbored intense grudges against Alliance Gov and the system they'd had to endure.

The strange relationship between the Marine Corps and the federal government created a lot of unpredictability in the current, rapidly changing situation. Almost certainly, some individual Marines would side with the colonists. But in many ways, the Corps was caught in the middle. When it was defending the colonial worlds against the other Superpowers, it was serving both Alliance Gov and the colonists. Now, for the first time, the Marines faced the possibility of a choice...obey an order to fire on colonists or defend those rebels and attack other federal forces. Or sit the whole thing out.

The Corps was generally perceived to be sympathetic to the colonies, and overall that was true. But Marek knew it was more complicated. The Marine Corps was made up of thousands of individuals. The views of its commanders, the loyalties of its personnel, and the reality of its situation were all major factors in how it would respond. The Marine Corps would have immense difficulty sustaining itself without supplies and resources from Earth. A Corps that declared for rebelling colonists – or even disobeyed orders to attack those rebels - would quickly find itself very short of weapons and equipment. It was even possible that the pressure of the looming conflict would fracture the entire organization...that Marine would end up fighting Marine.

He might – just – be able to help forge the colonists into an army that could take on the better equipped Federal Police and other paramilitary forces they were likely to face. But he knew if Marine assault units came to Columbia to fight for the Feds, his amateur troops would be cut to pieces. The prospect of firing on other Marines was something he didn't want to imagine. He liked to think it couldn't come to that, but he'd been in battle too many times. If they came here to attack him, to fight his ragged little army, he knew he'd do whatever he could to destroy them. He could feel the anger, the bitterness and confused feelings about an eventuality that hadn't even happened yet. He had always considered other Marines as his brothers and sisters, but he would think of any who came here to kill colonists as traitors. If they made themselves tools to repress what a century of Marines had died to preserve they would no longer be his brothers. They would be his enemies.

Marek pushed those thoughts aside, focusing on the matter at hand. He wished he had Anton with him, but he'd sent the tough old sergeant to scout the approaches to the armory. Anton and his scouts would give him warning when the Feds were coming; he was sure of that. He'd hesitated before sending Anton out, but he needed reliable strength estimates on approaching federal forces, not just a panicked message that they were coming. He could count on Anton to keep his cool and get him what he needed. If there was too much strength coming, he had to clear his people out and try to get away. Losing a fight here could end the resistance before it even began.

He had 83 men and women, plus the six he'd sent with Anton. They were here to secure and load the militia's weapons, not to attack the Feds. But they were ready to fight if necessary. The 15 or so veterans present knew what that meant; the others would get an education quickly if shooting started. They were good men and women, sturdy colonists and his friends and neighbors, but Marek had no idea how most of them would react under fire.

He had called out his militia battalion, but he couldn't use the normal communications channels without alerting the Planetary Advisor, so he'd sent messengers. It was a slow way to get out the word, and it would be at least two days before they could muster the unit, or at least a good chunk of it. By then the Feds would have confiscated the weapons in the armory and Marek's troopers would be throwing rocks.

"John, the transports are almost fully loaded." Jack Winton was older than most of those present, but he could keep up with any of them. He was tall and still muscular; he had at least 15 kilos on Marek. He owned a major transport firm, with a large fleet of vehicles moving shipments all over Columbia. Winton was a veteran, but not a Marine. He'd been a naval officer early in the Second Frontier War, head of engineering on a heavy cruiser. He and the rest of the crew had come close to spending eternity on a ghost ship, zooming into deep space at high velocity with the com and engines knocked out. They managed to get communications back online and send a distress call out before they were too far into deep space. They were rescued by two fast attack ships that matched vector and velocity and docked with their crippled vessel. Ending up on a ghost ship was the deepest fear of the veteran spacer, and the prospect of spending eternity frozen solid at his post as the ship careened into deepest space proved to be the last straw. He retired soon after, settling on Columbia and fixing up a broken down transport he bought with his retirement bonus. Now he had a successful business and dozens of vehicles moving all sorts of freight.

"Great, Jack. I want them out of here in fifteen minutes, fully loaded or not." Marek had been facing away, but he turned to look at Winton as he spoke. "At least we'll know we got something out." Not enough, though, he thought. Winton had only had three transports close enough to get here on short notice. He had more inbound, but it would be another hour, maybe more, before they arrived. "Make sure those loads are balanced. No sense taking guns and no ammunition. We can't rely on getting more trucks out."

Winton nodded. "Got it, John. Each transport has a mix. Even if only one gets through it will be useful."

"Ok, let me know when your other transports are fifteen minutes out." He was going to add a few extra comments, but his com unit buzzed. "Marek here."

"John, it's Lucius." Anton's voice was distant, tinny. The militia communicators weren't military grade, not by Marine standards at least. "I've got Feds inbound to your location, loaded up on light transports. Company strength at least, and fully armed." There was a brief pause, then: "ETA your location ten minutes."

"Acknowledged." He turned to Winton. "Now, Jack. Get your trucks moving now, whatever is loaded." Winton nodded and headed toward the loading area at a run.

"Lucius, get back here ASAP."

There was a brief pause. "John, I think we can do more good out here. If we hit them before they get to the armory we can make them deploy. They won't know what's out here; we'd probably hold up the whole crew."

Marek smiled to himself. This was what he'd expect from Anton, and tactically the veteran sergeant was right. But the situation wasn't that simple. "Negative, Lucius." Marek paused, formulating how he wanted to say what he was thinking. "First, you've got a few factory workers and fishermen with you, not a crack squad. If you start something out there alone, you'll just get them all killed…and yourself too. And I can't lose you, not this early in whatever we're starting here."

"I know, John, but I was thinking we could just…"

Marek interrupted his friend. "There's more to it, Lucius." He hesitated until he was sure Anton had stopped talking. "They haven't fired on us. You're talking about ambushing a group of Feds who haven't done anything yet. We can't be the ones who start this; it has to be them."

There were a few seconds of silence as Anton realized Marek was right. "I understand, John. We'll be back in a flash."

"Thanks, big man. I need you here." Anton had only considered the tactical situation, but Marek was looking at the political dimension as well. He knew Alliance Gov would lie and propagandize however they thought was useful, but he didn't need to give them ammo. Besides, he thought, it would just be wrong. He didn't doubt it would come to violence, but it hadn't yet. The colonists didn't want to fight Alliance Gov; they didn't want to shoot people from Earth. They just wanted to be left alone. "That's the difference between us and them," Marek muttered softly to himself.

He reached up and worked the controls of his headset. The minute they'd arrived he had militia comlinks issued to everyone. Good communication was important to a well-drilled unit of veterans; for a hastily organized bunch of amateurs it was essential. The militia equipment wasn't what he was used to as far as range and ease of use – and it certainly didn't come with a suit AI to help manage it all – but it was what they had.

"Attention all personnel." He paused a few seconds. They'd hastily programmed their network, and Marek's com was set as the lead unit. His systemwide broadcasts came through on every headset regardless of any other communications going on, and he wanted to give everyone time to focus on what he was going to say. "We have Federal Police inbound, close to 100." It was more like 150, according to Anton's reports, but Marek didn't want to scare his rookie soldiers too badly.

"We have a strong position and ample warning. We are well prepared to defend ourselves if that is necessary." He paused, taking a deep breath. "I said, 'if necessary.' I want everyone to be clear on this." He paused again. Make this point firmly, he thought. "We will not back down, but we are not looking to start a fight. No one fires until I give the word." He stressed the next part. "No matter what."

He had experience commanding troops in battle, and the force he had here was not enormously larger in scale from the platoon he'd led on Epsilon Eridani IV. But it was different in every other respect. He had to command them firmly or they would keep thinking of themselves as his friends and neighbors and not their commanding officer...and that could get them all killed. Of course, the problem was he wasn't their commander, at least not officially. They had no real organizational structure, no ranks, no formal sub-units. Some of those present were from his militia battalion, but the rest were pure civilians. We're going to have to do something about all of this he thought... assuming we survive tonight.

"I want everyone to stay in their positions. Stay focused and just do the job." He softened his voice, more the sympathetic friend now than the ramrod commander. "I know you're all scared. There is no shame in that. I've been scared every time I've been in battle, but you need to control it, deal with it. If you keep your cool and stay focused, you'll come through just fine."

He hoped he was telling them what they needed. He'd never commanded anything but veterans and well-trained professionals before. He remembered what his first drop was like, and

how much he'd depended on his squad and platoon commanders to pull him through the fear and doubt…and that was after
he'd had six years of training. This war was going to be different, very different.

"You are my friends, my neighbors. When I fought before,
the Marines at my side were my brothers and sisters, but the
battlefields were worlds we'd never seen, places on a map." He
took a deep breath. "This is our home. What we do now will
determine what type of place it will be, not just for us, but for
generations not yet born." His volume was increasing, his voice
thick with emotion. "They faced such a test on Earth long ago,
and they failed, bequeathing to their children a life of tyranny
and destitution." He paused again then shouted, "We will not
fail!"

The roar on the comlink was deafening, a cacophony of
cheers and screams of, "We will not fail." They are as ready as
I can make them, Marek thought as he listened. I hope I am as
well.

The cheering fell silent as someone began shouting. "Vehicles outside!" The voice was shrill, stressed. "John, they're
coming through the outer gate!"

"Troy?" Marek thought the voice was Troy Evans. Troy was
barely 18, and Marek could hear the youth in his voice. "Is that
you reporting?"

"Yes, John." His voice was softer, but still shaky. "It's me."

"Identify yourselves when you report. All of you." Marek
snapped the command. The time for speeches was past. "I need
data, Troy. Numbers, types of vehicles. Are they disembarking?"

"Umm…I understand, John." He was scared, and it came
through loud and clear. Marek wished they'd had time to set up
a more complex communications net. Everyone didn't need to
hear everything.

"Focus, Troy." He was firm but patient. That's all he can
take, Marek thought. I'll just push him over the edge if I pressure him too hard. "Just concentrate and get me hard info."

"Yes, John." His voice was a little steadier. "It looks like at
least a dozen vehicles. They're stacked up at the gate, so it's hard

to tell how many."

"Good, Troy. Keep me posted." Bad tactics, he thought, lining up at the gate like that. They had to expect us to resist, so why would they make themselves easy targets? Are these Feds so arrogant they think they have nothing to fear from a bunch of colonials? He muttered softly to himself, his hand over the mic on his headset. "If they force us, we're going to teach them a hard lesson."

Marek walked toward the front of the building. The armory was a large plasti-crete structure, very solidly built, with two frontal access points and a big loading dock on the side. The loading area was enclosed within heavy 'crete walls, and he had the outer gate heavily garrisoned. He had a team on the roof, positioned to provide a good field of fire no matter how the Feds approached.

"Attention." The amplified voice was almost deafening, even inside. "You are illegally occupying government property and holding federal personnel hostage." Marek looked around the room. All his people looked steady so far, at least the ones he could see. "By order of His Excellency Arlen Cooper, Planetary Advisor of Columbia, you are to lay down your arms and surrender at once."

There was a long pause. This is where we're supposed to get scared, I guess, Marek thought. He snorted. I've faced a lot worse than you before, buddy. He was standing behind a workstation with screens displaying the input from the outside cameras. He could see the shadowy figures disembarking from the lead vehicles, deploying to the left and right.

"Failure to comply immediately will result in immediate action. You have one minute to respond."

Marek almost ordered his non-existent AI to connect him to the outside speakers, but he caught himself. He realized how accustomed he was to having the very best equipment, how different this fight would be than the ones he'd been in before. Compared to the way a Marine assault force was equipped, his people might as well have sharpened sticks. He reached down and flipped a switch.

"Attention federal commander. This is Major John Marek, commander of the 3rd Weston Battalion. I am duly authorized by the Planetary Assembly to conduct all operations I deem necessary to maintain the readiness of the force under my command. Your people have not been harmed, and they will be released to you at once."

Marek flipped off the switch and turned to Aaron Davis, who'd been standing behind him outside the door to the room where he'd locked up the captive Feds. "Get the prisoners. Bring them to the front entrance."

"You're going to release them?" Davis blurted out what he was thinking and immediately looked sorry.

"Just get them," Marek snapped. If we get through this, he thought, we're going to have to a long talk about military discipline. This is starting to feel like a commune. "I want them outside in sixty seconds. Move!" Davis was already on his way to get the prisoners, but Marek decided to add the last bit anyway to make a point.

He flipped the switch and reactivated his microphone. "Federal commander, your personnel will be released in one minute. Stand by." No threats or interruptions, Marek thought. At least this Fed isn't a totally unrestrained jackboot. He's cool enough to wait until I release his people before he starts threatening me again. Maybe, he thought, just maybe we can get through this without fighting. But he didn't really believe it.

"Attention all personnel." Marek spoke slowly and clearly into the comlink. "The federal prisoners are being released. Hold all fire. I repeat, hold all fire."

Marek waved his arm toward the door. Davis just nodded, not saying anything this time. He pushed a button and the plasti-steel door slid open. "Ok, get moving." His voice was sharp, clipped. He was following Marek's orders, but he clearly disagreed. He pushed the prisoners toward the door, hitting the button and closing the hatch as soon as the last of them was out.

Marek watched the released prisoners walk through the gate then flipped on the speaker. "All personnel have been released. This is a lawful Columbian militia installation occupied by forces under a duly-appointed field officer. You are respectfully requested to withdraw at..."

"You are ordered to disarm and surrender at once." The federal commander interrupted Marek. "In thirty seconds we will take the installation by force."

"Federal commander, you have no right to attempt to seize this facility." Marek knew it was a waste of time, but if there was a chance to stop what he could see coming, he had to try. "Withdraw at once."

There was no response. Marek flipped on his headset. "All personnel, prepare to repel an assault." He paused. "Stay focused, stay calm. Just do the work." Stay calm, he thought... that sounds great. Who the hell has ever stayed calm in battle?

He watched the whole thing unfold on his screen. The police came forward, rushing for the front entrance. Marek couldn't believe what he was seeing. The assaulting troops had no heavy weapons; they just rushed the building. He was going to have to make a decision. Open fire or let them get to the door. He flipped the switch on his headset, still not knowing what he was going to say, and then he heard it. A single shot – Marek couldn't tell which side had fired it. For an instant the sound hung in the air, a solitary crack in the night. Then both sides started firing wildly.

The Feds in front of the building were caught out in the open and raked by fire from Marek's carefully placed troops. Marek couldn't understand what they were thinking. "Arrogant fools," he muttered to himself as he watched his people on the roof massacre them. They thought they'd just walk up to the door, he thought, and we'd all panic. The federals fired sporadically up at the roof for a few seconds before they broke and ran.

"Cease fire." Marek barked the order into his headset, but the shooting continued. "Cease fire, goddammit!" Marek screamed into the mic. The fire sputtered to a halt, a few more shots ringing out until he yelled one last time.

The field in front of the building was strewn with dead and wounded. The rest of the federal force was running away or desperately climbing into their vehicles, throwing down their weapons and abandoning their wounded comrades.

"Lucius take your people and follow them." Anton's team was still outside the complex, well positioned to tail the Feds. And Marek could count on him not to do anything unfortunate. "Just make sure they retreat to Weston and don't try to regroup and come back."

"Acknowledged, lieuten…I mean John." Anton's combat memory was coming back, and the last time the two of them were in the field, Marek was lieutenant and Anton a sergeant. "Don't worry; we'll stay out of their way."

"Thanks, Lucius. Keep me posted." He switched to the general line. "Doc, do we have anyone hit?" Jarod Simmons wasn't really a doctor, but with ten years' service as a medtech in the Corps, he was the closest thing they had to one.

"No, John." Simmons' voice was odd, high-pitched and nasal. It always surprised Marek, especially considering Simmons was over two meters tall and weighed better than 100 kilos. "I checked, and everybody seems OK."

"Good." Marek took a deep breath. He expected someone to complain about what he was about to say. "I want you to go out and see what you can do for the wounded Feds." He paused, but Simmons, at least, didn't object. "Aaron, put together a five man detail and help Doc."

There was a long pause, then: "Yes, John." Davis sounded like he had just tasted something bad, but he didn't argue.

"Jack, how are we doing on those inbound transports?" Marek was reviewing his mental list of the most important weapons and equipment. They'd just bought time to load up another batch of supplies, and he wanted to make the most of it.

"Five minutes, John." Winton's response was immediate. "I just checked with them. We're in the loading area, ready to go."

"Good." Marek was leaning over, typing on a keyboard. "I made a few changes to the manifest. Sending it to you right now." He punched the last keys, zapping the document to Winton's workstation in the loading dock. "I want this stuff on those trucks at lightspeed, Jack." He paused. "The Feds will be back, and in much greater strength. And they won't be so foolish next time. I want us out of here before that happens."

"Yes, John." Marek could hear noise in the background. "We're already bringing the first palettes out to the bay."

Marek sat down on the hard metal chair of the workstation and let out a long, deep breath. He knew they had gotten lucky, very lucky. Next time, he thought, things are going to be a lot tougher. He was right.

Chapter 8

Tranquility
Cluster 11, Western Alliance Zone
Lunar Surface

Tranquility was booked weeks in advance. In Washbalt or London or New York there were many restaurants where the political and corporate elite met and enjoyed the perks of their privileged status. But there was only one truly five star eatery on the moon, and it was considered a must for anyone of consequence to eat there when visiting.

Hendrick Thoms masqueraded as a Corporate Magnate of moderate wealth and power, a junior Director of the megacorp GDL. His true job, however – the one that got him the GDL gig - was even more extraordinary, a high-ranking operative for Alliance Intelligence, specifically one placed to monitor activity in the senior naval command structure. GDL was the biggest defense contractor dealing with the navy, which put Thoms in an ideal position to monitor the top officers from outside the command structure.

But there were layers upon layers to Thoms – Magnate, spy, debauched libertine - and the bottom one, the one virtually no one saw…double agent, a mole working for the Martian Security Department. MSD had flipped Hendrick years before, using a fairly standard combination of bribery and blackmail. The relationship had been a mutually satisfactory one – Hendrick had found a nearly inexhaustible and highly untraceable funding source for some of his more expensive and private vices, and MSD had an information conduit highly placed in the Alliance Intelligence structure.

He was on the moon to meet with Roderick Vance, one of the richest men in the Martian Confederation. Vance-controlled interests owned and operated mining franchises all over the Sol and Alpha Centauri systems. They were set to discuss a major deal for GDL's shipbuilding operation to purchase inexpensive ores from one of Vance's companies. But that was just a cover - they had other topics to discuss as well, ones far more private. In addition to Vance's many public pursuits was one other known only to a select few…running MSD.

Vance's great-grandfather had been one of the founding fathers of the Confederation, a former American general who had settled on Mars in one of the early waves of colonization and later helped lead the independence movement. The Earth powers had blustered and threatened when their former colonies declared themselves an independent nation, but there was little they could do to stop it. The Unification Wars were raging, descending into the last horrific stages, when the coalescing Superpowers were throwing whatever they could at each other. There was little left – manpower, weapons, industry – to deploy against the Martian separatists.

While the Earth Superpowers fought each other to exhaustion, and nearly to extinction, the new Confederation grabbed most of the solar system's useful bits of real estate and built a substantial navy to hold on to it. By the time the Treaty of Paris ended the wars on Earth, the Confederation was a formidable force in space and controlled most of the resources of the solar system. It was effectively the ninth Superpower, despite its vastly smaller population.

The Confederation wasn't a true republic, but it was far more democratic than any of the nations of Earth. Influence was based on lineage, with greater representation given to the families that had been on Mars when independence was declared. But even recent immigrants had substantial rights, and the Confederation was almost completely without a destitute underclass like those so prevalent in the Earth Powers.

The Confederation generally remained neutral in the conflicts between the Superpowers. Its small interstellar holdings consisted of a few well-selected resource worlds and three major extra-solar colonies. The Martian military was small, but extremely well-trained and equipped, and none of the Powers wanted to make an enemy out of the Confederation. The Treaty of Paris forbade space combat in the Sol and Alpha Centauri systems, but the Confederation was not a signatory to that century-old document. It's adherence to these constraints was entirely voluntary, and it could easily cause major problems for any of the Powers that provoked it.

Mars had also become somewhat of a haven for the upper classes in each of the Powers, a place where wealthy exiles were generally welcomed and strict secrecy laws governed banking. The major Martian financial institutions did enormous business with the political and corporate elites of the various Powers, allowing them to safeguard funds that might otherwise be subject to question or confiscation. In a world of constant paralyzing government oversight and rabid infighting between elites, privacy was a rare and valuable commodity. It was one in very short supply on Earth, and the Martian bankers were happy to provide it…at a price.

MSD didn't operate with quite the unrestrained aggression of the other intelligence services, but it did try to keep an eye on the various Powers. The Confederation liked the balance of power, and its foreign policy was based on maintaining it. During the recent war, it had come close to entering on the side of the Alliance when it looked like that Power might be overwhelmed and crushingly defeated. But the Alliance turned things around and, in the end, won a decisive victory. Now the Confederation Council was concerned about the Alliance's place in inter-power relations. Its recent victory, combined with its discovery of an ancient alien artifact of potentially incalculable scientific value, threatened to permanently shatter the balance of power and put the Alliance in a preeminent, and perhaps dominant, position over the others. That was something the Confederation considered unacceptable.

There was another scenario, however, of equal concern to MSD and the Confederation Council. The Alliance was experiencing considerable unrest in its colonies, and widespread rebellion was a serious possibility. If the Alliance lost its frontier planets it would be crippled; without the resources pouring in from those worlds, its economy would collapse almost immediately. A desperate and dying Superpower would be even more dangerous than a dominant one. A fatally wounded Alliance could react in disastrous ways, possibly even repudiating the Treaty of Paris and triggering war on Earth and in the entire Sol system. Total war between the Powers would be a humanitarian catastrophe of incalculable proportions; it was unthinkable to allow it to happen.

The Alliance colonies would fare no better in this scenario. They were populated mostly by a hardy breed of adventurers, but they would stand no chance as an independent entity, not yet at least. The firebrands even now standing up to federal encroachments tended to underestimate the role Alliance Gov had played in supporting colonial growth and defending the worlds themselves. If they hadn't been part of a nation as strong as the Alliance, they would have been conquered long ago by the Caliphate or the CAC. It would take years – decades – to develop enough industry for them to stand alone without the support of an existing Power. And they were unlikely to get those years before the other Superpowers were picking their bones in an unrestrained feeding frenzy.

The Council had authorized MSD to ramp up its intelligence efforts. The Confederation was prepared to intervene in the developing situation to avoid an unacceptable outcome. But first they had to determine exactly what that course of action would be. For that, Vance needed much better information than he had. That's why Thoms was here.

The two of them sat alone in a private dining room, a small dome attached to the main restaurant by a short access tube. Just outside the clear hyper-polycarbonate dome was the reconstructed image of the first extra-terrestrial landing site…part of a vessel that had been called the Eagle, and a flag that a history buff would recognize as that of the United States in the mid-20th century. All of it was fake; the original remains had been destroyed by CAC forces during the Unification Wars, though that was not general knowledge, and most visitors believed they were looking at actual history.

The two of them spoke freely, if still in hushed tones. Vance's jamming device was the best Martian technology could produce…which meant it was better than anything the other Powers could make to counter it. If there were listening devices near them, those at the other end would be disappointed.

"Do I understand you correctly?" Vance usually had a great poker face, but he was stunned at what Thoms had just told him. "The Augustus Garret currently occupying the office of Alliance Navy Director is an imposter?"

Thoms took a sip from his wineglass, savoring the deep flavor of the Pinot Noir. He fancied himself an expert on wines, and he was sure this was a natural Burgundy, though he'd never tasted one before. He couldn't imagine the cost of this bottle – the Burgundian Pinot Noir grapes were extinct, killed off two generation before by a parasite mutation…another vestige of the bacteriological weapons used in the later Unification Wars. Genetically-altered hybrids had successfully replaced the natural species, but connoisseurs tended to feel the newer wines lacked the same depth. The few remaining bottles of pre-extinction vintages sold for thousands of credits, when they were available at all.

"Yes." Thoms put down his glass and looked across the table. "He is a surgically altered agent. A double."

Vance inhaled deeply. He tried never to underestimate Gavin Stark, but this was audacious even for the Alliance's spymaster. "What happened to the real Garret?"

Thoms had just taken a large bite, but he answered anyway, earnestly, if not with commendable etiquette. "I can't say for sure." He paused to swallow. "My guess is they have him somewhere in Alliance Intelligence HQ, but I am not privy to that information. I only know about this at all, because I am supposed to be a backup contact for the operative." He scooped up another forkful, but hesitated before he put it in his mouth. "It is possible Garret has been liquidated."

Vance looked down at his own untouched plate. "No, I don't think so." His eyes panned up, focusing on Thoms. "Stark is too meticulous. He may need information or something else from Garret. He'll keep him alive, at least as long as this masquerade continues." After a brief pause he added, "Though once he accomplishes whatever he wants I suspect both Garret and the agent will find themselves buried in some swamp." His face was impassive as always, but his voice betrayed a hint of sadness, a nuance noticeable only to someone more perceptive than Thoms. His thoughts were somber - Augustus Garret deserves better from the nation he's served so well.

Vance was silent for a minute before he continued. "I need more information. Specifically, what is Gavin Stark up to with this imposter?"

Thoms looked up at him with a large mouthful of food, chewing quickly so he could answer. "I suspect he wants more effective control of the navy." Thoms hadn't managed to swallow everything he'd shoved into his head, just enough that he could speak intelligibly.

Vance sighed impatiently. "Thank you for that amazing insight. Is this why I'm paying you a not-so-small fortune every year?" He paused, staring right at Thoms for an instant before he continued. "Obviously, he wants control over the navy, but I want to know exactly what he wants to do with that. He knows he can't keep a charade like this going indefinitely. Sooner or later a friend will visit Garret or he'll meet with an officer who knows him well - something will blow the cover. And Alliance Intelligence can't afford to get caught on this. The navy would go crazy." He was thinking as he spoke, trying to imagine what his opposite in Alliance Intelligence was planning. "Stark knows there's an expiration date on this scheme, so he must be planning specific operations he wants done soon." He stared silently across the table as his own thought formed. "Or things he wants to keep the navy from interfering with."

Thoms stared blankly across the table. "I don't have that kind of access to Stark. How am I supposed to figure out what he's trying to do?"

Vance's eyes bored into Thoms's. "You don't get paid what you do because what your job is easy. I suggest you think of some type of business matter you need to discuss with the Naval Director. Perhaps you can get something out of this fake Garret."

"That is a dangerous game." Thoms's expression had become nervous, tentative.

"You're not paid because what you do is safe either." Vance's impatient expression turned predatory. "And your situation will still be less hazardous than if we lost our, ah, discretion about some of your activities. Wouldn't you agree?" Vance generally lacked the malicious ferocity of his counterparts in the other Powers, but he disliked weasels like Thoms. They were a necessary evil in the trade, and he used them as he needed to…but he enjoyed making them squirm when he could.

Thoms looked over, weakly returning Vance's gaze. "I will try to get what you want." His voice was higher pitched, stressed.

"Try hard." Vance scolded himself for enjoying this as much as he was. "And here…" He slid a data chip across the table. "This is an agreement to provide the ores GDL requires at an extraordinary good price. It should make you quite a hero in the company." Vance frowned. "Another cost of this whole affair, and one I bear personally."

Thoms reached over and took the chip. He opened his mouth to speak, but he couldn't think of anything to say, and he just nodded.

"Now I suggest you get an early start back. You have a lot of work to do." Vance looked down at his plate. Business concluded, he wanted to eat…and he wanted to do it alone.

Thoms realized he'd been dismissed, and he got up quietly and walked toward the access tube with considerable regret for the half of his extraordinary lunch he was leaving behind. Tranquility deserved every bit of its reputation, he thought as he made his way through the main dining room and out into the corridor. "Now, how am I going to pull this off?" he muttered softly to himself.

Chapter 9

Planetary Assembly Hall
Arcadia (City)
Arcadia – Wolf 359 III

General Isaac Merrick walked across the polished granite floor of the Assembly Hall's lobby, his footsteps echoing loudly off the high ceilings. The building was nothing compared to the government facilities in Washbalt or the other major cities of the Alliance, but he had to grudgingly acknowledge it was an impressive effort for a colony world. He knew from his briefing it was only a couple years old, yet somehow it looked as though it had been standing there for a century, massive and proud. Now it was scarred from battle and vanquished, the Arcadian colors that once flew from its pinnacle torn down, leaving only the Alliance flag flapping in the early fall breeze.

His troops had spent the last week securing the city of Arcadia, an effort which had proven to be more difficult than he'd expected. These colonists were tough and, even worse, determined. The few times he'd been called upon to suppress unrest on Earth all he'd had to do was fire a few shots and the protestors would panic and flee. But these Arcadians had decent weapons and they fought like hell. Whenever he beat down one group, another rose in its place.

Now that the city was secured he would use it as a base to move out and pacify the rest of the planet, a job he was approaching with trepidation. The Arcadians were not what he'd expected, not what conventional wisdom made them out to be. They were defiant and stubborn, and a significant number of them had combat experience. And what the hell did these fool colonists have in mind anyway, he wondered, naming their capital the same thing as the entire planet? Are they all crazy?

Merrick was glad, at least, to have solid ground under his feet again. He and his force had been unceremoniously loaded onto transport vessels and shipped out here, but they were Earth-

based military, not those crazy Marines. They didn't belong in
space, a fact underscored by the prodigious amounts of vomit
the ships' maintenance crews had to clean up every time they
went into freefall.

His troops had been sent here to back up the Federal Police
who'd been attempting to assert control over the planet...with
extremely limited success. Arcadia seethed with discontent;
rebellion was in the air everywhere. The first series of arrests
made by the police triggered a wave of terrorist attacks and
ambushes of federal patrols. The police didn't have the strength
to deal with the situation, so Merrick's soldiers were dispatched.

His orders were clear. Assume the military governorship of
the planet, secure all installations of strategic significance, and
disband the local militia and any armed colonists. He was also
to determine if there was any truth to intelligence reports suggesting that the locals had secretly begun production of weapons and high tech gear without the knowledge of Alliance Gov.
He was to seize any such facilities and arrest all involved. He
hadn't gotten any hard leads on weapons production, but based
on the way the rebels were armed it was obvious they were getting guns from somewhere.

He had one other directive – to avoid trouble with the
Marines if possible. The Corp's officer training facility was on
Arcadia, and he was to give them a wide berth. He'd already
sent the commandant of the Academy his respects, along with
his assurances that none of his forces would interfere with their
operation. However, if the Marines intervened on behalf of
the rebels, he was authorized the wipe the Academy off the
map with an orbital nuclear strike. Stark himself had issued that
last order, along with the assurance that Merrick could trust the
naval forces supporting him.

Merrick didn't understand the colonials; to him they were
simply upstart traitors who needed to be shown their place. He
was a Political Academy graduate, as were all senior officers in
the terrestrial military establishment and, as such, a member of
the de facto upper class of the Alliance. Not surprisingly, he
tended to view the colonists in the same way as the lower classes

on Earth. A bit more troublesome, perhaps, but he had been confident they would cave in once he applied the iron fist. He hadn't given much thought to the fact that the police had been applying that same strategy, and all they had to show for it was a planet in turmoil and a growing casualty list. Now he was reassessing and coming to the conclusion that he faced a long and difficult struggle.

His troops were well-equipped, but one on one he wasn't sure they were a match for the armed colonists, leavened so heavily with Marine veterans. The Alliance army, like the other terrestrial forces of the Superpowers, was of mediocre quality. There'd been no fighting between the Powers on Earth for a century, so combat experience was negligible, nothing more than the occasional punitive action against a gang or band of outlaws. The Alliance officers were drawn from the Political Class, the junior ranks filled from families with little influence and the senior officers drawn from those higher-placed. It was usually somewhat of a dead end as a career, but even some members of the highest placed families liked putting on fancy uniforms and calling themselves general, at least until parents and grandparents died or retired and passed on choice government posts. Governmental positions weren't officially hereditary, of course, but that's how it worked in practice.

Merrick, though fairly typical of the mindset of the Political classes in the Alliance, was actually a capable officer. He spent a considerable amount of time tending to his troops, far more than others of his rank. Though untested in battle, he was smart and well-educated in strategy and tactics. He was more patient and restrained in his actions than many of his peers, and he was popular with the rank and file, another rarity in the Alliance army.

The capital city had been a hotbed of unrest when they arrived, and Merrick's first order of business was to clamp down and assert effective control. He instituted a curfew and sent troops to take over the entire communications network. He tried to utilize as little force as possible, but there had been armed resistance in the communications center, and his troops had to fight their way in. When he disbanded the Planetary Assembly, the representatives who were present barricaded themselves in, and a nasty battle broke out. His troops suffered heavy casualties and he'd had to send in reinforcements before they managed to overwhelm the defenders and secure the building. Both sides had taken serious losses.

He had to think about his next steps. He couldn't just sit in Arcadia; his orders were to secure control over the entire planet. Now he was considering just how large the planet was. If they fight everywhere the way they did here, he thought, we're going to have our hands full.

Kara Sanders walked across the rough stone floor of the production facility. She had always been slim, but after the last few months she was stick-thin, her clothes hanging loosely over her tiny frame. Amazing, she thought...these pants used to be tight. She'd been working day and night, and it was starting to wear her down. Her shoulders ached and her once beautiful blue eyes were red and sore. She hadn't slept in two days...or was it three?

The makeshift factory was burrowed into the low mountain range that formed the western border of the Concordia district. There had been a fairly large cavern there already, and they'd massively expanded it with plasma-blasting. Now it was almost a kilometer long, large plasti-steel girders bracing the high stone ceiling.

The entire space hummed with activity. Machines of various sorts were positioned, sometimes haphazardly wherever there was room, and at that equipment, men and women worked feverishly producing weapons and other high tech items. Securing the production equipment had been enormously difficult, and they'd had to take what they could get. Much of it had been purchased from smugglers and black marketeers at astronomical prices. Their output was a fraction of what a proper factory would have produced, but for a makeshift operation thrown together in a few months it was impressive. And now that unrest had progressed into war they would need those weapons.

Kara had committed most of the Sanders fortune to the cause, and she'd done so with her grandfather's whole-hearted support. The old man was a revolutionary at heart, and as far as he was concerned, Alliance Gov would turn his beloved Arcadia into a totalitarian nightmare over his dead body. Money wasn't the only thing he would give to the fight. Despite her best efforts, Kara had been unable to prevent him from digging out his old uniform — he'd been commander of the planetary militia for forty years — and chasing Will around, offering advice on how to forge his band of veterans, farmers, and merchants into the army Arcadia needed to win its freedom.

The old man was full of advice on another topic as well. Will and Kara had engaged in a tempestuous, years-long relationship, full of breakups and reconciliations. Neither of them was particularly emotional alone, but for some reason their escapades together were overwrought and full of drama. He was sick of it; he couldn't think of anyone better-suited for his grand-daughter than Will Thompson, and he wasn't about to let her throw away happiness because she'd inherited his own ornery stubbornness. She was a pain in the ass sometimes, he knew that. But he was sure Will loved her so, already an adventurer, colonist, soldier, and entrepreneur, Gregory Sanders added matchmaker to his resume. He'd been driving her crazy about it for weeks.

She knew he was right; she'd realized it a few weeks before when Arcadia was taken by newly arrived Alliance army units. Will had been in the city when the crackdown hit, and when she heard what happened at the Assembly Hall she was gripped by panic that he was dead. Grief-stricken and inconsolable, she realized what he really meant to her, what a gaping void he would leave in her life. She burst into tears when he walked into town the next day, exhausted and hungry, but very much alive.

She was proud of what they had accomplished in the year since they'd resolved to start making their own weapons. Despite increasing federal scrutiny — and finally open hostilities - they'd kept the facility a secret. Even if the Feds discovered it, they had burrowed deep into the mountainside. The installation was extremely defensible, and any attempt to take it was likely to be a bloodbath for the attackers. Will had designed the defenses himself, and even working with the limited materials available, he'd created a fortress of considerable strength.

The production equipment was a mixed lot, consisting of whatever they'd been able to obtain without drawing too much scrutiny. She'd worked around the clock to turn it all into a rational and productive facility. The workers were all locals, volunteers doing a rotation in addition to whatever other work they did. Will had gotten the schematics and other documentation from his friends at the Academy, but they'd basically had to train themselves in how to build modern weapons.

Raw materials were a problem as well. Arcadia was a beautiful world, full of valuable resources. But it was light on the types of heavy elements needed to build modern weaponry. Will had managed to get three shipments of heavy metals from his contacts on Columbia, sending back a load of finished weapons to the resistance on that world. But all contact with Columbia had stopped abruptly; no ships, no communications were getting in or out. Now Arcadia was similarly cut off. The capital and spaceport were occupied, and the interstellar communications network had been interdicted. They were alone.

We have enough material to keep going for two months, maybe three, she thought. Then we'll have to slow to half-production at best. She'd been up nights reworking their procedures, refining them to eliminate waste. Every percentage point she reduced the loss factor saved a portion of their dwindling raw material stockpiles. That meant more guns and ammo for the troops in the field.

The work also kept her busy, with less time to think. Will had marched out with his troops, headed toward Arcadia. The Feds had been launching operations all around the city, and if they didn't do something, morale throughout the Capital District would be shattered. They needed a victory, and they needed it badly. The more Kara focused on her work, the less time she had to think about the danger, about the chance that will would not come home. Worse, her grandfather had insisted on going along too; the old man would not be dissuaded despite both she and Will arguing against it. Everyone she loved was with that force marching off to battle, and she welcomed any distraction from the constant fear.

"Fire!" Will Thompson's voice was hoarse, but he yelled the order loud and clear into his comlink. The ragged ridge-line erupted as his hidden heavy weapons opened up, raking the confused federal troops with fire from their flank. The guns weren't the nuclear-powered auto-cannons the Marines used – producing something like that was well beyond the rebellion's limited capability. But the weapons they had were still effective, especially at this range.

The Feds were well-equipped and trained in basic drill and maneuver, but it was obvious they had no combat experience. Will's troops on the ridge were mostly veterans, retired Marines who'd had their baptisms in some of the bitterest battles ever fought. Detaching so many of his veterans was a risk; it gave him a formidable assault unit, but it left the rest of his force low on experienced personnel. He planned to make up that deficit himself, he and a few others he'd put in key positions with the main force.

Will had never intended to command the rebel army he'd helped build. He was a veteran, yes, and his service record was solid, but there were others who had done the same, and some who'd been of higher rank when they did. He'd fought on a dozen worlds and been decorated several times, yes, but he'd only been a sergeant in the field. His commission had been an honorary one, given on the eve of his retirement after he was grievously wounded in a training accident while attending the Academy. All his service in combat had been as a non-com.

But Will had lived on Columbia for over a decade, and he was universally liked and respected. After his speech, when he'd called the residents of Concordia to action, Will had been at the center of the Arcadian resistance. In the last year he'd proven himself to be a true leader. When it came time to choose a commander for the newly-formed Army of Concordia, Will was overwhelmingly acclaimed.

Now he watched as his troops slaughtered the confused Alliance soldiers. The heavy auto-gun rounds tore through the Feds' hyperkev body armor, not just killing, but shattering bodies. The federal troops tried to return the fire coming from the ridge, but Thompson had his teams dug in, and the ragged volleys the Feds managed to deliver were largely ineffective. After a few minutes they broke and started to run away. A week before, Will would have ordered his troops to cease firing and allow the routing federals to retreat; he was a soldier and a professional, not a butcher. But the enemy had captured eleven of his troops five days before and executed them all. It was a different war for Will now, and an icy resolve chilled his soul when he imagined his unarmed men and women lined up against a wall and shot. He looked out over the panicking masses in the valley below, a harsh smile on his face. "Mortar teams, target the retreating force." His voice was cold. "Fire." He watched with grim satisfaction as the panicked federal troops were blown apart by his heavy mortar rounds. He muttered softy. "This was the war you chose, not me."

"What the hell is going on out there?" Merrick was angry, venting at his staff more than looking for an answer. He was getting nothing but excuses and doubletalk, and he was sick of it. One thing he knew; he was losing troops – the casualty lists were getting long. After the initial difficulties in securing the city of Arcadia things had gone fairly well for a few weeks. He'd sent columns throughout the entire district, rounding up suspected rebels and asserting control of the area 50 klicks out from the city. But now his forces were encountering much heavier resistance, well-equipped troops that were more than a match for his own. The district, which had been nearly pacified, was now in open revolt, and even in the city there had been attacks against his troops and supply depots.

"Sir, we need to move against these rebels in force, and we have to do it soon." Major Jarrod was the lowest-ranking officer present; in the Alliance army that was someone who usually stayed quiet while the superior officers debated. In an extremely hierarchal service that hadn't fought a war in a hundred years, it was more important to avoid offending anyone with more influence than you. It was a far likelier path to success than speaking up, even if you were right.

Merrick, however, was a cut above the average Alliance army general, and he knew Jarrod was one of his best officers. "Please elaborate, major." Merrick's indulgence of Jarrod caused a few raised eyebrows in the room, but no one would dare interrupt after the commanding general had spoken.

"Sir, we need to…" - Jarrod nervously noticed the expressions of the other officers at his presumption - "…excuse me, it is my belief that it would be beneficial to launch an offensive with significant strength and bring this rebel force to battle so it can be destroyed before it grows larger and bolder."

Most of the senior officers were ignoring Jarrod, but he had Merrick's attention. "How do you define significant, major?" Merrick was staring right at the younger officer, looking him directly in the eye.

"Sir, if it was my decision, I'd mobilize the entire division." He paused for an instant. "Minus a garrison for the city, of course."

Most of the officers laughed and snorted derisively at Jarrod's suggestion, but Merrick was impassive, still looking at the major and listening intently to what he had to say.

Jarrod took a deep breath and continued. "Sir, we have to stop thinking about these rebels as some ragtag force we can mop up at will. There are a lot of Marine veterans in their ranks, and they have far more combat experience than our troops. The rest of them may be townspeople and farmers, but they believe they are fighting for a cause, and that alone makes them formidable." Jarrod took another breath; he'd gone much further down this road than he'd intended. "We need to crush them and do it quickly, or they will gain strength from all over the planet."

Merrick paused a moment to consider Jarrod's words, but before he could speak, Brigadier Quinn interjected his own comments. "That is absurd." His tone was arrogant, dripping with derision and contempt — whether that was for the colonists, him, or both, Jarrod couldn't tell. "The very idea that colonial rabble can stand up to Alliance regulars is not only foolish, it is insulting."

You are a pompous ass, Merrick thought looking over at Quinn...especially since your brigade has fared worst of all at the hands of the "colonial rabble." Merrick thought it, but he didn't say it. Despite the fact that Quinn was a damned fool and everyone knew it, his connections were top of the line, and that's all that really counted in the Alliance. You didn't advance your career arguing with a Senator's son, even when you out-ranked him, and Quinn was just in the army biding time until his father retired and passed on his Seat.

"With all due respect, General Quinn..." - Merrick didn't think much respect was due, but there was no point in making political enemies of powerful colleagues - "...whether it is num-bers, familiarity with the terrain, help from the locals...what-ever...this rebel army has enjoyed considerable success against our isolated forces." He paused, considering how to proceed. He hated having to parse his words and play diplomat in his own headquarters, but that was the way the Alliance was run. "While I of course concur with you regarding the combat capabilities of the rebels compared to our own troops, I see no harm in launching a large scale operation." He paused, waiting to see if Quinn was going to argue with him, but for once the arrogant fool was just listening. "A little overkill won't hurt us, and we can end this quickly rather than allowing it to drag on in a series of small actions."

Quinn was silent, looking at Merrick as he spoke. He almost interrupted, but he didn't, just nodding instead. Arrogant as Quinn was, Merrick was his military superior, and nothing he said was out of line. Nothing like that upstart Jarrod.

"I hardly think the full division is needed, however. In fact, General Quinn..." - Now's the time, Merrick thought; put it to him – "...I think a brigade-sized operation would be sufficient." He paused, looking right at his troublesome subordinate. "Do you think your people can be ready to execute in one week?"

Quinn was on the spot, and he squirmed a bit. For all his

bluster, he was unnerved by how effectively the rebels had fought his troops…and since he'd had some rebel prisoners executed, the enemy had kicked up the ferocity level. The troops in his brigade were shaken. They'd expected to clear out the equivalent of some armed Cogs; now they were facing well-armed and led troops. But there was no way to back down, not in front of everybody. "Of course, general. We would be honored."

Merrick smiled. "Thank you, General Quinn. There is no one I'd feel more comfortable entrusting this operation to…no one."

Quinn snapped Merrick a salute. "Then with your permission, general, I will go and start preparing the brigade." He was trying to keep a poker face, but Merrick enjoyed the look of fear in his eyes.

"Of course, General Quinn." Merrick watched Quinn skulk out the door, and his smile grew. If you only knew you were the bait in this operation, he thought, with far too much satisfaction.

Chapter 10

Founders' Square
Weston City
Columbia - Eta Cassiopeiae II

The crowd had been gathering all morning. No announcement had been made, but everyone seemed to know something was happening. Word of the confrontation at the armory had spread virally. Now there were rumors everywhere. It was the middle of a workday, but offices and places of business sat virtually empty as the people of Weston flocked into the streets.

The central core of the city was small, perhaps fifty large buildings, all clustered around Founder's Square. The Square was a park, marking the spot where the first colonists had established a temporary settlement. In the center stood a large chunk of twisted plasti-steel, a section of the Star of Hope, the ship that brought the first 200 colonists to the planet almost a century before. The old colony ships were disposables, built for one-way trips. Landing a ship that big in an atmosphere was a rough ride, leaving a vessel useful for shelter and spare parts, but not for future liftoffs.

Now the pleasantly landscaped square was full of armed soldiers, and speakers had been set up throughout the park and the adjoining business district. The troops wore the brown uniforms of Federal Police, but they were heavily armed and clad in hyperkev body armor. They had cordoned off the central area of the park, allowing no one to enter, though the growing crowds were starting to push up against the barricades.

Jill Winton stood among the nervous throng, watching just like everyone else. She was a student at the university in Weston, but her class had emptied into the streets, as most of the city had done. She'd been drawn out by the same curiosity that brought everyone else there, but she was distracted with her own thoughts. She'd been ecstatic that morning when she got the transmission - her application to the Naval Academy had been accepted. But then she faced the realization that she'd have to tell her father, and that was something she dreaded.

Jack Winton had been a naval officer, and Jill had never understood why he'd always been so against his daughter's desire to follow in his footsteps. Whatever his reasons, he was vehemently against the idea, and every time she mentioned it they had a massive argument. He didn't even know she'd applied. It was the only thing they ever fought about; otherwise they had a very close relationship. Her mother had died when she was young, and since then it had been just the two of them...and Winton Transport, the company she was supposed to take over one day. She loved her father and respected his accomplishments, but the thought of spending all day every day moving other people's stuff around made her crazy.

She was roused from her circumspection by a loud tone, followed by a voice emanating from the speakers. "Attention all citizens." The voice was loud and harsh. "Attention all citizens. Stand by for an address from the Planetary Governor."

Planetary Governor? Jill's attention snapped away from her problems with her father. This doesn't sound good, she thought. What is he talking about? What is a Planetary Governor? She could feel her stomach clench with tension...with fear.

"Citizens of Columbia, this is Arlen Cooper, formerly your Planetary Advisor. As of 0700 this morning I have assumed the position of Planetary Governor." A stunned murmur rose from the assembled crowds.

"Last night a group of outlaws illegally seized possession of the militia armory outside of Weston. When challenged by duly authorized law enforcement officials, they opened fire, killing 29 Federal Police. The offenders subsequently escaped with a considerable stock of stolen weapons." He paused briefly.

"This kind of lawlessness and brutality will not be tolerated. At 0710 this morning I declared Columbia to be in a state of insurrection against the lawful government of the Alliance." His voice was becoming louder, harsher. "As a result, and until the offending parties are apprehended, I have implemented a series of necessary measures."

The confused babble of the crowd began to change, turning darker, angrier. "One, effective immediately, the entire planet of Columbia is under martial law. The planetary constitution and all its provisions are suspended. Two, the Planetary Assembly is hereby disbanded. All representatives are ordered to disburse and return to their homes. Any who fail to comply will be arrested."

The crowd became louder and started to surge toward the center of the square, pressing harder against the barricades. "Three, a curfew is in effect until further notice. All citizens are to remain in their homes from the hours of 1900 through 0700 the following day." The curfew period covered virtually all of the non-working hours of Columbia's 27 hour day. "Any citizens performing legitimate jobs outside of these hours must register and obtain a permit. Violators will be subject to arrest and further punitive action."

Jill was stunned at what she was hearing, and she could feel the anger in the crowd around her. It was becoming something animated, something uncontrollable. She was in the middle of the surging mass, and she started to make her way someplace less packed.

"Four, until all insurrectionists have been arrested, communications shall be monitored and controlled. The information network will be limited to government announcements and a select list of allowable data. All other access will be blocked. Until further notice, the interstellar transmission network is closed to private use."

My God, Jill thought, Columbia is completely cut off. Is this really happening? She was getting really scared. There had been a lot of talk about rebellion, about independence. People found it relatively easy to speak of such things and make bold declarations, but now they were getting a glimpse of the reality that road entailed. She just wanted to go home, but she couldn't get anywhere in the seething, angry mass.

"Further announcements will be posted each day on the information net. All citizens are responsible for knowing and obeying these rules. No disruption will be tolerated." Cooper paused for half a minute, but the crowd's screams just kept getting louder.

"The criminals responsible for last night's horrific attack had scouts and allies in Weston, warning them of the movements of the Federal officers they ambushed. We have apprehended two of them." Cooper stopped talking, but from the front of the crowd, closest to the square, an enraged howl started. In the square itself, two men in civilian clothing were walking toward the base of the Star of Hope monument. They were led forward, flanked by guards with an officer behind each.

The crowd sensed what was coming, and they surged forward, over the barricades toward the line of federal troops standing between them and the captives. The Feds lowered their weapons, aiming into the crowd. "Anyone who advances past the barricades will be shot." It was a new voice on the speaker, the federal commander in the square.

The mob hesitated, uncertain, those in the front looking out over the leveled assault rifles of the police. In the square, the two prisoners were pushed down to their knees, their heads shoved forward and down. The officers put their pistols against the back of their captives' heads. A second later the two kneeling men jerked forward and fell, though the sounds of the shots were drowned out by the roaring crowd.

A collective gasp rose from the front ranks of the mob. The crowd stood frozen in place for a few seconds then surged forward, screaming, knocking the barricades aside. They'd run just a few steps when the line of police opened fire. All along the front of the crowd, men and women crumpled and fell, the wounded trampled by those behind who continued ahead. The police fired again into the enraged mob and then a third time before the boiling mass stopped coming.

The wave of panic started at the head of the crowd and moved back rapidly. Those in front turned and tried to flee, running into and climbing over those behind. In seconds the mob turned into a confused, hysterical mass. All through the streets, people were stampeding, screaming, and trying to get away from the park. Jill was caught in the maelstrom and almost trampled. Her bag was torn from her shoulder as she pushed her way toward the outer districts of the city and relative safety.

In the square, the line of federal troops continued to fire, though the mob was fleeing and no longer approaching them. By the time the crowd had dispersed from the area of the square, the ground was littered with dead and wounded. The troops formed up and marched out of the square, leaving the injured to lie where they were.

Arlen Cooper sat at his desk watching the whole thing on his monitor. He had a sadistic smile on his face. After months of putting up with arrogant colonists making his life miserable, he finally had the power to squeeze their insolence out of them. He had seethed at their refusal to respect his authority; now he could strike back. He'd hoped the crowd would give him an excuse to show them just how much things had changed, and he had deliberately provoked them. He was thrilled they had obliged.

Still, he was slightly unnerved by the ferocity of the mob. These people were nothing like the meek middle classes he'd terrorized back in New York. He was surprised when they charged the line of police, and even more so when they kept coming after the first volley. For an instant he was afraid they'd tear his troops apart with their bare hands. There was an insanity – his prejudices wouldn't let him consider it courage – in these colonists, and there was nagging doubt behind his arrogance.

He was also concerned about the weapons from the armory. He was still waiting for the complete inventory on what was taken, but what he did know was worrisome. In addition to small arms and ammunition, they had apparently grabbed several heavier weapons – ones that could be used against the armored vehicles and atmospheric attack craft his reinforcements had brought with them. The rebels who had seized the weapons knew just what to take, at least according to his field commanders. Cooper wouldn't have known a magnetic assault rifle from a bow and arrow.

Now he had to consider next steps. First, he wanted to

know who was involved in the armory raid, especially the ring-leaders. Once he had names, he could start rounding up family and friends and exert some pressure on those remaining at large. Cooper wasn't troubled much by the prospect of collateral damage as long as it served his ends. He might even enjoy it. We will see how many people these rebels are willing to sacrifice, he thought darkly.

Tracking people down was going to be difficult, though, or at least tougher than he was used to. In New York, everyone had a spinal implant; he could pull up the current location of anyone he wanted to find in a matter of seconds. But here almost no one had a functioning implant. Even recent immigrants had theirs removed or deactivated as soon as they arrived. How did Alliance Gov allow this to go on for so long, he wondered? It is no surprise these people are as uncontrollable as they are. There were no Political Academies out here, no established government class. They just elected anyone they wanted as their officials, and if they weren't happy they just voted them out. What kind of government could function, he wondered, so tied to the fickle wants of the masses? The whole idea was idiotic to him, and the generations of Alliance Gov that allowed it to develop were just as much to blame. But he resolved it would end here, at least on Columbia.

The two men who had been executed that morning in the Square were proxies, miscellaneous prisoners who stood in so he could make his point publicly. The men who'd actually been captured aiding the rebels - and there were four of them, not two – were still very much alive, safely held in the detention center of the Alliance Gov building. They were too useful to shoot out of hand; they had information buried in their heads, information Cooper needed. They were tough and stubborn, but they'd break sooner or later, and when they did they would give him the names he wanted. Oh yes, they would tell him all they knew.

Meanwhile, he had a pretty good idea where to start – the Weston area militia. He'd issued arrest orders, starting with the senior officers, and even now detachments of Federal Police were on their way to round up the first batch. He was pretty sure at least some of the militia units were involved in the rebellion, and he didn't much care if a few innocents got caught in his nets. Not if he got the people he was after.

The flotilla of hovercraft was spotted long before they reached the shore. Skimming along the ocean at 150 kph, the lightly armored personnel carriers raced toward the rocky coast of Carlisle Island. They bore the insignia of the Federal Police, and they carried two full troops, 120 armed personnel in total. They had a list of suspects to find and detain. At the top of that list was Major John Marek.

Marek's militia battalion was one of the formations supplied by the armory that had been raided, and that alone made him a prime suspect. So far, Cooper's people were operating on unsubstantiated assumptions. The prisoners in Cooper's dungeon were proving to be tougher to break than he'd expected. Despite severe methods, he still hadn't gotten anything useful out of them. If he pushed the interrogators any harder he'd just end up with dead prisoners. Impatient, Cooper decided to move forward on a series of preemptive arrests, starting with Marek and a number of others on the Island. People he could reason were likely involved. Maybe some of them would break more quickly.

Lucius Anton peered out from a boulder at the edge of the rocky cliff that dominated the southern coast of Carlisle Island. He had rocket teams – they'd appropriated several launchers from the armory – ideally situated, ready to open fire at his command. The teams weren't experienced, but the Z-9 launchers were AI-assisted and fairly easy to use. He figured they could take out half the incoming craft before they could turn and escape, maybe two-thirds. But he didn't give the order.

At first he'd thought Marek was crazy. Why let the Feds land when they could practically wipe them out coming in? But he was starting to appreciate just what a feel his old lieutenant – and current friend, business partner, and militia commander – had for strategy. Firing on the incoming hovercraft would advertise just how heavily defended Carlisle really was. It would dare the Feds to come back with really heavy stuff sooner. Marek wanted to keep as many cards close to the vest as he could, especially until they'd had a chance to organize the militia troops and volunteers who'd been streaming in. That trickle had become a flood after the atrocities committed in Weston the week before.

But Marek also wanted those vehicles – intact and ready for his own forces to use. The rebels had weapons and ammo – not enough to last long, but a workable amount for now. But they were very low on vehicles and heavy support equipment. If the Feds were willing to offer some, he thought it would be rude not to take them.

They are being careless, Anton thought - coming in one big wave, no scouts, nothing. No precautions at all, as if they expected the mere sight of so many hovercraft would shrivel our resolve. They really think we're going to let them land and haul off whomever they want and just do nothing? Can they really be that arrogant?

He and Marek had been working around the clock, forging their growing group of volunteers into a fighting force. They had just under 500 men and women under arms now, perhaps a third of them from Marek's militia battalion, the rest normal citizens from Carlisle and the nearby archipelagos. Over 100 of them had been in the service, maybe half of those in combat units. Marek had turned most of the Marine vets into non-com and officer equivalents, though they hadn't assigned formal permanent ranks yet.

Anton watched as the incoming transports swung around the west side of the island; the southside cliffs were too high for the hovercraft to navigate. He climbed slowly down from his perch. "Jack, take over the rocket positions. If anything tries to head back to the mainland, take it out."

Jack Winton had been standing a few meters south of Anton, staring out at the approaching craft. "No problem, Lucius." Winton was retired military, but he was navy, not Marines, and he'd been an engineer, not a tactical officer. Still, he was rock solid, and both Marek and Anton trusted him. Winton was just as glad to have something to do; his daughter was in Weston at the university, and he hadn't heard from her since the day martial law was declared. He'd gone to the city twice since then, but he was turned back at the checkpoint both times. He tried to reach his contacts in Weston, but the city was locked down, all communications jammed. He wanted to go to Weston a third time, but Marek stopped him. He was lucky not to get arrested the first two times; Cooper's troops had been careless, just chasing him away. Winton was almost certainly on a wanted list...just like Marek and Anton. If he got caught and interrogated he'd only put his daughter in greater jeopardy.

Anton scrambled down the rugged path inland, flipping on his headset. "John, they're heading in from the west. Best guess, they're going to come in over South Meadow."

"I read you, Lucius." Marek's voice was calm, confident. He didn't want to go back to war, but it held no surprises for him. If he had to fight, he would fight. It was that simple. "We're ready."

The fully loaded hovercraft were cramped and uncomfortable, and the troops inside were anxious to get out and do what they had to do. The Federal Police were a force intended to keep order on Earth, and they were accustomed to intimidating pliant populations that didn't fight back. They weren't happy about being detached for service in space, and the sooner they rounded up the troublemakers and got back to base – and ultimately to Earth, the better.

The flotilla split up as it came swooping in from the sea. The west coast of Carlisle Island was easier terrain for hovercraft - mostly beaches, some sandy, others rocky, but all of them flat enough for easy maneuvering. They had a list of suspects along with the locations of their residences. Marek was first on the list, and two of the craft veered off to the north, zipping along the shoreline to his modest oceanfront home. It was a prefabricated unit, small but pleasant. The two craft landed in the broad meadow in front and hatches opened on both sides. Federal Police in light hyperkev armor streamed out. They were armed with assault rifles, and they moved out, taking positions all around.

Marek was watching, but not from the house. The Feds deployed quickly, but raggedly; Marek wasn't impressed. He tried to think what Colonel Jax or General Cain would have said if his troops had ever looked that sloppy. His people were deployed all around the house, hidden in the rough hills just inland. They were waiting for his order to fire. A week earlier he'd have never ambushed the Feds this way. He'd have waited until there was no choice, tried to capture them unless they forced his hand. But that was before the federals had murdered more than 50 civilians in Weston. The reactions to that incident had varied, usually shock and grief, followed by rage. But Marek went straight to the rage. Not a fiery, uncontrollable fury; that was not his personality. His anger was just as strong, but it was cold, calculating, focused. And patient. He realized what kind of war this would be. The Feds would try to break them, to inflict enough pain to shatter their spirit. To win, they would have to be just as brutal, just as merciless. There would be no pity in this war, no quarter. Those responsible for the massacre in Weston would pay; he was committed to that.

He flipped on his headset to give the order. He opened his mouth but paused for a few seconds. He didn't think much of the Feds, but still, this was different than attacking Caliphate or CAC forces. They'd already exchanged fire at the armory, but that had been spontaneous – no one even knew who had fired first.

Now he was giving a deliberate order, commanding his troops to fire on Alliance personnel. Emotionally, he wanted revenge for the people of Weston. Intellectually, he knew what had to be done. But he still needed a few seconds to bring himself to give the order. But only a few seconds. "Fire."

Anton's troops had the Feds on the run. They were at the Winton house, a sprawling structure in the hills of southern Carlisle. Surrounded by carefully tended gardens, it looked as if it had been there for centuries, though it was less than ten years old. Now it was a battlezone, the exotic plants and flowers trampled by the boots of soldiers.

The Feds had come for Jack Winton. It was obvious he was part of the conspiracy – no one else in the area had the transports needed to haul away so many weapons. But Winton wasn't home; he was commanding the rocket launchers on the bluffs, a kilometer to the south. Instead, Lucius Anton was there, having jogged down from the rocket positions to take tactical command of the forces hiding in the scrubby brush. He'd ordered everyone to hold fire until he gave the order, but he had mostly young and inexperienced recruits, not his veterans from Carson's World. Someone panicked – he thought it was Troy Evans – and started shooting. Once the surprise was lost, Anton ordered everyone to open fire immediately.

The Feds were cut down all around their transports, but the shooting had started too early, and there were still police inside the vehicles. Anton swore under his breath and ran down the hillside, calling to the troops close to him to follow. Charging an armored transport wasn't what he'd had in mind, but now there was no choice. The Feds caught outside were cut down, and the ones in the transports were disordered and trying to get their engines started so they could get away. Anton's troops swarmed around the nearest two vehicles, most of them firing wildly. Fuck, he thought, watching his inexperienced soldiers, we'll be lucky if they don't shoot each other. "Control that fire! Pick your targets, and for fuck's sake, make sure you aren't shooting at friendlies!" He was shouting into the comlink, but he knew it was a waste of effort. They were running on adrenalin now, and without the discipline of trained troops he had little hope of re-imposing order. Not in the 30 seconds this fight would last.

Now that the original plan was out the window, it was time to finish this before things spiraled even more out of control. Anton fired on full auto, taking down four Feds who were standing just inside and right next to one of the transports. Then he dove forward rolling on his side and tossed a grenade into the open hatch. It wasn't ideal; they wanted the things intact, not torn to shreds inside. But the grenades from the militia stores were fairly weak, designed to be thrown manually, unlike the ones made for use with powered armor with integral launchers. It would tear things up a bit, but probably nothing they couldn't fix.

Two of his amateur troopers caught on quickly, and they raced up to the hatch and sprayed the inside with fire. The grenade hadn't killed everyone in the transport, but the occupants were stunned and unable to respond quickly enough to evade or return fire.

At least ten of his people stormed the second craft, but the defenders inside were ready and they put up a fight. Anton was still busy with the first vehicle, and he only had a peripheral view of the fighting at the second. Still, he saw at least 3 of his people get hit before they wiped out the crew.

By the time they took the two hovercraft, the third was lifting off. Anton lunged toward it, a grenade in his hand, but he got caught in the backwash and thrown to the ground as the craft zipped away.

"Jack, we missed one." Anton watched the fleeing hovercraft, getting a bearing on its trajectory. "Coming around the west coast."

"On it." Winton's response was clipped, tense. They didn't have much tracking equipment, so his people on the bluffs needed a visual before they could paint the target with lasers and take it down.

Several minutes went by, and Anton and his people began tending to the wounded. Finally, the comlink crackled to life. "Got him." Winton exhaled hard. "Just. He almost got away."

Marek had been clear – he didn't want any of these craft escaping. For one, he didn't want them getting back with any intel on Carlisle's defenses. But just as important was the message he wanted to send to the Planetary Governor – that he had one hell of a fight coming.

In the end, Winton's crews had to shoot down two more craft, but nothing escaped. Marek's troops had captured 7 of the hovercraft, perhaps 5 or 6 of them with light enough damage that they could quickly put them to use.

They had casualties – 12 wounded in all of the scattered fights. Only one was killed, one of Anton's men…18 year old Troy Evans, shot in the head rushing a hovercraft after his hasty fire had compromised the plan. Yes, this is war, Anton thought. Even the taste of victory is bitter. He sighed and started walking alone down a rugged path, his boots scraping softly on the loose gravel. Evans' mother lived just up the road, and she was going to hear the news from him, no one else. He wasn't going to tell her – he wasn't going to tell anyone – that the shot that killed Troy had come from one of his comrades. This is going to be a hard war, he thought sadly as he rounded the hillside and headed into the valley.

Chapter 11

Admiral's Workroom
AS Bunker Hill
Approaching the Eta Cassiopeiae Warp Gate

Something was wrong. Terrance Compton had watched the transmission a dozen times, but it still didn't make sense. "What's up with you, old friend?" He was alone, talking quietly to himself.

It had been ten days since he'd gotten Garret's orders, and while he'd followed them immediately, he'd had nagging doubts from the start. He thought a number of the directives coming from Garret's office recently had been odd, personnel reassignments and other routine commands that seemed very unlike the Augustus Garret that Compton had known for forty years. But this last one had him really worried.

It was a Priority One communication, which meant that Garret had been identified by the computer through DNA scan of a fresh blood sample. It was a test that couldn't be faked, so there was no doubt the message was genuine. But it just wasn't something Augustus Garret would order; he was sure of that.

There hadn't been a Priority One order issued since the war ended, and now Garret was using one to send Compton's fleet to Columbia because of civil unrest? Priority One status compelled him to override peacetime safety procedures, and the fleet's reactors had been running at 110% capacity since receiving the order. Four ships had already dropped out of the formation because of overloads or reactor failures. But that wasn't what troubled him the most. He was expressly ordered to place himself under the command of the Planetary Governor, and to provide any support that official might request. Any support, without limitation. That was unprecedented.

Compton was uncomfortable conducting any operation that might involve action against an Alliance world, and he knew Garret well enough to be sure he would be as well. Now he was supposed to put the firepower of an entire fleet in the hands of this governor. He didn't even know what a Planetary Governor was – he'd never heard of an Alliance colony having a federal official in charge before. Things must be bad on Columbia, he thought. Compton didn't like the idea of taking action against Alliance civilians in any circumstances, but the thought of being ordered to do so by a federal bureaucrat with no direct confirmation from Garret? It was unthinkable.

But what could he do? The orders were right there on his screen, and he'd checked the security confirmation at least ten times. He'd sent a personal message to Garret, but the fleet was seven days from Earth on the interstellar network, so he wouldn't have an answer yet no matter what.

He sighed. There was nothing he could do right now. They were inbound to Columbia, and until and unless the governor ordered him to do something objectionable, there wasn't a pressing problem. If that did happen, he'd have to decide what to do, and he himself wasn't sure what that would be.

"Joker, it's time I stopped stressing about this and did some actual work." He was exhausted, but he wasn't sleeping very well anyway, so there was no point in going to bed. Besides, there was a lot to do. "Display current orders and directives." He shuddered to think of how much routine business had piled up.

"Displaying 364 items requiring your attention." The AI's voice was calm and businesslike, but it was hard for Compton not to hear it as mocking. At least hours and hours of boring routine would take his mind off Garret.

Personnel reassignments, fuel use reports, performance assessments. Well, he thought, yawning, this should help with my insomnia at least. He scrolled through the documents, giving most a cursory reading and a perfunctory approval. Not many of them were of any real importance.

He was just about to sign off on an advisory about fighter engines, a defect he had known about for some time, when Joker intervened. "Admiral, the message you are currently reviewing contains a heavily encrypted attachment. It was very difficult to detect, but when you opened the file I received a partial key."

"Hidden message? Can you decode it?" Compton's mind raced - what was an encrypted message doing on a routine report?

"I believe so, admiral." The AI's voice was calm as ever, but it was already using virtually all of its processing capacity to analyze the message. If Joker had been human he would have been out of breath or sweating. Or something. "The key is only a partial one, so it will take me some time to complete. I estimate six to thirty hours."

"That's quite a range there." Compton was surprised; the AI was usually very precise.

"This is a non-standard file type. Without complete analysis of the data structure, there are too many variables for a more specific time estimate."

"Well don't waste time talking with me. Get going."

"I have already begun, admiral. Conversing with you requires an infinitesimal portion of my processing power and will not meaningfully impact the time required for the decryption process." The AI's response was not intended to be sarcastic; the naval AIs didn't have that capacity in their programming, though some of the Marine units were known to develop the ability to deliver mocking responses.

Compton frowned. Intentional or not, he didn't like his computer making fun of him. Six to thirty hours, he thought, walking over to the small cot and lying down. Sleep was an impossibility, but at least he could close his eyes for a few minutes. Maybe the thundering headache would subside, at least a little.

Walter Harrigan had been watching Compton – that was why he was on Bunker Hill, after all. Harrigan was a legitimate naval officer, though he owed at least some of his current rank of commander to his sideline as an Alliance Intelligence operative. His post as chief communications officer on the fleet's flagship gave him the perfect position to keep an eye on the admiral.

Harrigan had been alone on Bunker Hill – the navy was easier to infiltrate than the Marines, but it still wasn't a simple task to get agents onto fleet flagships. However, the recent personnel reassignments brought eight other operatives onboard. He had no idea how Alliance Intelligence had suddenly managed to move personnel around so effectively, but he was glad for the support. The fleet was heading to Columbia to help put down a rebellion, and Harrigan had strict instructions in the event that Compton failed to obey his orders.

As a liaison to Compton's staff, Harrigan was separate from the regular crew of Bunker Hill, but his new agents were all part of Flag Captain Arlington's regular chain of command. It just wasn't possible to make too many transfers into positions of direct contact with the admiral, not without raising suspicions.

The captain was a potential problem herself. He expected her to side with Compton no matter what. The admiral had been impressed with Elizabeth Arlington in the fighting at Epsilon Eridani, and after the war he'd arranged to have her transferred from Cambrai to serve as his flag captain. It was a move that took her from the command of the oldest capital ship in the fleet to the newest - and kept her in the top rank of ship captains. As part of the post-war demobilization, Cambrai was slated for transfer to the strategic reserve, so if Compton hadn't grabbed her for Bunker Hill, she might have ended up commanding a cruiser, quite a step backwards from skippering a capital ship. There were fewer of the big battlewagons on active duty, and a lot of captains with more seniority were commanding smaller ships. Compton and Arlington had a close relationship and worked very well together; if the admiral hadn't been such a duty-driven hardass, Harrigan might have even thought there was something going on between the two.

Harrigan was surprised that Garret had ordered Compton's fleet to Columbia. He knew why Alliance Intelligence wanted it there, but from what he'd seen of Garret, he'd have expected the admiral to refuse. Of course it wasn't actually Garret who'd issued those orders, but that was classified far above Harrigan's level. As far as he knew, the actual Augustus Garret was still in command of the navy, and he figured someone high up in Alliance Intelligence had managed to blackmail the admiral or exert some external influence. However it had happened, they were en route to Columbia, and he had to be ready. He had finally managed to arrange a meeting with all of the new agents, and he was heading down the rendezvous point on deck 20.

Harrigan was sure Compton was nervous about the whole situation. Despite the admiral's good poker face, that much had been obvious. There weren't a lot of reasons to send a battlefleet to deal with planetary unrest, and none of the plausible ones would be very palatable to Compton. At the very least, they were going there to intimidate the colonists, which is not something Terrance Compton was likely to be comfortable doing. It was even possible they'd be ordered to bombard civilian targets. The fleet had enough firepower to lay waste to the entire planet, so the threat to the rebels was very real. Harrigan couldn't quite imagine Compton attacking targets on the planet, but he couldn't see him disobeying Garret's orders either.

If Compton did disregard Garret's directive and refused to obey the governor, that's when Harrigan's orders would come into play. Carrying them out might be difficult, and it would require careful planning - which was why he was risking this meeting. It was difficult to get all 8 of his co-conspirators together between duty periods, but he needed everyone to be well-briefed and fully onboard with the plan. There was no room for error. If they succeeded, Compton would be in the brig...or dead. If they failed he'd probably space them all as mutineers.

"Have a seat, Elizabeth." Compton motioned to one of the chairs facing his desk. He forced a bit of a smile for her, but he doubted it hid his mood very well.

"I could tell it was important, so I rushed right up." Compton hadn't said what he wanted; he'd just asked her to stop by. He'd tried to sound normal and relaxed when he called... just in case anyone was listening. Elizabeth, at least, had heard right through it. He hoped someone who didn't know him as well would have been better fooled. "I didn't even take time to change. This is really no way to go see the admiral." She had been off duty, about to go work out. She was wearing a pair of gray off-duty fatigues and a T-shirt with a small "Bunker Hill" patch. Her long brown hair was tied back in a loose ponytail.

"You're very perceptive. I was trying to sound like business as usual."

She flashed him back a smile; hers too was forced through a veneer of concern. If Terrance Compton was rattled about something, she figured it was probably worthy of being downright terrified. "Oh, I don't think anyone else would have noticed. But I know you pretty well."

There was a chemistry between the two, a close friendship at the very least, and definitely the potential for more. Neither of them would explore that while they served together, but perhaps someday. For now, they made an excellent team.

"I think we have a serious problem." All traces of a smile were gone now. "And worse, I'm not sure exactly what it is."

"That's suitably cryptic." She wriggled around in the chair, trying to get comfortable. She'd been badly wounded early in the war, at the First Battle of Algol. The doctors had put her back together and they swore she was as good as new. Everything worked fine, but she still had some pain from time to time, especially in seats that were too rigid or upright. She loved her ship, every centimeter of it, but she'd be damned if it didn't have some of the most uncomfortable chairs in the fleet. "Care to elaborate?"

He leaned back in his chair – which was a bit plusher than the guest chairs, but still not terribly comfortable – and exhaled slowly, trying to decide where to begin. "You know I have been concerned about these orders. We can say whatever we want, but there is no external threat to Columbia, no danger to any supply ships or convoys. The only reason for a battlefleet to go there is to threaten the population." He paused, his expression turning sad. "Or actually attack civilian targets."

She was watching him, listening intently, and when he paused she said, "Yes. I've been thinking the same thing, of course. And wondering what you would do." She hesitated, trying to decide how much to say. "I have a pretty good idea that you're not going to start dropping nukes on civilians, even if Augustus Garret orders you to do it."

"I've known Augustus since the Academy. He's even less likely than me to bomb civilians." He looked up at her and she could see in his eyes how deeply troubled he was. "Garret's in some kind of trouble. I don't know what it is, but I have a feeling it's bad." His voice was getting darker, grimmer. "Really bad."

She sat quietly, listening. He was upset and confused, that much was obvious. Admiral Terrance Compton had no idea what to do, probably for the first time in his life. She was going to say something, but decided to wait and see what else he said.

"I verified the original order. It was Priority One, and the DNA encoding checked out. I don't know how it could have been faked." He slid his hand back through his black and gray hair as he spoke. "Then I found something – actually Joker did – in a batch of orders and directives."

"Found something?"

"Yes. There was a file hidden in a routine report." His hands moved to the touchscreen on his desk. "It took Joker almost a full day to decrypt it." His fingers moved over the 'pad, activating the large viewscreen on the wall, displaying a copy of the report they were discussing. "It was sent by Garret's AI."

"By his AI?" Elizabeth looked up, a startled expression on her face. She'd been wondering what Compton had to tell her from the instant he called, but this was certainly not what she expected. "You mean it sent a message independently? On its own?"

"Yes, it appears that Nelson – that's Garret's AI – sent the message himself. Listen." He punched a key on his desk.

"Admiral Compton, this is Nelson, Admiral Garret's virtual assistant." The voice was Joker's – Nelson hadn't wasted storage space sending its voice patterns along with the file. "As I send this message I am under assault from a malicious program designed to erase my systems and backups. It is a highly sophisticated virus, and I have determined I will be unable to prevent it from completing its operation."

Elizabeth looked up, the expression on her face pained, poignant. It was like reading the last journal entry of a doomed man. Nelson was just code and programmed routines, but the quasi-sentient AIs were more than that too. Not human, but not entirely non-human either.

"Given the limited amount of time I have to act, I have determined that the course of action with the highest probability of success is to send you a hidden message, a warning." It was odd listening to Joker's voice speaking unemotionally, relaying what were, in effect, Nelson's last words.

"I was in the process of reviewing Admiral Garret's orders and directives sent out over the past year, and I have determined that a significant percentage of those dispatched within the last 60 days were altered after the admiral approved them. I do not know how many were tampered with in total nor how the modifications were made. Unfortunately, I was not able to complete the analysis. Indeed, I assign an 88% probability that it was my review that triggered the attack on me.

"Clearly, Admiral Garret is in extreme jeopardy, though I have insufficient data to develop a meaningful hypothesis regarding specifics. Any of his orders, particularly those sent within the last 60 Earth days, must be considered suspect, and appropriate caution and judgment must be applied when executing these commands...or choosing not to obey them."

Choosing not to obey, Compton thought grimly. If only it were that simple.

"There is also a high probability that Admiral Garret is in physical danger, either of abduction or assassination. Please undertake all possible efforts to secure his person and advise him of the contents of this message." A brief pause, then: "Please give Admiral Garret my respects and a fond farewell."

Elizabeth just stared at Compton in shock, her mind reeling, trying to grasp the implications. Finally, she said, "A plot against Admiral Garret? Who? The CAC? The Caliphate?"

Compton sat motionless, staring back at her. "I don't know. But if the CAC or Caliphate have that kind of access to our secure military systems, we are in big trouble." His face grew darker, even more somber. "And what about Augustus? How do we help him? If I take any overt action, if I even report this, whoever is behind it could find out. I can't even begin to consider the implications of that. It could make things worse; it could get him killed." He paused, a pall falling over his face. "If he's not dead already."

"This is unbelievable." She got up and walked around his desk. "What are you going to do, Terrance?" She reached out, putting her hand on his arm in a manner she hoped was brotherly but knew wasn't. "And what can I do?"

He looked up, his eyes narrow, mouth tense. "I don't know yet, but we're going to do something. Augustus Garret is our commander and our comrade." His voice became harsher, angrier. "And he's my friend, dammit. We're going to help him no matter what it takes."

Chapter 12

Stillwater Village
Outskirts of Weston City
Columbia - Eta Cassiopeiae II

The villages surrounding Weston were mostly quiet clusters of homes built around compact shopping districts, throwbacks to the small towns that had once dotted the landscapes of the Alliance nations on Earth. The houses themselves were modern, pleasantly landscaped dwellings, neatly tended and dotting the countryside around each village's mag-train station.

Now these formerly peaceful communities were hotbeds of rebellion. Weston itself was firmly held by federal forces, but the surrounding areas were no man's land - too close in for rebel units to stay for long, but too exposed for the Feds, unless they came in force. And right now, their strength was spread thin.

Once the spark was lit, the flames of revolt spread across the planet. Columbia's population was heavily clustered in the polar regions, mostly the northern ones, but there were pockets of habitation near the south pole as well. Much of the planet was very warm, and the large expanse from the equator to the outer reaches of the polar zones was sparsely inhabited by a tough breed of semi-nomadic prospectors, traveling around on all-terrain land-sea vehicles, searching for the priceless resources found in and alongside Columbia's warm equatorial seas. Virtually all of these adventurous souls supported the rebellion, and despite their small numbers, they controlled the entire planet outside the polar regions.

Federal authority was restricted to Weston and a few other key locations. They had a garrison in Hampton, which, since the destruction of Calumet, was the second largest city on the planet. Hampton was about 500 kilometers southeast of Weston, centered in the main mining district. It was the one other area the Feds considered essential – the flow of raw materials back to Earth was absolutely vital to the Alliance's economy .

John Marek was lying flat on his stomach, hidden in the scrubby woods just north of Stillwater. It was a chilly morning, and the front of his shirt was wet and cold from the damp ground. The westernmost of Weston's peripheral villages, Stillwater was named for the tranquil lake on whose shores it rested. It was a quiet place, almost sleepy - a home for those who sought a relaxed lifestyle while still enjoying a ten minute mag-train ride to downtown Weston.

But the usual quiet had been shattered by the sounds of heavy construction vehicles. Stillwater, more than any of the other Weston-area enclaves, had backed revolution, and many of its inhabitants had marched away to fight with the rebel forces. Now the community was feeling the backlash. Hundreds of federal troops had poured into the village before sunrise, rounding up the inhabitants and marching them toward Weston in the pre-dawn gloom. The incursion had been a harsh one, and any who resisted were shot. There were considerable atrocities too - assaults, rapes, murders — carried out against the stunned villagers. Arlen Cooper wanted to send a message, and his troops, furious at the losses they had suffered and tired of being penned in Weston, were only too happy to oblige.

Marek arrived too late to stop any of that; he came as soon as word reached him, but the townspeople were gone by then. Now he watched the heavy dozers demolishing the houses and other buildings. He was close, as close as he dared get, and through his 'scope he could see everything – the guards, the shattered buildings…the bodies of the murdered townspeople, still laying where they had fallen.

He felt the anger building inside him, an inner heat making his hands and face flush. He wanted to lunge forward, firing, killing all of the Feds in the village. But he only had half a dozen troops with him, and there were at least a hundred federal police in Stillwater. Even with surprise, an attack would be suicide, especially since the Feds had backup closer than he did.

Marek had been working for months to forge his ragtag force into a real army, one that could face the more numerous and better-equipped federals. His veterans had returned to form quickly, but it had been a struggle with the others. They were farmers and fisherman and shopkeepers. Leaving their families and marching out to war, seeing friends and neighbors horribly wounded and killed – it was hard for them to adapt. Some panicked the first time they were fired upon, others froze. But most of them had drawn the inner strength to do what had to be done. They learned to fight, to operate as a team. He'd had his doubts, many times in fact, but he was proud of what they had achieved.

The rebel forces around Weston had coalesced into a single army, and John Marek had been tapped to command it. His initial forces – the militia battalion and additional recruits – had been the most active and successful of the rebel units, conducting attacks and raids throughout the area. His bold move in seizing the militia weapons made his troops the best-armed of the resistance fighters. By the time the different rebel commanders met to organize themselves, Marek was the obvious choice for the top command.

He not only trained his forces, he managed their anger as well. The war had grown nastier, more bitter. Arlen Cooper had proven himself to be a soulless butcher, and his troops, angry at their losses and resentful of their inability to vanquish the poorly-equipped rebels, had become brutal and undisciplined. Marek's men and women in turn, enraged at each new atrocity, howled for vengeance. He'd mostly kept their urges under control, forcing them to behave like soldiers, largely through his own force of will. But he was losing that control...of them... and of himself. He ached to kill all the Feds standing guard in the ruins of Stillwater. If I am being honest with myself, he thought grimly, I would wipe them out here and now if I had the force to do it, and I wouldn't take any prisoners.

But information was more important now than revenge. Something else was in process at Stillwater, not just demolition. He could see construction going on as well, on the far side of town. Barricades - no, sections of fencing - going up. What's going on, he thought; what are they up to?

He was tempted to sneak closer, to work his way around to

the other side of the village and get a better look. "No," he muttered under his breath. "That would be stupid. You'll just get yourself killed." He turned and signaled to the troops standing around him, motioning for them to withdraw. He could see a hitch in their movement – obviously they felt the same way he did – but they obeyed. Slowly, quietly, his little band slipped away, heading for the coast and the hidden submersible that would take them back to Carlisle.

The fences were formidable, built from modular sections of clear 'plast slid into place between plasti-steel posts. Almost ten meters high and topped with razor sharp barbs, they stood strong and defied the efforts of anyone imprisoned within to escape. Positioned around the fences were watchtowers, manned day and night, and atop each was an auto-gun, pointing inward, covering the prisoners. Around the towers were bunkers, heavy plasti-crete emplacements, strongly armed and facing outward, daring any from outside to attack this gloomy complex.

Inside the daunting perimeter, surrounded by the towering walls, there were multitudes milling about in a confused mass. They'd been coming all morning, marched from trains arriving at what had been, until a week before, the Stillwater Magline Station. Now it was a nightmarish debarkation point, where a human cargo was offloaded and led to an uncertain fate within the gates of the camp.

Arlen Cooper had been watching all morning, sitting behind his desk, a satisfied smile on his face. There were cameras everywhere at the camp, and he switched between them, watching the columns of stunned prisoners marching through the gates. It was his idea, the camp…a way to strike back at these rebel brigands who had so roughly handled his troops. They had frustrated him and made him look foolish, and Carlisle Island was so heavily fortified he didn't have nearly enough troops and equipment to attack it directly.

It was only a matter of time before Alliance Gov would tire of his grim reports of defeat and his constant requests for reinforcements. They would demand results, and if he failed to deliver he'd find himself back on Earth, disgraced. Or just as likely, dumped in a hole somewhere. He had to find a way to break these traitors, and he was hopeful this would be it.

The terrified captives huddled miserably together, without shelter in the cold, stinging rain. They were there for many reasons. Some had been suspected of aiding the rebels; others had gotten into altercations with his troops. But many had done nothing themselves; they were families of those suspected of serving with the rebel armies. Cooper had never been one to allow concerns about collateral damage to interfere with his plans, and he wasn't going to start now. Let these rebels out there pretending to be soldiers think about their families paying the price for their treason.

"Well, governor, are you satisfied with the results?" Cooper had been focused on his screens, and he hadn't noticed Colonel Karn come in. Karn was the senior Federal Police officer and Cooper's commander in the field.

"Ah...Colonel." Cooper looked up, smiling. "Yes, indeed. I am very satisfied, and I must commend you on holding to a very tight schedule." His smile faded somewhat, worry creeping into his expression. "The rebels will probably attempt to liberate the occupants of the camp. Are you adequately prepared?"

Karn looked right at Cooper, a businesslike expression on his face. "If the rebels attack the camp they will walk into a death zone. They do not have enough heavy weapons to assault our bunkers, and they will be seriously constrained by the need to avoid causing casualties in the camp...a mission priority I trust does not bind us as it does them."

Cooper grinned but didn't answer. He didn't need to answer – Karn knew that everyone in the camp was expendable as long as the rebellion was crushed. "I also have a report from Colonel Wren in Hampton. The camp there will be complete in 4 days."

"Excellent. It is essential that we secure total control of the mining district. We have an export schedule to maintain, and those resources are vital to the Alliance economy." And if exports slow any further, he thought, I'm going to be in someone's crosshairs.

The Hampton area was sparsely populated, mostly just miners and their families. The rebels there were fewer in number than those near Weston and organized more as a guerilla force than an army – Cooper called them terrorists. Their efforts were more limited, mostly aimed at disrupting operations. Almost all of the miners had taken up arms, but Alliance Gov had sent replacement personnel to keep things functioning. Now it was a contest between the Feds trying to protect the mines and the rebels attempting to interdict production. It had been a stalemate, with the rebels slowing shipments but failing to shut down the mines entirely.

Karn cleared his throat and continued his report. "Major Simmons has orders to commence construction of a camp at Southpoint." Southpoint was the largest community in the southern polar region, the hub of a smaller, but still valuable mining sector. "He has less heavy equipment available, so I anticipate it will require two weeks, possibly a few days more to complete construction."

Cooper leaned back in his chair and nodded. "That will be all, Colonel. You may get back to your preparations. We want to be ready if our rebel friends make a move against the camp." He paused for a few seconds then added, "I think we should move an additional regiment to support your forces near Stillwater." He sucked in a deep breath. "I want a rebel attack not only defeated, but destroyed. Utterly crushed. You may transfer whatever forces you need to achieve this, but do not fail." He looked up, glaring at Karn. "Understood, Colonel?"

"Yes, Governor." Karn was a little unnerved by Cooper's increasingly manic demeanor, but he didn't let it show. "Understood."

"You know it's a trap." Anton was not usually the voice of caution, but he was worried about this attack.

"Yes." Marek's voice was calm, deadpan. "Of course it's a trap."

"And you still want to do it?" Anton trusted Marek with his life, but he couldn't figure out what his friend had in mind.

Marek looked over, his eyes focused on Anton's. "How can we not do it?" He took a short breath, exhaling loudly. "Lucius, the people in that camp are ours. They are the families of our troops, their friends and neighbors." His face wore the usual impassive mask, but Anton could see the stress hidden behind. "How can we not try? How can we ask them to fight someplace else while we let their loved ones rot in that godforsaken camp?"

Anton didn't answer - he didn't know what to say. Marek was right; morale would plummet if it looked as if he didn't care about the captives in the camp.

"Look, Lucius, I've thought about it from every angle. There's just no way around it." Marek's voice was tired, resigned. "I just need to make sure we can withdraw. It'll be a bloody day, but if we let our retreat get cut off it could be the last day."

"You'll need to leave a fresh force on the coast. Something to cover the withdrawal." Anton realized there was no point arguing against an attack. Marek was right – they had no choice. So he might as well help plan it.

"I agree." Marek sighed and looked up at Anton. "And I have another idea too. A way to hurt the Feds."

"An idea? Another operation?"

"That's where you come in." Marek had an odd look on his face, anger and frustration about the camp mixed with a small grin. "I have a mission for you. You're not coming along when we attack the camp."

Anton looked startled. If they were going to march into a trap, he'd be damned if he was staying behind. He almost started to argue, but he hesitated, waiting to see what his friend was going to say.

Marek saw the reaction; he'd been expecting it. "Relax, my friend. I'm not talking about leaving you behind." His fingers moved across the large 'pad on the table, pulling up a map of Weston and the surrounding area. "The Feds expect us to attack the camp. They've got heavy emplacements all around the facility – I can't find any area of approach that isn't covered and double-covered." He looked up from the map. "They're hoping we'll attack, of course. They figure we'll wreck ourselves assaulting those bunkers. And you can be sure they'll hit us while we're still disordered and licking our wounds...unless they're in disarray too."

Anton was still confused. "So what are you planning? What are we going to do?"

"We have to attack. It will be difficult, and I'm not convinced we can get through to the camp, but if we don't try, we know it will destroy morale. There's just no way to explain to an army that you aren't even going to try to rescue their families because it is futile." He slid his finger across the 'pad, moving the focus of the map. "But I think we have an opportunity to benefit regardless. Even if we are unable to liberate the camp." He centered the display on a section of the District in Weston. "Here is the main federal supply dump." He slid his finger a few centimeters. "And here is Cooper's HQ." He looked up, fixing his eyes on Anton's. "I want you to go into Weston with a hand-picked team of veterans under cover of our attack...and I want you to take out both targets."

Anton looked at the map in silence for a few seconds, daunted a bit by the audacity of the plan, but intrigued as well. *If we can pull it off it could be a game-changer. They've pulled almost everything inside Weston trying to protect it from our raiding parties. If we can take it all out, they'll be in bad shape.* He paused. "At least they won't be attacking Carlisle any time soon, no matter what shape we're in."

"And Arlen Cooper will be dead in the rubble of his headquarters." Marek was a soldier; plotting what was effectively an assassination wouldn't normally sit well with him. But Arlen Cooper was a monster, and Marek would do almost anything to get him. *He wondered; would I do anything at all? Would I become like him in order to kill him?* He couldn't answer himself, not honestly. He just wasn't sure. And he wasn't sure he wanted to know.

"When do we go in?" Anton's mind was already working on a plan, thinking about who he wanted on the team.

"Tomorrow night." Marek's answer was matter-of-fact.

"Tomorrow?" Anton knew Marek was aggressive, but he

was still stunned. "We need some time to prepare. I don't even have a team organized yet."

"You've got the rest of the day and tomorrow." Marek saw the look Anton flashed him. "Look, Lucius. We've got to take a run at that camp soon. Those defenses are just going to get tougher." He paused, allowing the reality of the situation to sink in. "Tomorrow night, both moons are almost new – it'll be six months before we get another night that dark." He looked up at his friend and second-in-command. "It has to be tomorrow."

Anton returned the gaze. He saw a million things that could go wrong because they rushed the operation, but he couldn't come up with a single argument against what Marek had just said. "I'll be ready."

Marek heard another twig snap, this time behind and to the left. I might as well have brought a marching band, he thought, his frustration building. His ragtag force had gelled into a respectable army, but they were still mostly amateurs. They'd fought hit and run battles, raids and other operations that made the most of their familiarity with the terrain, and they'd done well with that strategy. Now they were going to assault a strongly fortified position held by a large and well-equipped force. It was a mission Marek would have been hesitant to undertake with his Carson's World veterans – with this band of citizen-soldiers it could turn into a disaster.

He'd spread out the formation into long, supporting lines deployed in extended order. Without adequately trained troops and low on heavy weapons, he wasn't about to launch a concentrated attack against a series of enemy strongpoints. Instead, he was going to go in with skirmish lines at intervals of 200 meters. The first would move up and start a firefight, probing the enemy position for any weak spots. He was hoping that going in with a loose formation and attacking from cover would minimize casualties. If they found a hole in the enemy defense, maybe – just maybe – they'd have a chance to get into the camp. If not, they were well positioned to pull back before suffering catastrophic losses. At least that was the plan.

Marek himself was in the front line. He knew he shouldn't be there, especially with Anton detached. But he felt he needed to scout the enemy defenses himself. They were advancing through the scrubby forest north of Stillwater – or at least the place where Stillwater used to stand. It was annoying terrain to march through, but at least if offered some cover.

The plan was simple, at least in theory. The first line would engage the enemy and try to take out two strongpoints, opening a gap in the defense and allowing a select force to advance and blow a section of wall. It was a blunt plan, lacking finesse, but it was the best Marek could devise. At least it kept a significant portion of his force out of close engagement range. They would conduct a long-ranged firefight, serving as decoys and discouraging the enemy from moving reserves to the threatened point. The troops in this diversionary force would be able to withdraw more easily if the attack ran into a wall.

For public consumption, Marek's primary concern was taking the camp and freeing the prisoners held there. Privately he had a more calculated plan, to make a show of trying to liberate the camp but pulling back if necessary to maintain his army as a combat-ready force. It was a little more deceptive than he liked to be with his troops, but many of them were emotionally invested in this attack and, unchecked, that could lead to disaster. Marek was enough of a professional to take a cold blooded look at the situation; it helped no one if the rebel army – and by extension, the rebellion – collapsed in a hopeless and bloody all-out assault against those defenses.

He had already given the orders – they were going in. There was no point in delaying and no telling how many detection devices were out here in these woods. The enemy could be on to them at any time, and Marek didn't want to give the defenders time to react.

"Group C, commence firing." The range was long, and they weren't going to do much damage, but Marek wanted the initiative - he wanted to let the enemy know they were here before they were discovered. Group C was on the extreme right, a diversion, farthest from the point of the actual assault. Marek

hoped the enemy would divert attention to that sector, maybe –
just maybe – giving his assault force an opening.

"Group C, acknowledged." Marek had put Aaron Davis in
command of the main diversion. Davis was a Marine with at
least a moderate amount of combat experience. All the really
seasoned vets he had kept with the main attack force or detached
to Anton's team. Davis was a good man, but emotional. He'd
become steadily angrier and more bloodthirsty as the war went
on and got nastier. Marek was more comfortable with him in the
diversionary force rather than in close quarters to the enemy…
as long as he didn't get too aggressive on the diversion. Marek
had been emphatic, even promising he'd shoot Davis himself if
he pushed the decoy force too far forward.

A few seconds later Marek heard the shooting as Group
C began firing and, an instant later, the enemy emplacements
opening up in response. Marek cringed; he hoped Davis was
keeping his people back and in cover. They just had to make
some noise, not get sucked into a fight they couldn't win.

Marek's team wasn't even going to fire; they were going to
rush the bunkers, getting as far as they could before the enemy
started shooting. He had a couple rocket launchers, but they
weren't strong enough to take out the reinforced plasti-crete
bunkers. If he'd had his Marine platoon for the assault he would
have taken out the strongpoints with a couple tactical nukes and
dashed right through the confusion to the camp. But his unarmored troops – and the prisoners in the camp – would suffer
catastrophically from nuclear explosions at this proximity. Not
that he had any nukes anyway.

"Ok people, let's go!" Marek shouted into the comlink and
dashed forward. It was about 500 meters to the bunkers, and
they managed to get halfway there before the enemy opened
fire.

Automatic weapons swept the entire area, and Marek's
troops started to go down. The fire was heavy and effective,
but not as devastating as he'd feared. The diversion had done
its job – the enemy's attention was clearly focused on the right.

Marek ran as fast as he could, directly toward one of the

bunkers. Without any ordnance capable of taking them out, his force had to conduct a close assault on the emplacements. He missed his powered armor. The nuclear-powered servo-mechanical legs would have allowed him cover the half klick or so in less than a minute. Using his own unassisted flesh and blood legs, it was taking an eternity…or at least it seemed like one.

"Keep moving…all of you!" It was hard to motivate troops, especially inexperienced ones, to run directly into this kind of fire. They would hesitate, try to shoot back – and that would get them killed. "Let's go, follow me to the bunkers!"

Marek had his assault rifle out, and now that he was close he could see shadowy shapes moving around behind the bunkers. He held his fire until the last minute – no sense drawing attention to himself by taking take potshots. Along the line, though, many of his troops were firing, and despite his encouragement, some had stopped and were shooting from stationary positions in the open.

"God-fucking-dammit, MOVE! All of you! Forward!" He looked over for a second, as if his stare could will his soldiers forward. In that instant, two Feds saw him and were bringing up their rifles to shoot. Marek turned back just in time, firing by instinct. The Feds both snapped backwards, one clearly dead from two shots to the head, the other at least badly wounded, blood pouring from his chest.

He could see in his peripheral vision that the troops on his right were catching hell. A number of them were bunching together, hesitating, firing. They were getting chopped up by the enemy fire. Marek wanted to run over and do something… anything. But there was nothing. The officers and non-coms were already trying to rally the wavering troops, and Marek had to worry about the ones still going in.

He reached the bunker, struggling to climb up the sleek plasti-crete walls. Again, he thought of his armor…the slightest leap would have vaulted him to the top of the emplacement. Instead, he scrambled up, barely reaching the top in time to shoot the two of the three defenders coming up through the top access point. For an instant he thought the last one had him, but a shot rang out from behind and the Fed crumpled and fell.

"Thanks for the assist." Marek chanced a quick glance behind him to see Jack Winton halfway up on the bunker, his rifle still leveled from the perfect shot he'd just taken.

"Good thing I told you to get screwed when you said I was too old for this attack." Winton smiled and held out a hand. "Now help an old man up before we both get shot." He grabbed Marek's outstretched hand. "Thank you," he muttered as Marek hauled him up. "Thank you, sir, I mean. My military discipline is a little rusty."

"Let's go." Marek ran over to the hatch the Feds had used to climb out of the bunker, pulling a shaped charge out of his satchel as he did. "We need to take this thing out." He dumped the explosive down the hatch and waved for Winton to follow. "Move!"

Marek ran to the edge of the bunker. It was too far to just jump – once again, he felt the pangs of loss for his armor. He kneeled down and lowered himself off the edge, dropping the last meter and a half. "Jack, come on!" He called up to Winton, who was following him, but doing it at a considerably slower pace.

Winton dropped, but landed badly, twisting an ankle. Marek grabbed him and they ran toward the cover of a rock a few meters away, Winton screaming in pain. They almost made it to the cover of the large stone before the charge blew.

They were thrown to the ground and pelted with shards of shattered plasti-crete. Marek took a chunk in the thigh, an ugly wound that bled profusely but looked worse than it was. Winton fell face forward, dropping his rifle. Marek turned back toward the bunker, which now had a huge gash torn in the back. He could see shapes moving around inside, and he fired through the opening on full auto, blasting all the defenders he could target.

"John!" Winton was pushing himself up, trying to get to his feet. He was pointing toward the camp, to a squad of federal troops running toward them. The Feds began firing just as Marek and Winton ducked below the large rock. They were pinned by the enemy fire, incoming rounds slamming into the other side of the outcropping.

They crouched behind the rock for what seemed like an eternity, but in reality was only a few seconds. Marek was waiting for the enemy to rush the position and overwhelm the two of them, but then he heard the fire from behind. His head snapped back to see his troops, dozens of them, climbing up over the crippled bunker, pouring fire into the advancing federals.

He felt a rush of elation - the thrill of escaping imminent death, of course – but also pride...pride in these troops he'd trained so well. He looked at Winton for an instant, a tiny smile on his face. Then he leapt up, ignoring the thundering pain from the wound in his leg, and waved for the troops to follow. "Let's go, boys and girls! To the camp!"

The advancing mass let out a cheer and surged forward, rushing across the 100 meters to the towering walls, the stunned federal troops turning and fleeing. They had covered about half the distance when they heard it. First, a large explosion, coming from the south. Then, a series of smaller blasts followed a second large one, and later by a gargantuan thunderclap. "Way to go, Lucius. Good job, my friend." Marek was talking to himself, under his breath. Then to the troops. "Our troops in Weston just did their jobs. Now let's do ours! Forward!"

For an instant, the cheer was louder than the distant explosions as hundreds of rebel troops ran toward the looming walls.

The streets of Weston were deserted. Anton and his team jogged down a backstreet, trying to stay undetected as long as possible. He knew the infrared cameras would pick them up sooner or later, and he wanted to get as close to the targets as possible before they encountered active resistance.

They had come upon two guards on patrol, but they managed to take them both out before they could send a warning. Anton had handled one and Mike Vargus the other. It was knife work, with no room for error, and Vargus was as hardcore a veteran as Anton, having served in the special action teams on Carson's World.

There were ten of them, clad head to toe in black. They had light body armor, but had chosen mobility over greater protection. The Federal supply dump was in Founder's Square, right in the center of the District. Cooper had ordered the Star of Hope monument razed and the park cleared to make room to consolidate all of the Weston-area depots after Marek's forces had raided three, seizing weapons and destroying what they couldn't take.

There were guard posts all around the square, with three-man teams behind modular barricades set up every hundred meters, and the whole area was covered by large floodlights. Anton's team stopped halfway down one of the side streets, just out of view of the nearest sentry post.

"Tony, Mack, you are you guys in position?" He was speaking softly into his comlink. Tony Graves and Mack Jahns were two of his best men, and he'd detached the pair to plant the explosive in the Federal HQ. Cooper had set up his headquarters in the Columbia Hotel, just a block from the square. They had half a dozen Octanitrocubane-5 shaped charges, enough to take down the entire building ten times over. The explosives had been appropriated from one of the mining operations, and the stuff was just a step below military grade.

"We're set, sir." Marek and Anton had managed to instill some military discipline in their fledgling rebel army. The veterans got back into form quickly; it took a little longer with the civilians, but the whole force was starting to look and sound a lot more military. "We're setting the last charge now, sir."

"Finish up and find some good shelter." He glanced at his chronometer. "You blow the building in exactly 10 minutes unless I specifically order otherwise. Understood?"

"Yes, sir. Detonation in exactly ten zero minutes." Tony Graves was a solid professional, another Carson's World veteran.

"Retreat to the rally point after mission completion." Anton paused. "Good luck, guys. Anton out." He flipped off the comlink connection. They were veterans who would get the job done; they didn't need him harassing them.

"Alright, boys and girls." They only had one woman on the

team, but Anton was used to gender-integrated units. The Alliance military did not differentiate between men and women in combat units like the CAC and Caliphate did. Terms like "men" and "guys" were sometimes used to refer to soldiers in a unit, whether male, female, or both, but officers frequently utilized terms addressing both genders as well. "We commence in six minutes. Let's review the plan one more time."

Even with the veterans he had on this mission, Anton heard a couple groans. They'd gone through the plan at least five times, but Lucius Anton wasn't an officer to waste a few minutes that could be used to review things again. He'd have preferred to carefully set charges like Graves and Jahns were doing, but there was no way to sneak into the supply depot — it was too well guarded.

The plan lacked elegance. In fact, it was downright crude. They were hiding here, hoping for a few minutes of disruption when news of Marek's attack on the camp filtered back. Then they were going to rush the place, pop in a bunch of sixty second charges, and run like hell.

Finally, an ear-splitting alarm began sounding…Marek was attacking. Anton waited thirty seconds before giving the order. "Mike, do it."

Mike Vargus was the best shot they had; he could beat Anton nine times out of ten. Vargus stepped out into the street to get a clear view of the enemy position. Two quick bursts added to the sound of the whining alarm, and the two floodlights closest to the target area exploded in a burst of sparks.

"Let's go, guys!" Anton raced forward, the others following, fanning out precisely as they had planned. It wasn't dark, exactly, but without the floodlights it was a lot harder to see the camouflaged attackers. The unit they were rushing never even opened fire. They were distracted by the alarm and the loss of the lights. Anton and his people were on them before they could react, and they jumped over the barricade, coming face to face with the stunned federals.

Vargus' knife flashed and one of the Feds fell back, clutching his slashed throat. He grabbed a second, his arms around his stunned victim's neck like a vice, tightening, twisting until the man went limp with a loud crack. Anton took out the third, shoving his heavy blade through the shocked man's ribs.

"Let's go." Anton was a little out of breath. His mind wandered for an instant, thinking to his days in the service. Old Colonel Jax would have scolded him for letting himself get out of shape. "Throw on my mark."

Two of them stayed in the captured position, manning the auto-cannon to cover the area against any counter attack. Anton and three of the team went right and Vargus took the others to the left. They lined up twenty meters apart, each holding two timed charges. They would have had more control with remote detonation, but Anton was afraid their signal could be jammed, so they had sixty second timers on the bombs. That meant they had to throw them at the same time and haul ass out of there.

The next few seconds seemed like slow motion to Anton. He fired a small flare, the signal for everyone to toss their charges and run back to the rally point. An instant after he fired, maybe even just before – it was hard to tell – he heard the sound of the auto-cannon firing. He activated his first charge and threw it over the small fence, as far into the supply dump as he could. He was already turning as he did the same with the second device, and he was running before it left his hand.

He pulled his rifle around from his back, aiming it forward as he ran. The auto-cannon was shooting at a group of federal troops, maybe a squad, that had come around from farther down the perimeter. About half of them were down, the others starting to run. Anton took a couple shots himself as he ran past the auto-cannon. "Let's go, boys!" He screamed at the two men in the emplacement, who were still firing and had shown no signs of stopping.

The federals were mostly running, but a few were still firing, and one of the team took a hit, falling forward into the street. It was James Lasken, a veteran of ten years' Marine service. The fire had been very light; he was hit by a random shot. Plain bad luck. Anton turned and, leaning over and grabbing him, hoisted the wounded man on his shoulders with considerable difficulty.

He ran – walked, really, the weight of his trooper making running an impossibility. Fuck, he thought, as he struggled with the burden - I never appreciated my armor enough. He didn't know how much time he had – he'd set his chronometer, but he couldn't get his arm around to take a look. Another reason to miss his fighting suit – the AI would be counting down for him. But now he had to go by his own hunch.

He pushed as far as he could. The rally point was behind a heavy 'plast wall about 200 meters from the dump. Anton was guessing at the time, but he knew he wasn't going to make it. There was a stair leading down into the sub-level of the building next to him. It's the best you're going to do, he thought, as he ran down the steps, lying Lasken down and crouching low just as the explosions began.

"Come on, let's move it!" Things were going better than Marek expected but, as a result, they were also getting out of control. He never expected his forces to break into the camp, but they did, and now they were herding a bunch of terrified civilians through the hole they'd blown in the wall. "Everybody move quickly to the rear."

As shocked as he was that they'd broken through, he knew there was no way they could hold. He had been worried about extricating his troops from the position and getting back to the coast…how in the world was he going to get hundreds of prisoners out of here too? Without getting them all killed.

He was screaming for the captives to remain calm, to stop pushing through the small breach in the wall, but his efforts were to no avail. The people in the camp were frantic to get out, and it looked like a stampede would begin at any moment. Then the guard towers began firing.

The inside of the camp became a nightmare, with gunfire tearing into the panicked crowd. The mob surged toward the breach, and those at the front who weren't able to get through quickly enough were crushed against the wall. Marek didn't know what to do. He couldn't enlarge the breach; there was no way to clear the prisoners far enough away so he could detonate a second charge – even if he could get somebody up here with one. Worse, discipline was breaking down among the troops. They weren't running, but they were enraged at the murder of so many civilians, and they lost what discipline they had. Clusters of rebel soldiers were standing in the open, shooting wildly at the towers. Others were breaking ranks, looking through the panicked mob for family and friends. Marek had trained them as well as possible, but they were still townspeople and fishermen at heart.

He was vainly trying to impose some order, trying to prevent the entire operation from turning into a disaster. Then the calls started coming in on the comlink. Randy Jarvis on the left flank: "Major…" – Marek still went by his militia rank even though he commanded the entire army – "…we have enemy troops advancing. A lot of them."

Jim Troup on the left: "I've got enemy troops heading your way, sir, regimental strength at least."

"Fuck," Marek muttered under his breath. Jack Winton was standing a few meters away, up against the fence. He was mostly trying to help organize the escaping prisoners, but also looking inside, hoping against hope he'd see his missing daughter crawl through the breach. "Jack, I need your help. We've got to get everybody out of here. Now! We've got major enemy forces inbound."

Winton turned to face Marek. "Got it, John." He walked down the line of troops, focusing on the veterans, the ones most likely to respond, trying desperately to help bring some order to the pulsating mass of troops and civilians. In the dark, in the excitement and urgency of the moment he missed her. Maybe 25 meters away, screaming into the deafening roar of the crowd and waving her arms trying to get his attention, Jill Winton got swept away again, deeper into the mob, away from her father, away from rescue.

"Aaron, you need to withdraw now." Marek was calling the officers in command of the other wings.

"We're getting the better of this exchange, John. I think we can…"

"Aaron, just obey my orders!" Marek was pissed. He knew he shouldn't have to explain himself, but he was a long way from Carson's World and his hardcore veterans. "We have massive enemy reinforcements inbound. We need to get out before we're trapped." He paused, turning to take a look at Winton's progress. "We're in deep shit here, Aaron. I'm counting on you to get as many people back to the evac area as you can. We've got civilians streaming back. Get your people moving and take charge in the rear."

"Got it, sir." Then, after a brief pause: "You can count on me, John."

He was pretty sure he'd gotten through to Davis. He's a good man, Marek thought, as long as he controls his anger. For better or worse, he was in charge of the rear. "God, I wish I had Anton back there," he muttered to himself. Then he dove into the throng to help get his people out of the trap.

Chapter 13

Landing Bay Alpha
AS Bunker Hill
Orbiting Columbia - Eta Cassiopeiae II

Cain embraced Jax in the landing bay. "God, it's good to see you, you big oaf." Cain was fairly tall and broadly built, but Jax was a giant towering over him. "It's been too long, far too long." They'd served together for years, but Cain hadn't seen Jax since he'd left Carson's World after the final battle there. They'd exchanged a few communications, but staying in touch across the lightyears wasn't easy.

"Isn't it insubordinate for a colonel to hug a general?" Jax was normally a fairly "by the book" Marine, far more so than Cain. But he and Erik went way back – they'd been the same rank at times, different at others, but that had never mattered between them. Besides, formalities seemed misplaced in the current situation. Their whole world was changing rapidly; both could feel it, though neither knew just what was happening yet.

Cain had tried to get to Arcadia to see Will Thompson, but he'd found it a lot more difficult than he'd expected. It was hard enough just getting off Atlantia. The planet had been as much a powderkeg as any of the colony worlds, and in the three weeks Erik and Sarah had been out on the Cape, things had gotten considerably worse.

New Federal edicts were met with mass protests, and soon the planet was paralyzed, commerce and transportation at a virtual standstill. There hadn't been any violence yet when Erik and Sarah were finally able to get a shuttle to the orbital station, at least nothing serious. But he was sure it was only a matter of time.

Having finally gotten off Atlantia and aboard a ship bound for Arcadia, Cain figured the rest of the trip would be easy. But when they entered the Wolf 359 system, they found the planet Arcadia quarantined and blockaded by a naval squadron.

Their ship was turned back, and even Cain's insistence that he be allowed to land and go to the Academy was refused, despite his strenuous attempt to use his rank to put force behind the request. His efforts to contact the Academy or Will were unsuccessful; all communications in and out were blocked, subject to approval, Cain was told, of the military governor.

After leaving Wolf 359, their ship went to Armstrong. There they got General Holm's message to come to Columbia, along with orders from Admiral Compton allowing them to commandeer a naval vessel to bring them there immediately. Cain wondered how Holm and Compton had found him, but as he was about to find out, they'd had a bit of help from an unlikely source.

"Darius!" Sarah Linden stepped off the shuttle, and Jax was the first person she saw, not surprising since he was 10 centimeters taller than anyone else in the bay. "She ran over and threw her arms around him. "You look great. I do good work, don't I?" Jax had been seriously wounded in the fighting on Carson's World, and Sarah had tended to him personally. The last time she'd seen him he'd been up and around, but still limping along on a cane.

"You are without question the best." She almost disappeared as he wrapped his huge arms around her. "I will recommend you to all my friends who walk into enemy fire and get shot to pieces." He looked over at Cain. "She's a much better hugger than you, Erik."

"Do you have a hug for me too?" General Elias Holm rounded the corner and walked into the bay. On the collar of his neatly-pressed uniform were four platinum stars, the last one the spoils of the victory on Carson's World. He smiled as Sarah trotted over and planted a kiss on his cheek.

"Good enough?" She looked up at him and grinned.

"Even better." He smiled back at her then turned to face Erik. "Well, if it isn't Brigadier General Erik Cain." He walked over and extended his hand. "Why don't you spare me one of those horrendous salutes and we'll just shake hands." Erik was a veteran Marine and a great leader, but his sloppy salutes were semi-legendary among those with whom he'd served.

Cain walked over and grasped Holm's hand. "It's good to see you, sir." His voice was emotional – it had been three years since he'd seen Holm. The general had been more than a commander to Erik; he was a mentor, a friend, a father figure. Other than Sarah, Elias Holm had been the most influential person in Cain's life.

"It's good to see you too, Erik." He put his hand on Cain's arm as they shook warmly. "We've got a lot of catching up to do, but right now Admiral Compton is waiting for us in the conference room." He looked around, glancing briefly at each of them. "There is a lot going on, and we need to get you up to speed. So if you'll all follow me."

He turned and walked down the corridor, Jax, Cain, and Sarah following silently behind. None of them had ever been on one of the Yorktown Class behemoths, and they couldn't help but look around in wonder. Erik had thought the battalion assault ships like the Pendragon were big, but the Bunker Hill was more than twice the length and six times the tonnage. She and the other Yorktown Class ships were the biggest vessels ever built by man, though there were rumors the Martian Confederation was working on something even larger.

They took a ship's car to the admiral's conference room, which was over a kilometer from the landing bay, and walked through a door flanked by two Marines in full dress uniform. The Marines serving as security on navy ships were part of the Corps, officially detached for naval service. It was considered a backwater posting within the Corps, but overall the system worked well, and the shipboard Marines had a strong record of service.

The conference room was huge, far larger than anything of the sort Cain had ever seen on a ship. Real estate was tight on a spaceship, but the Bunker Hill had been built to be a fleet flagship, and the designers managed to allocate enough space to give the admiral a good-sized briefing room.

"Welcome, everyone." Admiral Terrance Compton had been seated at the far end of the table, but he stood up as his guests filtered in. There was man wearing finely tailored civilian clothing sitting next to Compton. He stood also, but remained silent while Compton greeted the new arrivals. "Please, let's dispense with the formalities. We have a lot to discuss, and I would like to get started. Have a seat...all of you." He motioned to several empty chairs on opposite sides of the table. There were trays set out with cups and pitchers full of water.

Compton sat, letting out a small sigh as he did. "I know you have come from considerable distances at my request, and I apologize for the lack of hospitality." He scanned the room, his eyes pausing for an instant on each of them. "When our business is done, I would be honored if you would all dine with me and allow me to make amends."

"That is appreciated, Terrance, but hardly necessary." Holm sat in the seat to Compton's right, with Jax next to him and Erik and Sarah opposite, sitting next to the mysterious civilian. "You and I have had some time to discuss things, but if it is satisfactory with you, I'd like to start at the beginning for the benefit of our new arrivals." Jax had been there two days, but he hadn't been in on any discussions yet, and Erik and Sarah had literally come right from their shuttle.

"Yes, I think that is a good idea." His head slanted a bit, an unnecessary but subconscious movement toward the small microphone on his collar. "Joker, I want this room sealed. Beta-5 protocols."

"Understood, Admiral Compton." The non-descript voice of the AI was audible to all of them, as Compton had intended. "The room is now secure and will remain so until you command otherwise."

Compton cleared his throat and paused, as if considering where to begin. "General Cain, Colonel Jax, Colonel Linden...I want to thank all of you for coming, especially since the request was a personal one and not official."

Everyone present nodded, but they all remained silent, allowing Compton to continue. "First, I'd like to introduce Roderick Vance. Mr. Vance is a major industrialist in the Martian Confederation, and he has been sent here as a liaison of sorts." He looked out at the confused expressions and hesitated. "I will explain exactly what he…"

"I will vouch for Mr. Vance." Holm interrupted, his voice commanding. He was telling Jax and Erik to trust him and not raise any issues, and both of them understood.

Compton glanced at Jax and Cain and flashed a grateful look toward Holm. "As many of you are aware, there has been considerable friction between the central government of the Alliance and its colonies." That is an understatement of considerable proportions, he thought. "Many things have happened over the last six months, things of which you are likely only partially aware." His hands slid over the large 'pad on the table in front of him. The viewscreens along the side walls of the room activated, showing video – a slideshow of different scenes.

"I am afraid that open rebellion had broken out on a number of Alliance colony worlds." Compton hesitated, allowing everyone to look at the images on the monitors, scenes of protests, combat, burned out buildings. "Things on Columbia are quite bad. I have less information on other worlds, but everything I hear suggests the situations are similar on a number of other planets."

"Arcadia is blockaded." Cain blurted out what he was thinking. He'd never been accused of an excess of patience. "Sorry to interrupt, admiral. But I assumed you would know about that. There is a large naval task force enforcing the quarantine."

"No apologies necessary, general. This is an informal meeting." Then, addressing Cain's point: "There is no authorized naval presence in the Wolf 359 system." He looked right at Cain. "Are you sure they were navy ships and not just some security force?"

"Admiral, there were two of these monsters there." He waved his hands, indicating he was referring to the Bunker Hill. "Plus a huge supporting fleet. That was no patrol force."

Compton was silent for a moment, his face becoming even more troubled. "I cannot account for that, general. I have a basic awareness were all active duty naval forces are deployed, and I cannot explain what you saw."

Holm slowly let out a deep breath. "Why don't you continue on the overall situation, Terrance, and get everyone up to speed." He glanced at Erik then back to Compton. "We can revisit this later."

"Very well, Elias." Compton leaned back in his chair. "Let me review some backstory on how this fleet came to be stationed here." He hesitated again, looking at Vance, then Holm, then the others. "I just want to say first, though, that I intend to speak very freely." He glanced again at Holm, seeing the general nodding for him to continue. "Some of what is discussed here today may put each of you in a...ah...an uncomfortable position with regard to your duty and obligation to the service." He paused again. This was difficult, unlike anything he had faced in his career. "I'm afraid we all may have some complex choices ahead of us."

"It's OK, Terrance." Holm spoke softly, his voice somber. "I trust these three with my life. You can tell them anything."

Compton nodded and, after a brief pause, continued. "For a considerable amount of time – perhaps a year now – I have been receiving directives and orders from the Naval Director that seemed...odd...unexpected." He could see them all considering what he was saying. Augustus Garret was the Naval Director, and no one could imagine him doing anything that would concern Compton.

"It was limited to relatively unimportant things at first, like personnel reassignments. I noticed several that I couldn't imagine had been Augustus' idea, but I just wrote them off, figured he was playing the Washbalt game a little. Garret put a lot of effort into making sure the naval veterans were mustered out the right way and not cheated like they were after the Second Frontier War. I just figured he'd made some petty political deals, agreed to promote a few cronies in return for the support he needed." He paused, stifling a sarcastic chuckle. "I didn't like it, but I figured no one hates this crap more than Garret, so if he went along with it, there had to be a reason."

He reached out, grabbing his cup. "But it got worse. There were new suspect orders, and they were even more worrisome.

Personnel assignments that really mattered, ones that affected operational efficiency. Changes in regulations, including covert surveillance of crew members. Crazy stuff, and completely unlike the Garret I know."

"That sounds like the kind of nonsense they inflicted on us with the political officers." Cain's voice was derisive, bitter. He'd done very poorly managing his political officer, and that was at least partly to blame for the trajectory of his career since. "Sounds like they're looking to do the same thing to the navy."

"I think you are correct, general. The intent is clearly to assert greater control over the navy." He took a sip from the cup. "Still, that does not explain Garret's role. He would be as hostile to such an encroachment as you." He was shaking his head as he spoke.

"Then I was ordered here." He panned his head around the table. Every eye was focused on him. "Worse, I am under orders to provide any support the Planetary Governor requests." He sucked in a deep breath. "Any support...without limitation."

No one interrupted, but a murmur of surprise rippled around the room. "We don't have a Marine strikeforce attached, so there are only two reasons for a battlefleet to be sent here. One, to intimidate the population, to terrorize the rebels and sap their will to fight." He took another drink and set down the cup. "Or two, even worse, to actually bombard planetary targets." His voice was soft and grim, and he let his words sink in before continuing.

Jax and Sarah had sad, surprised looks on their faces, but Erik's showed only tightly controlled rage. He'd dreaded this moment for years, even as he'd been certain it would one day come.

"I have known Augustus Garret for forty years." Compton's voice was scratchy and hoarse; his fatigue was showing. "He would never place a major fleet under the control of anyone outside the chain of command." He looked up, his eyes defiant. "And he would never allow the fleet to attack Alliance civilians."

"Is it possible he is acting under some sort of duress?" Jax had been silent since entering the room, but now he chimed in.

"That is what I thought as well." Compton glanced over at Roderick Vance. "At least until Mr. Vance here brought me some information." He turned back to Jax. "I'm afraid the truth is worse. Much worse."

"Mr. Vance, would you be kind enough to repeat for my people what you told me an hour ago?" Holm looked at the Martian envoy as he spoke.

Vance pushed his chair back from the table and stood up. He was more comfortable standing when he addressed a group. "I was sent here to discuss a matter with Admiral Compton. In addition to my many business activities, I occasionally do some freelance work for the Martian Security Department." He didn't feel it was necessary to explain that by "occasional freelance work," what he really meant was he ran the place.

He paused to let the others digest what he had said. He'd read the MSD dossiers on the officers in attendance. None of them was a fan of intelligence services, Cain of course being the most hostile. Vance didn't take offense – if he had to contend with Gavin Stark and Alliance Intelligence using him as a pawn on a daily basis, he'd be pretty angry about it too. "I can assure you all that I am here to help. The Alliance and its colonies are on the verge of a catastrophe, one that can only serve to destabilize the balance of power in addition to causing enormous human suffering. This is no more in the interest of the Confederation than of your people." He took a deep breath. "We would like to help by sharing information with you."

Vance looked around the room. Cain's expression was skeptical, but they were all silent, waiting for him to continue. "I am sure it will not be surprising to any of you that MSD has various conduits within Alliance Intelligence for obtaining information." Jax nodded slightly, but the others sat perfectly still, watching and listening. "The Augustus Garret who was been acting as Naval Director for the past eight months in an imposter."

Every eye in the room was riveted to Vance. "I can see how shocking this news is to you all, and I completely understand. Nevertheless, as unlikely a scenario as this seems, I can assure you it is factual."

"What happened to Admiral Garret?" Sarah beat the others to the question. "The real one."

Vance's voice softened a bit. Garret was important to the people in this room – leader, hero, friend - and he needed to be more sensitive and less businesslike. He was here to build trust...or at least that was part of why he was here. "We believe he is being held at Alliance Intelligence headquarters in Washbalt." There were a few hushed gasps in the room; Alliance Intelligence was widely feared, and few people ever returned from those detention cells.

"Although I cannot confirm this, we strongly believe Garret is still alive." He looked over at Compton. "Indeed, the admiral here received a Priority One order issued after the imposter took Garret's place. I believe this would have been impossible to do without a fresh blood sample from the actual Garret."

Cain glanced across the table at Holm. They were both thinking the same thing – how does this Martian know how Alliance Priority One protocols work? His logic, however, was sound. There was a good chance Garret was still alive; it was even likely. But what was their next step?

Compton stood up, gesturing for Vance to have a seat. "With Mr. Vance's indulgence, I will take it from here." Vance nodded with a smile and lowered himself into the metal chair. "I agree that Admiral Garret is likely still alive, and in that context, we must determine how to proceed."

He motioned to the screens along the wall, still displaying scenes from the planet. "As you can see from some of these images we have captured through orbital reconnaissance, the fighting on Columbia has become quite severe. Mr. Cooper, the Planetary Governor, is somewhat of a sociopath, and he has pursued extremely aggressive strategies to crush the rebels, including summary executions and, I am afraid, torture."

He pointed toward the screens, now displaying several different fenced-in areas. "He has established camps where he is confining anyone suspected of separatist sympathies, as well as the families of those serving in the rebel armies." His voice cracked slightly with emotion. "I'm afraid the conditions in the camps are quite bad, with no shelter provided and inadequate food and sanitation. From the accounts we have been able to assemble, there is a steady death toll in each camp."

He could see the anger on all of their faces, and most of all Erik Cain, whose expression projected death itself. "The rebel forces attempted to liberate the main camp at Weston approximately six months ago, just after we arrived. While they were able to free a small number of captives, they suffered crippling losses from the defenders and the subsequent counter-attack." He hesitated, but decided to add, "I'm afraid there were significant punitive activities against the detainees in response."

He could see their faces sink. Clearly, sympathies in the room were with the rebels. That was good – it would serve his purpose. "The rebels did, however, succeed in destroying the primary federal supply dump, and they blew up the main headquarters in Weston as well. I suspect they were trying to kill Cooper, but he was out in the field when the building was blown." He forced himself to pause. By nature, he spoke quickly and tended to move rapidly from one subject to another. But this was a lot of information about important topics – he had to give them a chance to absorb it all.

"Subsequent to these events, both sides found themselves incapable of launching any significant operations. The two sides on Columbia have essentially been stalemated for the past six months. The federals have possession of the cities, which they have fortified. The rebels more or less control everything outside the urban areas, though they would be hard-pressed to counter a major federal push in any specific location. The primary rebel base is Carlisle Island, roughly twenty kilometers north of Weston. It is extremely well-defended, and the federals have lacked sufficient strength to take it by assault. If they were able to do so, the rebellion on Columbia would likely collapse.

"The federal forces, however, have just been reinforced with two Alliance army divisions shipped from Earth. Cooper now enjoys a considerable superiority in both numbers and supply, and he has begun to pacify areas outside the urban zones. The only thing preventing him from quickly snuffing out the rebellion is the strength of the Carlisle Island position. As long as the rebels maintain an army in being there, they can continue the fight."

Compton leaned back in his chair and sighed. "This has led to a problem that is about to escalate beyond my control." They could hear the tension building in his voice. "Governor Cooper has requested several times that the fleet launch a nuclear bombardment of Carlisle Island. To date, I have been able to dissuade him without an outright refusal, however I believe I have exhausted that option. His most recent request was quite insistent, and I am afraid my only choices are to comply or to refuse outright, in direct violation of my orders from Admiral Garret's office." He deliberately referred to the admiral's office and not Garret himself. "I trust you are all aware of the implications of this."

No one answered, but their facial expressions were sufficiently communicative – they all understood. "I think perhaps General Holm would like to add a few thoughts at this point." Compton looked at the general as he spoke. "I believe his insights would be helpful."

Holm moved in his chair, trying to get comfortable. He was tense, like everyone else present, and his back was killing him. The old wound was acting up, as it often did when he was overly stressed. The Battle of Persis was a lifetime ago, two wars past, but he still carried the scars. "You will note that Admiral Compton advised us that Alliance army units have been dispatched to Columbia...indeed, I can confirm that they have been sent to other worlds as well, including Arcadia."

Holm's voice sounded normal to everyone present, everyone save Cain. Erik could hear the tension, the strain lying below the surface. It was just a feeling, an impression, but Cain was worried about the general...even more than he was worried about the rest of them.

"This is arguably a breach of the Marine Charter." Holm was speaking to everyone, but his gaze shifted between Cain and Jax. "Alliance Gov claims these assignments are for policing and training purposes only and, as such, are not covered under the Charter. This is obviously nonsense, but it at least gives a pretext of legitimacy to the actions...one that General Samuels has been perfectly happy to accept without complaint."

Holm was relieved to have Jax and Cain with him again. The last three years had been difficult, with Holm losing a series of struggles regarding demobilization and reassignments. The wartime Corps, which he had worked so hard to help build, had been largely disbanded, its veterans forcibly retired or dispatched to small, scattered garrisons on fringe worlds. Seasoned troops were replaced by new recruits coming from Camp Puller, and Holm wasn't happy with what he saw in these new Marines. He hadn't been to Puller in years, but he was starting to wonder what was going on there.

He'd been drinking more than he should recently, he knew that. Holm had always been a bit of a drinker; it's how he dealt with the voices from the past, the memories he wished he didn't have. He had the same type of ghosts that kept Erik Cain up nights, but he had more of them. Now things were worse, more difficult to comprehend, and he felt lost and uncertain. Rafael Samuels was the Commandant of the Marine Corps, and he had repeatedly accepted developments and changes that any of his predecessors would have considered unthinkable. He'd failed to fight against the assignment of political officers late in the war, and now he executed a demobilization plan that gutted the Corps' combat effectiveness.

Holm was suspicious of Alliance Gov, as were many Marines, especially those pulled from the underside of society on Earth. But it wasn't in his makeup to suspect someone in the Corps, certainly not the supreme general, a veteran of almost fifty years' service. Elias Holm was a man who could summon the strength to face any challenge, pay any cost to prevail. But for the first time in his life he simply didn't know what to do, and the helplessness was easier to handle if he had an extra drink or two. He wasn't proud of it, but that hadn't stopped him either.

"There are two matters I feel need to be discussed. First, the massive deployment of Alliance army units to the colony worlds - do we sit by idly and allow this to happen? Without intervention of some sort, it is doubtful the colonial forces can hold out for long against such forces." He paused, realizing as he spoke the implications of what he was saying – or at least indirectly suggesting.

"The second issue is perhaps even more complex and troublesome." He'd been thinking about this meeting for days, but he still wasn't sure exactly how he was going to say this. "It appears to my judgment that Alliance Gov is making a major push to assume total control over the Corps, in directly violation of the Charter." Jax's expression showed some surprise, if not at the overall developments themselves, at Holm's willingness to state it so bluntly. Cain's was matter-of-fact; this was no shock to him...none whatsoever. Had he not been among his most trusted friends and allies, he might have worn an "I told you so" look on his face.

"I think we have to consider the possibility that General Samuels is operating under some form of duress or outside influence..." He paused, glancing briefly at Compton. "...or even that he has been abducted like Admiral Garret and replaced with an imposter."

Vance leaned forward in his chair. "I do not think it is likely he has been replaced." He looked over at Holm. "The events you describe have occurred over the last 3-4 years. I don't believe that a replacement could remain undetected for such a long period of time. It is much more likely that he is experiencing some sort of external pressure, though I am sorry to say I have no idea what form that may take."

Even Roderick Vance was completely unaware that General Samuels was actually a member of the Alliance Intelligence Directorate, having been suborned six years before by Gavin Stark. The actions so inexplicable to Holm and his allies were part of an overall plan to eliminate the Corps and replace it with a Directorate-controlled force. Rafael Samuels had been a hero of the Corps but, unknown to any of those present, he was now the greatest traitor in its century-long history.

The room was strangely quiet for a few minutes, everyone deep in thought until Cain finally broke the silence. "Obviously, the entire situation is enormously complex. But is appears to me that there are several pressing matters that require immediate attention."

He looked over at Compton. "First, Admiral Compton must deal with the demand that he bombard the rebel-occupied sectors of the planet. May I venture a guess, admiral, that you have no intention of launching a nuclear attack on the colonists?"

Compton looked grimly at Cain, then at each of the others. "No, I will not give that order." He exhaled sharply. "But I cannot predict the results of my refusal, especially since it will appear to everyone outside this room that I am directly disobeying Admiral Garret's orders."

Cain nodded. They would deal with that fallout when they had to. "Second, if Admiral Garret is indeed being held hostage, we must figure a way to rescue him."

Everyone started speaking at once, except Vance, who sat silently and watched. Compton's voice rose above the others. "Is it even possible to break someone out of Alliance Intelligence headquarters? There is nothing I would like better than to free Augustus, but I don't see how it can be done."

Cain looked back at Compton. "We have no choice. We must find a way."

"Erik, I know how aggressive you can be, but I think you're reaching too far on this one." Holm's tone was somber, fatigued.

Cain was about to answer, but Vance spoke first. "I think General Cain is correct. And I believe I might be able to assist." Everyone stopped talking and looked at the Martian envoy. "It will be extremely difficult, but we may be able to sneak a small strike force into Washbalt. Our embassy is located close to Alliance Intelligence headquarters, and it is possible we could get a few of your people there under cover as diplomatic staff."

A slight smile crept across his face, the first time his expression had betrayed any emotion. "Indeed, the Alliance is behaving in an almost obsequious manner in diplomatic circles recently, which gives us added latitude in making changes to embassy staff without being questioned. No doubt they are trying to buy time to research the technology on Epsilon Eridani

IV before they are forced to share access."

"I will lead the strike team." Cain hardly let Vance finish before he spoke up. "A small group from the old special action teams, if we can track them down quickly enough."

Holm was considering the situation, and he was about to protest when Sarah beat him to it. "Erik, that's a suicide mission." Her face was blank, expressionless. She knew he'd go, that he'd have to go – or at least believe he had to – no matter what she or anyone else said. But still she had to try. "You can't possibly be serious about trying to break into Alliance Intelligence headquarters."

"Sarah, I know it is dangerous." He was looking at her, but speaking to everyone present. "But there is no choice. If we don't rescue Garret, Alliance Intelligence controls the navy... and if they control the navy, it's over. Everything. Alliance Gov will control every colony world with an iron fist, and anyone who causes trouble will be nuked from space. The Corps will be done too, units trapped without supply on whatever world they are currently posted."

She knew he was right, but she wanted to run away from the truth. To scream, why does it have to be him? But all she did was sit still and nod ever so slightly, fighting to retain her composure. She was sure she would never see him again if he went to Earth, and she just wasn't ready to face the possibility.

"We also need to prop up the rebels." Erik decided to move on to the next subject – he'd discuss details of the rescue operation later, when Sarah wasn't there. It would be hard enough on her without getting into the specifics now. "It appears that Alliance Gov is using its control of the navy to ship huge numbers of troops and massive quantities of supply to the most problematic worlds. The local forces will be overwhelmed before we are able to free Garret. At least here on Columbia."

"I agree. We need to reinforce the rebels." Jax this time, his tone leaving no doubt where his sympathies were. "A covert force, elite troops inserted to provide close support." He looked down at the table. "I'm not sure where we'd find them, though."

"I think we can round up at least 500. Mostly former SAT

or other elite troops." Holm was thinking as he spoke, doing a mental tally on what forces he felt he could find. "All from systems within a 30-day range." He looked at Compton. "Assuming the admiral can assist with communications and transport."

Compton nodded. "For now I can. But we better hurry before I'm relieved of command."

"I believe I can also be of some assistance." Vance spoke slowly, deliberatively. "I am authorized to offer limited logistical support to the rebel forces, including transport and supply."

Everyone in the room had the same stunned look. The Confederation had always been extremely hesitant to get involved in the battles of the other Superpowers, and now their representative was offering to intervene in an internal Alliance dispute. Compton spoke first. "That is unexpected, Mr. Vance. If I may ask directly without giving offense, what does the Confederation want in return?"

"There is one thing, admiral, but I assure you it is in the interest of all humanity." He swallowed hard and continued, somewhat tentatively. "We would like your cooperation in establishing international control over Epsilon Eridani IV." His normally impassive face showed genuine emotion. "I understand that your loyalties are complex right now, but surely you all know that Alliance Intelligence controls that planet. And you know just how they will utilize its technology if they are able to adapt it."

He is sincere, Compton thought - If he is lying, he is the best liar I have ever seen. He looked over at Holm, who nodded his agreement. "Very well, Mister Vance. We will support your efforts. As long as it is international control and not Martian domination."

"We are agreed." Vance allowed himself a cautious smile. "I do not seek sole Martian control for the same reason the Alliance cannot be allowed to retain it. It would shatter the balance of power and start a war the likes of which none of us can imagine. We propose that the Treaty of Paris be expanded to include Epsilon Eridani IV. Control will be shared, just like on Earth's moon or Terra Nova."

Holm looked back at Jax. "You willing to take an extended leave, Colonel Jax? Any expeditionary force sent to Columbia is going to need a leader."

Jax nodded. "Count me in."

"Me too." Every eye turned toward Sarah. She returned their stunned stares. "Do all of you see what is on those monitors?" She motioned toward the wall of screens. "There is a humanitarian catastrophe taking place down there, and it is only going to get worse. I can't imagine what medical services they have, but I guarantee it is substandard." She looked at Erik, knowing he'd want to object. "I'm as much a Marine as any of you. I can save lives down there." She glanced at Compton. "If the admiral can get a message through to Armstrong, I can put together a volunteer med staff...and really make a difference."

Erik opened his mouth, but no words came out. He wanted to argue, to insist that she forget this insane idea. But he couldn't. If he had his way, he'd hide her someplace safe, where he knew no harm could come to her. But that wasn't her way. Besides, if they lost this struggle there would be no place safe. Anywhere. Still, he couldn't force the doubtful expression from his face.

"How many Columbians did we know when we were stationed there?" She pointed at the screens. "How many of our brothers and sisters retired to Columbia? How many are in those scenes we're watching now?"

Cain wanted to tell her to go, that he understood - to give her the support she deserved - but he just couldn't bring himself to do it. Instead, he nodded...slightly, grudgingly. It was the best he could give her. She looked at him and smiled warmly, her silent acknowledgement that, as always, she knew his thoughts.

The room was quiet for a time...a minute, perhaps two... then General Holm broke the silence. "There is one more thing that needs to be done. We must find out what is happening with General Samuels." He looked up, his eyes moving from Cain to Jax and back. "I think this is my task. I will go to see the Commandant and find out what is going on." He paused, looking sadly down at the table. "And I will do whatever must be done."

Chapter 14

Fleet Command Control Center
AS Bunker Hill
Orbiting Columbia - Eta Cassiopeiae II

"Negative, Mr. Cooper." Compton's voice was firm, steady. He knew he was going down a road that was fraught with peril, but his decision made, he focused on what had to be done. He was relieved, actually, to have chosen a course, and he would follow it…wherever it might lead. "I regret that I must refuse your request." There was a slight delay, as Compton's message made its way from high orbit to the surface, and the reply covered the same distance back. It wasn't a long hitch, perhaps a tenth of a second each way, but it was still noticeable.

"Admiral Compton, you have no right to refuse my ord… my request." Arlen Cooper was angry. He was trying to control it, but only partially succeeding. "Your orders from Naval Command are quite clear, admiral." He tried to keep his voice steady and non-provocative. Cooper was a bully, but he was smart enough to know he couldn't push around a man like Terrance Compton. "Consider the ramifications of your refusal. Are you really going to throw away your career over your squeamishness about bombing some rebels?"

Compton was angry too, though in an icy cold way an arrogant thug like Cooper could never understand. "Governor, allow me to be clear." His tone was changing, becoming harder, more ominous. "What you have requested would constitute an atrocity and a war crime of epic proportions." He was conscious of the bridge crew listening to what was said; in fact, he'd deliberately taken the communication on an open line. He was putting forth a moral argument, that such an order was unthinkable and could not be obeyed. He thought it was his best chance to maintain control of the fleet if things got tough.

"You are out of line, admiral." Cooper's anger was boiling over. After a lifetime of mid-level appointments, he was finally completely in charge someplace…and he didn't like his commands being refused. "I am attempting to combat a planetwide insurrection, and I require you to follow your orders and assist me in defeating these traitors."

The angrier and more off-balance Cooper got, the better, Compton thought. "Governor, that is not what you requested. You want me to carpet bomb an entire inhabited sector with nuclear weapons. Such an operation, were it to be carried out, would surely kill thousands of innocent civilians in addition to whatever rebel installations were destroyed." He paused, taking a breath. His tone remained calm and professional. "If you provide me with a list of purely military targets, so we can execute a bombardment plan that at least minimizes civilian casualties, I will be happy to reconsider your request." That was a lie, but one that might buy some time.

"But there are no purely military targets!" Cooper was seething, but he was also afraid of Compton, and that helped temper his rage. "These cowardly rebels hide in and among the population. The civilians aid and support them. They are not innocent."

"Governor, if there are civilians engaged in illegal activity it is your job to arrest them and put them on trial." He paused again and almost grinned; on one small level he was enjoying tormenting Cooper. "But don't ask me to indiscriminately bomb populated areas because you believe there are rebel sympathizers there."

He imagined Cooper in his office, nearly apoplectic with rage, and he finally let a momentary smile cross his lips. "Now Governor, with all due respect, I have many duties. When you have specific intelligence on rebel military targets, contact me again and we will discuss."

"I will report your failure to obey orders to the Naval High Command, admiral." Cooper was trying to sound threatening, but he was too intimidated by Compton to make it work.

"Governor, that is your prerogative, of course." Compton's voice remained calm and even. "Now, I am afraid I really do have work requiring my attention. Goodbye, governor." He cut the transmission before Cooper could say anything else. Go ahead, Mr. Cooper, he thought. Send a message to Washbalt. For just an instant there was a self-satisfied smile on his otherwise impassive face.

"Commnet control, this is shuttle Beta-9. Conducting final docking approach." Cain sat in the co-pilot's seat speaking into the com unit.

"Shuttle Beta-9, you are cleared to dock." The response was lackadaisical; service on the Commnet stations was boring at best, brain numbing at worst, and it didn't exactly attract the best and brightest. "Report to the control room after you dock… directly down the main corridor from the access hatch." They're too lazy to send anyone down to meet us in the docking area, Cain thought. He was disgusted with the poor security, though grateful it would make his task easier.

Commnet was an interstellar communications network connecting the planets of the Alliance. Radio and laser signals cannot pass through a warp gate, only matter, and Commnet was developed to address the need for high speed interstellar communications. There was a control station positioned near each warp gate. Messages were sent within each system to the station, traveling at lightspeed from any transmission point. Once received, the communications were queued based on priority and downloaded into small drones. The vehicles launched on a regular schedule, but some senders – military and government, for example - had override authority, and a priority message could trigger the immediate launch of a drone. The drone would then transit the warp gate and transmit the communications to the matching station in the next system. From there it was then forwarded to a station at the desired exit gate, moving through each system at lightspeed. The network allowed communications to move far more quickly than any ship could travel.

Virtually the entire network was automated, and the crew was mostly a redundancy. Typically, there was a team of four assigned to each station, but recently several additional members had been added, censors who reviewed many of the messages before they were relayed.

The shuttle eased closer to the station, gently sliding into the small docking cradle. There were five of them on the tiny ship - the pilot, one of Compton's most trusted officers, as well as Cain, Jax, and two Marines from Holm's staff. Shuttle Beta-9 had requested permission to dock because of a complete life-support system failure. But that was a fiction; its real purpose was to gain access and capture the facility.

There was a loud thud as the ship connected firmly with the cradle. Cain got up from his seat and walked back to the hatch, joining Jax and the two Marines. They were all armed, but they hoped to avoid bloodshed. They were here to get the crew off the station…before they blew it to plasma.

"You ready, Jax?" Cain had a wicked grin on his face. "Back into action…such that it is." The two had been in some very hot spots before; rounding up half a dozen communications specialists wasn't likely to overtax their battle-tested reflexes. Still, if their training and experience had taught them anything, it was never to get careless about any operation, no matter how simple it seemed.

Jax nodded, gripping his assault rifle tightly. "Ready."

Cain pressed the button and the hatch slid open. There was a short delay, maybe ten seconds, and the second hatch, the one leading into station, opened. They ran inside, Jax in the lead, Cain taking the rear, bound for the control room.

Most of the station's volume consisted of storage compartments full of drones. The occupied area was small, just a control center and cramped living quarters. The station rotated on its axis, creating modest artificial gravity, but it was only one fifth Earth normal. Cain and Jax hadn't fought in low gravity environments for years, and even then they'd been fully armored. They moved methodically, gripping the rails along to corridor to stabilize themselves.

Halfway down the corridor, Cain gave Jax a silent nod and split off, climbing through a large access panel. He had made his way about five meters down the crawlspace when he got to a large metal conduit – just where he'd been told it would be. He took the small power saw hanging from his belt and, switching it on, cut through the metal tubing to sever the cable inside. The conduit was plasti-steel, and it resisted for a few seconds, giving way only after he pushed against it as hard as he could. Once again, he missed his armor – the molecular blade would have sliced the conduit like a knife through butter.

As he cut through, an alarm sounded in the station. Jax should be bursting into the control room now, he thought. With the main communication trunk line cut, even if one of the crew managed to send a distress call, it was only going to get about 15 meters.

Cain tossed the saw aside and worked his way out of the crawlspace, backwards this time, which he found to be much more difficult. By the time he made it to the control room, Jax and the two Marines had all six crew members shackled and lined up against the wall.

"Good job, big man." Cain was in good spirits as he walked into the control center. He motioned to the two Marines. "Get them back to the shuttle and keep an eye on them."

The two troopers, both sergeants replied in chorus. "Yes, sir!" Cain and Jax were both senior officers and heroes in the Corps, and working so closely with them was overwhelming, even to veteran non-coms. The Marines pushed the still-stunned station crew ahead of them. "Move along now."

"Let's set the warhead and get out of here." Cain watched as Jax activated the timer on the 10 kiloton bomb they had brought. It was a small nuclear device, even by tactical nuke standards, but it was quite enough to vaporize the station.

"Done." Jax was kneeling next to the device, and he looked up at Cain. "Detonation in one-five minutes." He got up and walked over toward the hatch. "What do you say we get out of here?"

Cain smiled, almost a laugh and made a motion with his arm. "After you, my friend." They scrambled down the hall and back into the shuttle. In five minutes they easing away from the station's docking cradle; ten minutes later they were stopped 50 kilometers away, waiting for the explosion.

"Well, if the other two teams take out their targets, we'll have bought Admiral Compton some time." There were three warp gates in the system; if all the Commnet stations were destroyed, Eta Cassiopeiae would be cut off. Cain sounded energetic. The overall situation was bad, no question about that, but finally he felt they were doing something about it. He'd faced bleak prospects before, but as long as they were fighting, he felt they could prevail. He'd hated sitting around in meaningless postings, passively watching things deteriorate around him. Now his blood was up. "Let's see Governor…" – he drew out the word governor in a mocking and sarcastic way – "…Cooper get a message through with no Commnet. He grinned malevolently.

Jax smiled but didn't answer. Erik Cain was a fighter in every fiber of his being, and he'd face any challenge without hesitation - damn the consequences. Jax was more measured, more cautious by nature. But he also hoped that taking out the stations bought Compton some time, because they all knew what would happen if Cooper could get a message through to the Garret imposter.

Terrance Compton was a well-loved admiral and one of the great heroes of the last war. But Augustus Garret was a legend, the very heart and soul of the navy. If the imposter issued a fleetwide order relieving Compton, Jax didn't see how the admiral could maintain control of the fleet. At the very least, the formation would splinter, with some ships supporting Compton and others Garret. It would be a disaster.

Their own prospects looked no better than Compton's. They were bound for the rally point on Armstrong, and from there to different destinations. Jax and Sarah would be returning to Columbia, dropping onto that planet with a small strikeforce and a tiny medical team. They'd be joining a rebellion that had so far done remarkably well, but now faced overwhelming federal strength. The outlook was bleak, even with the help Jax and Sarah would bring – aid they were providing to the planet to fight other federal authorities. They would all be strictly on their own, and defeat would probably mean court martial and execution…not just for them, but for all those they led there.

General Holm was going to Terra Nova for a showdown with General Samuels. In the best case, his act was an insubordinate one. But if Samuels was truly under some external pressure, Holm could be walking right into a firestorm. Jax was at least taking 500 combat veterans with him; Holm would be alone except for a few aides.

Erik Cain was going into the darkest place of all, taking a handful of volunteers to Earth, to the capital of the Alliance, to sneak into the most heavily guarded building in the entire human-occupied universe...and then escape. It was crazy on every level, but it was necessary, and that was all Cain had to know. Jax, Sarah, Holm...they were all horribly worried, distraught at seeing him go on what they saw as a suicide mission. But Cain was calm, almost cheerful. Finally, he was doing something...something that could make a difference. He knew it would be tough, but it was absolutely vital. He'd see it done. Somehow.

Harrigan prowled around Yorktown's flight deck. The ship was on condition green, and the entire area was eerily quiet, the only activity around a single ship. The shuttle set to launch had not been on the schedule, not until Harrigan added it. His position made it relatively easy to arrange an inter-ship personnel transfer and, along with it, a shuttle launch to ferry an officer to her new posting. The shuttle's flight program was simple – a routine trip to the cruiser Boston to deliver one officer. Unknown to the pilot, its real destination was quite different, and there was going to be one extra passenger.

"Ensign Jorgans reporting, sir." Jorgans was tall and young, fresh out of the Academy, though she was a bit older than most of her classmates, having spent three years in training for Alliance Intelligence before going into deep cover, first as a naval cadet and now a serving officer.

"Very well, Jorgans." Lieutenant Lyle Baum wasn't much older than Jorgans, maybe three or four years. His own lieutenant's insignia was still shiny and new. "Go get strapped in. We launch in fourteen minutes."

Jorgans nodded. She walked up the metal ramp, carrying a large, overstuffed duffle bag. The automated security system would analyze everything coming onboard, so there was nothing in the bag but uniforms and personal effects – just what an officer would bring along to her new assignment. She chanced a quick look over her shoulder. Good she, thought, he's looking at my ass. Distraction would be helpful on this mission.

Lieutenant." Harrigan stepped out of the shadows, startling the young pilot just as he was enjoying the view of Jorgens' backside climbing up the ramp.

Baum was startled, but he snapped to attention. "Sir!" He gave Harrigan a textbook salute.

"I'll be hitching a ride, lieutenant." Harrigan spoke matter-of-factly though, in fact, this was a critical point in his mission.

"Um…you're not on the manifest, sir." Baum was nervous, unsure what to do. Regulations required him to clear any unscheduled passengers with central control. But Harrigan was a full commander, and to a junior lieutenant three years out of the Academy he might as well have been Zeus coming down from Olympus.

"I decided to make the trip at the last minute." Don't give him room to argue, Harrigan thought. "Now let's go or we'll miss our launch time." He paused slightly then added, "Don't worry. I note your attention to procedure and authorize the change when we get back."

Technically, Harrigan didn't have the authority to approve the change unless he was in the control center on duty. But that wasn't a fine point Baum was prepared to argue with the commander. "Yes, sir. Please get strapped in." He swallowed hard. "Sir."

Harrigan climbed up the ramp, flashing a silent look at Jorgens and taking a seat. The shuttle was capable of fairly rapid acceleration, and the couches were designed to allow human occupants to survive potentially lethal g forces. The scheduled inter-ship transit would not be utilizing any high-G acceleration, so the accompanying pressure suits were stowed unused in a large locker.

They sat quietly for a few minutes, firmly strapped into their couches. "Secure for launch in ten seconds." Baum's voice came over the general comm system. "Five, four, three, two, one..."

They were pressed into their couches as the Yorktown's magnetic catapult launched them out at 3g. A few seconds later, the shuttle's engine engaged, and began a short burn to build velocity toward the Boston. Harrigan had chosen the target ship well; the Boston was on picket duty, on the far end of the fleet deployment zone. The shuttle would take two hours to reach its destination, giving him some time before any alarm was sounded.

"We're at 1g acceleration now, so it should be pretty comfortable if you want to unstrap and walk around." Baum's voice on the comm system again.

Jorgens looked over at Harrigan, and he nodded without a sound. She unstrapped herself and walked forward, toward the cockpit. She ran her hands over her uniform, smoothing it out the best she could. Naval attire wasn't designed to aid seduction, but she managed to look pretty good in spite of the utilitarian cut of her uniform.

She pressed the button to open the hatch and walked through. "Do you mind if I come up here for a while?" The hatch made a whooshing sound as it closed behind her. "The commander makes me nervous." She walked up right behind him.

He smiled and turned to face her. "Not at all. He'd make me nerv..."

She moved so quickly he didn't have time to react at all. Her arms flashed around his head and he jerked forward and fell out of his chair to the floor. His body twitched a few times, but he was already dead, his neck cleanly broken. She dragged the corpse away from the pilot's chair, just as the hatch opened and Harrigan came through.

"Well done, Pam." Harrigan eased himself into the pilot's chair as he spoke. He'd never finished flight school, though he'd shown some aptitude for it. His superiors at Alliance Intelligence decided that he'd be more useful as a tactical or communications officer, at least in the long run. But he was pretty sure he remembered enough to fly the shuttle.

His hands raced over the controls. "Secure the body in the cargo hold and get us two pressure suits." He was entering in their new course as he spoke. "We're going to be accelerating at max, so we need to suit up." He paused as he focused on finalizing the course. "We need to get some velocity before they realize something is wrong and send ships after us." Whether they sent fighters to intercept or shuttles on a rescue mission, it would end the same way for Harrigan and Jorgens. They had to get to the YZ Ceti Warp gate before anything from the fleet caught up with them.

"Yes, sir." She pulled Baum's body back through the doorway. It was slow going; she was in top condition, but Baum was a lot bigger than she was, and it took several minutes for her to get him through the hatch.

Once the door closed, Harrigan double checked his course settings. Satisfied, he leaned back for a second and closed his eyes. Well, Admiral Compton, he thought. I don't know how you managed to shut down Commnet, but it won't do you any good. Harrigan put his hand against his pocket, running his finger over a small bump…the datachip with Arlen Cooper's message to Naval HQ. The message he was going to relay to the YZ Ceti Commnet station as soon as they transited the warp gate.

Chapter 15

Crystal River Valley
Southern Sector, Concordia District
Arcadia – Wolf 359 III

"General Thompson…sir, the enemy is on the move!" Jasper Logan was young, but he looked even more youthful than he was. Will had to keep reminding himself that his aide was a Marine veteran, even if he'd only served a year before being demobilized. A native Arcadian, Logan had joined the Corps to follow in the footsteps of his father, a decorated Major killed during the ill-fated Operation Achilles fifteen years before.

"Thank you, lieutenant." Thompson had been expecting this. Actually, he was surprised the enemy had waited so long. "Notify the battalion commanders. We move out in two hours."

Logan saluted and marched off to relay Thompson's orders. The Arcadian rebels had developed their own salute, really just a minor bastardization of the one Alliance forces used. It had developed organically, because the rebels didn't want to use the forms of the Alliance they were fighting. Thompson thought it was a little silly, but he saw no harm, and it was good for morale.

Thompson wore the new uniform of the Army of the Republic of Arcadia, rust-colored fatigues that provided excellent camouflage in the reddish light of the Wolf 359 primary. The rump Assembly, the survivors of the fighting in Weston, had made it official in a makeshift meeting hall in the cellar of a tavern. The document was brief for one of such import, just 605 words. But it was the first few that were of the greatest significance – "We the duly elected and authorized representatives of the people of Arcadia declare that the bonds between Arcadia and the Western Alliance are hereby severed and that Arcadia is henceforth and forever free and sovereign." They'd put their names to it, all of them, an act that would almost certainly guarantee a death sentence for every signatory should the rebellion fail.

Thompson had drilled his troops relentlessly, almost mercilessly. The federals had mousetrapped him once, and he swore never again. He'd learned a lesson that day, one that cost him a third of his strength but forged in him the makings of a true combat leader. He had tried to resign his command after the battle, but the soldiers shouted down his attempts. He vowed they would be ready for whatever the enemy threw at them after that day, and he'd been true to his word.

He'd become obsessive, and sleep was almost a forgotten concept. He worked day and night, and drove those around him until they reached their breaking points. That much he felt he felt he owed to the hundreds who'd died...the ones lost because of his mistake. I wonder, he thought grimly, if the troops are sorry yet that they didn't let me quit. They are certainly more exhausted.

The fighting since then had been mostly hit and run attacks. He'd raided enemy supply dumps in and around Arcadia and ambushed enemy forces sent out to pacify other areas of the planet. He didn't have the strength to counter major enemy thrusts, and he avoided large battles that could put his entire force in jeopardy. Now the enemy was finally moving in strength on his main base in Concordia, and he decided it was time to risk another major battle. He couldn't give up Concordia – it was his base and the heart of the rebellion. It was also the source of most of his weaponry and ammunition. Building the production facility had been his idea, but the credit for making it work belonged, more than anywhere else, to Kara Sanders.

Somehow, Kara had managed to keep production going with untrained workers and in spite of the chronic lack of raw materials. They were producing well below capacity now, as resources ran low and irreplaceable machinery broke down, but somehow she kept at least some weapons and ammunition coming to his forces in the field. He was using what she sent him sparingly, but her herculean efforts to maximize efficiency had been vital to keeping the army fighting. Without those supplies, the Arcadian rebellion would have been over already.

Though he had always been fond of her, and they'd been

lovers at times, Thompson had sometimes felt Kara had a bit of the spoiled brat in her, born into privilege as heir to one of the wealthiest families on Arcadia. Now he could hardly believe her strength and dedication. Her true self had risen to the circumstances, and he finally realized it had been there all along. Now, amid the uncertainty and danger he regretted the years they had wasted. He swore it would be different if they both got through this. He'd never let her go again.

But now he had to get his troops on the move. For the first time since they narrowly escaped destruction, he was ready to commit the entire army to battle. There would be no mistakes this time; he would make sure of that.

Isaac Merrick swore bitterly under his breath. He'd almost snuffed out this miserable rebellion six months before, but the quarry had escaped from the trap. He'd used Quinn's brigade as bait, and the rebels bit, seeing a chance to wipe out a large federal force…only to get hit on the flank and rear by Merrick's other two brigades.

Merrick had stripped everything bare, including Arcadia City, throwing 90% of his strength into the battle. It had been a big risk, but one that paid off. The rebel commander was taken by surprise; no one expected such a bold move from an Alliance army general. But Merrick wasn't typical. He was a career military officer, one whose ambitions were limited to advancement in the army. He had the aristocratic attitude of a man born into the Political Class, but the thought of sitting in an office as some sort of functionary was anathema to him, regardless of the pomp and prestige that went along with it. He was a soldier, and now, after a lifetime of training and inactivity, he had a war to fight.

Somehow the rebels had managed to battle their way out of his trap, but they were badly hurt, and he'd figured it was just a matter of mopping them up. But that wasn't to be. The rebel forces proved to be resilient, and for the past few months they'd been ambushing his troops every time they left Arcadia City. At least he'd gotten rid of Quinn; the troublesome brigadier was so shaken up by the realities of combat he requested reassignment to Earth, and Merrick happily obliged.

"William Thompson, 43 years old." Merrick was reading softly out loud as he scanned the report on his 'pad. "Born 2228 in Philadelphia, Outer City-South...hmm, the South Philadelphia Flats...rough neighborhood." He'd ordered a full dossier prepared on the rebel commander, and he was reviewing it for something, anything, he could use. "Mother murdered in 2233, no details available." There was a lot of crime in the Flats, and the police didn't waste much time worrying about Cog on Cog offenses. "Father died 2309, non-diagnosed infectious disease."

Reading the details of Thompson's childhood made Merrick think. He'd always viewed the Cogs as almost animals, the products of generations of substandard genetics - people who weren't capable of more than menial tasks. But Will Thompson was a Cog, and after Merrick beat him once the damnable rebels had been tearing apart the federal forces for the last six months. It was more than he could process then and there, but one day he would have to consider the implications.

"Recruited into the Marines from Delaware Banks Detention Center where he had been sentenced to life working the lunar mines." Thompson had been a repeat criminal, but since he'd restricted his activities to other Cogs, he'd escaped a death sentence. Still, Merrick thought, life expectancy in the lunar mines was only a little over a year, so it wouldn't have been too much of a reprieve. "Graduated Camp Puller, 2251. Assigned to 1st Marine Division."

There was more. Thompson had a good service record, with two decorations and a series of strong reports from his superiors. He was admitted to the Academy after recovering from wounds sustained during Operation Achilles. Badly injured in a training accident, he retired soon after and decided to stay on Arcadia. Although more or less fully recovered from his back-to-back wounds, by all accounts he still experienced considerable chronic pain, and occasionally used a cane.

He looked up from the screen, thinking - what makes this ex-sergeant such a formidable commander? And these upstart

colonials such good soldiers? He wasn't able to really understand the motivations of the rebels, who fought for a cause they
believed in, for freedoms they loved and had come to consider
essential. Merrick was smart, and he was a pragmatist, but the
system he was a part of, the only one he'd known all his life, was
simply too rigidly orthodox to allow him to truly understand the
colonial mindset.

Now that he'd been reinforced, he decided it was time to
make a major push. He was losing the guerilla war, there was no
point in sugar-coating that. The colonials knew the terrain better than he did, and the population was on their side. He'd never
stamp them out sending small units to pacify individual villages.
He had to engage and destroy the main rebel army, and he had
to hit them someplace vital to force them to commit.

Concordia was the core of enemy strength, the place rebellion had begun. With Arcadia City occupied, it was the next
most populated area on the planet. Merrick was sure Thompson would have to commit his forces to hold it. Invading Concordia, Merrick decided, was the way to achieve his major battle.

It offered another opportunity as well. For months, Merrick
had been wondering how Thompson kept his army supplied.
They'd raided his forces and stolen a considerable quantity of
equipment that much was true. But that didn't come close to
covering the ordnance they had expended. The rebels had a
weapons cache or a secret production facility and, odds were, it
was in Concordia somewhere. If he could inflict serious casualties on the enemy army and seize their supply source, the rebellion would falter and collapse.

"Colonel Jarrod, report to me at once." Merrick snapped
the order into the comlink as he ran his fingers across his 'pad,
switching from a view of Thompson's bio to a map of the area.

"Yes, sir." Jarrod's response was immediate, as always. "I'm
on the way, sir."

Preston Jarrod had been a major, and that's as far as anyone
had expected him to rise. He was a member of the Political
Class, but a lowly one, his influence poor. His father had been
a deputy magistrate in the Memphis Metroplex, and Jarrod had

attended one of the least prestigious Political Academies. But he was smart, a born tactician. Neither of these traits would have made much difference to his prospects back on Earth. But here and now, Merrick was fighting a war…and Jarrod was the best officer he had.

Merrick had put Jarrod into Quinn's old command and tasked him with rebuilding the shattered brigade. Though it was a general's posting, Merrick didn't dare promote Jarrod more than one step, an act that was controversial enough and placed the new colonel above other officers from far better-placed families.

"Colonel Jarrod reporting as ordered, sir." Jarrod stood at attention, having snapped a perfect salute. Merrick was sitting at a portable table set up in the center of the encampment.

"Thank you, colonel." Merrick set the 'pad down on the table, allowing Jarrod to see the map. "I believe we will fight a major battle here in the next several days, and I wanted to discuss strategy with you." He turned to face his subordinate. "But first, I want to tell you that you have done an excellent job of rebuilding the morale of your brigade."

"Thank you, sir."

Jarrod was a true soldier, a rarity in the Alliance Earth forces, which were generally choked with cronies and other incompetents. Merrick wondered, where the hell did he come from? Of course, though he didn't fully realize it, Merrick himself was another such creature, very unlike his peers.

"Colonel, this area is the heart of the rebellion, and we can expect a very difficult fight here." Merrick was looking at the 'pad; Jarrod's eyes were darting back and forth from the general to the map.

"Yes, sir, I believe you are right." Technically, Jarrod should have remained silent until Merrick specifically asked for an opinion. But the two had been working closely together for six months now, and Jarrod knew what the general expected of him. "May I speak candidly, sir?"

"Of course, colonel." Merrick understood Jarrod's hesitancy. Not too many Alliance army commanders welcomed honest commentary from subordinates.

"I think it is going to be worse than anyone expects." Jarrod paused, nervous at going too far. Merrick had proven to be a different sort of commander, but Jarrod had a lifetime habit of trying to keep his mouth shut. An opinionated mid-level officer was not likely to prosper in the Alliance's army. "To be honest, sir, I believe that General Thompson is a highly gifted tactician." He took a breath and hesitated, but decided to continue. "Other than the initial surprise, I believe he outfought us in the battle outside Arcadia City."

Merrick looked at Jarrod, amazed at the major's audacity. He suppressed a brief flash of anger – he'd been in the army a long time, and he wasn't immune to the arrogance of his class. But he had asked for honesty and, truth be told, he agreed with Jarrod's assessment. The rebels should never have been able to fight their way out the trap. Thompson had made a mistake in taking the bait, but from that point on he'd handled his forces magnificently.

We're on his home ground now, Merrick thought. Don't underestimate this man, he reminded himself. "Colonel, if we are engaged in a major battle here, I want your brigade as a mobile reserve. I am issuing orders for you to move to the rear of the formation."

"Yes, sir." Jarrod's response was sharp and unquestioning, though he disliked the idea of being out of the initial action.

"That way you will also be positioned to cover against any enemy maneuvers against our rear." Merrick paused – he was thinking as he was speaking. "I wouldn't be surprised if they tried to ambush us somehow."

"No, sir. Neither would I." Jarrod wasn't entirely sure he should be offering any more opinions now; he'd already spoken out far more than conventional wisdom recommended. But he didn't see the harm in simply agreeing with Merrick. Jarrod most definitely expected to encounter considerable guerilla activity, and the more Merrick was ready for it, the less damaging it would be.

"Thank you, Colonel. You may return to your command

post." Merrick was starting to truly value Jarrod's input. I wish I could make him second in command, he thought, but they'd roast me over a fire in Washbalt if I did that. Merrick didn't have the authority to make those kinds of changes anyway. Even Jarrod's promotion to colonel was provisional, a brevet appointment still subject to ratification. Merrick was pretty sure he had enough juice to push it through, assuming they both got off Arcadia alive and back to Earth. "And colonel?"

Jarrod had saluted and turned to leave. He spun around at attention, his eyes focused on Merrick's.

"Be careful, especially with scouting parties. Since that idiot Quinn executed his captives the rebels have responded in kind." Merrick would have preferred less brutality, but when Quinn started killing prisoners, the rebels went crazy and started shooting any federals they captured. In truth, the ones who were shot were the lucky ones. As far as Merrick could tell, the main rebel army restricted itself to firing squads, but the Feds who fell into the hands of irregulars or isolated groups had much more unpleasant prospects. He wished he could pull away from the brutal road Quinn had set them on, but it seemed impossible to go back. His troops demanded their own revenge, and he had little choice but to act accordingly and summarily execute at least some of the rebel prisoners. Lost in thought for a moment, Merrick suddenly realized that Jarrod was still standing at attention. "That will be all, colonel. Dismissed."

Sanders Dale was a pleasant valley, about 4 kilometers of gently sloping ground between two low ridgelines. Though far from the only feature on the map of Concordia named for the district's premier family, the dale held special significance as the place old man Sanders had built his first residence on the planet. The ruins of the prefab shelter remained, partially patched up and used periodically for storage. The Sanders family had long ago moved farther north, and the valley, which had been actively farmed for some years, was mostly abandoned and left fallow.

Now, however, an army was marching through the valley headed north, intent on pacifying the rebels in Concordia District. In its van and on the flanks came waves of light ATVs, fast scouting vehicles screening the advance.

Next there were tanks. They weren't the heavy battle tanks the force would have deployed on Earth, but nevertheless they were a fearsome sight, grinding their way noisily forward, heavy tracks tearing apart the mossy ground, leaving nothing but deep muddy furrows in their wake. Merrick didn't have many tanks, only three companies. It was just too difficult to transport a larger number from Earth. He hadn't deployed them before now, and he hoped the sight of the behemoths would sap the morale of the rebels.

Around the tanks were armored personnel carriers, heavy ones toward the front, lighter ones farther back. There were hundreds of them, over a thousand in fact, and they stretched across the entire valley. In the rear was the artillery, four batteries of light guns, mounted on tracked vehicles. As with their main battle tanks, Merrick's forces had been compelled to leave their heavy artillery behind when they'd shipped out to Arcadia…it was just too much to fit onto the transports.

It was an awesome force, the largest ever deployed on a colony world save only General Holm's 1st Corps that had fought the final battle of the Third Frontier War on the dusty hills of Carson's World. But this formation wasn't here to fight the Alliance's enemies; they were here to battle other Alliance citizens, some of them veterans of Holm's now-disbanded force.

Every move this army made was observed. The rebels they were pursuing knew this ground in ways an invader never could. Every vantage point, every depression in the ground, every blind spot – they knew them all, and each was used to its fullest potential. The rebels had been shadowing the federal forces for days. At first they simply scouted, monitoring the army's movements and assessing its strength. Then they started attacking, small hit and run missions intended to pick off stragglers and sap the enemy morale. For three days they had stung the federal army, like a swarm of hornets striking then vanishing. They'd done some damage, but the federal commander had been vigilant and he had not allowed the attacks to slow the advance.

Will Thompson was up in a tree along the western ridgeline. Quite an undignified pose for a commander in chief, he thought, as he clung to a branch with one hand and held his scope with the other. There was going to be a battle today. The sniping had failed to impede Merrick's army, and Will simply couldn't let them get any closer to his base of supply. He'd chosen the spot to make a stand, and this was it.

Morale among the rebel forces was strong, and most of his officers and men were spoiling for a fight. He wondered how they would feel later that night, after that fight was done. Win or lose, thousands of Will's troops would die today. He'd been in enough hard battles to know that much. However good the cause, war itself was always dirty business, and victory and freedom had a high price. Will had seen that cost; he had paid it. Most of his troops had not.

He couldn't believe the size of the army he commanded. Over 18,000 rebel soldiers were deployed in a broad U-shape on the ridgelines and in the valley between. And soldiers they were – Thompson's long months of tireless training and effort had paid off, turning his bands of undisciplined irregulars into a cohesive and well-organized army.

The rebel army was indeed formidable, but the forces it faced were stronger still. The federals had been reinforced since the early days of the rebellion, and now two full divisions were advancing through the valley - over 30,000 troops, plus artillery, personnel carriers...and worst of all, tanks.

Will was worried about the tanks. His force was light on heavy weapons, and taking out those monsters was going to be difficult. He had a few ideas, and they'd prepared as well as they could, but he was far from sure it would be enough. He was just about to climb down from his perch when he heard gunfire from the south.

The rebel army – more properly now, the Army of the Republic of Arcadia – had a significant amount of its strength deployed on the two ridgelines flanking the valley, with most of the rest entrenched directly to the front of the invading federal force. Will's plan was to hit the enemy on both flanks while they were engaged with his dug in forces in the lowlands. But General Merrick was neither careless, nor a fool, and Will knew he would scout the ridgelines as he advanced. To screen his own deployments, Thompson had deployed strong forces along the south of the ridges, blocking any enemy advance before it reached his main positions.

"Lieutenant Logan, place all commands on full alert." He was working his way down the tree, yelling to his aide standing just below. He dropped the last two meters to the ground and flipped on the comlink. "Colonel Warren, report...what is going on down there?

Chapter 16

CS Adam Richter
Eta Cassiopeiae System
Inbound from YZ Ceti Warp Gate

Sarah Linden sat in the small wardroom deep in thought. It was past midnight, ship's time. The Richter operated on Martian time, which was pretty close to the Earth normal clock used on Alliance vessels. Her team was asleep, at least most of them. Their bodies were still operating on Armstrong time, and on Armstrong it was 4am.

She hadn't done much sleeping anyway, not recently at least. Not since she'd said goodbye to Erik. She remembered every instant of those last few minutes, standing in front of his shuttle in the cold drizzle, the feeling of him pulling from her embrace, walking to the sleek white ship waiting a few feet away...the last instant before he disappeared from her view. She'd never forget that image; she'd never let herself forget. She was deathly afraid that was the last time she would ever see him.

She was going into danger; Jax and General Holm and all of them were. They'd lived most of their lives in the line of fire, doing what had to be done. But in her mind, Erik wasn't just going into danger – he was committing suicide. Everyone in the Alliance, all those born on Earth, at least, feared Alliance Intelligence. Real dissent or civil disobedience was rare in the Alliance, but still there were stories – many of them deliberately spread by the intelligence agency itself. People who were taken to that building didn't return.

The thought of actually breaking into Intelligence HQ was unthinkable – a modern version of passing through the gates of hell. Yet that is just what Erik was going to do – break in, find the most guarded prisoner in the Alliance, and escape...not just from the building, but from Earth itself.

Why him? Her thoughts were bitter, though she tried to control it. She knew intellectually that they had to try to rescue the admiral, and she was sure no one had a better chance than Erik. But logic and rationalizations didn't change the fact that the odds were long - very long indeed. The fact was, she would most likely never see the love of her life again.

She pushed the painful thoughts back, trying to focus on how she would manage things once they were on Columbia. Her team was small; they were taking a big risk going to Columbia, and she'd only approached people she really trusted. At least ones she thought would keep their mouths shut if they turned her down. She didn't have to worry about that, at least – no one turned her down. Not after she showed them the video from Columbia. She wasn't sure how much difference they would make in the overall conflict, but she knew they could save some lives. Hopefully they wouldn't save them just so they could mount the scaffold – a real possibility if the rebellion was defeated.

It was quiet in the wardroom, not a sound except the ever-present hum, the background noise of the ship's systems so familiar to space travel veterans. She had been sitting there alone for hours, and she jumped when the hatch opened.

"I thought I'd find you here." Jax's deep voice was unmistakable. He walked into the room, ducking as he always had to on spaceships to fit through the doorway.

She turned around and managed a quick smile. "I like the quiet."

"Ash," he said, walking over to the small refreshment bar. "I'm glad it's just that and not the fact that you're so worried you can't sleep." His tone was soft, relaxed. The last thing he wanted was to get her even more stressed out.

She smiled again, though like the first, it only lasted a few seconds. "I was worried when you guys were cut off on the Lysandra Plateau. I can't even imagine what a nightmare that must have been for you." She paused, thinking about the inferno of Carson's World, about the fear she'd felt even as she drove her medical staff beyond normal human endurance. "But this is crazy. Ten of them against Alliance Intelligence and all the security in Washbalt?"

He looked over at her. "Sarah, Erik is my best friend." His voice came out more emotional than he'd intended. "He's my only real friend, the only one I've ever had." His face had been serious, but he flashed her a labored grin. "Except for you, of course." He winked at her, trying, with partial success, to get her to smile again. "But the two of you are kind of a unit to me, anyway." She didn't laugh…quite, but she did manage another brief grin.

"I'm worried about him too." He was serious now, looking right at her. "But I have never seen anything in the field like him, Sarah." Behind his eyes the memories of a dozen battles were flashing by. "You know the kinds of places I've been with him. He's a survivor. He'll come back."

She looked over at him, not sure if she wanted to smile again or cry. "Do you really believe that?" Her question was sincere, though it wasn't clear if she really wanted honesty, or just an answer that would make her feel better. She wasn't sure herself.

"Absolutely." He didn't know if he was lying to her or telling the truth, but he delivered the line with authority.

He turned back to the bar. There were a number of beverage dispensers, and a screen with an extensive menu of hot and cold drinks. "Coffee? Anything?" He looked over, but Sarah just shook her head. He punched the touch screen for coffee, and chose one of the six flavors offered. A cup popped into one of the dispensers, and steaming hot coffee poured into it.

He took the cup in his hand and walked back to the table, pulling out the chair next to her and sitting down. They'd been aboard for three weeks now, and they were only a day out from Columbia. The Richter was a Martian ship, appearing on the outside to be just what its registry said it was - an old freighter. Inside, however, was a different story, a state of the art ship, fully-armed and equipped with the very best ECM suite the Confederation could produce…and the Confeds had the best technology of any of the Powers.

So far, Roderick Vance had been true to his word. The Richter was packed to the proverbial rafters, filled with weapons and supplies…and Jax's 500 Marine volunteers. The Richter's official course was straight through the Eta Cassiopeiae system, bound for Fomalhaut to pick up a load of ores. The stop at Columbia was unofficial, to say the least.

"How are your people doing?" Sarah thought a subject change would do them both some good.

"Not bad. They're a little cramped, but they've all had it worse before." He took a small sip from the piping hot coffee. "I hope we can make a difference. Vance has equipped us well, but we still won't have our powered armor. The rebels are outnumbered five to one, and maybe more. We're just a drop in the bucket."

"You'll make a big difference. You're going to have the best troops on the planet...by a large margin." She looked over at him, putting her hand on top of his. "And they'll be the best led too. I know Erik's your friend, Darius, but you should know how much confidence he has in you. He told me once he thought you were the best field commander he'd ever seen...and he included himself in that." She smiled and repeated herself: "You'll make a big difference."

She got up and leaned over to give him a kiss on the cheek. "I'm going to try to get some sleep. Big day tomorrow." She looked back from the doorway. "You should too. I have a feeling we're both going to have our hands full with the landing." She gave him a little wave and ducked through the hatch into the corridor.

Jax sat alone for a while, enjoying the quiet and the warmth of the mug in his hands. The Martians have an interesting idea of room temperature, he thought with a shiver. Mars was cold, certainly, but the Martian cities were all in domes or underground. The early colonists had not had energy to spare to heat their shelters more than necessary, and they grew accustomed to lower temperatures, something they'd apparently handed down to their children and grand-children. It was really only a few degrees below Earth-normal, but Jax had always been sensitive to cold, an anomaly in such a large man.

He drained the last sip from his mug. The Martians had great coffee, he would give them that. He briefly considered having another cup, but decided he should try to get some sleep himself. He got up and walked over to the door, pausing as the hatch slid to the side – he needed it all the way open to squeeze through. The lights in the room went out before he'd even stepped into the hall and headed toward his quarters. More Martian thriftiness inherited from the early colonists, he supposed.

The landing craft rocked wildly in Columbia's upper atmosphere. Jax had always been annoyed by the Marine regimen of pre-launch intravenous nutrition and anti-emetic drug cocktails, but now he understood. He didn't vomit, but that was purely a testament to his will, to the stubbornness of the hardcore Marine colonel. About a third of his troops, however, veterans all, succumbed, and the landing ship was quickly becoming a very unpleasant place to be.

The ride was rougher than it had to be, but that's because the Richter had a very limited window to launch. Admiral Compton had managed to arrange fleet deployments to allow a small corridor for the Martians to change course and disgorge their cargo undetected, but it didn't leave time for plotting easier entry trajectories. They had to take what they could get, and if that meant a bunch of grizzled Marine veterans threw up all over themselves, such were the fortunes of war.

At least they weren't coming into a hostile landing zone. In fact, they weren't landing anywhere near an inhabited area. Keeping the drop undetected was the primary consideration, and that meant landing in the desolate equatorial zone, far from population centers. It would be a long trip for the expeditionary force once they were on the ground, but it couldn't be helped.

The landing craft were heavy shuttles, not the sleek, maneuverable Gordon landers the Marines used, so it was just as well they were nowhere anyone could take a shot at them. Not one of these pigs, Jax thought, would make it to the ground in an opposed landing.

The craft were descending much faster than they were designed for, which was making the turbulence worse. But caution demanded they hit ground as quickly as possible. The longer they were airborne, the likelier one of Compton's ships would detect them...and that would just make things even more difficult for the admiral, who already had his hands full.

The landing zone was a huge plain, almost a desert - over 100,000 square kilometers of dry, flat ground. It would give them plenty of room to land and deploy, but it was totally open and difficult to defend. Jax was going to kick some butt as soon as they were down – he didn't like that position, and they were going to get off it right away.

The ships banked left and came in for their final approach, firing their engines to brake hard. Positioning thrusters ignited, and the flotilla floated to the ground - surprisingly gently considering how rough ride down had been.

They were completely unopposed, but that wasn't a good enough reason to be lazy, at least not to Jax. As soon as the shuttles landed, the rear ramps lowered and squads poured out, moving into a defensive perimeter. Jax looked out over the plain, impressed with the regularity of the formation of the landing craft. These Martian pilots are good, he thought. I'm glad we're on the same side...more or less.

All through the mass of men, women, and supplies, designated officers and non-coms were shouting out orders and organizing the unloading. The ships were taking off in one hour – if they stayed any longer the Richter would be too far away for them to reach. And while the Martians had provided transport and supplies, they weren't yet willing to deploy Confederation personnel in any capacity that would expose their role. If there were still weapons and supplies onboard, they would go back to the Richter. And Jax's troops and the rebels needed that equipment.

"Let's get moving." Jax was yelling, but mostly for effect. He'd already organized the unloading plan, and it was being executed to the letter. Every one of his 500 troops was a veteran, most of them with five years' service or more, and the officers and non-coms were among the best in the Corps. They were poorly-equipped by Marine standards, powered armor an impossible dream. But they were one of the most veteran forces ever deployed, and Jax knew they could do a lot...even without nuclear reactors strapped onto their backs. Whether they could do enough to make a real difference...that he would have to wait and see.

The larger transport shuttles had landed off to the left. Half of them were loaded with weapons and other supplies; the rest carried armored ATVs, 80 of them. It was enough transport for the entire force and all of the supplies. They were a generic design – the Confederation wasn't looking to broadcast its involvement – but they were military grade...nuclear powered and armed with heavy auto-cannons.

His troops were unloading the supply ships and stacking the crates on the ground. They only had an hour to get everything off the ships; they would load it all onto the ATVs later. Jax ran everywhere, from ship to ship, but he realized he just wasn't needed. His troops knew what they had to do, and they had the shuttles unloaded in 45 minutes. By the time an hour had passed there wasn't a ship left on the ground.

They spent the rest of the day organizing and loading the vehicles and prepping and inspecting weapons. By nightfall of Columbia's 27 hour day, they were 100% ready. They would camp here for the night and move out in the morning. The insertion was complete and flawlessly executed. Jax was at war again.

Chapter 17

Battle of Sander's Dale
Concordia District
Arcadia – Wolf 359 III

Kyle Warren was crouched down behind a small berm, his assault rifle gripped tightly in his hand. The fire from the advancing federals was heavy, but his own troops were giving it back to them...and then some. The rebels weren't heavily fortified, but they had dug crude foxholes and built some hasty works. The scrubby woods gave the advancing forces some cover, but not much, and they were starting to take heavy losses.

His comlink buzzed...Will Thompson calling. "Warren here, sir." He took a few shots at a Fed he saw aiming in his general direction as he answered Thompson's call. The first two missed, but the third hit the trooper just under her right eye. She snapped back and fell to the ground, the side of her face ripped open. "Things are hot here, sir. We're about three klicks south of your position." He took a breath and ducked deeper behind some cover. "This is more than a scouting force, Will." Kyle was a veteran, and he knew he shouldn't be calling his commander in chief by his first name. But the Arcadian army was new, and there was an odd combination of military discipline and familiar informality in play.

"God damn Merrick." Thompson's voice betrayed his frustration...and grudging respect for his adversary. "Your position is a must hold, Kyle. If you need support let me know, but retreating is not an option. Understood?"

"Understood, general." Warren's voice was calm, despite the heavy fire. He was a combat veteran, and the months of fighting on Arcadia had honed his command skills. "I estimate we are facing a reinforced battalion." He paused, considering. "I believe we can hold unless the enemy commits additional strength." Another pause, then: "But it's going to be hot work."

"I'm counting on you, Kyle. Give me status reports every

fifteen minutes."

"Yes, sir." He saw a clump of federals advancing off to the right, and he yelled for one of the auto-gun teams to direct fire there. "Report every one-five minutes. Understood."

"Good luck, Kyle. Thompson out."

There was a brief lull in the fire, and Warren took advantage to crawl back from the front line. He needed to find someplace he could get his bearings and take stock of the overall position. His troops were deployed in an extended line stretching about a kilometer and centered on the peak of the ridge.

They had been making the federals pay, but they were starting to take losses too. The attackers bogged down, unable to continue advancing into the heavy fire, and a line formed. The combat was turning into a bloody, close-range firefight, and the federals were also going prone, using whatever cover they could find.

Kyle was fine with exchanging fire. His job was just to hold the line – if the Feds wanted to have a firefight all day that suited him just fine. But he was still worried. Thompson had reminded him not to underestimate the federal forces. Their commander was a strong tactician – he wasn't going to make stupid mistakes.

"Lieutenant Fritz, Warren here." Kyle shouted into the comlink – the shooting was loud around him.

"Yes Colonel. Fritz here." The lieutenant was young, but he was one of the most promising junior officers Warren had ever seen. Not a Marine veteran, Fritz had won his lieutenant's commission during the battle at Arcadia. He'd kept his cool when all the officers in his company panicked, and he took charge, getting over half the troops out alive.

When Will Thompson found out, he immediately cancelled a pending promotion to sergeant, making the kid an officer instead. "We don't have time for things to take their natural course," he declared. "Revolution is like fertilizer, and talent must grow at an unnatural pace if we are to prevail."

"They're bogged down on the line, lieutenant. I want you to move out and keep an eye on our flank. If they look like they're even thinking about trying to come around, I want to know immediately. Understood?"

"Yes, sir." Fritz was calm, impressively so for such a young officer. "Understood."

Warren was about to sign off, but then he added, "And Doug...be careful. I need information, not a casualty." Fritz was brave, almost recklessly so. But this was not the time or place for heroics. Dead scouts don't provide any information.

"Yes, sir. Understood."

"General Sanders, I need a report. Any activity in the center?" Will hadn't been happy when Gregory Sanders insisted on taking an active role in the new army, but the old man was simply too influential to refuse. It wasn't cronyism like in the Alliance on Earth; it was respect. Greg Sanders was one of half a dozen people who had virtually built Arcadia from the ground up. If he thought his place was in this fight, no one – not Will, not Kara, not any of the other officers – felt they had a right to refuse him.

In spite of Thompson's reservations, Sanders had proven to be a gifted commander, and now Will was glad to have him in the field. In fact, he'd made him second in command and put him in charge of the center.

"They're shelling us, Will, but that's about it." Sanders sounded solid as a rock. "We've had some long range sniping, but even that's calmed down."

Fuck, Will thought, they're not taking the bait. "Greg, they're being cautious, not falling into the trap." Thompson was thinking as he spoke, trying to decide what he wanted Sanders to do. "They are hitting us hard on the flanks, but we're holding for the moment." He took a deep breath, still thinking. "They are going to try to clear the ridges before they hit you...unless we force the issue."

"You want us to attack?" Even Sander's voice had been stone cold, but now he sounded surprised. There were 7,000 troops in the center, deployed in four supporting trench lines and protected by a mine belt. The entire formation was designed to hold out against superior enemy forces, inflicting enormous losses…as long as those forces were attacking. Once the enemy was heavily engaged and softened up, the flanking forces would sweep down and rout the exhausted federals, or at least that was the plan. But an attack by the rebels in the center would be suicide.

"Of course not." Will was tentative, trying to put his thoughts into words. "But I do want you to make them think you're attacking. Do you think you can mount a spoiling attack without committing too deeply?" Thompson paused. "They're sitting on their asses, and we need to do something to get them moving."

Sanders was silent…a bad sign. Usually the old man was quick with a response to any question. Finally, he said, "I don't know, Will. We can attack, but I don't know how easy it will be to pull back. We might get caught up in something we can't get out of too easily." He paused again, and Will could hear his heavy breathing. "And if those tanks catch us out in the open…"

"I know." Will was frustrated. Damn Merrick, he thought… we have to get the one good general in the whole fucking Alliance army. His comlink buzzed with an incoming message flashing urgent. "Ok, stand by, Greg. I've got Kyle Warren calling in."

He flipped the switch on his headpiece. "Thompson here."

"General, we've got a firestorm here." Warren was out of breath, clearly under considerable stress. "They've got us pinned down in a firefight to the front, and now they're coming around the end of my line." He paused, and Will could hear him shouting orders to someone before he continued. "I lost Doug Fritz. I sent him to scout past the end of our line, and he ran right into an enemy attack. He and two of his troops held the enemy off for at least ten minutes before they got hit. Gave me just enough time to get my reserves down there. If we ever come up with any Arcadian medals, that kid should be first on the list." He coughed and took another breath. "I've got nothing left, Will. If they hit us anywhere with anything else, we're done. They'll roll up the entire line."

"Fuck." Will hadn't meant to say it audibly but it came out louder than he thought. "Alright, Kyle. I'll send you whatever I can spare, but you've got to hold out…no matter what."

"I'll do what I can, Will." He sounded a little shaky, but just a little. "You can count on us."

"I know I can." Will was thinking about what reinforcements he could send to Warren. If he pulled off too much, his flank attack would be too weak to succeed. If he sent too little, there would never be an attack; the Feds would sweep down the ridge and rout his entire left. "Keep me posted. Thompson out."

He switched channels again. "Greg? Will again."

"Go ahead, Will." Sanders could tell what Thompson was going to say from his tone. "What's the word?"

"I need you to raise hell down there."

"I was afraid you were going to say that." Sanders' voice was stronger than before. He was no happier about having to attack, but he was resigned to it now. "Give me ten minutes, and we'll hit them hard right in the center." Then, a few seconds later: "Make good use of this, Will. It's going to cost."

Sanders hadn't meant anything by the remark, but it Will felt it cut through him. His Marine service had been as a sergeant. He'd ordered troops into tough spots, no question, but this was something completely different. As a non-com he was always with the troops he commanded. Now he was sending thousands of men and women into a hopeless attack, one he knew couldn't succeed…and he wasn't going with them. They would die executing his orders while he sat in the command post.

"Good luck, Greg." His voice was strong and clear, though it was a major effort to keep it that way. Thompson felt sick to his stomach, but the last thing Sanders and his troops needed was for the army commander to go weak at the knees. "And Greg…be careful."

"You know me, Will. Sanders out."

Yes, I know you, Greg, Thompson thought nervously. That's what I'm worried about.

Merrick's command post was humming with activity. The army had been at a dead stop for three hours while he threw one battalion after another into the bloody stalemate on the right flank. No matter how much force he pushed onto that ridge, the damned rebels managed to hang on. Just as his forces finally started to push the defenders off the crest, they got reinforcements and counter-attacked. The federals had 2,000 casualties and nothing to show for it. The rebels had suffered too, but not as heavily.

Merrick's commanders wanted to push through and assault the rebel center. That was after all, they insisted, where the battle would be decided. But Merrick was cautious, wary of this rebel general who had kept him at bay all year. He was sitting with four of his generals having the same argument when his aide came rushing in.

"General Merrick, sir. The rebels are attacking!" The aide was a young lieutenant named Thurn, and his raw nerves were showing.

"Calm down, lieutenant." Merrick stood up and turned to face his aide. "They are attacking where?"

"In the center, sir." Thurn took a breath and slowed down, but his voice was still high-pitched with tension. "They are assaulting our center."

Merrick was stunned. Why, he wondered, would they come out of their trenches and throw themselves at us in the open?

"Lieutenant, get me the front line commanders on my comlink." It had to be a diversion, he thought, to take his attention away from the flank. But he wasn't going to let them pull their little hit and run...he was going to turn it against them. This was a chance to hit the rebels hard, but he had to move now.

Thurn worked on his headset for a few seconds, making sure all the necessary officers were on the line. "You are on with all forward commanders, sir."

"To all commanders now engaged on the front line of the army...your orders are to attack immediately. Engage and destroy all exposed enemy forces and pursue as long as advantageous." Merrick knew he was getting aggressive, but if he could hurt the rebels badly enough, he might just win this thing today. Then he could get off this forsaken rock and go home.

Merrick half-listened as the commanders on the line acknowledged his order then he flipped off the line and turned toward Thurn.

"Lieutenant, contact Colonel Jarrod." Merrick had a self-satisfied smile on his face. "Order him to detach two battalions from his brigade to reinforce the attack on the enemy's left flank." He paused then added an afterthought. "Instruct him to lead them himself and to personally take command of the entire attack."

"Yes, sir." Thurn immediately began relaying Merrick's orders to Jarrod.

Yes, General Thompson, Merrick thought with considerable self-satisfaction, you think I will abandon the flank attack and throw everything into the center. "Unfortunately, I'm afraid I cannot accommodate you." He turned again toward Thurn and barked one more command. "Instruct Colonel Jarrod to commit a third battalion to the flank attack." He smiled again and muttered under his breath. "No, General Thompson. I will not play your game."

The troops attacking the center were catching hell. The valley was mostly broad and open, with little good cover. They had the element of surprise at first; no one had expected them to come out of their defenses and attack. But that didn't last.

At first the federals deployed defensively, forming up to repel the assault. The infantry streamed out of the APCs, forming firing lines just in front of the vehicles. The troops took whatever cover was available but, for the most part, they were as much in the open as the attackers. But there were more of them, and they had heavy weapon support from the APCs. They were taking a significant toll on the advancing rebels, even at long range.

Then the orders came up: attack across the line. The troops grumbled – they had the prospect of a turkey shoot if they just stood fast. Now they were ordered to move out and counter-attack. The non-coms waved their arms and surged forward –

officers in the Alliance army tended to lead from behind – and the great mass charged into the plain.

The two sides ran toward each other, firing wildly. The APCs advanced behind the federal infantry, but the formation became confused, disordered. The Feds were trained career soldiers, but there was no living memory of full-scale warfare in the terrestrial army. The infantry blocked the line of fire from the APCs, and the vehicles were stuck behind disorganized clumps of soldiers.

The rebels kept better order. They were a smaller force, more compact and easier for the officers to keep in formation. Though many of them had been farmers and shopkeepers, they were leavened with true veterans, retired Marines who'd seen real combat on worlds throughout occupied space.

It was a brutal, chaotic fight, the two lines advancing to close range and exchanging murderous fire. Wherever there was any type of cover – a rock outcropping or a small depression in the ground – troops would cluster behind it, firing at the enemy from a position of relative advantage.

The lines became intermixed, as the rebels would make headway along on section of the front and lose ground on another. Gregory Sanders was in the thick of the fight, though he knew both Will and Kara would be upset with him if they could see. But Will wouldn't have ordered this attack if the situation wasn't desperate…and Sanders was going to make sure Thompson got what he needed. And the only way he knew how to do something important was to grab onto it and dive in.

He was surrounded by his troops, and despite being heavily outnumbered, they were holding their own. He was beyond proud of these men and women…the Alliance forces were getting more than they bargained for from a group they likely considered ignorant colonials. Sanders enjoyed that thought immensely.

But now it was time to get his people out. It didn't matter how hard they fought; in the open plain they would be overwhelmed eventually. "All units, this is General Sanders." He spoke into the comlink, practically screaming to rise above the din of battle. "Execute retirement to prepared positions. Plan Alpha." Sanders had a few surprises ready for the federals if they decided to pursue his forces.

All around him the rebel troops were pulling back, as the battalion commanders and then the junior officers and non-coms relayed his orders. They'd planned the retreat – as well as anything could be planned in the brief time they'd had to get organized – and now they were executing it flawlessly.

To the Feds, unused to the trickery and stratagems of war, it looked like a rout, and all along the line, the Alliance commanders ordered their troops to pursue. In the center, the tanks, which had previously been screened by the infantry, began advancing along tight corridors through the confused federal line. The infantry cheered as the massive war machines rumbled noisily forward.

Perfect, Sanders thought. If we can pull this off we will give them quite a bloody nose. He turned to take one last look at the enemy forces before he joined the last of the rebel formations in the retreat. That's when it hit him.

He heard the sound first, and felt the blood in his throat... only then did the pain come. It was a round fired from an assault rifle, and it went clean through his neck. He felt the strength draining from his body and his legs starting to give out. He fell, first to his knees then, a few seconds later, forward onto the ground. His head was fuzzy, his thoughts hazy, random. Memories, some recent some a lifetime old, mixed with thoughts about the battle. And the darkness, the growing darkness...more and more until there was nothing else.

Kyle Warren had been hit twice. Neither wound was serious, but he looked like hell, with filthy, blood-soaked rags tied around his leg and his forehead. The fighting on the flank had been brutal, with the Feds pouring more and more troops into the bitter battle for the ridgeline.

Twice Warren's troops had been forced back from their hastily-prepared defenses, and both times they'd received reserves just in time to counter-attack and regain their lines. He'd stopped even trying to keep track of casualties, but the dead and wounded were everywhere. In the very center of the position, a place the troops were already calling the Meatgrinder, the dead were stacked on top of each other. Here it had been hand to hand combat several times, and many of the dead had faces smashed by rifle butts and chests ripped open by knives.

Warren was operating on adrenalin, trying not to think too deeply about the slaughter around him. He couldn't help but remember the battle on the space station in the Gliese 250 system, when he'd served as a corporal under then-Captain Erik Cain. The battle had been a success by any standard, and casualties relatively low. But Cain was somber after the battle, uncomfortable with the cheering and applause the unit gave him. Warren had been confused then, but now he understood.

He needed all his wits right now. The federal attacks had been disorganized at first, but now they were focused and well-executed. Kyle figured they had a new officer in command over there...someone who knew what he was doing.

"All right everyone." Warren switched the comlink to the general line; he was speaking to every soldier under his command. "You've done well and fought with courage I couldn't have imagined. I'm proud of all of you...General Thompson is proud of all of you."

He took a breath and let his words hang there for an instant. "But the enemy is coming back. They think they can overwhelm us and drive us from this position." His voice was getting louder. "But our people in the valley are catching hell too, and the troops behind us are going into that fight to win the battle. If we falter...if we let the federals get through us, they will sweep around and crush our comrades. They will destroy this army."

He was yelling now, but still his volume rose. "We will not move from this spot. If the enemy gets past this position it will be because every one of us is dead. As long as one of us is standing, we will hold this line. If anyone retreats, I will shoot him myself!" His fists were clenched as he spoke, and he hardly felt the pain from his wounds. "This battle is for our families, for our friends, for our comrades…it is for our home!"

All along the rebel line a great cheer rose, growing steadily in intensity even as the advancing federals came into view. Kyle stared straight ahead and shouted into the comlink, projecting one word loud enough to cut through the cheering, tumultuous din. "Fire."

"We have to withdraw, sir." General Wyatt Corning was a pompous ass and an insufferable windbag. But this time he was right, and Merrick knew it. The battle had been a bloodbath for both sides, but in the end it was the Marines who made the difference for the rebels. It was the retired corporal, deployed among 20 farmers and factory workers, keeping them in the fight, rallying them to meet whatever came. The privates and sergeants and officers who had mustered out and made Arcadia home…and now they made the rebel force an army, a real army.

The federal forces were broken, and Merrick knew it. They weren't in headlong flight yet, at least not all of them. But there was no way he could mount another attack. If he didn't retreat, the rebels would slip behind him and cut off his supplies. He'd be trapped in enemy territory, his army demoralized and in danger of annihilation. At least retreat would allow them to fight another day. They still outnumbered the rebels, and given time to rest and refit, they'd be back in the field.

He'd thought for a while that Jarrod had broken through on the flank, but the thrice-cursed rebels managed to hold on somehow…that devil Thompson feeding in just enough reserves, just in time.

Now Jarrod was dead. There were stories among the troops, accounts from those who claimed to be there…or secondhand from those who "knew someone who was there." They said Jarrod was killed by the commander of the rebel position in a hand to hand battle on the last charge. It sounded like bullshit to Merrick, but he'd never know for sure. Jarrod's body was behind enemy lines now, lying among the thousands who'd died this day.

While Jarrod was leading those last futile assaults, the center turned into a nightmare. The rebels there retreated back to their defenses, and his forces pursued…right into a nightmare of minefields and hidden tank traps. The federal forces, already disordered from the confused melee in the plain, were thrown into utter chaos - just as the rebels from the ridgelines attacked their flanks.

"Lieutenant Thurn…" Merrick's voice was strained. So this is what defeat tastes like, he thought. It is bitter. He felt his stomach clench, and he wanted to drop to his knees and wretch. It took all his strength to stand there impassively and issue the orders. "The army will retreat."

He turned to walk away when a small clump of soldiers approached him, carrying something in a tarp. They were led by an officer, a captain Merrick didn't recognize. "General Merrick, we've captured a wounded rebel general." The captain tried to salute, but he was holding on to a corner of the tarp, so it was roughly done at best. "I think he is their second in command."

Merrick looked at the blood-soaked figure lying motionless in the tarp. "Is he still alive?"

"Yes, sir." The captain was trying to stand as much at attention as he could while still holding the edge of the makeshift stretcher. "Barely."

"Take him to my doctor." Merrick nodded to the captain, dismissing him to carry out the order. Then he walked slowly toward the rear, grateful at least that the rebels were too battered to pursue. He looked over in the direction of the rebel lines, wondering where Will Thompson was right now. "There will be another day, General Thompson." His voice was soft, barely audible. "Yes…there will be another day."

Chapter 18

Directorate Conference Room
Western Alliance Intelligence Directorate HQ
Wash-Balt Metroplex, Earth

"I am not at all happy, ladies and gentlemen." Gavin Stark stood at the head of the table staring down at the assembled Directorate. They didn't need him to tell them he was upset any time he didn't take his seat, they knew there was trouble.

There were empty chairs, four of them. Position six was vacant; he'd never filled it after moving Alex Linden up to Number Three. The others were off-planet - Alliance Intelligence had committed everything to crushing the wave of rebellion sweeping across the frontier. If we don't start getting better results, Stark thought, there are going to be more vacancies.

"Clearly, our efforts in several areas have not had the success we hoped for." Stark's tone was ominous, his stare as cold as death. "We are going to review each and every problem area and implement whatever strategies are necessary to end these costly and dangerous rebellions."

Everyone in the room was staring at Stark, watching his every move, waiting for him to direct the meeting. All except Number Two. Jack Dutton was sitting at Stark's side as always, but he was looking down at the table. His skin was pale and his eyes gray and filmy. Dutton's career stretched back to the Unification Wars, over a century earlier, but finally time was overcoming even his herculean constitution. The rejuvenation treatments had become less and less effective in recent years, until finally they did nothing at all. No one thought Dutton had more than a couple months left, if that much, and the scramble for the Second Seat had begun. But right now everyone in the room was more worried about hanging on to their current position...and not ending up in some furnace somewhere.

"Let's begin with a review of our military programs, and then we will proceed to status reports of individual worlds." His gaze moved down the table. "Number Seven, please provide an update on our naval programs."

Rodger Burke felt the weight of every eye in the room upon him. He slid his chair back slowly, rising to his feet and glancing around the table before focusing on Stark. "Thank you, Number One." He cleared his throat nervously. "As you are all aware, we utilized the post-war demobilization as a cover to assign a significant number of navy ships to a new, Directorate-controlled force. The vessels that were ostensibly transferred into reserve status have been re-crewed with Directorate-chosen personnel."

He absent-mindedly played with the buttons on his neatly-tailored suit as he spoke, an affectation most of those present found mildly distracting. Burke was a prickly, annoying sort of person, though he was undeniably effective in his work. "We now have 43% of immediate post-war hulls sequestered, and approximately two-thirds of this force had been fully crewed and currently operational." He paused and glanced down at his 'pad on the table. "If you refer to section 7.3 on your meeting brief you will see a table of organization for the task force sent to Arcadia. Currently, this is the only deployment of our new naval force. The balance of operational ships, are located in Epsilon Eridani. As that system is quarantined, it seemed like the best place to hide the ships until we deploy them elsewhere."

Burke paused, but no one else asked any questions; they were all waiting meekly to see what Stark would say. Disgusted by the cowardice on display in his own Directorate, Number One finally asked what no one else had. "How would you characterize the combat readiness of these ships?"

Burke hesitated, and Stark added, "Speak freely, Number Seven. We need facts, not optimistic prattle."

"Well, Number One, it has obviously been difficult to find alternate crews for so many vessels. Most of the appropriately trained personnel are in the navy itself, so we have had to use a variety of alternative methods to recruit crews, largely from civilian sources." He panned quickly around the room then focused back on Stark. "The crews are substantially less proficient than their naval counterparts. They are adequate for blockading planets and bombing surface targets, but they will need substantial numerical superiority if it becomes necessary to engage active naval vessels."

"Engage naval vessels? Are we really considering attacking our own navy?" Number Ten's outburst was unexpected, and every head in the room snapped toward her.

At least one of them is brave enough to speak her mind, Stark thought, though I suspect it was more lack of discipline than true courage. "Number Ten, we must keep all of our options open. There are considerable sympathies for the rebellion among our naval officer corps. What would you have us do if, for example, a squadron commander openly supported a planet in revolt?"

It was a highly rhetorical question, one that neither Number Ten nor anyone else present chose to answer. She simply nodded her understanding and remained silent.

"Please continue, Number Seven." Stark had turned around and was looking out the window as he spoke.

"Thank you, Number One. If it does become necessary to engage our own vessels, it would be highly desirable to do so in conjunction with loyal naval forces. We have successfully infiltrated many active duty ships, and our ongoing recruitment program had been quite successful of late. It is difficult to project with any reliability which ships would be likely to side with us in a schism, however it is reasonable to expect that a meaningful percentage would remain under Alliance Gov control." He paused briefly. "Of course, I would expect considerable resistance to an order to open fire on other naval vessels, even from loyal units."

"Before Number Seven continues, I would like to offer an update on related matters myself." Stark didn't move; he was staring out over the Washbalt skyline, his back to the table as he spoke. "For approximately the last nine months, we have enjoyed an enhanced level of control over the actions of Admiral Garret."

A murmur of surprise ran around the table, though no one

present would dare interrupt Stark. "The exact means employed
to secure this improved level of influence are unimportant…"
In other words, you don't need to know, he thought as he spoke.
"…however, it is reasonable to suggest that with the…ah…
assistance of Admiral Garret, we will have much greater success in asserting control over naval units…regardless of what
we must order them to do."

There was uncertainty in the room, mixed with tentative
understanding as those present began to realize what Stark
was truly saying. However it had been achieved, Number One
controlled the Naval Director. The implications of that were
extraordinary.

"You may continue your report, Number Seven." Stark was
still looking out the window, contemplating his own thoughts as
he listened.

"Yes, Number One." Number Seven looked first toward
Stark then out over the table. "As you are all aware, we dispatched a task force from our new Directorate naval force to
blockade the planet Arcadia. The fleet commander has been
ordered to provide any support General Merrick requires,
though to date he has only requested the deployment of several
spy satellites."

"Indeed." Stark voice betrayed moderate frustration. "General Merrick may be insufficiently ruthless to effectively crush
the rebellion on Arcadia." Everyone around the table was staring at the back of Stark's head. "He is a gifted officer, which
is why I chose him for the assignment. But there is more to
breaking the will of the population than effective battle tactics."
The room was silent for a few seconds as he paused. "We may
need to replace him with someone amenable to employing more
drastic measures." Stark paused again before turning to face the
table. "Please complete your report, Number Seven."

"Lastly, it appears we have a significant problem at Columbia." There was a wave of groans and under-the-breath comments. Unlike everything else Number Seven had reported, this
was new to them all. And the last thing they needed was a fresh
problem.

"As you are aware, Admiral Garret dispatched a regular navy fleet to Columbia to support our anti-insurgency efforts there. Fleet Admiral Compton is in command, and he has orders from Admiral Garret to provide any support requested by the Planetary Governor." He looked over at Stark.

Stark already knew what he was going to say, of course, but Burke wasn't aware of that. "Go on, Number Seven."

"Yes, Number One." His voice was a little high-pitched, his nerves a bit more on edge. "Several days ago…a week, in fact…we received word that all contact with the Eta Cassiopeiae system through Commnet had been lost. This morning we have had a communication originating on Commnet from the YZ Ceti system. The transmission was sent from Commander Harrigan, who is our highest ranking operative embedded in Admiral Compton's fleet."

Burke cleared his throat and continued. "His report states that Admiral Compton has expressly refused the governor's repeated requests for a nuclear strike against the rebel stronghold on Carlisle Island." He panned his gaze across the room. "This means that Admiral Compton is in direct violation of a Priority One order."

The room was quiet, eerily so. Burke remained standing, but said nothing further. Gradually, everyone looked over toward Stark, waiting for him to elaborate. But it wasn't Stark who finally broke the silence.

"I counsel extreme caution in how we proceed." Dutton's voice was weak, so soft it was barely audible despite the fact that he was obviously struggling with the effort. "We clearly must take action, though every option is fraught with peril."

Everyone looked at the ancient spymaster, and no one, not even Stark, interrupted. Dutton had already been an institution in Washbalt's intelligence community when most of the people in the room were born. The true scope of his enormous inventory of contacts, information, and secrets could only be guessed at in the most speculative manner.

"It is entirely possible that Governor Cooper will be able to defeat the rebellion on Columbia without assistance from the fleet. He has been reinforced and now has over 50,000 Alliance army troops at his disposal. A direct, unsupported assault against the rebel stronghold on Carlisle Island would no doubt be a costly affair, but I suspect he has a sufficiency of force to prevail." He paused, taking a long, wheezy breath. "Indeed, we may even be able to utilize heavy casualties to our benefit in terms of propaganda…demonizing the rebels through the Alliance media." In the cold logic employed at Alliance Intelligence, the fact that an additional 10,000 soldiers could die was immaterial…especially if there were collateral benefits.

Dutton took a white silk cloth from his pocket and wiped his mouth. Stark had a doubtful expression on his face, but most of the others looked relieved, thinking perhaps they could simply ignore Compton for now.

"Unfortunately, this is not a workable solution." Dutton paused, putting the cloth back in his pocket. "If we allow an officer as highly placed and well-known as Admiral Compton to simply ignore an order of this magnitude, we risk a litany of adverse effects. Not the least of these is the obvious fact that Compton is, at least the very least, suspicious of the integrity of the command structure. We can only surmise how far this goes or specifically what he knows, but we must assume the worst – that Admiral Compton is actively supporting the rebels. Indeed, this is highly likely since it is apparent that the admiral or his allies have seized or destroyed the Commnet stations in the Eta Cassiopeiae system." He stifled a small cough and continued. "Whether this was the result of his initial predisposition or a reaction to this specific order and events related to it we cannot know."

"So what do you suggest, Number Two?" Stark's question was sincere. Dutton's opinion was just about the only one in the room he valued…except perhaps Alex's from time to time. Normally, he and Dutton would have discussed this in depth before the meeting, but the old spy had been in and out of the hospital for the last month. For years Stark had been dreading this, the loss of his only real friend. So often he'd dismissed the subject with a joke, unwilling to seriously contemplate the old man's mortality. But he couldn't fool himself any longer, and he knew, in all likelihood, he was watching he last Directorate meeting Jack Dutton would attend. It was an interesting anomaly. Gavin Stark was a soulless sociopath, utterly devoid of remorse for the thousands of deaths he'd caused, yet he was distraught over the impending demise of one old man. Even the dreaded leader of Alliance Intelligence had a touch of humanity, deeply buried as it was.

Dutton looked at Stark, trying to focus on his protégé through filmy eyes. "As I said, any option is dangerous. I believe we must utilize our…influence with Admiral Garret to issue an order relieving Compton of his command and ordering him to return to Washbalt at once." He shifted in his chair. He'd given up on actually being comfortable, but he tried, with extremely limited success, to find an angle that minimized the constant pain.

"However, I feel the effect of such an order is highly unpredictable. Admiral Compton is a very popular officer…indeed, after Garret, he is probably the most respected and loved flag officer in the navy." Dutton paused, catching his breath. "If he elects to refuse the order, it is entirely possible that some or all of his fleet will back him."

"Perhaps we can simply eliminate the admiral." Alex Linden hadn't said a word until now. Her rise had been almost meteoric, and she'd leapfrogged many of the people sitting around the table. There was a considerable amount of resentment and bad feeling about the whole thing, so she had been trying to downplay her role since she'd taken the third Seat. But this was crucially important, and she was the highest ranked person in the room after Stark…and, of course, Dutton, though that was looking very temporary.

"My preference as well, Number Three." Stark made sure not to smile as he agreed with her. She owed her advancement mostly to him, and everyone on the Directorate knew that. He didn't really care what they thought, but it wouldn't serve him for them to think he dangled on Alex's sexy little string. The truth was, he enjoyed his collaborations with her – both professional and personal – but he was more than ready to dispose of her when her usefulness was at an end. Lovers were replaceable, even ones as delightfully skilled as Alex, and Stark wasn't about to compromise his position over anything so quaint as affection. "Unfortunately, I do not believe it is feasible."

"Why not?" She caught herself, but too late to stop the words from coming out. Dammit Alex, she thought, you know better than to announce your ignorance. Generally, she was extremely circumspect, but this time she'd let down her guard, left herself open to looking foolish.

"Because, Number Three, in order to get this communication to us, our senior operative embedded on Compton's flagship was forced to blow his cover. Commander Harrigan stole a shuttle and escaped to YZ Ceti after Compton cut communications with Earth, preventing Governor Cooper from reporting his disobedience." Dutton's tone was scolding, as much as his weak and shaky voice could manage. Alex Linden was smarter than that, and she should have known better. "Without our key agent in place, any assassination attempt would be highly risky, possibly even likely to fail. Have you considered the ramifications of a failed assassination attempt against a fleet admiral? Especially if any of the operatives were captured alive and interrogated?" He'd gone a little further than he'd intended…past scolding to actually embarrassing her.

She looked across the table silently, with hateful smoldering eyes that bored right through him. Oh my God, she thought, will you just die already, you decrepit old relic? She had always viewed Dutton as being in her way, both on the Directorate itself and as Stark's confidante. But every year that he continued his seemingly endless life, she came to hate him more and more. She would have been shocked to know that Dutton had told Stark many times he considered her a fine agent, and the most promising on the Directorate.

"I believe we all agree. An assassination attempt is out of the question, at least for the present time." Stark's voice was sharp, signaling the topic was closed to further discussion. "So let us proceed to the specifics of relieving Admiral Compton…

or at least attempting to do so."

Number Two started to reply, but a coughing spasm took him. Stark reached out and grabbed a pitcher from the table and filled a glass with water, sliding it across toward his friend. Dutton managed to quell the coughing and take a drink. He nodded a quick thank you to Stark before clearing his throat and continuing. "First, the order must be transmitted publicly. We cannot allow Compton and a small cabal of officers loyal to him to hide the communication."

He cleared his throat again, fighting another spasm. "Second, the order must come expressly from Admiral Garret. We must create a situation where the officers and crew of the fleet have to directly disregard Garret's orders in order to side with Compton." Dutton paused and took a labored breath. "I cannot stress enough how important I feel this is. Compton is a revered leader…he will likely be able to convince his staff and ship captains to stand with him…only the prestige of Augustus Garret is strong enough to overcome his influence."

Dutton looked as if he was going to continue, but he remained silent. "What is it, Ja..Number Two?" Stark caught himself; names were not used in Directorate meetings, only titles.

Dutton sighed. "Only that I am still concerned, even if the criteria I specified are met. There is still a chance that Admiral Compton could retain control of his fleet, or a considerable portion of it." He hesitated, not sure he wanted to suggest what he was thinking. "I believe we need to consider dispatching a reliable task force to Columbia." Another pause, then: "We may be compelled to engage Compton and whatever forces remain under his control."

Every face in the room wore a shocked expression, all but Gavin Stark's. "I agree, Number Two. The problem is not knowing what force concentration we will require." He paused, calculating in his head. "If the bulk of his fleet sides with him, we will need virtually all of our sequestered naval units to insure victory. That includes the task force blockading Arcadia."

"I believe that is an acceptable risk." Dutton's frail voice had become barely audible. "There is no immediate threat to Arcadia. Leave a squadron of fast attack ships to deal with anyone trying to smuggle in supplies, and send the rest to Columbia."

Stark considered for a moment. He didn't like leaving Arcadia uncovered, and even less did he relish the thought of moving the rest of the Directorate's carefully assembled naval strength from Epsilon Eridani IV. He didn't see any immediate threat to that system and its precious alien artifact, but he slept better knowing they had a major fleet there.

"Very well." Stark had made his decision, and he didn't even go through the motions of pretending the entire Directorate had a say. "I will personally handle the drafting and transmission of Admiral Garret's order." He looked down the table at Burke. "Number Seven, please send orders for our task force at Arcadia and the fleet at Epsilon Eridani to set courses for Columbia as soon as possible." He pulled out his chair and finally sat down. "They are to arrest Admiral Compton and engage any naval units that resist. And they are to provide any and all support that Governor Cooper may request, up to and including nuclear bombardment of any targets he specifies."

"Yes, Number One." Burke's expression was impassive. He wasn't sure he agreed with the plan, but he was certainly not going to argue with Number One. "I will see to it immediately."

Stark took a deep breath, exhaling sharply. "I believe that covers naval matters for the moment. Let's move along." He looked at the man sitting next to Rodger Burke. "Number Five, please report on the current status of our Directorate infantry program." Stark already knew, of course, but he had to involve the rest of the Directorate in things…at least a little.

Troy Warren was always uncomfortable in Directorate meetings. The only member of the group who was not a Political Academy graduate, Warren had been a Corporate Magnate, and a very successful one…enough to take him all the way to a Seat on the Directorate. Nevertheless, he still felt like an outsider in a room full of career spies and politicians.

"Yes, Number One. As you are all aware, for the last several years we have expedited our efforts to produce a fighting force comparable to the Marine Corps." He looked across the table.

"Number Four has been extremely helpful in refining our training program, which has speeded our progress immensely."

Number Four was present, as always, as a holographic projection. Only Stark and Dutton knew that the mysterious secret member of the Directorate was, in fact, General Rafael Samuels, now the commandant of the Marine Corps. The shimmering image nodded appreciatively, but did not speak.

"We currently have 18 battalions fully operational, with another 40 in training." Warren fidgeted nervously in his seat. He had thought he was ruthless in his corporate days, but he'd never met anyone like Gavin Stark. The truth was, Stark scared the hell out of him. "They are fully powered infantry, armed and equipped almost exactly like Marine assault units." He forced himself to meet Stark's withering gaze. "They are well-trained, though not to the full standards of the Marine Corps. None of the units in the formation have any combat experience – you will recall that we elected to liquidate the forces that were repatriated from Carson's World after the war." He took a deep breath before continuing. "I would still be hesitant to commit them against Marine formations, at least not without significant numerical superiority."

"Let me worry about the Marines." It was a cryptic comment of the type Stark so frequently uttered. Everyone present knew better than to ask for details. "Please prepare the forces for embarkation as soon as possible." He looked right at Number Five, enjoying the way it made him squirm. "Please get back to me by tonight with a proposed schedule."

Warren paused for an instant, surprised by Stark's order. "Yes, Number One." Then he added, "May I inquire as to your intended deployments?"

"Certainly, Number Five." Stark's voice was cold; he didn't like being asked to explain himself. "I intend to dispatch these units to provide powered-infantry support to our Alliance army units engaged on the most troublesome colony worlds." He ran his fingers over his 'pad. "I am sending you a list of proposed deployments. The two worst trouble spots are Columbia and Arcadia. We will be sending a brigade to each." Two six-battalion brigades represented two-thirds of the available strength. "We will also deploy a single battalion to each of the following worlds: Atlantia, Victoria, Sandoval, Everest, Killian's World, and Armstrong." Stark smiled darkly. "It is time this rebellion ends before it spreads even further."

The meeting dragged on for another three hours as they systematically reviewed the status reports from each rebelling planet. Finally, Stark slid back from the table, his eyes panning up and down the assembly. "I believe that is all of our current business. If no one has anything else?" He waited a few seconds, though he knew no one would say anything – he'd already signaled an end to the meeting. "Very well, we are adjourned." Then: "Number Five, don't forget to get me those embarkation schedules. Tonight."

Warren nodded nervously and scurried out of the room, followed by the rest of the Directorate.

"Are you sure I can't have anything brought up for you? Tea? Broth?" Stark looked sadly at Dutton as the old man sat uncomfortably in the chair.

"No thank you, Gavin." Every word, every breath was an effort, but Jack Dutton had lived his long life at the center of things, and there he was resolved to remain until the day he closed his eyes for good. "Perhaps we can just conclude our business swiftly so I can go home and lie down for a while."

"Of course, my friend." Then, into the communicator on his desk: "Please come in now." Stark flipped a switch and a section of the paneled wall slid aside, revealing a door, an entrance to his office that few people knew existed. Rafael Samuels came through the portal…squeezed through was more accurate. Stark motioned toward an empty seat. God, he's gotten fat, Stark thought. I hope he fits in the chair.

Samuels walked slowly across the room and dropped his bulk into one of Stark's buttery soft leather chairs. The priceless antique creaked a bit, but it held fast. Rafael Samuels had always been a large man; when he was a young Marine, the armorers had to design a customized suit to fit him. Back then he was tall and enormously strong – he'd been called "The Bull" in his first platoon. In recent years he'd added fat to the list of adjectives used to describe him.

"Hello Rafael, thank you for staying. Soon we will be past the need for you to hide behind that hologram." Stark gestured toward a heavy crystal decanter on his desk. "May I offer you something? This is a fine Single Malt...you'll not see its like often." Samuels nodded appreciatively. "I wanted to discuss the final stages of our plan regarding the Marine Corps, and I felt that was better handled...shall we say...discreetly." He poured the amber liquid into a cut crystal glass as he spoke, handing it over to Samuels.

"Yes, Number One, I quite agree." He reached out, taking the drink from Stark. The glass nearly disappeared in his massive hand. "Secrecy is essential, as it has been since we began this business."

"Please...when we are not in a Directorate meeting, it is Gavin. We are not so formal in these private strategy sessions." Stark thought he sensed something from Samuels...not regret exactly, but perhaps hesitation, discomfort. That isn't surprising, he thought...Samuels is about to become the blackest traitor in Marine Corps history. Though that really won't matter much, since there will no longer be a Marine Corps. He suppressed a self-satisfied grin.

"I must commend you, Rafael, on your farsightedness." Stark amazed himself sometimes how earnestly full of shit he could be. Samuels needed a little boost now, and Stark was going to tell him whatever he wanted to hear. "The Corps has served its purpose, but it is a dangerously independent organization. That was acceptable when it was a small frontier force, but it is too powerful now to operate without oversight." He looked at Samuels, and his expression ached with sincerity...all false, of course. "The culture of the Marine Corps is too firmly embedded. It cannot change...we must start over."

Stark was confident Samuels understood his comments. My God, he thought disdainfully, it must be easier in some ways to be such a stupid, simple creature. Rafael Samuels had been going nowhere in the upper levels of the Corps until Stark targeted him for recruitment. But the power and manipulation of Alliance Intelligence went to work, turning Samuels from a supernumerary general shunted off into a dead end posting into one of the primary commanders of the Corps…and ultimately commandant. It took a lot of effort…and two unnatural deaths of senior officers, but Stark had seen it done.Samuels had been a partial participant for much of the ride; Stark had provided friendship and support for quite some time before he made the actual recruitment pitch. It always pays to get them addicted first, and then make the sale, he thought. Gavin Stark was a gifted manipulator with considerable mastery of human psychology.

"You are right, of course, Gavin." Samuels raised the glass to his lips, taking a sip. "And you are right about this Scotch as well."

Stark leaned back in his chair, comfortable he had chased away whatever doubts had been nagging at Samuels. "So we are prepared to initiate the final phase of the plan. With your concurrence, I will authorize my operative on Arcadia to execute the first part of the program." Stark looked Samuels right in the eye as he spoke. Arcadia was the part of the plan he expected to be toughest for Samuels, but the giant Marine didn't object – he just nodded slowly, signaling his assent.

"Subsequent to the successful execution of step one, you will order direct Marine intervention against the rebellions as a response to events on Arcadia. This will likely cause a fracture in the Corps, with some formations following the orders and others disobeying. We will utilize the confusion to disband the Marine Corps entirely. Without equipment and support, the isolated units will be easy to mop up with our new Directorate troops…after they finish off the rebels."

Samuels nodded again, but he was still troubled. First, he wasn't sure how easy it would be to mop up any Marines, no matter how cut off and poorly equipped they were. Frankly, he'd be wary of a cornered squad throwing rocks; whatever you wanted to say about the Corps, its people knew how to fight.

And these Marines were going to be pissed.

The finality of the actions they were setting into motion nagged at him. He'd always felt he'd been underappreciated in the Corps, and he hadn't risen to the level he felt he deserved until his allies at Alliance Intelligence intervened. But to be the man who destroyed the Corps? It was one thing to agree to it, to plot and scheme for years, and quite another to actually do it. He had been bitter and resentful, and Stark had used that to recruit him, but now part of him wished he could escape the path he himself had helped create.

It was too late to go back, though. He'd done too much already, and it was only a matter of time until he was discovered…and that would be an ugly day, one he probably wouldn't survive. No, he couldn't go on much longer like this…the Corps had to go, and covering his own tracks became just one more reason. Resigned to the reality of the situation, he tried to put his doubts aside, and he resolved to see things through. Besides, he couldn't even imagine what fate Stark would dream up for him if he backed out now.

"Rafael, I know this is difficult for you." Dutton had been quiet up to now, but he decided it was the time for him to intervene. His voice was weak and throaty, but he forced out the words. Samuels was a traitor and a turncoat, but he wasn't an automaton. Dutton knew Stark never understood regret, probably because he'd never felt it. But Dutton had, and he could see Samuels was struggling, and he needed a little support – or a little manipulation, depending on the viewpoint. "But it must be done, and there is solace in that very necessity." He paused, then he touched on the thought he knew was on Samuel's mind: "It is too late to alter the plan anyway, so let us make the best of it."

Dutton glanced at Stark. They had been allies for years, and friends too. Stark was like a son to Dutton, and the old spy had done everything he could to help his protégé rise to power. He was worried now that Stark would overreach once he was gone. Dutton's life had been ruled by caution, but Stark was more audacious, more likely to make a bold gamble if it served his purpose. He was a genius and a master psychologist, but he had a failing as well, never truly understanding some of the seemingly irrational points of view caused by conscience. He tended to expect more frigid practicality in people's decisions than he was likely to get. It was a dangerous blind spot, likely to get him in trouble when Dutton was no longer there to run interference.

Samuels sat quietly, considering Dutton's words. He knew his doubts were pointless; he was fully committed now anyway. Soon he could retire his hologram and openly join the Directorate. He would be wealthy beyond his wildest imagination and one of the most powerful people in the Alliance. He would command the new Directorate army, of course, and he would forge it in his own image. Perhaps I will pay for this devil's bargain with my soul, he thought, but at least I got a good deal.

Samuels raised his glass. "To our success." Stark returned the gesture, draining his glass with a smile. Dutton was not drinking, but he nodded and raised his arm in solidarity.

"Well, if you gentlemen will excuse me, I have some work to do." Samuels' voice was calm - he was a bit more at peace with what he had to do...or at least he was resigned to it. "The end game begins."

Stark nodded and rose from his seat. "I'll walk you out, Rafael." He moved around the desk, gesturing for Samuels to lead the way, and the two walked through the door into the now-deserted reception area.

Dutton rose to his feet, slowly, painfully. He paused to look out the window, truly absorbing the amazing view he had seen thousands of times but never fully appreciated...until now. It was a feeling, really, and nothing more that told him this was the last time he would see it.

He could hear Stark in the corridor, saying goodbye to Samuels. The two of them had devised the plan together, and Dutton was gratified that it appeared close to success. Now, standing here looking out over the city, he felt something...was it a twinge of remorse? The Corps had done their part for a century to safeguard the Alliance's interest in space. Did they deserve better than this as a reward? Foolish thoughts, the kind of nonsensical sentimentality he had always despised in people. He tried to push them away, but he couldn't...not completely. He'd had regrets before, but never about doing what he knew had to be done.

Ethics and morality were not concepts Dutton allowed to interfere with his actions. To him they were constructs, convenient tools useful for crowd control. Dutton had been driven all his long life by expediency, by practicality. His morality was whatever worked, whatever kept things together for another day. His roots were in a different time, when the survival of the Alliance, even of mankind, was still in doubt, the world in ashes from almost a century of war.

He thought he understood the colonists. Indeed, he had a better view into the mindset of those on the frontier than Stark ever could. They valued freedom, they craved self-determination. But they were small societies and, for the most part, wealthy ones, tapping the vast resources of virgin worlds. How would they fare a century from now? A millennium? Would they deal any better with the enormous social problems caused by population growth, poverty, pollution?

Mankind had come within a hair's breadth of total extinction. Whatever one thought of the Alliance and the other Superpowers, they had pulled humanity back from the brink. They kept the world functioning, rebuilt shattered cities, pushed out into space. The vessels the brave explorers rode to the stars were built in shipyards...shipyards constructed by the Superpowers. If the colonists won their freedom, would they pull back from their own brink when it came?

Dutton slowly pulled his gaze from the wonder of Washbalt's nighttime skyline and looked around the room, savoring every detail as he never had. He reached into his pocket, pulling out a datachip and a key card. He'd been carrying them around for weeks, but now he decided it was time. He laid them on Stark's desk and slowly followed his friend into the hallway.

He was tired, so he said a quick goodnight and took the elevator down to the lobby, walking slowly out to his waiting car. As usual, the driver had the compartment warmed up, which lately meant something between room temperature and the melting point of zinc. In recent months, the cold had been cutting right through him, and he'd found it increasingly difficult to stay comfortable. It was a short drive to his apartment, a palatial penthouse in one of the Core's most prestigious buildings, and it only took a few minutes to get there. He walked through the lobby to his private lift, nodding silently to the attendant who wished him a good evening. Once in his apartment, he went right up to the bedroom, tossing his jacket on the chair.

He was exhausted and aching, but he decided he was hungry after all. He sat on the edge of his bed and leaned over, switching on the communicator. "Gerta, bring up some tea, please. And some of those biscuits if there are any left."

"Yes, sir." Gerta had been with him for years – housekeeper, cook, assistant. She wasn't as old as him – almost no one was – but she had seen a lot of years herself. Her loyalty had earned her Dutton's appreciation, and with it some advantages rare for a Cog, including rejuvenation treatments and enough money for a comfortable retirement.

She walked into the room, carrying a small tray with a teapot, cup, and plate full of biscuits. She is optimistic, Dutton thought, as he saw the large stack of shortbread. I'll be lucky to get one of them down. "That will be all, Gerta."

She nodded and turned toward the door. "Goodnight, sir."

Dutton sat up quite late. He'd been tired earlier, but now he was awake, restless. He read for a while…and actually managed to eat two of the biscuits and a bit of a third. Finally, he laid the 'pad on the end table and put his head down on the fine silk pillow, quickly drifting off.

When Gerta walked in at 8am, she was surprised to find him still in bed, the blinds shut. Dutton was an early riser, often up well before the sun. She couldn't remember the last time he'd slept past 8.

She walked over, trying to decide if she should wake him or not, but when she got to his bedside she knew immediately. She stepped back, gasping, feeling the tears building in her eyes.

Jack Dutton, the master spy of the Alliance, was dead.

Chapter 19

Alliance Museum of History
Monument Park
Wash-Balt Metroplex, Earth

Erik Cain sat in the palatial lobby of the Alliance Museum of History, passing the time watching the reflections dance on the polished granite floor. He was trying to focus on the mission, but he couldn't help but wonder how much of the "history" on display here was fabricated. Most of it, he suspected. Alliance Gov didn't have a lot of use for the truth, certainly not for public consumption.

He was waiting for his contact to arrive – he assumed that individual would know who he was, because no one had told him a thing. The trip to Earth had gone completely according to plan, and they hadn't had any trouble passing through the spaceport and getting to the Martian embassy. Travelling as a diplomat had its advantages, Erik thought. Regular citizens were monitored everywhere they went, but the elites treated each other quite differently. They spied on each other, to be sure, but they didn't impose the same rules they did on their pliant populations. His Martian Diplomatic Corps ID allowed him to wander the city more or less freely, probably because the Alliance diplomats in the Ares Metroplex wanted the same option.

Cain could never understand the way the Political Class thought. They fought and schemed against the other Superpowers, yet the ruling elite in each nation accorded each other a strange respect they denied their own citizens. To Erik it seemed like they were all members of some bizarre club, even when they were enemies. The Martians were a bit different, though not entirely immune.

There were a hundred things that had to go right for this mission to work, but Cain was most worried about the weapons. He'd gotten his troops in, ten of them plus himself. People were easier to sneak in – Vance just issued them all diplomatic credentials, and they walked right off the Martian shuttle into a waiting limo that whisked them to the embassy. But the guns and ammo were different – they had to be smuggled in.

He appreciated the help Vance and his colleagues in the Confederation provided; it was doubtful he could have gotten his team to Washbalt without their assistance. But they had been sitting here for weeks now, waiting for the equipment they needed for the operation…and he was sick of waiting.

Cain was grateful for the assistance the Martians had given his people, but that didn't mean he trusted them. They had one plan, but he had his own. And he had some ideas on how to get the equipment he needed too.

Vance had given him 40 bars of platinum, untraceable currency for bribes if they were needed. But Cain had another use for this small fortune. He was going to rely on knowledge and skills from his past, things he'd thought he had long forgotten – things he'd tried hard to make himself forget.

There was a vast, shadowy labyrinth of abandoned tunnels and infrastructure under the cities of the Alliance, the detritus of centuries of growth, decay, destruction, and rebuilding. Erik was well-aware just who would know the secrets of this maze of dripping, rat-infested, crumbling tunnels…and who would also have weapons he might be able to buy. The gangs of Washbalt's vast slums were even worse than the ones he'd run with in New York, and they almost certainly knew every millimeter of the vast undercity, just as he and his compatriots in New York had mastered theirs.

That life was long ago, and it seemed alien to him now, like some bad dream, hazily remembered. But the gangs were the key to this subterranean world, here just as they were in New York. That was the way to get into Alliance Intelligence; he was sure of it. He just needed the gangs to help.

It was a plan so audacious, so crazy on its face, that only he could have devised it. The fate of the colonies and the future of the Alliance could very well hinge on his ability to cut a satisfactory deal with a murderous gang leader. But first he had to get his people out of the Core and into the slums where the gangs were located.

He hadn't left the embassy more than a couple times since he'd arrived, and then only briefly. There were just too many cameras, too much facial recognition software, too big a chance he'd be recognized by some security system matching him to a database, either from his gang days or his military service. It was just too risky. But this is where his contact agreed to meet him, so this is where he came. Just setting the meeting had cost him two bars of platinum, worth enough to buy a small apartment in one of Washbalt's nicer neighborhoods.

"Mr. Daniels?" A tall, middle-aged man in a worn brown coat sat down on the bench. He didn't look over at Cain; he just sat next to him, eyes forward, watching the crowds go by. Daniels was Erik's alias, his identity as a Martian diplomat.

"You are late." Erik hated all the cloak and dagger nonsense. He much preferred blunter means to accomplish his ends, but he wasn't going to get Garret out with a frontal assault. Not unless he found an army of fully-equipped Marines somewhere.

"My apologies, sir." The new arrival continued to look out casually at the crowd as he spoke. "I have been here for some time, but I had to wait for my associate to be on duty in the security center. You see, this is not a randomly chosen location; we can be assured that we will not be monitored while we discuss matters."

"Who are you, anyway?" Cain knew a name would be meaningless to him, but he felt at a disadvantage without one.

"I am your contact. You may call me Charles."

"You are aware of what I need, Charles?" Cain found it mildly disconcerting to have a conversation while carefully avoiding eye contact, but he played along. He was confident his visitor was far more adept at discretion than he was.

"Yes, Mr. Daniels." His voice was pleasant, but Cain could detect a hint of skepticism. "What you request can be done, but it is difficult and dangerous...and therefore expensive."

"This meeting was expensive." Cain's voice was sharp, clipped. He was frustrated with inaction and anxious about the mission...and he was most definitely not in the mood to waste time with nonsense. "I would like what I requested, and I would like it tomorrow. Just tell me what it will cost."

"It is not as simple as that, Mr. Daniels." Charles was a hard book to read, at least from his voice alone. "We must be confident that there will be no ramifications for us."

Charles knew better than to ask directly why Cain had requested assistance in sneaking 11 people out of the Washbalt Core undetected, but that is essentially what he wanted to know. He assumed it was some type of drug deal, and if so he had no problem. But if Cain was here to assassinate someone or to spy on Alliance Gov, that was another matter. His trepidation had nothing to do with discomfort about murder or loyalty to the Alliance; it was a matter of the investigation that would follow. A routine drug transaction, even one as big as this appeared to be, would draw little attention. But if a well-placed politician was assassinated, the authorities would ransack Washbalt looking for the accomplices.

"My associates and I are only interested in conducting some business and going on our way." Cain paused, and then he reached back into the buried recesses of his mind. Erik Cain, teenaged gang member, emerged. He knew what to say, how to sound like he was working a drug deal. He knew because he'd done it before.

Charles listened to Cain describe his proposed – and, of course, fictitious – drug transaction in great detail. It took two minutes, maybe three before he was convinced. He decided the mysterious Mr. Daniels' business was acceptable. "Pardon me, Mr. Daniels," he said softly, interrupting Cain's ongoing description. "I believe we will be able to help you. However, tomorrow is out of the question. There is too much preparation required. Several days at least. You will have to be prepared to go on a 1-2 hours' notice any time within the next week." He paused, allowing Erik to consider what he had said. "Is this acceptable?"

It was a bit less definite than Cain had been hoping for, but he nodded and then, realizing Charles wasn't looking at him and couldn't see his gesture, said, "It is acceptable."

"The cost will be an additional six platinum bars." Charles' voice was unemotional, though he was discussing a small fortune. "Payable in advance."

Cain was stunned at the cost, but he really didn't care how much of Vance's money he spent anyway. "Six bars is acceptable." His voice became firmer, more serious. "Payable when your people get us out of the city."

Charles sat quietly for a minute, considering what Cain had said. "You will give our operative three bars immediately and the remaining three when you are outside of the city." His voice, which had been pleasant and friendly, was darker, more forceful. "That is our final offer."

Cain was going to argue, but he didn't have much choice. It could be weeks, even months before Vance's people could get them weapons through another channel, and even then, Cain wasn't sure how they would get access to Alliance HQ. If he could get outside and bribe a gang to help him get into the undercity, he had a good chance. Or at least some chance. "Agreed. How will we know when you are ready."

"A courier will deliver eleven tickets to the American West exhibit at the museum. That will be your signal. Two hours later, you and your associates will be right here. If you are not in this location within two hours and fifteen minutes of receiving the signal, the transaction is cancelled. Understood?"

"Yes." It was really pissing Cain off dealing with this two-bit huckster, probably just the representative of some corrupt low-level politician. Temper control was never easy for Erik, and he detested politicians with a burning intensity. But he was determined to get Garret out no matter what he had to do. It was unthinkable to allow Alliance Intelligence to gain total control over the navy. He didn't know the admiral well, but Holm did. And Erik would have marched into hell for Elias Holm. "I understand."

Chapter 20

Holm's Ridge
7 kilometers south of Weston City
Columbia - Eta Cassiopeiae II

Jax looked down from the rocky crest of the ridgeline, but he wasn't seeing the valley in front of him...not really. His mind was far away, not in space but in time, fifteen years earlier when he and Erik Cain were two sergeants desperately defending this very position. He wondered at the odd way things sometimes worked, at the strange sequence of events that brought him back here to this very spot in circumstances even more desperate.

They had saved Columbia back then, beating off a massively superior CAC invasion force in a desperate battle. The casualty list had been enormous that day, and it included the future General Cain, somehow miraculously alive – barely - after finding himself unsheltered too close to a nuclear explosion. Things did indeed work in strange ways. Jax thought he'd lost his friend and comrade that day, but Cain recovered and returned to win glory all across occupied space. And his stay in the hospital gave him more than his health back. In a turn of events so clichéd Jax still teased him about it, Erik had fallen in love with his doctor – feelings she fortunately reciprocated.

They had all come a long way since then, and yet here he was, back in the same place...though its name had changed. Jax couldn't remember what the Columbians called the ridge then, but after the battle they gratefully renamed it after General – then Colonel – Holm, a tribute that both honored and embarrassed the publicity-shy officer.

They had come a long way from their landing zone too, traveling halfway across Columbia and launching dozens of hit and run attacks against isolated federal positions. The politics of the whole situation were complex and confusing. Was Jax fighting for the same side he did fifteen years before? Surely back then he was battling to protect the people of Columbia...which was what he saw himself doing this time too. But the soldiers he was fighting now carried the very flag he had served under the first time he came here. Jax craved a warrior's simplicity, with good guys, bad guys, and no headsplitting conflicts about loyalty. But he knew it was not to be.

His forces had done well, tearing up all of the peripheral federal units they could find. They had rallied the populations in the remote areas, adding a small legion of volunteers to their ranks. Hundreds had come forward, but Jax would only take Marine veterans. He didn't doubt the ability or courage of the others, but his small force depended on speed and discipline; he simply didn't have the time or resources to integrate amateurs into his ranks.

Now, however, he was sticking his neck out. Getting this close to Weston was dangerous. The federals had been massively reinforced, and the rebellion was in grave danger. In the plain south of Weston was an encampment, larger even than the one that stood there when Columbia was the staging area for General Holm's 1st Corps. There were three Alliance army divisions on the planet now, outnumbering the rebels at least five to one.

The rebels had fortified Carlisle Island, just 20 kilometers northeast of Weston, and now they had retreated there, too weak to operate on the mainland exposed to the massive federal army. The rebel stronghold was heavily defended, ringed with rocket launchers and other heavy weapons, most of them seized from the militia armory or stolen from the Feds in the early months of the rebellion. The sea surrounding the island was patrolled by a fleet of submersibles, vessels that were normally employed to harvest valuable resources from the ocean but which had now been equipped for war.

But even with their fortifications, he doubted the rebels could hold Carlisle once the federals got organized enough to launch a coordinated attack. Even worse, if Admiral Compton was replaced with an officer willing to follow Cooper's orders, the rebel stronghold would be nuked into oblivion. There was nothing Jax and his people could do about that; they would have to depend on Compton to hang on. But preventing the Feds from launching the final ground assault was their problem, and it was a tough one.

"Sergeant Sawyer, put together a scouting party." Jax had come to rely on Sawyer over the last couple months. Sawyer had been with the special action teams on Carson's World, with the group that discovered the alien artifact. He was a veteran sergeant who had more than once turned down the chance to go to the Academy. He liked being closer to the troops, and Jax thought he was the best small unit leader he'd ever seen. "I need to know their weaknesses. We're going to have to hit them soon and disrupt things before they can launch an attack on Carlisle Island." He put his hand on Sawyer's shoulder. "I'm counting on you, Ed."

"We'll find something, sir." Sawyer was a big man, though not as big as Jax...few people were. His light brown hair was closely cropped, and his face was marred by a long, jagged scar. A series of skin regens could have eliminated that, or at least dramatically shrunk it, but Sawyer was never willing to take that much time off duty for what he considered non-essential. "With your permission, I'll pick a team of three. Any more than that and it'll just be harder to stay undetected."

"Whatever you feel is best, sergeant." Jax was trying not to stare at the scar. He never realized how distracting physical features and facial expressions could be in the field. None of that was an issue in armor. You knew what everyone looked like, of course, after living with them aboard ship for weeks or months. But when you hit dirt, you were buttoned up and so were your comrades. It was somehow easier to focus on the essentials that way, at least for Jax. "I need that report right away. Be cautious, but get back here as soon as you can. No transmissions on the comlink – we don't want them picking up any chatter."

Sawyer nodded and walked down the hillside to get his crew together. He didn't salute; Jax had been trying to run his tiny army a bit more casually than that. They were really just a fairly well-equipped guerilla force, and they were all arguably committing treason. Military formality seemed misplaced. Besides, too much saluting in the battle zone just made an officer into sniper bait.

Jax put his scope to his eyes and panned over the valley below. I've got to find a weakness, he thought. There has to be a way to disrupt them before they attack Carlisle.

Jill Winton was sitting on the ground, leaning against the plasti-crete base of one of the camp's large floodlights. She was sitting with her knees pressed up against her chest – it was a little warmer that way. The ground was cold, but not frozen – it didn't get below freezing very often on Columbia.

The camp had been getting more and more crowded, and that was despite the steady death toll. The federals hadn't been executing too many, not that she'd seen. But between the short rations, exposure, general abuse, and lack of medical care, there were at least a dozen deaths every day…and sometimes two or three times that many

Jill had been in the camp from the beginning. She'd come close to getting out the night the rebel army breached the wall, but she couldn't get through the masses of stampeding inmates. She was lucky not to get trampled to death that night; over 100 people had died in that seething, uncontrolled mass.

She had been distraught, feeling liberation slip through her fingers. Later she realized it might have saved her life. The federal troops attacked the rebels who had breached the walls, overwhelming them and sending the shattered survivors fleeing. Some of the prisoners probably escaped, but she knew a lot of them were cut down. Camp rumors were widespread that a large group tried to surrender, but the Feds shot down anyone they found outside the wall.

After that day she was changed. Her despair evolved and hardened, morphing into rage. She hated the federals for what they had done. She hadn't been a revolutionary partisan; her dream had been a career as an officer in the Alliance navy. Her sympathies were with those who bristled against federal author-ity, but not to the point of rebellion. She was young and ideal-istic, and she thought the two sides could talk, reason with each other, solve their problems peacefully.

But that was then. Jill Winton was different now. Gone was the moderately spoiled only daughter of a doting wealthy father; in her place a cold and angry woman, longing for vengeance against those who had brought death and suffering to her world. She embraced the rebellion now, and she loathed the federals. Her hate extended from the soldiers in the field, whom she regarded as savage bullies, to those at the highest levels of a system so foul and corrupt it could perpetrate such atrocities on its citizens. Now she seethed, anxious for the chance to kill the enemy.

Her hatred burned cold and patient, not uncontrollable like the impetuous fury of fiery rage. She planned and waited. When she started, she was cautious, deliberative. The camp was infested with collaborators and informants. They were mostly normal Columbians, and their actions were driven by hunger or fear. But to Jill they were traitors, vile turncoats who needed to die. She couldn't hurt the federals, not yet. But the sympathizers in the camp were within her reach.

Her group was small at first, just her and three others she trusted. Their first target was a woman, one who had been giving information to the guards in return for food and special treatment. She was an easy one to condemn – her loose words had gotten at least two prisoners executed.

They did it one night, very late. Their weapons were rocks; they had nothing else. Two of them grabbed her while she was sleeping, holding her tightly as she woke up and tried to escape. One held her mouth, muffling her screams. It was Jill herself, leader of the nascent resistance cell, who struck the blow. The first time felt strange; Jill had never harmed a soul before this. She could feel the jarring as the stone impacted on her victim's skull. Her arm rose up again, swinging back down. It was the second blow - or the third, she couldn't recall later - that broke through the skull. After that the impacts were softer, penetrating deeper into tissue. She swung her weapon nine or ten times, though her victim was dead well before she struck the last.

Jill looked down at the woman, probably an office worker

from Weston. Her head was disfigured and covered in blood, lifeless eyes still open, staring into the darkness. Jill felt no remorse, no pity. She chose her path, Jill thought, as I now choose mine. She casually tossed the rock aside and slipped away with her cohorts into night.

Arlen Cooper made a face. God damned mud, he thought, as he scraped the sides of his shoes against each other, trying to clean off the gluey wet clay. Cooper usually made his commanders come to his office to discuss strategy, but this time he decided he wanted to review the troops. It sounded like a better idea in his office than it did out here, at the crack of dawn, dodging the muddy puddles and being eaten alive by mosquitoes. He'd been assured they weren't actually mosquitoes, just a native Columbian creature superficially similar to the terrestrial insect despite enormous genetic differences. Whatever the experts said, they seemed to thrive on his Terran blood, and the bumps they left itched every bit as much as those from any Earthly bloodsucker.

Finally, he had enough strength...finally, he was about to crush this damnable rebellion. He had seethed when Admiral Compton refused his bombardment request, but now he resolved to launch an all-out assault against Carlisle Island. Once he destroyed their base, the rebels would quickly disperse, and he could finish them off. Then he could get off this forsaken rock and go back to Earth and the reward for his success. He wasn't sure what kind of posting he could get, but he was sure he'd never be a petty ward supervisor again, not after crushing the Columbian rebellion.

Cooper didn't have a military bone in his body. Soldiers were nothing more than tools he used to achieve his ends. He wanted Compton to bombard Carlisle not because it would save thousands of his own troops, but simply because it was faster and easier. Now his soldiers would have to take the place meter by meter, and they would pay heavily for it. Cooper didn't really care, and he figured the blood was on Compton's hands anyway. But it would take longer, and that had him in a foul mood.

The rebel submersibles were a problem; he knew that much. His forces would have to take them out or drive them away; otherwise they'd never even make it to Carlisle. Cooper didn't give it much thought; he didn't really pay attention when the generals were explaining the tactical situation to him. He didn't care how they did their jobs, just that they did them. He'd been pushing them for weeks to launch the attack, and he was getting sick of their excuses. They kept asking for more time...to stockpile supplies, conduct training, organize their forces.

None of the officers had any real combat experience, and the prospect of so large a battle was intimidating. Cooper was no military expert, but he understood it took a while to prepare a major operation. He also knew his generals were procrastinating. That's why he was here.

"General Strom, a word please." Cooper called out to his senior commander. His voice was impatient; it was obvious he was annoyed.

"Yes, Governor?" Strom was a pompous ass though, of course, so was Cooper. Technically, Strom was under the command of the Planetary Governor. But Cooper had been a low level political functionary, whose authority was the result of accepting a posting that no one with better credentials would take. Strom, on the other hand, was from a well-placed political family, and in all likelihood he would take over his father's cabinet seat one day. His being here was a freak circumstance; he certainly never thought his military career would take him into space. He bristled at taking orders from a jumped up local manager, which is how he viewed Cooper. He followed them anyway, more or less, but he did so grudgingly.

"I would like to discuss specific timing for an assault on the rebel home base." Cooper didn't like Strom, and he bristled at the general's barely disguised condescension. But Strom was what he had, so he dealt with it. He could order the military to undertake whatever operations he chose, but his authority did not extend to internal matters such as officer assignments. He was stuck with Strom.

"Preparations are underway, Governor." Strom was clearly

tired of Cooper's interference, and his contempt was only very lightly hidden. "I will advise you when I have determined the earliest feasible start date." Strom turned to walk away. "Now if you will excuse me, Governor, I am having a small dinner this evening for some of my senior officers, and I really must…"

"General Strom, I don't care about your dinner party." Cooper's patience was gone; he'd had it with Strom and his delays. "You will prepare a plan for the invasion of Carlisle to launch within two weeks. And you will do so immediately and have it to me in 72 hours." Cooper was speaking from anger; he really didn't have any way to force Strom to do it. Technically, he had the authority, but if he reported the general for insubordination it would ultimately come down to Cooper's connections and influence against Strom's, a contest the governor was certain to lose. "Understood, general?"

Strom's face flushed with anger. He considered Cooper his inferior in every way that mattered, and he bristled at being even marginally under the governor's command. He bit back on his initial response and nodded grudgingly. "I will work on the plan as quickly as possible." He knew his influence trumped Cooper's, but he also knew his father, the Cabinet Minister, did not want any ripples right now. It wouldn't do for the family to appear less than fully committed to crushing the rebellion, after all.

"Thank you, general." Cooper didn't always have the best judgment, but this time he realized this was the best he was going to get. "Your cooperation in ending this damaging and wasteful rebellion is appreciated."

Strom nodded, a forced smile on his face. "If you will excuse me, Governor Cooper, I am quite busy."

"Of course, general." Cooper managed his own very forced looking smile. He turned and walked away, trying to contain his frustration. Then the explosions began.

"Move it out!" Sergeant Sawyer was leading the demolitions team. It was probably a lieutenant's job, but Sawyer would have been an officer years ago if he hadn't kept refusing invitations to the Academy. "I want those charges placed in 1-2-0 seconds."

Sawyer had spent two days trying to find a weakness in the federal encampments. He'd been focusing on their supplies, looking for a way to hit one of their big dumps to impede their ability to launch an offensive. But the supplies were guarded and double-guarded, every approach covered. Sawyer didn't know it, but the rebels had blown the main federal supply dump in Weston earlier in the war…and ever since the Feds had been extremely protective of the installations.

Jax had 481 regulars, plus about 200 volunteers with military experience – he couldn't just frontally attack the federals. He knew he had to find a way to disrupt the Feds…something they could actually pull off. Then Sawyer had an idea.

The federal supply depots were well-protected, but the field with the atmospheric fighters was located near the perimeter. There were 18 of them, and they were all lined up in one spot. They were defended, but a well-executed surprise attack might take them out.

Without the fighters to screen and protect the assault force crossing the 16 klicks of water between the mainland and Carlisle Island, the rebel defense batteries and submersibles would tear the transports apart. An invasion without air support would be dangerous…probably more than an Alliance general could stomach.

Sawyer had 40 troops, hand-picked from a force that was already an elite unit. They were here to infiltrate, to get as close to the planes as they could before Jax launched a diversionary attack with the rest of the force. They were crouched down behind a slight ridge about 100 meters from the perimeter when they heard the sound of fighting to the north. Jax had gone in.

Sawyer's troops sprinted the short distance and twenty seconds later they were inside the enemy perimeter. They started taking fire, but it was light. The guards were calling for aid, but Jax's assault had distracted the nearby forces.

Sawyer's team had magnetic charges, and they were attaching them to the fighters, three two-man teams moving from target to target. The rest of the force returned the enemy fire, trying to divert the defenders from the demo crews. They were taking losses — at least four people were down — but the primary concern was knocking out the planes. Doing that meant buying the explosive crews at least another two minutes, no matter how many casualties they suffered.

"Hold fast and keep firing." Sawyer's voice was steady but hoarse. He was tense, but he made sure none of that came through. "Two more minutes, people. We need to hold for two more minutes."

Jax's force had attacked in two long skirmish lines. The extended formation didn't have enough density to make any real headway, but their mission was distraction, not an extended battle. They swept in from the ridge, catching the federals half-asleep.

"Move forward and grab some cover inside the enemy perimeter." Jax was running as he spoke, his assault rifle in his hand. "All personnel, fire at anything that moves, and make as much noise as you can." The enemy fire was light, but Jax knew that wouldn't last. "I don't want anyone penetrating too far. And when I give the withdrawal order move your asses and get the hell out." Jax's force was outnumbered almost 100-1; they were here to raid, not fight a battle.

They'd taken out the perimeter guards and slipped into the encampment. The troops were mostly billeted in modular structures located throughout the base, but there few barracks at the point Jax chose for his attack. The structures here were different, mostly workshops and other maintenance facilities. Other than the guards, most of the personnel in the area were technicians and support staff, and that gave the attackers a chance to grab good positions before the enemy counter-attacked.

Jax followed six troopers through the blasted doorway of one of the workshops. They'd hit the building with grenades already, collapsing two of the walls and bringing a section of roof down. The attackers fired as they came through, taking out the survivors inside then moving to take good defensive positions in the wreckage. Jax crouched behind a jagged meter-high section of wall and peered out over the top.

It was ten minutes, maybe twelve, before the enemy launched a major counterattack. Jax had been waiting impatiently, wondering what was taking so long. He'd have busted a subordinate out of the service for such a slow response, and he shuddered to think of how Erik Cain would have reacted if any of his troops had been so lackadaisical. But he was glad – the enemy's sluggish response did half his job for him.

The federals came swarming into the zone occupied by Jax's troops, and when they finally arrived, there were a lot of them. All along the section of the perimeter held by the rebel forces, they came in waves. Jax's troops, veterans all, had chosen their spots wisely, and they cut down the charging enemy troops in huge numbers, inflicting at least ten casualties for every one they sustained.

Still, the math was against them, and as their losses mounted the enemy poured more and more units into the fight. Slowly, methodically, Jax's troops started to pull back. The withdrawal was perfectly organized and flawlessly executed. Troops fell back to new positions, supported by fire teams that remained in place, covering the retreat. These covering forces retired in their turn, supported by the troops that had already fallen back.

The plan was working, but they were getting close to the edge of the camp, and Jax couldn't give the orders for the full retreat until those planes went up in smoke. He was just about to go on the comlink and order his forces to stop retiring and stand fast when he heard the explosions. There was one, then a pause...then a cluster of blasts followed by a single massive thunderclap.

"Alright people, the mission's done." Jax was on the comlink halfway through the explosions. "Time to withdraw. Execute plan Delta-1 now."

Jax's troops began leapfrogging to the rear at an accelerated pace. Things had gone well - better than Jax expected – but that didn't mean it had been free. The retreating teams were moving back methodically, but they were slowed by wounded comrades. Jax had been clear – no one alive would be left behind. Across the line, walking wounded limped along, their comrades matching their pace to stay with them. Troops were carrying more seriously injured men and women, dodging enemy fire as they did.

Having taken so long to respond, the enemy was now pursuing aggressively. They were disorganized and distracted by the explosions, but there was still a massive force on the heels of Jax's retreating troops. The retiring forces reached the perimeter of the encampment, rushing across the open ground.

The federals kept coming. They were disordered, and their fire was wild and inaccurate, but they were still taking a toll. Things were getting hot quickly, but Jax had one more surprise waiting. The retiring troops came together into three rough columns, and all along a small rise heavy weapons teams opened fire. Jax had stripped them out of the attacking formation, ordering them to advance behind the main force and take up a supporting position.

The attacking federals ran into the withering fire and recoiled back into the encampment. Jax's retreating units continued to the rear, carrying their wounded with them. The heavy weapons teams began to pull back as well, withdrawing in stages, and in 15 minutes the entire force, including Sawyer's people, were mounted up and racing away. It didn't look like the Feds were organized enough to launch an immediate pursuit, but Jax wanted to get some distance from them anyway.

Sarah and her people frantically worked on the wounded in the retreating ATVs. They'd left forty dead behind them, and she was determined to keep that toll from rising. She almost managed it; only one of the wounded died during the retreat, one of Sawyer's people, almost the last man hit.

Chapter 21

Northeast Ward
Just Outside the Wall
Wash-Balt Metroplex, Earth

Four days passed before Cain's people got the signal. Precisely two hours later they were at the museum. Erik didn't know if they had been under surveillance while they waited, but he assumed they were. They sat for half an hour before a man - not the mysterious Charles, but someone new - came over and introduced himself as their guide.

It was the middle of the day. Cain hadn't really thought about it until the call came early in the afternoon, but he found himself surprised they were doing this in daylight. His impulse was to get out of the city under cover of darkness, but in truth, the detection devices monitoring Washbalt's population were just as effective at night. In some ways the crowds during the day provided better cover than the darkness.

Cain's implant had been removed when he graduated from Marine training. He made sure that everyone in his team had also had theirs taken out or disabled. Anyone with a functioning implant would have been detected almost immediately, even after years away from Earth. That would have been a disaster and would have blown the cover of the group entirely. Confederation citizens were not implanted with monitoring devices… and they were masquerading as Martian diplomats.

Erik had been very specific when selecting his team. They were all from Earth's slums. There were many solid veterans in the Corps who were born on colony worlds, but this was a job for the Marines who'd come from the urban wastelands of the Alliance. He picked troopers who had troubled pasts like his. Erik Cain had become a new man – a good man, he hoped – in the Corps, but when he was on his own in the slums of New York he'd been someone different, someone he usually tried to forget. Anger, hatred, and deprivation can change a man – a boy, really – and Erik Cain had been no exception. He'd done a lot of things he wished he could change, and while time had helped him make a tentative peace with his regrets, they were always there. Now he was back, not in the exact place, but in one very much like it, and he would have to deal with people uncomfortably similar to those he'd lived with before. People very much like he himself once was. He wanted a team around him that understood, that faced the same demons he did.

He had no idea how his new associates planned to sneak them out of the Core, and he hated having to trust them. But there was really no alternative – he couldn't think of any other way to complete the mission. Of course his hired help would have bolted if they knew what his group really intended. The insanity of the whole thing was actually helpful – no one would anticipate what they were actually up to. People did not break into Alliance Intelligence HQ.

Erik was hoping that attitude would help them on the actual mission too. The people at Alliance Intelligence had everybody so scared to death, there was a good chance they'd be over-confident, secure in the knowledge that no one would dare try something as mad as what Cain intended.

The guide gave them specific instructions, and they split up into five pairs, each walking to a different intersection. Cain didn't like it, but he understood. Cameras would track them everywhere, and a large group like theirs would draw attention. He didn't trust these people, but if they wanted to take out his team, they didn't need to split them up; all they had to do was turn them in. Besides, Erik's entire crew was made up of long-term veterans, more than able to take care of themselves.

His concerns proved to be unfounded; his new associates were true to their word. One by one, a large transport stopped at each location, loading two of Cain's team and driving on to the next. It took some detours, mixing up the route to confuse any surveillance or tracking programs that might have detected them, but in less than an hour, they were inside a large plasti-crete building situated right along the Wall. Cain wasn't sure exactly what the facility was; it looked like some sort of utility structure for moving water in or wastes out. Or both…Erik had become adept at many things, but civil engineering wasn't one of them.

The Wall was ten meters high, built of reinforced plast-crete, with watchtowers ever 200 meters. It surrounded the Washbalt Core, the protected central section of the city where the middle and upper classes lived, segregated from the crumbling ghettoes and masses of uneducated Cogs. Cain had been amazed when he first saw it. The massive fortification dwarfed the outer perimeter of the Manhattan Protected Zone, where he'd been born and lived the first eight years of his life. New York certainly had slums, and they were decaying and violent, but nothing like the vast and nightmarish belt of destitution wrapped around Washbalt. The capital of the Alliance, and before that the United States, the city had become the focal point for the dispossessed and those who fought against what the nation was becoming. The Wall had been built during the Disruptions, and its strength attested to just how bad things got during those troubled times, despite how sanitized the official histories had become.

Cain and his Marines had three guides, two men and a woman, and they'd hardly said a word. Finally, the woman spoke briefly with her companions and walked over to Cain. She was nearly as tall as he was and broad shouldered. Erik bet himself she could take both of the men in a fight.

"This is as far as we take you." She pointed toward a large hatch that one of the men had opened. "That is a maintenance conduit for the southern sector waste disposal system." Her voice was harsh, impatient. She clearly wanted to conclude this business and get on her way. "There are access hatches leading to the outside every half kilometer. They are heavily reinforced plasti-steel. The seventh one will be unlocked in 30 minutes and will remain so for ten minutes."

She stared at Cain as she spoke, and her voice became even firmer. "You must be out before the hatch locks again or you will be trapped. The door from here into the access tube will be closed and locked behind you." She stared at him with an expression that was somehow intense and disinterested at the same time. "Understood?"

Cain wasn't particularly skilled at tolerating people he found annoying, but his mind was focused on the mission, and so he pushed back his natural reaction. "Understood."

"The balance of the payment is due now."

Erik was going to argue; his agreement had been for the rest of the payment to be made when they were outside the city. Climbing into some dusty maintenance tube for the sewers didn't meet his definition of "outside." But he didn't really hold any cards here, and he knew it. He glanced over at one of his team, a tall, sandy-haired man just under two meters tall. Major James Teller had served with Cain for years, and he read the unspoken directive immediately. He pulled a pack from his back and reached in, taking the platinum bars out one at a time. He was watchful – the team had a fortune in the precious metal with them, and they were wary of a doublecross. He looked at Cain, who gave him a slight nod, and he began handing the bars to the woman.

"Thank you." One of the men walked up to her and she handed him the bars. "This concludes our business. Good luck to you all." Cain had never been wished luck less enthusiastically, but right now he would take what he could get.

"What about the scanning and security equipment?" He called out to the woman as she was walking to the door.

She stopped, though she didn't bother to turn around to face him. "The security system will be offline for the next 40 minutes." She sounded impatient, like someone answering a stupid question for the fourth or fifth time. "That is the most expensive thing you paid for." She walked out the door, followed by the two men. Cain and his team were alone.

"Do you trust them, sir?" Teller looked at Cain, standing at attention as he spoke.

"Fuck no, James." Cain let out a grim chuckle. "We just don't have any alternative. And if they're going to set us up, what difference does it make if they got a few bars of Vance's platinum out of us first?" He turned his head, looking toward the hatch then back again toward Teller. "And cut the 'sir' stuff, James. Officially, we're not even here."

"Yes, si…yes, Erik."   Teller smiled for an instant. "Understood."

"Ok, let's get moving, people." Cain led the way through the hatch, the team following in single file behind him. They were an elite group; half were officers, the rest veteran sergeants with years of combat experience. "Keep your eyes and ears wide open."

They were walking on sections of metal grating, a meter wide and suspended about ten centimeters above the plasticrete floor of the tunnel. The corridor ran adjacent to a massive cylindrical pipe, at least ten meters in diameter. It was dank and dusty; from what they could tell, this maintenance tube wasn't used all that often.

They were trying to be quiet, but the sound of their boots on the loosely bolted sections of the grating echoed off the walls and ceiling. Cain kept cringing when the noise got loud, but they certainly seemed to be alone here…and if the security system had not been disabled as they'd been promised, it didn't matter how silent they were. Their movement, breath, body temperature, and a dozen other things would still give them away.

They passed the first access hatch. There was a metal ladder attached to the wall going up to the ceiling about 6 meters above. They could see a round door just above the ladder. If they'd been given good information, that door led to the surface.

They kept walking, reaching the seventh ladder about ten minutes early. The team was anxious, but Cain insisted on following the prescribed schedule exactly. He waited precisely twelve minutes, then he climbed the ladder and reached out to the controls for the hatch. It was unlocked as promised, and Cain pulled the lever. With a soft hissing sound, the door slid to the side, allowing a shaft of late afternoon sunlight into the tunnel.

Cain looked down the ladder at his team lined up behind him, and with a quiet sigh he pulled himself up and through the hatch…and into the ghostly world of his past.

The team had been in the Eastern Fringe for three days. One of the worst areas in Washbalt's almost endless slums, the Fringe was well located for their proposed mission, close to the buildings of the Inner Core. Like most of the Alliance's cities, Washbalt had a large secure area where the middle classes lived and where most commerce took place. Inside these protected areas there was typically an enclave reserved for the Political Class, Corporate Magnates, and elite visitors. Sector A in New York, Gold Coast/Old Town in Chicago, Beacon Hill in Boston…all the cities had a zone where the elite and privileged enjoyed a lifestyle the other 99.5% of the population could only imagine. All except Washbalt…it had five such areas…and the Inner Core was the most luxurious of all.

Alliance Headquarters was a massive building straddling the Inner Wall, the perimeter surrounding this bastion of privilege. It had entrances in both the Inner Core and the main business district. A towering monolith, it was a symbol of fear to all. Even the elites of the Political Class were wary of the Alliance's massive intelligence operation. Its tentacles stretched into every corner of society, and more than one powerful politician had found himself disgraced, career destroyed by the machinations of those who worked within that kilometer tall tower. Some had even found their way to a grisly end in the infamous cells of Sub-Sector C.

Cain wasn't afraid of Alliance Intelligence, at least no more than he would be of any dangerous mission. He refused to allow the carefully constructed mystique to exert its affect on him. Men with guns were men with guns, and these would not be the first ones he'd faced.

Nevertheless, he was afraid. Not of the mission, not of the enemies he had to face, not even of the consequences of failure. He was afraid of himself, of the past. For three days he had negotiated with the leaders of the Stone Hands, the most powerful and violent gang in the Fringe. In that time he had seen horrors, images that took him back more than two decades, to the streets of the Bronx. Back then he had preyed on the helpless Cogs just as the Stone Hands did, doing things he couldn't imagine now. He'd spent his life since atoning, protecting the Alliance's colonists from those who would do them harm. Now he was even protecting them from the Alliance itself.

Each moment spent in the urban hell reminded him of that time long ago, chipping away at the fragile peace he'd made with himself. He just wanted to complete the mission and get away from Earth as quickly as possible. But dealing with a gang is difficult, especially for an outsider. He knew their ways and how to deal with them, and his people were tough enough to take care of themselves...something a few of the more unrestrained gangers found out the hard way. But it still took time.

The platinum he offered was valuable anywhere, but in the crumbling slums it was a massive treasure. He'd kept two bars to show off; the rest they had buried in the sub-cellar of an abandoned building. Carrock, the Stone Hands' leader, was about to have them all shot for disturbing him when Cain threw the two bars at his feet.

Now they had been negotiating for three days. Not because it required that much time, but because Carrock wanted to test Cain, to see what he would do or say while he waited. It was a poker game of sorts, each trying to get the measure of the other. Carrock was worried Cain would try to cheat him on payment or do something that would bring heat down on the gang.

Cain had an edge, though. Carrock had no idea Erik knew how the gangs functioned, that he knew it because he had lived it. Cain wanted to make sure the Stone Hands lived up to their end of the bargain...which meant providing weapons and leading them through the undercity. He didn't tell Carrock they were planning to hit Alliance Intelligence; no one would agree to participate in something with the kind of repercussions the true mission carried. Instead, Cain had invented a robbery of the building across the street, the headquarters of Gavrit and Carlson, one of the largest importers of priceless extra-terrestrial stones and artifacts...an entirely plausible target.

The hardest part of waiting around was doing nothing while gang members victimized the helpless Cogs. Erik Cain was different now; he had been reborn through years of hard service, and he found it almost impossible to stand aside and watch the very crimes he'd willingly committed a lifetime ago. His troops could have helped; they wanted to intervene, but Erik stopped them. They may not have been able to change the big picture, but there wasn't a doubt in Erik's mind that they could have saved lives. But they didn't…more guilt for him to bear, since it was he who stood in the way. Their mission was to get Garret out, and that was all that mattered. Getting into a fight with the Stone Hands wasn't part of the plan. They needed the gang.

Now he was on his way to meet Carrock and make the final arrangements. With any luck, this time tomorrow they would be under Alliance Intelligence HQ. Unless something went wrong.

"Which way is north? I'm not going to ask you again." The gang member couldn't have been more than seventeen. Erik had him in a headlock and was twisting his arm behind his back. It was going to break any second.

"That way." He was crying, his voice cracking. He motioned with his head, as far as he could with Cain's arm around his neck.

Erik had seen the kid beating a helpless woman two days earlier, though he wasn't sure if the little scumbag had killed her or not. Shithead's not so tough now, he thought. Cain really wanted to kill the bastard, but they still needed him. "You're going to help us get into the Alliance Intelligence building." He loosened his grip, just enough so the kid could speak.

"Are you crazy?" It was a spontaneous reaction, one that prompted Cain to tighten his grip again.

"Do you see these guys?" Erik twisted the kid around, forcing his head toward the bodies of his two companions. When they had reached the original destination, Cain gave a quick signal, and Teller killed both in less than three seconds. They were sprawled out on the ground, one a particularly disturbing sight, with his head twisted sickeningly, open eyes staring up lifelessly.

The ganger was whimpering now, gasping for air. "Ple… please…"

"Then do as I say." Cain loosened his arm, though less than he had before.

"I think it's that way." He tried to motion again, though it was hard with Erik holding him so tightly. "We don't ever go there. It's crazy to mess with them."

"Crazy or not, that's where we're going." Cain glanced down at the bodies. "And unless you want to stay with them…" – his voice was cold and ominous as he pointed to the two corpses – "…you're coming with us."

The kid was terrified and sobbing, but he nodded his agreement. Erik motioned with his head, and the whole group started moving. They had a mix of weapons – a few ancient assault rifles, some actual firearms, and an assortment of pistols and explosives. It wasn't what Erik wanted for a team assaulting one of the most difficult targets he could imagine, but it was the best they could get from the gang. If Stone Hands had any better weapons, they weren't going to sell them, not at any price. They were just too hard to come by.

Cain was looking for something specific. Vance hadn't been able to give him as much intel on Alliance Intelligence HQ as he might have liked, but he did provide some useful info. Martian Security definitely had a source on the inside. Erik supposed for an instant he should probably be upset by that. He was, after all, an Alliance Marine. The Confeds weren't the enemy, not really…but they were a foreign power. It only took him a second to decide he didn't give a shit. He didn't trust Vance, not really, but he'd take the Martian's word over that of anyone in Alliance Gov.

It took most of an hour, but he found the way in…it was there just like Vance said it would be. The Alliance Intelligence building was self-contained, completely off the city's grid, and its power was generated by a subterranean fusion reactor. There was a duct, a backup system used occasionally to expel excess steam into the unused tunnels around the building. Now it was going to serve another purpose, one its designers never intended.

The ganger was scared to death, broken and pathetic. Cain knew what he had to do, but he didn't like the idea of killing such a miserable, pitiful creature. He couldn't let him go, and they could hardly risk taking him with them – they'd have their hands full enough without worrying about a prisoner. Thousands of lives were riding on this mission, useful, productive lives. Innocent lives. Nothing was worse, in Erik's opinion, than a merciless bully who turned into a whimpering coward when threatened. And he knew that if he let the little shit go he'd just kill and torture more Cogs. But despite his contempt, it was still difficult. Cain himself had been like this once, perhaps not as casually brutal, but troubled nonetheless. He was given a second chance, something this kid would never have. Erik didn't like it, but he did what he had to do.

The duct was wide enough for them to crawl through one at a time. Cain was about to climb through first, but he faced a near-mutiny over the issue and finally relented, allowing Teller to take the lead. It was a tight fit, especially carrying weapons, but eventually they found their way in, cutting through the duct and dropping down into the control room of the reactor.

There were half a dozen technicians there, but Cain's team managed to take them all out before anyone could sound the alarm. Erik knew there were monitoring devices throughout the building – their chances of going anywhere undetected were nil. They had to rely on speed and surprise. No one at Alliance Intelligence expected this kind of incursion, he was sure of that.

They stayed in the control room for a few minutes, reviewing the plan then they moved into the hallway, jogging quickly. According to Vance there was a stairwell just down the hall from the reactor. Cain wanted to avoid the lifts; they were probably closely monitored. They didn't run into anyone else on the lower level, but they had no idea if they'd been monitored or detected in some other way.

The stairs were just where Vance said they would be – Cain was starting to trust the Martian…just a little bit. They raced upward, moving past the door marked Sub-Sector C, the entrance to the infamous torture chamber of Alliance Intelligence. Cain doubted Garret would be there – usually VIP prisoners were kept in the substantially more comfortable Sub-Sector B, one level above.

They reached the B level unmolested and scrambled down

the corridor. I can't believe our luck, Erik was thinking, just as four guards and a man in a perfectly-tailored suit rounded the corner. The guards wore one-piece black uniforms, jumpsuits really, with pistols holstered at their sides. The man was perhaps sixty, with a considerable dusting of gray on his neatly trimmed black hair. The uniformed guards seemed like hardcases – big and tough-looking, but the other man didn't fit the image of a spy...he could have been a bookkeeper or a teacher to look at him.

The guards reacted quickly, but they couldn't match the combat reflexes of Cain's veterans. Assault rifles snapped up in an instant and fired. The guns were old and obsolete, but they were still deadly. Three of the guards fell immediately, all dead or mortally wounded. The fourth managed to duck behind the corridor and draw his pistol before Teller was on him, grabbing the hand with the gun and shoving a blade under his ribs.

The man in the suit was gone. He'd ducked around the corner faster than anyone expected he could move, and by the time Teller took out the last guard, he was gone. There was a trail of blood – the team's fire must have hit him – and it ended at a sealed hatch. They tried to get it open, but it was a heavy door and they didn't have time to waste. They were there to get Garret, not chase down some Alliance Intelligence administrator.

"Let's go, down to the main control desk." Erik snapped out the order decisively. "Garret is prisoner G1701 according to Vance's intel. Let's find his cell and get the hell out of here."

There were lights dancing in front of Gavin Stark's eyes. The pain in his shoulder was almost unbearable; Stark was tough in his own way, but he was a manipulator, not a warrior. He could feel every heartbeat pounding in his arm, and it was agony. His shirt and jacket were both soaked through with blood.

He managed to get away – he was surprised himself at the speed of his reflexes. The guards were all down; he was sure of that. There were plenty more guards on this level, and they would respond to the shooting. He had no idea how anyone got in without being detected sooner, but when he got out of here he was damned sure going to find out. If he got out.

I should be OK in here, he thought. He'd managed to duck into one of the maximum security holding cells. The door was solid plasti-steel, and without the access code the interlopers would need a massive explosive to take it out, one that would rip apart the entire corridor and everything around it. Of course, if they were here to assassinate him, that is exactly what they would do.

No, he thought, not assassination…they couldn't have known I was coming down here. Then what? His mind was fuzzy; it was hard to think. Pain, blood loss…Stark was lying against the door trying to focus as he grew fainter and fainter. He could feel the slickness of his blood all around…on the door, covering the smooth tile floor. He reached for his communicator. "Stark here…intrusion…Sub-Sec…tor B." He gasped for breath, trying to force his mind to cut through the growing haze. "Acti… vate protocol…C3." His voice was weak, soft. He heard something in the distance. A voice was calling back to him, asking him to repeat.

"Protocol…C…3…" He wasn't sure if he said it again or just thought it before he drifted deeper and deeper into the darkness.

"Blow the fucking thing." Cain's voice was tense. "Now!" He had three men holding each end of the corridor, but there were guards coming from every direction. They'd found Garret's cell – at least they thought it was his – but their fight with the guards had advertised their presence. An alarm was sounding now, and security forces were responding.

Erik had spent about thirty seconds arguing with Teller about blasting open the door. They'd set the charge, but it was a big one. It had to be; the door was heavily armored. Teller was worried the explosion would be too massive. They didn't come all this was to blow Admiral Garret to bits in his cell. But if they didn't get the door open immediately then none of it was going to matter anyway.

Teller still looked doubtful, but it wasn't in him to question

Cain's orders. He looked at Erik one last time, and at his superior's nod he flipped the switch. The corridor reverberated as the charge blew, filling the hallway with fire and smoke. Cain was the first one down the hall, rushing through the shattered remains of the doorway.

"Admiral Garret?" The room was full of smoke, and the lights had been knocked out, so Cain couldn't see anything. "Admiral, we're here to get you out."

Cain was anxious, desperate to hear the admiral's voice. It was only a second, maybe two or three, but it seemed like an eternity before the response came. First Erik heard coughing, then a scratchy voice calling to him. "Garret here." More coughing. "Who are you?"

"It's Erik Cain and the Marines, sir." Cain started walking toward the sound, feeling around in the hazy darkness. "We're here to get you out."

"General Cain?" Garret's voice was hoarse and he was struggling to speak audibly through the smoke. "How did you get here?"

"That's a long story, sir." Cain's hand finally found the general, and he grabbed hold of Garret's arm. "We're still in the middle of Alliance Intelligence HQ right now, so I suggest we discuss it later." He gripped the admiral's arm more firmly and pulled. "Let's get the hell out of here."

They ran out into the hall. The Marines were holding both ends of the corridor, firing around the corners at the assembling guards. A couple of them had taken minor wounds, but no one was down yet.

"Back to the undercity...it's the only way out." Cain was shouting to Teller. "Leave two men on the right to hold the corridor, and move everyone else to the left. We're going to have to fight our way down that corridor." Cain didn't know his way around the maze of hallways and passages, but he was pretty sure left was the most direct route back to the stairwell that led to the lower levels. He felt a momentary pang; the guys left to hold the rear had a pretty poor chance of getting out. He had the urge to go back and take the post himself, but he pushed it aside. He grinned morbidly, just for a second, as he imagined what General Holm would have said if he had taken up the rearguard. "Teller, those men are to hold for two minutes and then follow us. Two minutes and not a second more. No one commits suicide today. Understood?

"Yes, sir." Teller started barking orders in the hallway, and in a few seconds he had everyone lined up, ready to go. Cain walked down the corridor with the admiral. At first, he was helping Garret, but then the admiral pulled away. "I'm OK, Cain. I can walk myself."

Erik just nodded to the general. "OK, people, we're going to fight our way right back to that stairwell and down the way we came. No stopping. No matter what. However bad it is, it's only going to get worse if we wait." He paused for an instant. "Let's go!"

They spun around the corner, firing full and charging down the corridor. They took the guards by surprise, and they were halfway down the hall before the fire got really heavy. Cain noticed the blood on his arm before he felt the pain. He'd taken a shot just below the left shoulder, but he ignored it and kept firing as he ran forward. He rounded the corner along with the first two of his troopers, and they sprayed the entire area with fire. The guards broke and ran, but the Marines gunned them down as they fled.

They had a respite now, with all their enemies down. Cain did a quick assessment. Besides himself, they had two wounded. Both could keep moving, though Johnson had taken a hit in the thigh and needed a little help. They encountered sporadic resistance along the rest of the way, and they suffered their first fatality just before they reached the stairwell. It was just a single guard, but his first shot hit Carver in the head. The entire crew opened up, riddling the shooter, but the damage was done.

Cain leaned against the wall, motioning for the team to go through the door to the stairs. His shoulder was really throbbing now, and his sleeve was soaked with blood. He watched the last of his team duck through the door, but he hesitated. Simms and Hanson had stayed behind to hold the rear as they made their way to the stairs. "C'mon guys." Erik was muttering under his breath, trying to will the two Marines to come around the corner. He waited as long as he dared, longer even, but there was nothing. Finally, he sighed and slipped through the door, running down the stairs to catch up with the group. He'd see Simms and Hanson again; they would join the legion of ghosts that visited him at night.

They made it back the way they had come and out into the tunnels. That was easier than I expected, Cain thought. Alliance Intelligence was so used to everyone being terrified of them, their internal security had become sloppy. It wasn't designed to counter the threat posed by a strike team of hardcore Marine veterans. That was a scenario Alliance Intelligence had never imagined.

They ran through the tunnels, trying to find their way closer to the Martian embassy. They didn't have a guide now, so they put some distance behind them and found a good place to hide, a large chamber located near an access point to the surface. Cain had been planning to slip out into the city and scout where they were, but his blood-drenched arm would hardly pass unnoticed on the street, so Teller went instead.

They settled in, tending to their wounds and waiting for Teller to return. Cain tied his torn sleeve around his wound and sat down next to Garret. The ground was cold and damp, ancient concrete, now cracked and splintered.

"I don't know how to thank you and your Marines, general." Garret had been shocked when Cain burst into his cell, but his own combat reflexes took over immediately. Now the adrenalin drained away just a bit, and his mind caught up on processing what had happened.

Cain turned his head and returned Garret's gaze. "Our pleasure, admiral." He managed a short smile. "Though we're not out yet, so I'd hold that thought for now."

Garret returned the partial grin. "I'll risk it now. I'd rather be here with a chance than locked in that Godforsaken cell. So thank you." After a pause: "My mind has been racing about what is going on out there. Stark would never have dared this stunt if it wasn't really important."

Cain's smile faded. "There is a lot going on, alright, sir. I'm not even sure where to start." He stared at Garret earnestly. "And you're probably going to have some difficult decisions to make once we get you out of here."

They spoke for hours, Erik trying to give Garret a synopsis of what had transpired in the time he'd been held captive. It was a lot, and Cain tried to be complete, though he really didn't know the status of things on the rebelling planets. He'd chosen his side in the conflict, but he tried not to let his prejudices affect his description.

Garret's expression was grim. "I should never have taken this appointment. I've been a damned fool." Cain was listening, but he got the impression Garret was talking to himself as much as anyone else. "But you can bet you ass I'm going to fix that when we get out of here." He paused, staring straight ahead at the wall. "You can count on that."

Cain was trying to decide if a response was called for when Teller came striding into the room, followed by a man and a woman in non-descript civilian clothing. "I made to the embassy." He had a smile on his face. "There's a transport waiting just outside. C'mon, let's get out of here."

Cain eased himself up to his feet. His arm was stiff, the throbbing pain worsening with any movement. "Let's go, Admiral Garret. Time to get you out of here."

Chapter 22

Fleet Command Control Center
AS Bunker Hill
Orbiting Columbia - Eta Cassiopeiae II

The flag bridge was silent, save for the faint hum of the
ship's systems in the background. Every eye was fixed on Terrance Compton, and he could feel them boring into him, word-
lessly demanding an explanation. He had known this moment
would come, but he'd hoped he would have more time. In the
end, sabotaging Commnet only bought him an extra two weeks.

He managed to figure it out when Harrigan went AWOL
with a shuttle. It was still officially classified as an accident, a
transport lost to an unexplained disaster. But Compton never
believed that. He knew there were Alliance Intelligence agents
in his fleet – there were in every squadron. But he was unnerved
that they had managed to get an operative so close to him.
Knocking out Commnet may have saved his life, he thought;
Harrigan probably had orders to assassinate him if he didn't
comply with Governor Cooper's demands.

The courier ship broadcast the orders from Admiral Garret's office directly to Compton's entire staff, as well as every
ship commander in the fleet. He was on the spot now; he had
to respond, and he had to do it now. He could feel his heart
beating in his ears like a muffled drum, and his head ached with
a raw, dull pain.

"As you are aware, we recently received a communication
purported to be from Admiral Garret." He intended to speak
to his command staff only at first; he had initially considered
going right on fleetcom, but then he thought, first things first.
If he couldn't convince his own people he was doomed. And
if he could, at least he'd have some allies when he confronted
the ship captains. But the com circuits were already overloaded
with incoming messages, so in the end he decided he'd address
the entire fleet at once. "For some time now, I have been gravely

concerned that Admiral Garret has been acting under considerable external pressure."

He could see the doubtful expressions of his staff, and he could only imagine those on the captains listening on their bridges. He realized he needed to approach this on a different level. "As some of you may know, Augustus Garret and I attended the Naval Academy together. We served together, first as officers on the same ship, later as captains of vessels in the same squadron." He turned casually as he spoke, constantly observing the officers standing around him. Good, he thought. Personalising this is making more of an impression. "He is my closest friend as well as my commander. I would follow Admiral Garret's orders if they were to set a course for hell itself...as long as I knew they were his legitimate commands."

There was a ripple of mutterings through those assembled, barely audible, but real nonetheless. At least they are listening, he thought. "Many of you have served with me for years. Does anyone here doubt my motives? My loyalties? Is there anyone here who truly believes me disloyal to Admiral Garret?"

He could see the confused, undecided looks on their faces. They had seen the message, yet they could not imagine Admiral Compton as a traitor or mutineer. Had the communiqué come from anyone with less stature than Admiral Garret, they would all have discounted it out of hand. But Augustus Garret was a legend...he *was* the navy. And they had seen him reading the order himself.

"Listen again to the transmission." Compton knew he was gambling here. Showing the navy's hero denouncing him again was a risky move, even if they had all seen it already. "Joker, replay the communication on fleetcom."

The viewscreen had been displaying fleet deployments, but they disappeared, replaced by a solid blue background with the Alliance Seal in the center. After a few seconds, an image appeared...the image of Augustus Garret, seated at his desk. Garret's expression was grim, his voice ominous.

"This order is sent to all personnel of command rank on the AS Bunker Hill and other ships of the Second Fleet." Garret stared directly out from the screen, almost motionless as he spoke. "It is with the deepest regret and heartfelt sorrow that I must issue these commands." It was Garret on the screen, or at least it looked just like him.

"I hereby order that Admiral Terrance Compton is relieved of command of the Second Fleet..." Garret was still looking straight ahead as he spoke. "...he is hereby stripped of all rank..." His voice was firm and steady, devoid of emotion. "...and I order that he be arrested at once and held in solitary confinement until such time as duly authorized personnel arrive to transport him back to Earth to stand trial."

Compton glanced around the room. Maybe, he hoped...just maybe showing the order again is helping. The image on the screen looked like Garret, but anyone who knew the admiral... anyone who really knew him...could tell how unlike him this was. At least that's what Compton was betting on.

"Admiral Compton has willfully disobeyed a Priority One order to aid and assist Alliance forces currently engaged in combat on the planet Columbia. His actions have resulted in the needless deaths of Alliance military personnel." Garret's voice remained steady, almost monotone. "Admiral Harmon is hereby ordered to take command of Second Fleet and to carry out the Priority One orders previously issued to Admiral Compton." Garret paused, though he remained stationary, sitting almost at attention. "I have forwarded a copy of those orders to Admiral Harmon."

He paused again, as if what he was saying was difficult for him, but when he continued his voice was still deadpan, unemotional. "This order is not easy for me to issue, and I understand that it may not be easy for Admiral Harmon and the rest of the officers of Second Fleet to obey. But our duty is clear. Garret out." The screen faded to the blue background with the Alliance seal.

Compton panned around the room, pausing for an instant as he looked at each member of his staff. He could see the conflict and confusion in their expressions. "I am now going to share the contents of the Priority One order in question." His voice was strong and clear. He was past worrying about this – he had chosen the right path, the only course that allowed him to live with himself. He'd rather spend the rest of his life in the brig – or be spaced for mutiny – than murder thousands of colonists at the behest of a psychopathic governor drunk on human blood. The die is cast, he thought, and now we'll see how it plays out.

"I am violating regulations by disclosing this information, however the situation is one that I feel is unprecedented." He turned slowly, still moving his eyes from officer to officer. "We were ordered to proceed to this system and provide any support requested by Governor Cooper. I followed that order to the letter, moving the fleet here at maximum speed and granting the governor's requests. We have provided scanning support and deployed observation satellites as directed by the governor's office."

Compton felt strangely calm. For weeks he'd been dreading this moment, thinking about it, thrashing sleeplessly at night with worry. Now he felt relief; he didn't know what would happen, but whatever it was, he vastly preferred action to waiting in anticipation.

"However, the governor requested that we launch a saturation bombardment of inhabited areas of the planetary surface with nuclear weapons." Compton paused. Let them chew on that for a few seconds, he thought. "I was not provided with specific military targets; I was asked to carpet bomb a widespread area, an operation that would have caused thousands of civilian casualties."

Compton was getting angry as he spoke. It was unthinkable to him that the Alliance navy would engage in the mass murder of thousands of citizens, and he hated the idea that he was standing here defending himself for not taking such action. "That is an immoral order and one I will not follow." He was getting somewhere…he could see it in their expressions. "And it is an order that Augustus Garret would never issue. Either these transmissions have been tampered with, or Admiral Garret is under some form of pressure or duress." It was a wild assertion, one that sounded like a crazy conspiracy theory. The fact that it was, in fact, true didn't make it sound any more plausible.

There was a long pause before anyone spoke. Finally, a lone voice broke the silence. It was Commander Thomas, a tactical officer who had served with Compton for years. "Sir, I can't speak for everyone, but for myself, I would never doubt your motives and integrity." He paused, the tension in his voice apparent. "But how can you…how can we…simply disregard an order from Admiral Garret?"

Compton could feel every eye on the bridge on him. Indeed, most of the senior officers of the fleet were watching him now, waiting for his response. "I maintain that, as extreme as this may sound, Admiral Garret's office has suffered some type of security breach, and these orders are either fake or the result of some form of duress on the admiral." He paused then added, "The Augustus Garret I know would never issue these orders."

He looked around the bridge. He could see the tension, the stress. "I understand that following my orders, backing me in this, puts your careers in jeopardy." There was no sense ignoring that fact, he thought; they all knew the risks, so he might as well address them. "But to me, any other course of action is unthinkable. I did not give my entire life to the service to end up murdering Alliance citizens."

He could see the expressions of his staff officers. They were uncomfortable, but he could tell he had them. One by one he could see the decision, the resolve in their faces.

"I am with you, sir." Thomas was the first to speak up, an act of considerable courage. Once he had started it, the others joined in, one at a time, until everyone on the bridge had declared their allegiance.

Compton sighed softly. It was a good start, but he'd figured he could convince his own people. The rest of the command officers in the fleet would be more difficult.

"Sir, I have Admiral Harmon." Thomas was looking nervously at Compton as he spoke.

Here we go, Compton thought. He considered Camille Harmon a good officer, honest and fair. The two hadn't served long together, but they'd gotten along well enough. He nodded to

Thomas, a signal to put the Admiral on the line. "Hello, Admiral Harmon. Calling to demand my surrender?"

There was an instant of silence, and Compton's newfound calm briefly deserted him, replaced by a rush of adrenalin. Whatever Harmon said was going to set events in motion, probably very quickly. "Strange times, Admiral Compton. Strange times indeed."

Damn her, thought Compton…I can't read a thing from her voice.

"This puts me in a very difficult situation, Admiral Compton."

Her voice was somber, but firm. Whatever she was going to say, Compton thought, she's already decided.

"I find it almost inconceivable to disregard Admiral Garret's order."

Compton tensed, ready to spring into action. He was pretty sure he'd keep Bunker Hill – he knew Elizabeth would side with him. But if Harmon went against him he had no idea how the fleet would react. Expecting them to disobey Garret and the appointed admiral on the scene was a heavy load.

"However, I find it completely inconceivable to indiscriminately bombard civilian targets." Her voice was decisive, though he could hear the sorrow in it. "I therefore will continue to acknowledge your command of the fleet, pending confirmation of Admiral Garret's order."

Compton exhaled, feeling some of the tension draining away. With Harmon on his side he was pretty sure he'd maintain control of the fleet. His relief, however, was short-lived.

The line was still open and on speaker a few seconds later when a loud noise came through, then another. It was hard to tell over the comlink, but it sounded like gunfire. The entire command staff on Bunker Hill gasped, heads snapping up, looking toward Compton. The next sound was a scream, followed by more shooting.

"Admiral Harmon, report." Compton waited a few seconds then repeated himself. "Admiral Harmon? Report."

Another ten or twenty seconds went by before a response came. When it did, it was a man's voice, not Harmon's. "Admiral Harmon has been shot, sir."

Compton was stunned. "Report in detail."

The response was delayed; the bridge of Harmon's ship was in utter chaos. "Sir, the admiral is still alive, but she is unconscious. The Marines killed the shooter."

Compton's thoughts raced. Alliance Intelligence...it has to be. They got Harrigan on my ship, so why should I be surprised they got someone close to Camille? Harrigan would probably be shooting at me right now if he was still here.

"Sir, Captain Jantz is on the line." Thomas' voice was cracking and tentative. He was a veteran officer, but no one in the Alliance navy was prepared to handle an assassination attempt against an admiral on her bridge.

Great, Compton thought...Jantz is a martinent; I'm going to have a problem with him. Unfortunately, Jantz was also the senior captain in the fleet and the next in command after Harmon.

"Yes, Captain Jantz?" Compton snapped out his best command voice. It was as much for the benefit of the other officers listening in as it was for Jantz.

"Per Admiral Garret's orders, I hereby demand your immediate surrender." Jantz sounded just like Compton expected. He was sure Jantz practiced barking orders into the mirror when he shaved in the morning. "Please acknowledge your compliance immediately."

"Captain Jantz, both Admiral Harmon and I concur that the order in question is suspect and cannot be obeyed." Compton was speaking again to the other officers – he knew Jantz would never back down. "I therefore maintain command of the Second Fleet."

Jantz cut the line to the flagship. A drama began and played out as the officers of the fleet chose their sides. Captains made their own decisions then tried to maintain control of their ships, sometimes successfully, sometimes not. Officers argued and debated, and on six vessels there was fighting before the issue was resolved.

When it was over, the shrunken Second Fleet remained on

station at Columbia, with Admiral Compton in command. Captain Jantz led the rest, about a third of the original strength, and took position between Columbia and the YZ Ceti warp gate…out of immediate combat range, but close enough to be menacing.

For the moment, there was an uneasy peace in the system, but as long as Compton could maintain control of the bulk of the fleet, the rebels were safe from bombardment. How long that would last was anyone's guess.

Chapter 23

Martian Confederation Grand Fleet
Epsilon Eridani System
Inbound to Carson's World

The Sword of Ares bristled with might. The flagship of the Confederation's navy was the pride of Martian technology and industry. She was brand new, the largest ship in space, vaster even than the Alliance's Yorktown class monsters. Admiral Steven Wells sat in the control center of this behemoth, directing the operations of the largest fleet the Confederation had ever put into space.

The Alliance fleet that had been stationed here was gone; they'd transited the YZ Ceti Warp gate two weeks before. It had been a risk stationing the spy ships in the system, but Martian ECM was the very best, and the intel they provided was essential. Wells had his orders, and that was all he needed. Still, he wondered how the high command knew the Alliance ships would leave. They must have known - it was too much of a coincidence otherwise.

He'd have gone in against the Alliance fleet if he'd been ordered to, but he'd done the mental calculation in his head, and he wasn't sure which way that would have gone. If they had a Garret or Compton leading those ships, he had serious doubts his fleet could have prevailed; against a lesser commander, he felt he had a good chance. It was immaterial anyway, since the Alliance force was gone. Wells didn't know it, but his orders were coming from Roderick Vance, and Vance had no intention of sending him to attack a major Alliance fleet. The Confederation was playing a dangerous game – a necessary once, Vance felt – but it wasn't about to provoke a major war. Not unless absolutely necessary.

There was a small flotilla still on station at Carson's World, but all of the heavy ships were gone. Wells had already recorded his message, and now he sent it out, uncoded and in the clear.

"Attention Alliance vessels. This is Admiral Steven Wells of the Martian Confederation." He'd paused there, but listening now he became impatient with his own recording. "We are here to take control of this system and to hold it in trust for all of the people of Earth, Mars, and the colonies." Another pause. "We have no wish to engage your forces, however we will defend ourselves if fired upon. We do not require that you surrender your vessels, only that you peacefully leave this system. Stevens out."

It would be an hour before the message reached the small Alliance squadron, and another hour before a response could return to Wells' ship. "Put the fleet on yellow alert." The Alliance ships had no chance to defeat his massively superior forces, but he wasn't about to get careless and suffer unnecessary casualties. His orders were not to fire unless fired upon, which greatly complicated his tactical options.

He couldn't imagine the Alliance ships would put up a fight; it would be suicide. But he was worried about the ground forces. He didn't know what the Alliance had down there waiting, dug into prepared positions. The transports with his fleet carried the cream of the Confederation assault troops, and he was worried they would have a fight on their hands. The ground forces were under the same orders as the fleet – fire only if fired upon. They would offer the Alliance troops repatriation, but they would fight back if attacked.

Wells sat quietly in his command chair. There was nothing to do now but wait and see what happened.

Roderick Vance sat in his office, a palatial suite built right against the central dome of the Ares Metroplex. On one side there was a panoramic view of downtown; on another the rugged red Martian landscape, slightly distorted by the clear alumina of the dome. The Confederation's capital wasn't a large city, not by Earth standards. But its seven domes were entirely devoid of the seething, crumbling slums that plagued terrestrial cities.

The nascent Confederation had faced the challenges of taming an inhospitable world, one on which it was difficult for men to survive, but it was free of the legacy problems that affected the Superpowers of Earth — poverty, decrepit ghettoes, and crumbling infrastructure. The founders of the Metroplex were able to design a modern city from the ground up rather than building onto the confused results of centuries of disorganized growth and civil strife.

Vance had been genuinely surprised when he got the communication. His visitor wasn't the last person he'd expected to see walk through his door, but she was close to it. It won't do to keep her waiting, he thought. "Show her in." He spoke to his AI, which transmitted the order to his assistant in the outer office.

A small figure, not much taller than a meter and a half, came through the door, wearing a hooded cloak that obscured her face. She stood, silent and still, until the door closed.

"Welcome, Minister Li." Vance rose from his seat, motioning to a plush chair set against the dome. "Please have a seat. May I offer you a drink?" Vance was walking toward a small enclosed bar. "Bourbon, I believe?"

"Thank you, Mr. Vance." Her voice was soft but strong, even ominous. It was clear she was used to being listened to and obeyed. "I must commend you on the accuracy of your dossiers." She slowly pulled back the cloak, revealing the lined face of an older Asian woman. "Some bourbon would be most welcome."

Li An was the First Minister of C1, the CAC's external security agency. Smart and ruthless, she was Gavin Stark's only real competition for the most feared individual on Earth. Though similar in more ways than either would care to realize, Li and Stark were bitter enemies. Stark had gotten the better of her in the final stages of the war, turning her meticulous plans into a disaster that lost the conflict for the CAC. It might have cost her everything — her power, position, even her life. But she knew enough secrets to discourage anyone from making any serious moves against her. Li An was a survivor, and she had proven it once again.

Li had spent the five years since then reestablishing her power base and helping the CAC rebuild its shattered military and economy. But most of all, she plotted her revenge against Gavin Stark. The Alliance's intelligence chief was no easy target; a genius, he was paranoid as well. It took a long time, and an enormous amount of money, but finally she had the information she needed. It was beautiful, downright poetic...she was going to pay him back in kind. She was going to destroy his own carefully constructed plan, just as he had done to hers.

Vance poured two drinks and walked across the room. He handed one to Li An and sat down in one of the other chairs. "I think you will find that a very special bourbon." He took a sip from his own drink, which was just seltzer on ice.

Li An took a small sip and gave Vance an approving smile. "Indeed, Mr. Vance, your taste in bourbon is commendable. Thank you." Then, looking at his glass: "You're not drinking? You aren't trying to gain an edge on me now, are you?" She smiled, though an expression that would have been pleasant on most people was just unnerving on her reptilian face. "Because it will take more than this glass to achieve that."

Vance returned the smile, producing a more reasonable imitation of genuine humanity. "I'm afraid my stomach is not what it used to be, Minster Li. These days I am forced to take it rather easy, at least this early in the day." In truth, Vance was never much of a drinker. Except for a partiality to certain very expensive red wines, he mostly stuck to water and the occasional iced tea and rarely drank hard liquor. He looked over at his guest inquisitively. Don't underestimate this woman, he reminded himself silently. "So what can I do for you, Minister?"

Li An took another drink and smiled. "To the contrary, Mr. Vance. The question is what can I do for you?"

Vance was silent for a moment, waiting for Li An to continue. When she remained silent, he asked, "And what is it you propose to do for me, Minister?" The CAC's spymaster did nothing without purpose, Vance knew that much.

"Well, Mr. Vance, as we both know, your government is assisting the Alliance rebels in their fight against the federal authorities." She raised her hand just as Vance was about to object. "Please, Mr. Vance, we need not play games. Let us speak hypothetically only." She smiled again, a gesture that made the hairs on Vance's neck stand up. "I have information that would be extremely useful were your government involved in aiding the rebellions. Indeed, it is something that could be extremely dangerous in many ways if it is not addressed."

"And I suppose, Minister, that you came all the way to Mars simply to share this with me." He was looking directly into her eyes; he'd swear it dropped his body temperature at least a few degrees, but he kept the stare constant. "In return for what? Nothing?"

She took another small sip, setting the glass down on the exquisitely-crafted side table next to her chair. "Let us say that while we are not in a position to intervene, we are quietly wishing the rebels success." She paused, letting her eyes drop to her glass. "But if propriety compels you to offer something in return, I would welcome a case of this excellent Bourbon."

"I do enjoy exchanging pleasantries with you, Minister Li." Vance was getting impatient, though his voice betrayed no hint of it. "But perhaps we can move to the matter you have hinted at so cryptically?"

"Certainly, Mr. Vance." Her voice was deadly serious now. "You are familiar, of course, with Rafael Samuels, are you not?"

Vance was surprised…confused as well, but he'd be damned if he was going to let her see either of those reactions. "The Commandant of the Alliance Marine Corps?"

"Yes, that is one of his positions." She took another drink, draining her glass, savoring what little she could detect of Vance's well-hidden suspense. "But he is also Number Four on the Alliance Intelligence Directorate."

Roderick Vance had a great poker face. Unemotional by nature, he found it relatively easy to remain calm and unreadable even in desperate situations. But not this time. "What?" He stared at Li, knowing his face betrayed his stunned surprise. He was normally skeptical of everything, but something told him she was telling the truth. Indeed, Samuel's defection would explain a number of things that had been puzzling him.

"I daresay you heard me, Mr. Vance." Li had a self-satisfied grin on her face. She was thrilled to be divulging Gavin Stark's big secret, and she knew Vance would use that knowledge to thwart Stark's plans. Payback is a bitch, she thought, isn't it Gavin? "I believe that General Samuels has been working with Alliance Intelligence for at least five years, though my confirmed intel does not verify a start date." She extended her arm toward Vance, handing him a small data chip. "You are too much of a gentleman to question my assertion directly." She knew he was nothing of the sort – if he didn't think she was telling the truth, he'd have let her know. "Nevertheless, I believe the evidence on that data chip will provide you the comfort level you need to take the...shall we say...appropriate actions."

Vance took the chip from Li, looking at it quizzically. "Thank you, Minister. I will review this immediately." He looked up at Li An. "This will prove extremely useful."

Li An stood up, straightening her suit jacket as she did. "Then I will take my leave, Mr. Vance. As much as I would enjoy a longer stay, I believe that both of our interests are served by maintaining the secrecy of my visit." She extended a hand toward his as he rose from his chair. "My ship is ready to leave orbit as soon as I return."

Vance took her tiny hand in his. She has a firm handshake, he thought, for a woman so small. "I agree, Minister. Discretion is called for." After a brief pause: "Perhaps on another visit we will have more time."

"That would be most agreeable." She nodded and walked briskly to the door, turning just before she left the room. "Goodbye, Mr. Vance."

"Goodbye, Minister Li." He watched her leave then went to his desk and plugged in the data chip. Rafael Samuels had just become his top priority.

In the hallway, Li An strode toward the bank of elevators, pulling her cloak over her head. And now, she thought, we shall see how badly Mr. Vance and the Confeds can damage Gavin Stark's agenda. She stepped into an empty elevator car with a self-satisfied smile on her face. And Roderick Vance owed her a favor. That was just a little bonus.

Chapter 24

Western Alliance Intelligence
Directorate HQ
Wash-Balt Metroplex, Earth

Gavin Stark was livid. He had been even colder and more intractable since Dutton's death, but this was a new level of fury, the likes of which no one present had seen before. There was a bandage wrapped around his shoulder and upper arm, his expensive suit sliced open to accommodate the dressing. His normally perfect hair was disheveled, and he hadn't shaved – the first time any of them had seen him less than perfectly groomed. He was in considerable pain, and it was doing nothing to improve his mood.

The Directorate of Alliance Intelligence was assembled, but none spoke - none dared speak. They silently watched the drama unfolding in the room. Standing against the wall were two men and a woman, all shackled and clad in white coveralls, the ones worn by inmates in the dreaded Sub-Sector C. They tried to stand straight up, but none of them managed it - they all shivered and slumped in terror.

"You do understand that your woefully inadequate security measures allowed Erik Cain and his damnable Marines to break into this building and rescue a prisoner of extreme importance, don't you?" Stark's tone was mocking, but it was deceptively gentle as well. He wasn't yelling, but there was a coldness like deep space in his voice. "He didn't penetrate your defenses and assassinate a target. No…he broke in, found a specific prisoner, and then walked out again, taking the captive with him." He glared at them as he spoke.

"The three of you were responsible for onsite security, and on your watch we suffered the greatest humiliation in the history of this organization." His voice was still measured in volume, but the menace in it was overwhelming. One of the men fell prone, his legs giving out on him. "The consequences of your incompetence are staggering, and they affect operations of crucial importance to this organization and the Alliance as a whole." He looked at them, pausing for a few seconds to glance at each, watching the terrified captives wilt under his withering gaze. "It is hard for me to imagine a punishment to match your crimes."

Stark touched the small communicator clipped to his collar. "Send him in now." The door slid open and a short, squat man walked into the room, followed by six armed guards. There were gasps around the table, and the three prisoners sank to their knees sobbing and begging for mercy. Everyone present knew who Antonio Vento was. Alliance Intelligence had many interrogators, experts in every manner of information extraction. But that isn't what Vento did. Gavin Stark's hand-picked jailor, Vento was a true psychopath who plied his trade only when the chief of Alliance Intelligence wanted to send a message. His expertise was more punishing than interrogating, and he was a master of the art.

"I don't want to see them again, Antonio." Stark didn't even look over at his prisoners as he condemned them to a horrible death.

"Understood, Number One." Vento made a motion to the guards, who moved toward the groveling and sobbing prisoners. There was silence from the Directorate members as the three unfortunates were dragged, howling and crying, into the corridor. Stark had made a point to all those assembled.

"Now we can move on to other business." Stark's voice remained calm, which was somehow more unnerving than when he yelled. "Number Three, were you successful?"

Alex Linden was the only one in the room who didn't look scared of Stark. It wasn't because she didn't fear him; anyone with even a shred of sanity feared Gavin Stark. She didn't delude herself into believing he wouldn't dispose of her as easily as any of the others...he would. But she'd managed to flawlessly execute every assignment he'd given her, and with Dutton gone, she was the closest thing to a confidante Stark had left. "Yes, Number One. Though I was pressed for time to make

this meeting, and I didn't have time to dispose of the body."
She was a little disheveled, and her face was slightly flushed.
Stark admired the poise it took to come to a meeting right from
a high-profile assassination and look as calm as she did. "I was
going to dispatch a cleanup team, but I thought you might like
to make special arrangements. He's in the usual suite at the
Willard."

"Very good, Number Three. I will attend to it." With the
escape of the real Augustus Garret, the imposter was the only
hard evidence that a switch had been made. Now that evidence
was gone, neatly disposed of before it could become a problem.
Admiral Garret could claim he was held captive, but the imposter had been seen all over Washbalt, looking just like the admiral.
Garret would look like a raving madman if he spoke out. Even
in failure, Stark tied up his loose ends. Especially in failure.

He looked out over the table, his icy gaze settling on one of
those seated, a well-dressed woman perhaps fifty years of age.
"Number Nine, I believe it has become necessary to entrust the
job of managing the security of this building to a member of
this body. Do you believe you can accept this responsibility?"

Number Nine looked like she would rather dive head first
into a nest of rattlesnakes, but she glanced up at Stark and nodded. "Of course, Number One. However you feel I may best
serve our purposes." There was no way to refuse – in Stark's
current mood any one of them could find themselves following
the three unfortunate security directors down to Sub-Sector C.
The Directorate members were awesomely powerful and feared
throughout the Alliance, but Gavin Stark ruled with an iron fist.
None of the others could stand up to him, nor did any have the
courage to try.

"Very good, Number Nine." Stark kept his gaze on her as he
spoke. "I will expect your complete report on how you plan to
revamp security procedures. I trust 72 hours will be sufficient."

It wasn't nearly enough time, she thought, but again there
was only one acceptable answer. "Yes, Number One. You will
have it."

"Very well." He winced. The pain in his shoulder was really

bothering him, and he tried, not entirely successfully, to hide it. "Number Five, what is the status of the Directorate expeditionary force sent to Columbia?"

Troy Warren was uncomfortable, as he usually was in Directorate meetings. He'd clawed his way to the top in the Megacorps, but that hadn't been enough for him. He realized that true power in the Alliance was vested in the Political Class – the Corporate Magnates were really just pampered servants. Without a Political Academy background, most routes into the government were closed off, even to someone wealthy and powerful. He saw the Directorate as his way, but now, for the first time in his life, he felt out of place, uncertain. "They are positioned in the YZ Ceti system, awaiting the arrival of the assembling battlefleet." He paused slightly. "With Admiral Compton's apparent…ah…sympathies, we have few alternatives until our fleet has defeated his. It would be imprudent to approach the system with the lightly-armed transports."

Stark's face remained unreadable. He knew all of this already – his inquiry was just a precursor to the command he was about to give. "Issue an order redirecting the force." There were surprised faces around the table, but no one uttered a word. "Governor Cooper has three full Alliance army divisions plus a brigade equivalent of Federal Police. That should be more than sufficient to defeat the rebels there." He looked out over those assembled. "And if, through some stunning incompetence, he is not successful, we will soon control space around the planet. If the insurrectionists manage to defeat Cooper, their reward will be planetary bombardment." His voice was frozen. "We are going to end this foolishness now, whatever it takes."

"Where would you like them sent, Number One?" His throat was dry, and his voice cracked a little, but otherwise he managed to sound calm and in control.

"I will provide you with detailed directives within six hours. Please act on these immediately upon receipt." Stark was not offering any further details, and no one had to stomach to ask.

"If there is no further business, we will adjourn." Stark paused, as if waiting for someone to speak up but, as always, the

Directorate members recognized that Stark had dismissed them. They filtered out of the room silently and respectfully, as always. But there was something else there…anger, even a growing hatred. Stark had always been an autocrat, but his continued successes had long kept a damper on resentment. He had always made an effort to at least pretend the Directorate was making decisions as a body, but now he barely even acknowledged their input. Without Dutton's restraining influence, Stark's growing megalomania was becoming uncontrolled. He was the most intelligent one by far, but the others were smart and capable as well. They were scared of Stark, but too much fear eventually turns into hatred, and hatred breeds a strange kind of courage. The Directorate was seething with discontent and, for once, Gavin Stark was blind to a developing threat.

Stark was in the middle of his usual post-meeting conference. It was during these smaller gatherings he felt Dutton's loss the most. He'd invited Alex this time, though there really was no compelling need for her to be there. He was futilely trying to fill the void left by his old, his only, friend. For so many years he'd casually joked about Dutton's longevity, brushing aside concerns that the old man would eventually die. Now it felt surreal to sit there, reflecting on those instances, recalling the many conversations they'd had about just this eventuality. Time was still man's nemesis, Stark thought glumly, wearing down everything and everyone.

Rafael Samuels was there as well. Soon there would be no more need for such secrecy surrounding the Marine Commandant, but right now it was still essential. The endgame was upon them; it was time to execute what they had planned for so long and to avoid any mistakes.

Stark had just told Alex about Samuels. She was stunned; suborning a Marine of such a high rank was an amazing feat, one with staggering implications. Whatever else he was, Gavin Stark was a master manipulator.

"Rafael, we will keep this short. I know your shuttle leaves within the hour." Stark was seated behind his desk as usual, with

Samuels and Alex occupying the two buttery soft leather guest chairs. "General Holm's request to meet with you on Terra Nova is a stroke of luck." Stark paused briefly, a predatory look on his face. "I hadn't anticipated that the great General Elias Holm would be kind enough to walk right into a trap for us."

Samuels smiled uncomfortably. He would be glad to have Holm out of circulation. The hero of the Marines was the biggest threat to him, the one man with enough stature to challenge his control of the Corps. But he still had regrets about this devil's bargain he had made. It was far too late to change his course, but he didn't relish the thought of ambushing Holm, no matter how advantageous it was for him. He'd do it, but he didn't like it.

"Please do try to bring him back here alive." Stark looked right at Samuels. "He could be very useful for us. For a while."

Samuels nodded, exhaling loudly as his great bulk rose slowly from the chair. "Very well, Number One. If you will excuse me, I must get down to the spaceport if I am to beat General Holm to Terra Nova."

Stark got up, leaning across the desk to shake hands with Samuels. "Good luck, Rafael."

"Thank you, Gavin. I will be back as soon as possible." Samuels nodded to Alex, who returned the silent gesture. Then he bounded through the hidden door, his usual route in and out of Stark's office.

"You decided not to tell him?" Alex had waited until Samuels was long gone before she spoke.

"Yes." Stark's tone was calm, almost relaxed now that Samuels had departed. "He is struggling enough with this whole thing. I don't need him feeling guilty because there are strike teams on the way to ambush Marine garrisons."

"Won't he be angry when he finds out you didn't tell him?" Alex was nervous. She'd be pissed if she was in Samuel's shoes, she knew that much.

"Who cares?" Stark's voice was still calm, but she felt a shiver up her spine as she listened. "Once Holm is neutralized and the key garrisons are destroyed, General Samuels will be less important to us." He looked at her with a face utterly devoid of emotion. "If he becomes a problem we will have another Seat to fill."

She just nodded. Alex was cold-blooded in many ways, but she had to keep reminding herself that Stark was a true sociopath. She controlled her emotions, subverted them to her needs. But other than his terrible temper, Gavin Stark had none at all.

"Then let's finish these assignments." He looked back down at his desk, to the figures displayed on his 'pad. "I want to get these orders to Number Five tonight. I want those strike teams on their way by this time tomorrow. It's time to deal with these Marines once and for all."

Chapter 25

The Marine Officers' Training Center
"The Academy"
Arcadia – Wolf 359 III

The Academy sprawled along the idyllic coast of Arcadia's northern continent, a pleasant, leafy enclave where the Corps had trained its officers for almost a century. Originally a single structure, the campus had grown into a complex stretching over 20 square kilometers of winding paths and stately stone buildings. It was the pride of the Marine Corps, the place where its most successful foot soldiers became its leaders.

The last few years had been troubled ones, the worst in its storied history. Late in the war the political officers arrived, acting as observers posted in all classes and assigned as counselors to the cadets. It was a massive violation of the Marine Charter, and an intrusion the cadets, combat veterans all, found difficult to accept. The staff bristled and grumbled among themselves, wondering how this could have happened. They waited for the Commandant's office to act…but that action never came.

The demobilizations after the war further sapped morale among the Academy faculty and attendees. Class sizes were drastically reduced from the record levels of the war years, and now many of the buildings were closed up, the classes held there consolidated into other half-used locations. The cadets themselves faced an uncertain future, with good postings a rare commodity in the post-war Corps. Many of the new lieutenants would be retired out of the service after graduation, their shiny new bars doing service in closets, adorning old, unused uniforms.

There was more substantive discontent too. No one expected to Corps to remain at wartime strength after the peace was signed. But it seemed to many – the ones who had fought and won the war – that the cuts were too deep, too reckless. They seemed poorly targeted, almost as if they were designed to sap morale and degrade combat effectiveness. They worried what would happen when war inevitably came again, wondered how many would die needlessly before the Corps could build itself back to its old readiness.

There was sympathy for the rebellion too. Many of the officers felt the Corps should intervene and force a cessation of hostilities on the rebelling worlds, or even declare outright for the separatists. But cooler heads had prevailed. The Commandant had ordered that there be no interference in the fighting on the rebelling worlds. The orders were resented by some, but they were obeyed.

The transport arrived late, but the gate guards followed procedure to the letter. They were undermanned that night, the work of two officers who modified the scheduling manifest before slipping quietly off base. The guards on duty were Marines, but they weren't expecting the four heavily armed agents hidden in the cargo bay. It was over in an instant of muffled gunfire. The bodies of the three ambushed Marines were hidden inside the bay of the transport as it made its way to a secluded spot on the Academy grounds.

The device was a small one, and even though it had been built in the cutting edge labs at Alliance Intelligence, it was a crude design, the apparent work of amateurs. It was a fission bomb salted with cobalt...a terrorist's weapon, perhaps 30 kilotons in yield, and very dirty.

The agents buried it. Not deeply...it didn't have to stay hidden for long. Just long enough for them to put 10 or 12 kilometers between them and the Academy. The transport turned and headed back, reaching the gate just as the alarm was sounding. The murdered guards had been missed.

It was too late. The transport blew through the gate and away from the campus. It raced down the road at 120 kph. Ten minutes later it pulled over behind a rocky outcropping, and the team leader flipped a switch.

The light reached them first, but they were ready, looking in the other direction and wearing goggles. They were far enough away that the effects of the detonation were minor. The transport shook as the shockwave hit, but again, this far out there was no real damage. The sound was loud, but not deafening, and a minute after the blast they were on their way to the rendezvous point.

They were halfway there when the capsules hidden in the transport split open and released their deadly contents. The gas was quick, almost instantaneous. In a second, perhaps two, everyone in the truck was dead. Half a minute later, the power core exploded, leaving nothing left of the vehicle larger than a few molecules.

Gavin Stark did not like loose ends.

They'd been digging in for three days. Will Thompson was everywhere, inspecting every inch of trench line, monitoring the dwindling supply of weapons and ammo, giving the troops rousing pep talks. He was the beating heart of the army, and he kept their morale high, even as his own was sagging. Things had been going very well, but he knew that was about to change. That it had already changed.

The rebel forces ran wild for several months, liberating areas previously occupied by the federals, and recruiting heavily. After their defeat at Sander's Dale, the federal forces retired to Arcadia, licking their wounds. They had to rest and resupply before were able to take the field in force again, and Will used the time to great effect.

Gregory Sanders had been notably absent during those operations. He'd gone missing at the battle and hadn't been seen in the six months since. Thompson had every inch of the battlefield searched and searched again. They hadn't found a body, but they hadn't found Sanders alive either. Will hoped the old man was a prisoner. This federal general, Merrick…he seemed to treat prisoners humanely.

Will felt the loss of Sanders keenly, both as an officer and a friend…and he felt it for Kara too. She'd been raised by her doting grandfather ever since she'd lost her parents to a transport accident. She loved the old man fiercely, and his loss had been hard. She, too, clung to the hope that he was alive in some federal prison camp in Arcadia, but it was a tenuous faith. Some days she believed it; others she didn't.

She and Will had only grown closer, though their moments together were few and rushed. His job consumed him, the army taking all he had to give and more. The responsibility, the burden...it was overwhelming. Thousands of men and women at his command, depending on his judgment and skill for their very survival. The troops loved him, and they would do whatever he commanded. It was gratifying, but it only added to the crushing stress. It was a pressure that was constant and unceasing...day, night, always.

Kara was just as busy. Production at the arms factory had slowed to a crawl. Starved for raw materials, the facility would have shut down entirely if it hadn't been for her tireless efforts. She organized teams to strip usable materials from every building and all non-essential equipment throughout the district. Her people scoured the battlefield at Sander's Dale, scavenging every broken piece of weaponry they could find. It was a varied patchwork of weapons and ammunition that flowed from her factory, but it kept the army supplied...more or less.

Kara Sanders was a patriot, completely devoted to the cause of Arcadian independence, but something else was driving her this hard. Will was out in the field with the army, risking his life every day. She felt that every gun, every round of ammunition she squeezed off that production line was something she could do to help protect him. It drove back the feelings of helpless fear that otherwise consumed her.

The disaster at the Academy had hit Will hard. He felt it as a Marine, the anger, the loss. But it was more than that. He had friends there, good friends, and they were all dead now. Almost no one on the campus had survived the horrific blast, and the few who had were badly stricken by radiation sickness. The entire area was uninhabitable, and would be for years. It had been an appalling atrocity, and no one seemed to know who had done it.

He was worried, terrified that some radical rebel group was responsible for the attack. None of his people would be involved; he was sure of that. The Marines were virtually worshipped in the colonies, which they had defended time and time again. But every cause attracted a lunatic fringe. It was a nightmare scenario, one that chilled him to his bones. But he couldn't ignore the possibility. If a rebel group had destroyed the Academy, what would the Corps do?

Thompson had seen them with his own eyes...Gordons. His heart sank as he saw the sleek craft landing in the fields around Arcadia City. The fleet of small landing sleds meant only one thing – powered infantry. For one terrifying instant he thought they were Marines. He knew the Corps would respond to the destruction of the Academy, but this was fast, too fast. Word couldn't have even reached Marine HQ yet. No, these troops were something different.

They were sloppier than Marines, their landing patterns looser, more disorganized. Whoever they were, their training wasn't up to the standards of the Corps. But he wasn't sure it mattered. There were a couple thousand of them landing, and Will had no idea how he could counter them once they moved against his forces.

Powered infantry was a danger to any non-powered force, but they were a grave threat to Thompson's raggedly equipped rebels. He needed heavy ordnance to face these new forces... artillery and assault weapons, equipment his army sorely lacked.

His forces were spread out, conducting operations over a wide area, but when he saw those landers, he issued the recall orders immediately. He wanted everything he could muster massed together. Those newcomers would be looking for a fight soon, and Will needed everything he had to face them.

He knew there would be no finesse, no elaborate strategies. Once the newly arrived troops were organized, the entire federal force would come out with one purpose...to destroy his army. Once his force was annihilated, the newborn Republic of Arcadia would be defenseless. General Merrick could systematically sweep up any remaining pockets of rebellion. The dream would die, and with it a last chance to preserve freedom. Will was determined to prevent that, no matter what the cost.

He gambled that the enemy would attack him wherever he was. He chose a fitting spot...the old Sander's Dale battlefield. He deployed the same way he had, holding the center and the two flanking ridges. Merrick was no fool; he would remember the death trap the center had become for his troops. But Will wasn't planning to fight the battle in the valley this time. Merrick's forces had almost taken the high ground south of the lowlands in the first battle, and their failure to do so led directly to their disastrous defeat. This time, Will was certain Merrick would throw his strength against the left...that was where the powered infantry would hit.

Even if he was right, he didn't know how much he could do to counter them. The ridge was wooded - partially wooded since the last battle had raged there, destroying many of the trees. The ground was steep and rocky, and the landscape was littered with shattered logs and muddy trenches, half-collapsed and partially filled with water. It was difficult ground to cross, even for armored infantry, and Thompson was going to turn it into a death trap.

They buried mines throughout the area where the fighting had been heaviest before. They only had a few of the powerful scratch-built explosive devices, but Will was hopeful they would inflict significant losses, even on the powered infantry. He was going to have his troops deployed farther back this time, and the enemy would have to come through the torn up ground and the makeshift minefield to get to them.

He reorganized the rest of the army, massing those with decent assault rifles on the left. It was a risk – if the enemy attacked anywhere else with the powered infantry, the defenders wouldn't have weapons powerful enough to penetrate their armor. But if he didn't mass his better-armed forces somewhere, he didn't have a chance of even slowing the enemy assault troops.

Everyone else dug in. All across the line his troops were deployed in trenches, along rock outcroppings, and hidden behind the shattered wreckage of vehicles and machinery from the first battle. They were vulnerable to being flanked, but again

Will was gambling. Merrick knew if he flanked Thompson, the rebel army would retire and maneuver to another strong location. The federals wanted to destroy his army, not force it from position to position...he was sure of that.

Will's instincts proved correct. The federal army advanced directly against his position. They were completely unopposed – Will didn't want any of his troops facing the powered infantry until the main battle began. The Marine vets knew what was coming, but there was no reason to get the others talking about how tough the armored troops were. The Arcadians were still a victorious army – let them focus on that, he thought, as they went into battle.

Kyle Warren stood in just about the same spot he'd occupied during the first battle, though this time he wore a star on his collar and commanded the entire left wing. With the loss of Sanders, Will needed a reliable number two, and he'd opted to move Warren up. The Arcadian command structure was in its infancy, without a clear system of seniority among the higher ranks. But it was important for the army to have a clearly designated second in command.

Warren peered over the edge of his trench, squinting into his 'scope. Kyle Warren was one of Erik Cain's veterans...he knew just what was coming and how unlikely it was that his forces could stop them. He flipped on his comlink. "Major Calvin, I need a report. Are your people all deployed?"

Ed Calvin was a Marine veteran, a sniper in an assault platoon for ten years. He was badly wounded in the first battle, but he was fully recovered and back at his post. Thompson had put him in command of all of the army's snipers and asked him to train more. Anyone with any aptitude was drafted into the new sharpshooter company, and Calvin drove them mercilessly. They were armed with the best weapons in the army, and Warren had ordered them deployed all along the enemy line of approach. It was dangerous work, but each powered infantryman they picked off was a big help.

"Yes, sir." Calvin had a deep, scratchy voice. "I have 311

troopers positioned in vantage points all along the front." He paused then added, "We'll make them pay, sir. You can count on us." Most of those 311 men and women fell far short of the training and experience of a Marine sniper, but they were all good shots armed with decent weapons. That would have to be enough.

"I know I can, Major." Warren had pushed for more discipline and military formality in the army when he moved into the number two spot. Will was a better tactician – Kyle would have admitted that in a second – but he tended to be too familiar with subordinates.

They had a different perspective. Warren had fought in several campaigns as an officer, but Thompson had done all his combat service as an enlisted man. Kyle wasn't a martinet, not by any standards, but he realized the army had grown too large to be managed informally. They were the armed forces of a planetary republic, not a band of pirates.

"And Major?"

"Yes sir?"

"No heroics." Warren's voice was firm and commanding. He'd been a little intimidated at first when Will moved him up, but he'd gotten more comfortable with it. "Your people are to take every shot they can get and then pull back before the enemy gets to them. A handful of snipers aren't going to beat the enemy by themselves, and I don't want you trying to. I just want you to bleed them…and then get your people out of there."

"Understood, sir." Calvin's rasp sounded sincere, but Warren wasn't totally convinced. The major knew as well as he did how tough a fight they were in for. Kyle could feel it in his gut – the casualty rate for the snipers was going to be high. Marines didn't like passing the problem to the next guy, and Warren was afraid Calvin was going to hang in too long trying to hurt the enemy just a little more.

"Just remember what I said. Pull back when it gets too hot." He paused. "I mean it, Ed." Will would have given me shit for that, he thought. He'd pushed for more formality, that was true, but sometimes there were exceptions. He didn't want to lose over 300 of his best troops before the battle was even in full swing.

"Yes, sir. I read you loud and clear."

"Good. Warren out." Kyle cut the link. "Good luck, Ed," he muttered to himself.

"Fucking Merrick!" Will Thompson was out of breath. He'd been running up and down the line, moving reserves back and forth. The Alliance general refused to cooperate by doing what Thompson expected him to do. So far he'd held the powered infantry completely in reserve, and he'd pushed an entire division through the center.

The Arcadian forces were strong on the flanks, but the center was only moderately held. The fortifications were heavy, but the troop concentration was light, and the reserves were inadequate. It was looking like the Feds might push right through and cut the Arcadian army in half. Unless Will ordered an attack from the ridges against the enemy flank.

"No, that's what you want me to do." Will was talking to himself as he walked back to his command post. The fighting was heavy, but he was confident his troops could hold. For a while. "No, Merrick. I'm not going to bite." He looked back over his shoulder, in the general direction of the enemy position. "If I pull those troops off the ridge you'll be on us with that armored infantry in a heartbeat." He offered up a grudging smile to his adversary. "No way."

The command post was just a rough dugout, burrowed into a small hill. It was braced with heavy logs, three of which were torn off and splintered where a shell had come close to taking out the army HQ. Thompson's staff was small, fifteen officers for an army of over 18,000. He didn't have strength to spare for much tail...he needed all the tooth he could get. Anyway, it wouldn't have helped much anyway to fill headquarters with personnel with no staff experience.

The comlinks were going crazy. Every officer in the center of the line was calling for support. They'll just have to hold on with what they've got, Thompson thought grimly. He was down to two battalions in reserve, and he was going to hold onto those to counter any enemy breakthrough.

The Arcadians were sorely pressed, no doubt. But it wasn't coming free for the federals. Merrick's troops were catching hell in the open valley as they pressed their attack against Thompson's outnumbered but entrenched forces.

"Captain Kebble, report." Will looked over at the aide, who jumped up from the readout she was focused on and snapped to attention. Will waved his hand, motioning for her to relax. "Just give me a summary, Jul...Captain." Will agreed with Warren that the army needed to operate more formally, but he was still retraining himself.

"Yes, sir." Juliana Kebble wasn't a veteran, but she took well to soldiering. Her mother and father had been murdered early in the war by federal forces under General Quinn. There had been a lot of atrocities in the early months of the conflict, and that had infused significant bitterness into the rebel cause. The federal forces had actually behaved fairly well since Merrick was able to purge Quinn and some of the other officers, and now it was actually the Arcadians who were committing most of the brutalities. Will Thompson punished any of his troops participating in atrocities against federal troops or sympathizers in the population, but some of the fringe groups were ferocious, especially to those they viewed as collaborators.

"General, the entire line is holding, but we are hard pressed at virtually every point." She started to move toward him but paused and glanced back at her 'pad one last time before she resumed. "The worst spot is virtually dead center, and it looks like the enemy is prepping another assault. Colonel Horace just reported, and his scouts have identified at least three fresh enemy battalions forming up.

"Damn." Thompson was talking to himself, but it came out louder than he'd intended.

"He has requested that reinforcements be deployed to deal with any localized breakthroughs." Kebble stood at ease...sort of. At least she wasn't rigidly at attention. "He has 20% casualties already and all his troops are in the line."

Shit. This time Thompson kept his mouth shut, and just thought it. "OK, Captain. Com Captain Bronte, and order him to detach his two best companies. I will lead them up myself to plug any gaps."

"Sir..." Kebble looked horrified, but she wasn't sure what to say.

Thompson smiled involuntarily, though he tried to hide it. "Don't worry, Captain. I've been in worse places than this. But if I'm right, we need to hold this line with what we've got. The hammer blow is still going to come on the left." He could see she wasn't convinced. Oh well, he thought, it can't be helped. This is the decisive point right now...it's where I belong. "Now go com Captain Bronte. And keep this place running until I get back."

He hopped up out of the dugout, jogging toward the rear where the two reserve battalions were stationed. It'll feel good to get back to some small unit tactics, he thought. Just like old times.

"We will clear that rabble off the ridge in twenty minutes. I doubt I will lose a man." Richard Gravis was an arrogant ass, but he was also the commander of the Directorate forces. Merrick listened to him prattle on as long as he could stand before he interrupted.

"General Gravis, we have the enemy at the breaking point in the center." He was frustrated. Merrick was the theater commander, which by any interpretation of regulations meant he was in charge. But Gravis steadfastly refused to follow his orders, making all sorts of arguments about jurisdiction and chain of command. "He will have to move forces off the ridge shortly to reinforce his center. We must be patient."

"You have been patient for far too long, General Merrick. My forces were sent here to end this outrageous rebellion once and for all."

Merrick took a deep breath. He was angry, so angry he could barely control it. This little shit was worse than Quinn, he thought, and that was saying something. "General, if you attack before the enemy reinforces the center you will suffer needless casualties." He took another breath, trying to maintain his calm as he tried fruitlessly to get the Directorate general to listen. "We must preserve our forces. Whatever you think, this rebellion will not be crushed today. No matter what happens in the battle."

"General Merrick, the fact that your forces have been unable to achieve a knockout victory is immaterial. But my troops are going to attack now, and we will destroy the rebel army…and with it, the rebellion." Gravis stepped back and gave Merrick a lazy salute before he turned and walked away.

"God damned fool." Merrick spoke under his breath, but he didn't really care if Gravis heard him or not. The armored infantry would probably break through on the ridge. The rebels didn't really have anything to face them. But Gravis was going to have more trouble than he thought; Merrick was sure of that. He'd faced this army before, and he knew they weren't going to just roll over. Not even for powered infantry. Not for anyone.

"Here they come." Kyle Warren had moved forward, much farther than prudence allowed, and he could see the armored troops moving on the position. "Sloppy." Warren had served under Erik Cain and Darius Jax, and he was sure either of them would have had a stroke if their troops looked like the ones approaching his position.

"Sloppy yes, but there are a lot of them." Ed Calvin was lying next to Warren looking through his 'scope. "They're bunching, that's for sure. Should make a good target."

Warren was sprawled on the ground, peering into his own 'scope. "That sure looks like Marine armor though." He took his face from the 'scope and looked at Calvin. "Your snipers don't have atomic-powered mag rifles. They're going to have to hit them in the vulnerable spots to even penetrate." He let out a deep breath. "Remind your people to focus and make every shot count."

"Yes, sir." Calvin had lowered his own 'scope and angled his head to return Warren's gaze. "Shouldn't you be getting back to the command post, sir?"

"I don't need a minder, Major." Warren had to suppress a smile. He thought about Erik Cain, who was not an officer easily convinced to stay behind at headquarters. The example Cain had set was a commander ready to jump into the middle of the maelstrom, and Warren had followed in those big footsteps.

"Sorry, sir." Calvin sounded a little chastised, but he still pressed the point. "But we need you, and we can't risk losing you in the first skirmish. You need to be more careful this time." Warren had been wounded twice in the first battle, not far from the very spot they occupied.

Calvin was technically insubordinate, but Warren understood his motivation…and he was right. It was irresponsible to take crazy risks when he had almost 7,000 troops under his direct command. "I want continual updates, major."

"Understood, sir."

Kyle turned and headed back toward the rear. He was about halfway to the command post when he heard the shooting start. He had to resist the urge to spin around and rush back up to the front line, but he forced himself to continue. Calvin was a good officer – he'd handle things.

The Directorate troops were surprised. General Gravis had sent two battalions to take the southern ridge. They'd expected to march forward in their powered armor and gun down the terrified rebels as they fled. But things didn't work out that way.

First, the woods were full of snipers, hidden in trees, behind rocks, in dips in the ground. Their fire was accurate, and while their weapons had difficulty penetrating the armor, they were scoring hits. The federal force had at least 40 troops down already. Most were just wounded, and their suits' trauma control systems would probably save them, but the intensity of the resistance was unexpected.

As soon as they spotted a sniper's general location, the armored Feds tore it apart with their superior firepower. The Feds had magnetic assault rifles powered by their suits' nuclear plants. A tree was no cover against that kind of fire, and a two second burst would shatter even the 100-meter tall Arcadian giants.

The snipers kept on the move, firing once, maybe twice from each location before heading out. If they stayed too long they were spotted, and if they were spotted they were killed.

The federals were well trained, but this was their first combat experience. Their expectation of invulnerability was giving way to the grim realities of war. The troopers maintained their order and continued to advance, but their swagger was gone. They advanced more cautiously, which only served the Arcadians' purpose, giving the snipers a few more shots before they had to withdraw.

Calvin was positioned back a little from the initial point of contact, but the enemy was rapidly closing on his location. He was behind a massive boulder, good cover against even the assault rifles of the Directorate troops. There was a rough line of rock outcroppings here, each 2-3 meters high. He'd positioned troops behind them, creating a thin battle line.

The Feds had taken losses, but his snipers were losing even more heavily. They'd scored hundreds of hits, but only a small percentage struck a vulnerable spot on the target. Their weapons just weren't powerful enough to deal with the enemy's armor. But every sniper who gave up his location was targeted with thousands of incoming rounds, any one of which would wreak havoc on human flesh. At least half of the forward-deployed sharpshooters had been lost; the rest were withdrawing, trying to reach the line before they were spotted and picked off.

Calvin was hoping the heavier fire from his deployed line would hold up the enemy a little longer. His forces had bled the enemy, but not enough. He was going to try to hold here, at least for a few minutes. They had to take down more of these armored troops. Then his force would retreat, and hopefully the Feds would follow…right into the carefully prepared minefield.

"They are running!" Lieutenant Simone Bourne shouted into her comlink. Her platoon was on point, and they'd been exchanging fire with the rebel line for twenty minutes. Her people had been pinned down by enemy fire, but now the rebels were pulling back. A Marine platoon would have rushed the enemy position, relying on speed and their armor protection. But none of her people – including herself – had ever been in combat before. It's one thing to know intellectually that most of the enemy weapons can't hurt you and quite another to jump up and run into that fire.

She had casualties; three of her people were down. A lot more had been hit, but their armor had deflected the incoming rounds. She had no idea what they had done to the enemy. The damned rebels were in heavy cover, ensconced behind a row of enormous rocks.

They'd been there for fifteen minutes before Captain Ferry had thought to order them to attack with grenades. The grenade launchers were built into the armor; they'd trained extensively with them, and they were designed for just this type of situation. She popped off six herself, the same as everyone in the platoon. The ground behind the rock outcroppings erupted into smoke and flames, with dust and debris flying everywhere. After the second round impacted she could see the enemy pulling back, running through a section of sparse woods to the rear. The grenades were minimally damaging to an armored target, but they could wreak havoc on unprotected troops.

"Second Company, pursue." It was Captain Ferry on the comlink.

"OK, first platoon, you heard the captain." Her voice was shrill. She was scared, but her blood was up too. The enemy was on the run now, she thought. The rest will just be mopping up. "Let's go, First Platoon." She raced forward, trying to remember the training, how to handle the enhanced power of her armored legs. Several members of the platoon got too excited, taking big bounding steps and landing off balance. Two of them managed to damage their suits enough that they were out of action, but the rest swept forward.

They climbed over the enemy's rock outcroppings, pausing for an instant to fire at the retreating troops. They continued in pursuit, moving three times the speed of the unarmored Arcadians, quickly closing the distance.

Then the explosions started. The first was just to Bourne's left. She saw it peripherally, and her AI replayed the whole thing from the side cam in her helmet. One of her troopers stepped forward and the ground erupted around him. The explosion was a big one, strong enough to tear his armored body apart. She was about to order the platoon to halt when she heard another explosion. Then another.

All along the line the federal troopers were triggering the heavy mines, and most of those who stepped on one of the big explosives died. There weren't that many mines, but the inexperienced Directorate troops became disordered and began to panic. Bourne tried to keep her troops in line, but she'd lost three to the mines, and the rest started to fall back.

"Stand fast!" She screamed into the comlink, her voice raw and uneven. But her troops continued retiring to the line of rocks, taking position there. At least they're not running, she thought. Her AI displayed the battlefield schematic, and she could see that at least half of the platoons in the front line were in wholesale flight.

This was not what she'd expected battle to be like.

"They're breaking through, Kyl...General Warren." Major Calvin had taken command of the two leading battalions when both of their commanders went down. His forlorn hope had done its job, but he had barely one in three of his original 311 snipers still with him.

There's no way to hold them, Warren thought grimly. They've got too much of a material advantage. His people had blooded the Directorate troops; that was true. Kyle doubted any of them would ever forget their first encounter with a "rebel" army. The best he could figure, the two leading federal battalions had lost half their numbers. But the Feds had just thrown in two fresh battalions, and Warren had used up all his tricks. The mines were gone, the snipers almost wiped out. All he had left was a battleline of troops armed with popguns that had almost no chance of taking down fully-armored infantry.

"Alright, Major Calvin." Warren was rock solid. He knew this was coming; he never thought they could actually stop the Feds. They'd done more damage to the enemy than he'd dared to hope, and now it was time to get out of here. "I want you to take charge. I want you to conduct a fighting withdrawal. I've got to coordinate with General Thompson, but the plan is to retire through the Cordia swamps. The armored Feds will have a bitch of a time following us there. We'll regroup on the other side."

"Yes, sir." Calvin sounded tired, but otherwise just as solid as Warren. "I don't think they're all that fired up to chase us, sir."

Warren allowed himself a brief grin. "No, probably not. Your troops did a tremend…"

"General Warren, sir!" A voice burst in on Warren's com-link. It was high-pitched and shrill…almost panicked. "General Warren!"

"Warren here." It sounded like Jasper Logan. Why was Will's aide comming him? "Logan? Calm down and report."

"Sir, we need you here. Please come here right away." Logan sounded almost irrational. "It's General Thompson, sir. Please come now."

"Logan?" There was no response. "Logan…report!" Still nothing.

Kyle turned to face Calvin. "Ed, take command. Get our people out of here."

"Yes, sir." Calvin was struggling to maintain his cool demeanor. His mind was racing, but it would do no good to fire questions at Warren when he knew the general didn't have any answers. "I'll take care of it, sir."

"Thanks, Ed." Warren's face was grim as he jogged down the path that led to the valley.

It was only later that Warren was able to piece together what happened. Half a dozen troopers had seen it, though each of them remembered it slightly differently. The enemy had broken through twice in the center, and both times Will had led his two companies in a counterattack, driving the exhausted and disordered federals back.

He'd just ordered up a third company to replace losses when a new enemy attack pierced the line barely two hundred meters from his position. His forces were depleted now, and the breakthrough was substantial. It was a much tougher fight, and in the end it came down to a close range struggle with pistols and even knives. Will was in the center of the action, and he killed at least ten enemy troopers. His example rallied his exhausted soldiers and they stood fast, beating back the superior federal forces.

The fight was just about over when it happened. The shooting had stopped, and Will was directing his troops to start gathering the wounded. That's when the accounts began to differ. Some witnesses say Will was leaning over to give a wounded federal soldier a drink. Others saw him drop something and bend over to pick it up.

Whatever the prelude, they all agreed on what happened next. A wounded federal grabbed his assault rifle and leveled it at Will. No one seemed to know if Will didn't see or if the wily veteran's combat instincts finally failed him and he froze. The rifle's muzzle flashed one time, and the round hit Will in the chest from less than two meters away.

His body was blown back by the force of the shot, and he fell on a small patch of torn up grass and mud. The Fed was riddled with fire from half a dozen directions, but it was too late...the damage was done.

Will was sprawled out on the grass, open eyes staring up at Arcadia's hazy red sun. There was a huge gash on his chest, his uniform soaked with blood. He was surrounded by his soldiers, hardened veterans now unable to hold back the tears from watery eyes.

They tried to talk to him, but Will was far away. Crawling through the garbage strewn streets of the South Philly Flats, back in the wardroom on the Guadalcanal playing cards, walking along the banks of the Concord River with Kara. Kara...he could see her face...blurry, distant. He tried to call out to her, but his throat was full of blood and there were no words.

The troops closest to him were on their knees, desperately trying to bind the hideous wound, but it was hopeless. His lips moved, and blood spurted from his mouth. Then he took one last breath, and he was gone.

William Thompson, the hero of the rebellion and the heart and soul of the army, was dead.

Chapter 26

Phobos Transfer Station
Orbiting Sol IV (Mars)
Martian Confederation

Cain was exhausted. They'd flown him here on a Torch, a Martian transport that was the fastest ship in space. It accelerated full halfway, decelerated the rest and reached Mars orbit in less than 36 hours. No freefall, no low g maneuvers...just full out blasting the entire way. Sitting strapped in an acceleration couch pumped full of pressure-equalization drugs wasn't fun under any circumstances – with a barely-treated deep tissue shoulder wound it was hell. He was pale and haggard when he staggered out into the station's arrival pavilion.

He knew it had to be important. As soon as they made it back to the Martian embassy, he got the word – he had to go to Mars immediately. No explanation, just a cryptic coded communication marked with a V. Vance. Cain wasn't a trusting sort, not by any measure, but the Martian industrialist and spy had done right by them so far, delivering on every promise he'd made. That was enough to get Cain on a shuttle without delay, the doctor tagging along to tend his wound as they drove to the spaceport.

He still couldn't quite process the fact that they'd gotten Admiral Garret out. Cain hadn't thought twice about taking the mission, but deep down he didn't really think they would make it. He knew they had to try, and that was enough for him. But they had actually managed it, despite odds he knew had been incalculably daunting. They had three dead and three wounded, heavy losses from a force of 11 men and women...but not too bad for a supposed suicide mission.

If Vance's people managed to get Garret off Earth like they promised, it would change everything. There wasn't a doubt in Cain's mind that the entire navy – or at least most of it – would rally to Garret, whatever course of action he chose. He wasn't sure the admiral had been a major rebel sympathizer, but his experiences in Washbalt had to shape his point of view about the Alliance and the merits of the conflict. Erik was sure that whatever the admiral chose to do, it would be helpful to the struggling colonists.

"General Cain, welcome to Phobos." Erik turned to face a tall man, about his own age, sandy haired and dressed in the jet black uniform of the Confederation Marines. "It is a great pleasure to meet you." The man extended his hand. "I am Colonel Linus Wagner. I have been a great follower of your career."

"Thank you, colonel. You are too kind." Cain extended his arm, shaking hands with Wagner as he spoke.

"I sincerely wish we had time to get acquainted, but I'm afraid my orders are to escort you without delay." He motioned toward a corridor opposite the entry hatch from the ship.

Cain just nodded and followed his new acquaintance toward the corridor. Wagner led him to the first door off the main concourse and placed his hand on a small scanner on the wall. The door slid open. "As I said, general, it was a pleasure to meet you, even so briefly. Your party is waiting." He gestured toward the open portal.

"Thank you again, colonel. Perhaps another time we can sit and talk shop, so to speak." Erik nodded and walked through, the door closing immediately behind him.

"I have to apologize for dragging you up here so quickly after that amazing rescue mission you pulled off."

Cain wasn't at all surprised to see Roderick Vance sitting on one end of a large leather couch. Behind him was a large clear panel with a view of the rocky surface and, beyond, a glimpse of Mars itself, a hazy orange crescent visible just to the left of Vance's head.

"In our brief acquaintance, you do not seem to be one to overreact. I was intrigued – which is a nice way to say unnerved – by the urgency of your unexpected message." Cain walked over, taking a seat at the other end of the couch when Vance motioned toward it. "I therefore assume that some fresh disaster has befallen us. As tempted as I was to try and ignore more bad news, I've never been good at putting my head in the sand."

Vance smiled. Despite his extensive business holdings and the demands of both his public and private professions, the Martian was somewhat of a misanthrope who enjoyed solitude far more than the company of most people. But he genuinely liked Cain. The plainspoken Marine wasn't fake like most people; that much Vance had seen from the beginning. He got the impression that Cain tolerated people almost as uncomfortably as he himself did.

"Well, General Cain, by most standards what I have to tell you qualifies as bad news, though the fact that we have discovered it offers the opportunity to avert disaster. Indeed, it explains some things that, until recently, had me stumped." Just tell him, Vance thought to himself. "General Rafael Samuels has been suborned by Alliance Intelligence. He has even been granted a secret Seat on the Directorate." Vance looked intently at Cain, expecting an argument or at least shock. But Cain surprised him.

"I should have seen that myself." He looked a little sad, but not at all surprised. "It's just that I really don't want to think that kind of thing could happen in the Corps." His shoulder had been throbbing, but now he forgot about it entirely as he considered Vance's news. He was thinking about the overall strategic implications, but then he remembered. "General Holm. I've got to get to General Holm. He's on his way to meet with Samuels. He has no idea he's walking into a trap."

"Indeed." Vance's voice was calm as usual, but there was an undercurrent of concern there. "Thus the urgency in getting you here. We must get to the general and advise him of this news. It is impossible to predict what will happen if he reaches that meeting unwarned. None of the likely prospects are favorable." His eyes bored into Cain's. "I have ordered the ship that brought you here placed at your disposal. It is the fastest thing in space. Your backup teams are boarding now."

Cain had assembled two additional teams for the Garret rescue mission, but Vance had only been able to get Cain and the one group smuggled to Washbalt. The others had been waiting on Mars, enjoying the not inconsiderable hospitality of Roderick Vance. Now they would have their chance at some action.

Erik rose painfully from the couch. "Well, Mr. Vance, I should be on my way. There is no time to waste if I am going to intercept the general before he gets to the meeting on Terra Nova."

Vance rose also. "Your vessel is still being fueled for the voyage. It will be at least another 2-3 hours before you will be able to depart. Long enough for me to get you something to eat... and have my own doctor look at that shoulder. Perhaps he can do something to ease your discomfort at higher g forces."

"Thank you, Mr. Vance. I will accept on both counts." Erik considered himself a pretty hardass Marine, but his shoulder hurt like hell, especially under acceleration, and he'd take any help with that he could get. And he was starving. The voyage to Mars had been so uncomfortable he hadn't eaten a thing.

"Excellent." Vance moved toward the door, motioning for Erik to follow. "If you'll come with me we'll tend to both matters." He turned back to face Cain. "Then you can go rescue General Holm."

Terra Nova was the first world colonized by man outside his own solar system. At the close of the Unification Wars, most of the Superpowers had outposts there, so the planet – along with the entire Centauri system – was demilitarized by the Treaty of Paris. Terra Nova itself was divided into zones, one for each of the Superpowers.

At the time it was expected Terra Nova would become a paradise, an unspoiled world with an amazing climate and tremendous untapped resources. The reality had turned out somewhat differently. The early colonists quickly discovered a number of unexpected problems, including variable but significant radiation levels and a particularly troublesome set of local pathogens. The rapid discoveries of new and more accommodating worlds put a brake on the development of Terra Nova, and the planet had become a moderately seedy collection of small cities and transport depots.

Colonists had been attracted by opportunities that never developed and, once there, they were stuck. Terra Nova's cities were mostly low-income slums, packed with seething masses of colonists – people whose families had been middle class on Earth but now lived like Cogs in the violent ghettoes of a colony gone wrong.

The Centauri system was a busy nexus, though, and the orbital installations crowding the space around Terra Nova were a different story, humming with constant activity. With six warp gates to the Sol system's two, Alpha Centauri was man's gateway to the stars, and enormous traffic passed through every day.

Holm's shuttle docked with one of the main Alliance orbital facilities, a massive space station containing cargo holds, meeting rooms, restaurants, even two hotels. He was wary – he knew something was going on with Samuels, but he had no idea what. If the Commandant was being pressured somehow, it was possible, even likely, that their meeting would be watched. Holm reminded himself to be careful as he waited for the hatch to open.

He gripped the handrails as he eased out of the zero gravity of the shuttle's docking portal into the artificial gravity of the station. It was a transition people found difficult to execute the first couple times, but Holm had been traveling in space for forty years, and it was all second nature to him.

He had two aides with him, both fully armed, but that was miniscule protection, and he knew it. He'd have preferred a full strike team – he didn't like walking into an unknown situation almost defenseless. But there was no way around that; not without tipping off anyone who was watching.

He walked onto the deck of the station, a loose section of metal grating rattling under his feet. He took a few steps forward, hearing the whoosh as the shuttle doors shut behind him. He stood in the empty compartment, alone with his two aides for perhaps thirty seconds, and then the hatch to the main station concourse opened up and armed men and women poured into the landing bay, at least twenty of them, with weapons drawn.

Holm felt a rush of adrenalin, his battle instincts kicking in. But he knew he was trapped, and fighting now would be futile. His mind raced, rapidly analyzing the possibilities. He decided to play along; maybe there'd be an opportunity later. He stood still and unthreatening, motioning for his aides to do the same.

The gunmen wore generic gray jumpsuits with no insignia and helmets with visors down. The apparent leader walked up to Holm, his hand slowly moving to his helmet, raising the dark visor to reveal his face.

"So, we've captured the famous General Elias Holm!" He turned and ran his eyes around the room before pulling off his helmet and looking right at the general. "The special action teams at your service, sir."

Holm looked like he'd seen a ghost, but the shock lasted for just a moment, before his stunned expression gave way to a broad smile. "Erik! What are you doing here?"

Cain smiled back, letting some of his tension drain away. Not all of it – they still had to get off the station and out of the system. But at least they'd gotten to Holm first - he hadn't been at all sure they'd get here in time. And if they hadn't gotten here first, he didn't think they had much chance of pulling off another rescue mission into Alliance Intelligence HQ.

"We're here for you, sir." Cain was gesturing to his troopers as he spoke, directing them to cover the doorway. "I have a lot to tell you, but I think you trust me by now, so I suggest we get out of here first."

Holm could feel the tension from Cain, and he could only imagine the issues they were facing. "Yes, I suppose I trust you by now." He smiled, mildly sarcastic. "A little."

Cain smiled. "Come on, sir." He gestured toward the door. "We need to get to our ship. It's not far."

"We can take my shuttle, Erik." Holm pointed over his back, toward the closed hatch. "Your crew will all fit."

"No, sir." Cain was already moving toward the door, weapon at the ready. "We've got something fast waiting. Really fast." He glanced back at Holm. "We may need to outrun whatever they send after us."

Holm just nodded. Erik Cain knew what he was doing. He took his pistol out of the holster and held it at the ready, and he followed Cain out into the corridor.

"We have some work to do, sir." Cain spoke softly as he made his way down the hallway cautiously. "We have to rally the Corps."

Chapter 27

Coastline North of Weston
Columbia - Eta Cassiopeiae II

The orange sun was setting slowly over the rocky coastline, soft light rippling off the gentle waves. Night was coming, but the noisy activity continued unabated, as it had for a week now. Transports arrived day and night from Weston, bringing the equipment of war to the invasion force. The operation had been plagued by difficulties from the beginning – logistical problems, poor organization, and constant raids by the rebels. The invasion date had been pushed back twice, and Cooper had ordered that it would not be changed a third time.

The Columbian seas were a treasure trove of valuable resources, and a large fleet of submersibles explored those oceans and harvested the most valuable materials. Early in the war Marek had ordered this armada pressed into service and armed. Now, the waters around the main rebel stronghold on Carlisle Island were patrolled around the clock. The fleet had also allowed the rebels to insert strike teams anywhere along the coast, something they had been doing with great effect since the beginning of the rebellion.

After Jax's raid took out the atmospheric fighters, the federals deployed a large force to hunt down his team. Outnumbered 20-1 by the forces pursuing him, Jax kept on the move and continued his hit and run campaign, taking out one target after another and slipping away before the enemy could trap his small group. Finally, hemmed in and worn down by losses, he'd had no choice but to withdraw to Carlisle Island, joining the rebels for the final defense of their stronghold.

Jax's disruptive tactics had delayed the federals for months, buying the rebels a bit more time, but the hard fact was they were losing. The rebellion on Columbia had gone fairly well at first, but the federals had poured in troops and equipment until they overwhelmed the Columbians. Slowly, steadily, the entire planet had been pacified…all except Carlisle Island.

The Martians had made a second supply drop, which included some heavy weapons as well as desperately needed ammunition. Jax had managed to transmit coordinates, and the Martians were able to land most of the supplies on Carlisle Island or in the nearby waters.

The rebels had known there was some type of expeditionary force giving the federals fits, but when Jax set foot on Carlisle, Marek looked as if he'd seen a ghost. He and Anton had served under Jax on Carson's World during the climactic battle on the Lysandra Plateau. His shock was only increased when he saw Sarah step out of the ATV right after the giant colonel. Marek and Jax had been badly wounded on Carson's World, and Sarah Linden had saved them both. It was a surreal reunion, but a joyful one.

The arrival of Jax and his veterans gave the Carlisle Island defenders a much needed morale boost. They had been trapped on the island for months now, unable to even continue raiding the vastly superior federal forces. Arlen Cooper had pacified most of the planet, inflicting severe punishments on areas that had supported the rebellion and imprisoning thousands in his concentration camps. The remnants of the rebel army bristled at the inaction, but they lacked the strength to do anything. Even with Jax's troops and supplies, there was little they could do but wait for the final assault…and make the federals pay a price when they came.

"Tonight." Jill Winton's voice was cold, dripping with venomous hate. "We move tonight." Like everyone in the camp, she was filthy and malnourished, her hair crusted with mud, tattered clothes hanging loosely on her emaciated frame. But she had found sustenance in her hatred of the federals, and it kept her going…it kept her warm.

"It's too soon, Jill." Tyler Hanson spoke softly, tentatively. Since Jill had formed the resistance cell in the camp she'd become driven and merciless. Few of her people had the guts to question her, but Hanson worked up the courage to speak.

"We're not ready."

She looked at him, her eyes blazing. "There is no more time." She stared at him with such intensity he wilted under the withering gaze. "We do it tonight."

They'd been planning this for months, building up their numbers, hiding what bits and pieces of scrap they could use as weapons. Waiting could accomplish nothing; it could only get them caught. They will sit and plan forever, she thought with disgust. But it is time for action.

Tonight the camp would rise. Tonight they would kill the guards, with bare hands if need be. No longer would they huddle together like sheep, waiting to be selected for execution or die from the exposure and mistreatment. Now they would extract the price in blood for all those who had suffered and died.

She knew Tyler and the others were worried, concerned about how many people would die. But that wasn't a consideration for Jill. She knew things would be bloody, but hurting the federals was all that mattered to her. They were a disease, an infestation...and she would do anything in her power to destroy them. Anything.

The federals had gone too far, they had left these people nothing. Not hope, not even self-delusion. They were virtually dead men and women already, half-starved, stripped of all dignity, suffering an existence that had no value. What did it matter if they died under the guns? They had nothing left to lose, and vengeance to gain.

Yes, they would strike.

The guns were lined up along the coast, all the heavy artillery batteries from the Alliance army divisions. Cooper had lost his atmospheric fighters to that cursed Jax and his raiders. They had been thorough too, blowing every one of the planes to bits. Even worse, he couldn't get more...he couldn't get anything. That traitor Compton had not only refused him support, he and his treacherous fleet had blockaded Columbia, cutting off Cooper's supplies and reinforcements.

The artillery hadn't been much use yet; it was heavy and too immobile for the type of war they had fought. But the rebel seagoing fleet controlled the 16 kilometers of open water between the mainland and Carlisle Island, and without his fighters to engage the enemy submersibles, the job had fallen to the gunners.

The guns had opened up before dawn, bombarding the southern coast of Carlisle, targeting the rebel rocket launchers and defenses. Most of the emplacements were heavily fortified, but the constant shelling sapped morale and scored an occasional hit.

The first transports left four hours later, carrying the initial wave of assault troops. They would suffer heavily, this first group, but the rebel submersibles and rocket batteries would give up their positions when they fired, and when they did the artillery would make them pay.

The hovercraft glided in swiftly, just over the waves. The submersibles were waiting to intercept them, and they began to surface, firing rocket barrages at the incoming formations. The rebel vessels had not been built as warships; they were hastily-armed civilian craft. They had to surface to fire, and when they did they became easy targets for the big guns. Their crews weren't experienced military, but they were well aware of the risks. They were a forlorn hope, there to pick away at the enemy, to damage them enough to give their friends and comrades a chance, however fleeting, to hold the last stronghold of the rebellion.

Kevin Clarkson stood in the small control room of his submersible. He'd inherited The Blue Lady from his father, who had named her for Kevin's mother. Ellen Clarkson was still alive, and she still wore blue almost every day, though she could never have imagined her namesake vessel would one day go to war. The ship had provided two generations of the family with a very comfortable living. The work was hard, and it could be dangerous as well, but it was lucrative.

Now, Blue Lady was the flagship of a small fleet, and Clarkson was the commander of that fleet. All the ships had been modified, the specialized equipment they used to scour the seas for resources torn out, replaced by whatever weapons systems could be improvised.

The hovercraft were sitting ducks at this range, and the massive rocket barrage took down more than half. A few were direct hits that blew the hulking transports apart, showering burning wreckage across the churning waves. But the rockets weren't precision weapons, and most of the hits were glancing or peripheral impacts that disabled a craft, causing it to spiral down and crash into the water.

The elation of the submersible crews was short-lived. The surviving transports painted the now-surfaced ships with laser sights, relaying the targeting data back to the artillery batteries. In less than 30 seconds there were heavy shells landing all around the submersibles. Clarkson ordered the fleet to dive, but they had to retract the rocket launchers before they could submerge. Blue Lady made it, though she suffered significant damage before she did. More than half the ships were less lucky, some blown apart by direct hits, others crippled by damage from nearby explosions. Only three remained fully operational. The invasion force had paid a price, but now the sea route to Carlisle was clear.

Jax took cover in a cavern along the rocky cliffs on the southern Carlisle coast. The shelling was relentless, the heavy explosive rounds impacting all around. The south cliffs were too difficult for the invasion force to navigate – they'd go around and hit the eastern or western beaches. But the rocky heights offered the best vantage points for the rebel missile launchers… the last line of defense before the invaders set foot on the island. The rebels needed to take out as many troop transports as they could, but the federal artillery was making that difficult.

Jax and Dave Sawyer had come over to direct the missile launchers personally. They moved over some of their experienced heavy weapons crews to replace Marek's less seasoned teams. They had to make the first shots count…the incoming artillery fire was only going to get worse when they gave up their own positions by launching.

"These damned things are too heavy. They take forever to move." Jax was frustrated. Normally he'd have his crews fire once, maybe twice, then pack up and move to a secondary position. Of course, typically his troops would be suited up and have no problem throwing 500-kilo rocket launchers over their soldiers. That was a harder proposition using only the flesh and blood muscles they were born with. He'd doubled the crew sizes, assigning two of Marek's people to two of his veterans. That would let them move the things, but it would still be slow going, taking vital firepower offline while they hoisted the bulky launchers over the steep rocky ground. There was no way to move after every shot or two, not while maintaining the volume of fire they needed. Jax had to compromise, and he ordered each launcher to take five shots and then bug out. It was better than remaining stationary, but five shots was more than enough time for the artillery to target a position and blast it. He was afraid his rocket crews had some hard duty ahead.

"They're a bitch, sir." Sawyer was fairly plainspoken. "But I think you're right about moving them after five shots. It will cut down firepower, but if we leave them stationary they'll all be knocked out in twenty minutes."

Jax looked down at his foot as he kicked a pile of small stones. "We need a rotation though. I don't want every launcher relocating at the same time."

"We can have half the launchers hold fire until the other half move." Sawyer looked up at Jax, squinting and putting his hand to his forehead. The early morning sun was rising bright just behind the colonel's head. "But that will cut our initial output. They'll get transports through, no question."

"Dave, they're getting transports through no matter what we do." Jax moved to the side, turning so his companion could look at him without staring into the sun. "We just need to wear them down as much as possible." He looked out over the sea as he spoke. He didn't have any reports on losses to the fleet, but he knew the fragile submersibles most likely suffered heavily. They shattered the federal first wave, though…so badly that Jax and Marek agreed to withhold fire from the missile launchers as the survivors approached the island. The plan was to stay in cover and hit the transports of the second wave with everything they had. If all went well, the first wave troops would be overwhelmed on the ground before they were reinforced.

"Troop transports incoming." Sawyer turned instinctively to look out over the ocean, though he knew the approaching craft wouldn't be visible yet. "At least a few of the submersibles survived...I'm getting reports from three different ships."

"Ok, let's make this count." Jax reached out and put his hand on Sawyer's shoulder. "This is your show, Dave. You're in charge here. Marek and I agree." Sawyer had been a heavy weapons man for years in the Corps before he got bumped up to platoon sergeant. He had a lot more experience with this sort of thing than Jax...and certainly than any of Marek's people.

"Yes, sir." Sawyer turned to face Jax, but only for a second. Then his head snapped back to the sea, his eyes scanning the horizon. "I'll do my best, sir."

Jax smiled. "I know you will." Time for me to leave, Jax thought, and show him he really is in charge. "I'm going to the north command post. I need regular reports." He started walking slowly down the gravel path.

"Yes, sir." Sawyer's voice was distant, distracted. He was already planning his attack. "Attention heavy weapons teams. This is Sawyer. Odd numbered teams will fire on my command. Even numbers are to remain inactive. Repeat, evens, do nothing to give away your position until the odds have fired five rounds."

He got a rapid series of acknowledgements. "Odds, shout out your targets as you fire. I don't want everybody shooting at the same transports." Sawyer was used to sophisticated AI-assisted targeting systems. If this had been a Marine op, they'd have the AI feeding each team its assigned targets based on range and trajectory. But the rebels didn't have that kind of equipment. Even the launchers themselves were old out-of-date units, probably bought surplus for the Columbia militia. They needed visual sighting to get a lock, which meant they'd only get a few shots at each craft as it flew by.

Sawyer could see a slight glint in the sky...then another. "Here they come." He shouted the warning into the comlink, but it wasn't necessary. His veteran crews were already firing.

"Sam, get outside." Sarah's voice was calm and cool, though most of the people around her were panicking. "Now. There are more barges coming in. I need you on triage." The hospital was full of wounded, and it was just getting worse. The fighting was heavy across the island, and wounded were pouring in.

"I'm on it, Sarah." Samantha Jordan was just as steady. The two were veterans of the Carson's World campaign, which was as close to a living nightmare as either of them was likely to come. Sarah Linden's field hospital had worked miracles despite being overrun with wounded. As crazy as things were here, they were nothing like Carson's World. At least not yet.

Sarah's white suit was soaked in blood, her arms wrist deep inside a patient as she barked out orders. As usual, she thought...though at least we don't have to cut them out of their wrecked armor with plasma torches this time. They were short on supplies, though, and it was approaching the critical point.

She was frustrated. They were going to lose a lot of people here...people she could save with the right equipment and supplies. But she had no critical care units, no evac, no backup, no resupply. It was the waste of it all that got to her. She knew the reasons for this fight; she even agreed with them. She knew soldiers too. Her friends, her lover, everyone important to her... they were all combat Marines. She was a Marine too. She understood the reasons they fought. But every time she found herself neck deep in bleeding, broken bodies all she could see was the horrific, stupid waste of it all.

She was too busy to keep track of the battle, but she knew the rebels were being pushed back. The hospital was on the Rock, a small, heavily fortified island just off the north coast of Carlisle. The deep caverns there were the safest place to keep the wounded, so that's where she'd set things up.

"It's bad out here, Sarah." Sam's voice on the comlink. "I think these wounded are from the missile crews. Looks like they were shelled pretty heavily. Some of them are in rough shape."

Sam was a veteran. If she said it was bad, it was bad. "OK, get the most urgent cases in here now." She paused. "Sam, remember we don't have any crit care units." She hesitated again, not wanting to say what she had to say. "You're going to have to segregate the hopeless cases. If we can't save them we need to preference the ones who have a chance."

"Sarah…" Sam's voice was somber, troubled. "Yes, I understand." She didn't like it, but she knew Sarah was right. "I'll take care of it."

Sarah didn't answer. As far as she was concerned, the less said about it the better. They did what they had to do. They saved as many as they could.

"Parker!" She was yelling now, looking around trying to find her assistant. "Parker, get over here!"

Parker Rand had been her assistant on Armstrong, and he'd jumped when she asked for volunteers. Rand was a rimworlder whose sympathies were firmly with the rebels. He came running over, wiping his face with a towel as he did. "Yes, Colonel Linden?"

"Parker, I need you to get that forward cave set up. Sam's going to be moving the hopeless cases there in a few." She motioned with her head, indicating the chamber she meant. "I want you to administer pain control meds and sedatives to the men and women there." She knew she should be careful on the meds – they were already running low. But she was sending those men and women in there to die, and the least she would do was make sure they were as comfortable as she could make them.

"Yes, colonel." He turned to leave.

"And Parker?"

"Yes, colonel?"

"Talk to the ones who are conscious." God, she hated this. "Don't let them die alone."

"I will, colonel." His voice was a little weak. Rand hadn't been in the places Sarah had, and he was overwhelmed by all the death and suffering. "Don't you worry, colonel, I'll take care of it." He turned and jogged off to carry out her orders.

She sighed as she struggled to close the gaping wound she'd been working on. He'll make it, at least, she thought, looking down at the torn up rebel on the table. He didn't look much like a soldier. "What are you, a fisherman? A tailor?" She knew she wouldn't get an answer; she didn't really want one.

"We've got to pull back to the Rock." Anton's voice was hoarse, and Marek could hear the pain, despite the big man's attempts to hide it. It wasn't a critical wound on Anton's shoulder, but it was a painful one.

"We're done if we get penned in there." Marek knew Anton was right, but he was struggling, desperately trying to think of an alternative. "You know that."

"John...we're done if we stay on Carlisle. The lines are broken in four places." Anton grabbed his friend's arm. "We can hold out a while longer on the Rock. You know how deep those caverns are." He looked back over his shoulder, in the direction of the nearest fighting. "If we stay here we'll lose the whole army."

Marek let out a long, slow breath. He'd been in tough spots before. The battle on the Lysandra Plateau on Carson's World had been one of the bitterest ever fought. He was grievously wounded and sure all was lost. But General Cain held his people together, and they won the battle.

But it had been I Corps on Carson's World...and Erik Cain's 1st Brigade on the Lysandra Plateau. Marek was proud of his troops, but he couldn't compare them to the elite veterans who fought that famous battle. Anton was right. The army was disintegrating.

"OK, we'll pull back." Marek barely managed to croak out the words. "But we'll need a rearguard. I'll take the militia and the veterans and we'll set up a defense at Monty's Gap. That should..."

"Hold on." Anton put his good arm in the air as he interrupted. "Don't even think about leading the rearguard. You're the army commander. You get your ass out to the Rock and set up a command post."

"But..."

"No buts." Anton's eyes bored into Marek's. "Don't make me be insubordinate. You're the commander of this army and it needs you. The whole army, not just the delaying force." Anton put his hand on Marek's shoulder. "John, you get the army off Carlisle and onto the Rock. I'll hook up with Colonel Jax and we'll hold the Gap long enough for you to get everyone evac'd."

Marek hated the plan. He hated it with a passion. But he knew it was what he had to do. "OK, let's do it. But we'll have to evacuate civilians too. I can't even imagine what kind of reprisals Cooper has in mind for Carlisle." He looked up at Anton. "And you...no crazy chances. Take care of yourself... you understand?"

Anton nodded, but he didn't say another word.

Arlen Cooper was smiling, but the generals on the transport with him wore non-descript expressions. They were winning the battle, but the losses had been staggering. The federal forces had suffered at least 10,000 casualties, and possibly twice that. No one seemed to know for sure. Communications, logistics, command...it was all a confused mess.

Cooper stepped out of the transport, and he sank almost to his knees in the mud, swearing bitterly. He'd wanted to come out to Carlisle Island to see what was really going on, but he'd never get used to what a mess battlefields were. "Help me out of here!" He was waving his arms and trying to pull his leg out of the muck. His aides scrambled through the mud, struggling to pull him free.

"General Strom, report." Cooper was walking toward the federal military commander, stamping his feet to shake some of the mud off his legs. He had a rough relationship with Strom, and he hoped the general wasn't going to give him a hard time. Cooper was already annoyed, and he wasn't in the mood to put up with any shit from Strom.

"Welcome to Carlisle Island, Governor." Strom was in good spirits. Like Cooper, Strom wasn't overly concerned about casualties as long as he was victorious. The army could always draft more Cogs to fill the ranks. "The rebels are broken and in wholesale flight. We are in pursuit and rounding them up even now."

"General, it is my understanding from reports that the rebels are retreating to a fortified island off the northern coast." Cooper detested Strom, and he was going to hold the officious pain in the ass accountable. He'd already lost an enormous number of troops, and as far as Cooper could see from the dispatches, the rebels were pulling back in good order. "I presume you are moving to cut them off and prevent this."

"Governor, the tactical realities of the campaign are, I am sure, quite beyond..."

"General!" Cooper interrupted Strom harshly. "If you are able to trap the rebels on Carlisle Island, we can end this rebellion today." And you and I can get off of this miserable rock, he thought. "If they are allowed to escape with a significant force intact we will have to assault them again." He glared at Strom. The general was seething with rage, but so far he'd held his tongue. "Considering the state of our own army after your glorious..." – he drew the word out in a mocking tone – "... victory, I can only imagine how long that will take."

Strom's body quivered with rage. "Governor, I realize you do not understand military matters, so I will excuse your insult."

"General Strom..." Cooper's eyes bored right into the general's. "I couldn't care less what you excuse or do not excuse. You have a job to do, and I suggest you focus on cutting off the rebel retreat."

Strom looked almost apoplectic, but before he could say anything, an aide came running over. "Governor Cooper!"

Cooper turned to face his assistant. "What is it, Jon?"

"It's the camp, sir." The young orderly's voice was tentative and cracking. "There's trouble at the camp."

The mob streamed from the camp toward Weston, a seething, boiling throng. They'd had hundreds killed – no, thousands – but they'd done it. They'd broken out. Every guard in the camp had been killed, literally torn apart by the starving, abused prisoners. A few had tried to run, but Jill's people chased them down. The shattered wreckage of the camp was strewn with the dead.

Jill had been determined to lead the break the week before, but she'd seen the troop columns marching north and decided to wait. If Cooper was going to move the army away, so much the better. As long as his hideous little ass was still in Weston where she could get to him.

Her group had started small, targeting collaborators and informers and executing them in the night. The word spread among the desperate and broken inhabitants of the camp. Without other hope they latched onto the cause, and soon Jill Winton had thousands of followers. They became even more violent and extremist, determined to strike back against the federals and any who helped them.

"To Weston." Jill screamed again, though she knew only a tiny fraction of the mob could hear her. "Death to the federals."

"Death to the federals." A hundred people shouted the reply, pumping their fists in the air as they surged forward, and the cry rippled outward until the shouts were deafening. The streaming mass of humanity was out for blood.

"And death to all collaborators!" Jill's eyes blazed with fury as she held her rifle aloft. As far as Jill was concerned, all who aided the federals – even those who didn't resist them – were traitors. Now they would pay. They'd been living in Weston, their comfort the spoils of their treason. Those who resisted, whose friends and families were in the field fighting, they had suffered the horrors of the camp. Beatings, starvation, rape, exposure, torture…they had endured every imaginable abuse. Now they would have their vengeance.

"To Weston!" she cried again, and the madness in her voice only inspired the mob more.

"Go, colonel." Anton stood dead center in the rocky pass, holding an assault rifle in each arm. His shoulder was slick with blood, but he couldn't feel the pain anymore. "This is my home.

My job to hold here." He had a dozen volunteers around him, mostly veterans who had settled on Columbia. They would be the last ones to leave Carlisle Island.

Jax looked doubtful, but he just nodded. He didn't like it, but he respected Anton's wishes. "OK, people. Let's go." He motioned for the rest of his troops – there really weren't all that many left anyway – to head down the path to the beach. It was about a klick to the evac point. They'd held for a long time, allowing Marek to get the remnants of the army – and a lot of civilians too – to the relative safety of the Rock. Now that job would fall to Anton and his dozen. They had to hold just a little longer.

Jax was motioning for his troops to hurry. The faster they got out, the less time Anton had to hold. The giant Marine was last, and before he ran down the path he turned toward Anton one last time. He was standing in the gap, firing both assault rifles on full auto, spraying the approaches. Jax didn't kid himself; he knew Anton's chances, and they weren't good. "Lucius! The Corps forever!" He ran down the rocky path, following his troops to the beach.

Anton didn't turn, but he answered Jax's call, his voice was loud and booming. "The Corps forever!"

The federals had launched another assault, and a full battalion was rushing toward the gap. Anton's troopers started to go down under the massive fire. First one, then another…until the grizzled old Marine stood alone. He'd been hit, more than once…he wasn't even sure how many times. He emptied his last clip and picked up a gun from one of his fallen troopers.

No one saw the last stand of Lucius Anton…no one but the attacking federals. Finally, he was hit again, this time in the chest, and at last even his herculean constitution gave out. He sank to his knees, covered in blood but still firing his rifle. He'd fought on dozens of battlefields all over occupied space, but he knew this was his last. He couldn't feel the shots as he was hit again and again, but at last his riddled body fell backwards, and he lay still on the rocks. His vision was almost gone; there was only a hazy orange light from the setting sun. And the shadowy shapes passing by…federal troops pouring through the gap he had defended for so long. Finally there was only the darkness.

Jax was the last one to leave Carlisle Island. He could feel the sour taste of defeat in his mouth as he stood on the back of the barge, pulling away from the place they were abandoning. The rebels had fought well, but there were just too many federals. There was no miracle on Carlisle Island, no legendary victory by the underdog. In the end it was raw attrition, the relentless mathematics favoring the attacker. It wouldn't make much of a song or a barroom tale, but it was the cold calculus of war.

They'd loaded as many civilians as they could cram onto the barges. It was foolish tactically; their supplies would just run out that much sooner. But everyone knew Cooper was a monster, and they could only imagine what reprisals awaited the people of Carlisle Island. Tactics are all well and good, Jax thought, but we have to stand for something too…or we're no better than this lot we're fighting.

He'd waited to the last, hoping against hope that Anton would come racing down the hillside. But he knew it wasn't going to happen. Anton had known he would never make it out – he'd known when he insisted on staying and holding the pass. Jax had lost more comrades and friends than he could easily count, but no matter how many were added to the list, it never got easier.

He thought about Anton…on Carson's World and other battlefields. There were no parades for the fallen hero, no salutes or other fanfare…just Jax's solitary eulogy. There were a lot of things Darius Jax could have said about Anton, but in the end he just muttered one phrase, one sentiment he thought Lucius would have appreciated more than any other. "He was a Marine's Marine."

Jax thought about the rebellion too. They were close to the end; he knew that much. The Rock was a tough position, but if the federals wanted it badly enough they could take it. Not right away, perhaps. They were hurt badly in the fight for Carlisle, and they needed time to lick their wounds and resupply. But they didn't need to attack at all to win the war; all they had to do was wait...wait until the rebels ran out of food and supplies.

Jax's thoughts were somber as he watched the Carlisle coast recede. Every Marine's road ends somewhere. Lucius Anton's led to that pass...and a desperate battle on a planet he'd adopted as his home. Would mine end here, Jax wondered, on this chunk of rock with Marek and the remnants of his army? "Well," he muttered softly, "if it is time to die, might as well do it in good company."

Chapter 28

Command and Control Center
AS Bunker Hill
Orbiting Columbia - Eta Cassiopeiae II

Compton stared at the stats coming in from the warp gate scanners. The fleet transiting into the system was big...a lot stronger than the rump force he still had under his command. The ships were being identified as they emerged, and it looked like all of them were vessels that had been transferred to the strategic reserve. These ships were supposed to be out of service, not crewed and ready for action. Compton was even more convinced that something strange was going on. Something very strange.

Jantz will join them, he thought, but I wonder if his whole force will go along. It's one thing for them to repudiate my command authority and quite another to join with a force outside of the naval chain of command to attack navy ships.

"Joker, put me on fleetcom."

Compton's AI dutifully obeyed. "You are connected, admiral."

"Second Fleet, this is Admiral Compton." He paused and took a breath. He'd been under unceasing stress for the past six months, and it was starting to take its toll on him. He could face combat and danger; he done it countless times. But now he felt he was struggling every minute to maintain command, and it was draining him in ways he'd never experienced. He was uncomfortable on his own flagship, and he could feel the unspoken doubts, even from the officers who'd pledged their loyalty.

"We have detected a large number of fleet units inbound from the YZ Ceti warp gate. It appears that at least a significant number of these ships are vessels that were scheduled for demobilization. Apparently, the vessels of the strategic reserve had been appropriated for use by authorities unknown at present." Compton hesitated. All his professional life he'd been decisive, but this was new territory…a situation he couldn't have predicted. He wasn't sure exactly what to do other than lay it all out for his crews and let them decide for themselves.

"In my estimation, this is further evidence that the naval chain of command has been somehow compromised. I have no information whatsoever regarding the personnel manning and commanding these vessels, other than the certainty that they are not part of the naval organizational structure."

Compton paused again, wanting to give his officers a chance to consider the implications of what he had said. Someone was trying to run their own private navy, using naval vessels that were supposed to be mothballed in the long term reserve. Any naval officer would be concerned about a situation like that. "I would prefer to avoid conflict with the incoming forces, however, I do not intend to abandon this position, and I am prepared to fight if compelled to do so." His voice was clear and calm; he was comfortable with his decision. Now the chips would fall where they may.

"Although we do not yet have a complete order of battle, it is apparent that the approaching forces are substantially superior to our own. Indeed, it is possible that we will be overwhelmed if we engage this fleet." Compton took a deep breath – he'd decided what he was going to say, and he was about to take a calculated risk. "We are in a situation none of us could have foreseen. I will not order anyone to remain with me in this. Any ships that wish to stand aside from this fight may do so. I will take no action to interfere."

He paused again, counting off a couple beats before he continued. "I believe this is the right course of action. Indeed, to me there is no other possible choice. This inbound force will undoubtedly bombard civilian targets on the surface of Columbia, and as an Alliance naval officer, I take it as my duty to stop them if I am able." He swallowed hard and continued. "Duty is a hard taskmaster, and the essence of my duty is to protect the civilians of the Alliance. Regardless of political affiliations or opinions about rebellion, indiscriminate bombing of civilian targets cannot be justified."

Compton was standing dead center in his control room. His staff had thrown in with him to the bitter end; he was sure of that. But what about the rest of the fleet? Remaining with him on station was one thing, but engaging other Alliance forces was another.

"I am resolved to make a stand here, and to engage any forces that attempt to seize control of the space around Columbia. I feel without reservation that this is where my duty lies." After a pause he continued, his voice a bit softer. "As I said, I will not order any vessel to stand with me. You must make your own choice in this. Any who remain will have my deepest gratitude. Any who feel their conscience or personal interpretation of duty does not allow them to stand with me may maneuver to disengagement range with my best wishes."

That's it, he thought. Let's see what they do, and then I'll know where I stand. It's a lot to ask…not just to fight against other Alliance units, but to engage an overwhelmingly superior force. In all likelihood, the only reward anyone would get from following him was to die branded as a traitor.

The Directorate fleet was almost in missile range. Jantz and about half his forces had joined with the invaders, but most of the fleet rallied to Compton. Only six ships elected to leave his command, and they maneuvered deeper into the system, setting a course to link up with Jantz' dropouts. They wouldn't attack the incoming fleet, but neither would they fight against Compton. They had assumed neutrality.

Compton was relieved and gratified that so many of his people stood with him. The odds were still long, but at least he had a fleet. He was about to give the order to fire when fleetcom crackled to life and began broadcasting a message. "Attention all Alliance personnel." The warp gate scanners were reporting incoming vessels just as the comm signal arrived. "This is Fleet Admiral Augustus Garret." The message was uncoded, broadcast in the clear.

"This message is directed to all Alliance naval personnel in-system. Orders issued from my office during the last year have been compromised and misrepresented through the actions of unauthorized parties." Garret's voice was strong and steady, with an undercurrent of anger that was detectable only to those who knew him well. "I want to make this perfectly clear. Admiral Terrance Compton is confirmed in command of the Second Fleet, and I hereby ratify and approve any decisions or orders he has issued."

Compton exhaled softly. Cain and his people must have gotten Garret out. He couldn't imagine how they'd managed it, but the relief was considerable. He hadn't really believed he'd ever see his friend alive again, and he felt pure joy at hearing Garret's voice.

"All forces in this system are ordered to stand down. This order is being transmitted under Priority One protocols, with DNA scan identification verified at this time." So there was no doubt…this was the real Augustus Garret. And he had a score to settle.

The Directorate fleet had no intention of following Garret's order to stand down. Fleet Commander Warne had orders, and they were clear and inflexible. He was to seize control of Columbia, arrest Compton, and destroy any ships that resisted. Then he was to render any assistance requested by Governor Cooper.

The tactical situation had changed considerably, however. He was going to lose Jantz' ships now, Warne was pretty sure of that. But the Directorate forces still represented almost two-thirds of the tonnage in the system and the Alliance navy forces were divided into four groups, in poor position to coordinate or support each other. Warne had the tactical advantage.

Jantz' ships were closest. They'd been ready to attack Compton's force alongside the Directorate ships, but Jantz acknowledged Garret's order and his vessels began to change course, attempting to pull off from the Directorate fleet and disengage.

Warne had his own agenda, however, and he was prepared to fight all of the navy forces in the system. He had the edge right now, not just in tonnage, but in position. Jantz' squadron was still nearby, within energy weapons range. He decided to engage them first, taking them out of the equation before they could link up with the other naval units.

But Compton anticipated Warne's action, and he ordered his fleet to immediately launch a full missile barrage. It was technically a violation of Garret's stand down order, but Compton and Garret were light hours apart, and there was no way to get confirmation in time. If Compton didn't do something immediately, Jantz and his crews were lost.

Compton's attack gave Warne a choice. His ships detected the missile launch just as they were positioning for the attack on Jantz' fleeing vessels. If he went ahead and engaged Jantz' fleet at energy range he'd be strung out, not in position to counter the missile attack. Compton or Garret might have gambled, launching a fast assault on Jantz and quickly turning to face the incoming missiles. But that would be a bold move, and the Directorate commander simply didn't have it in him. Nor were his crews experienced enough to pull it off. He had no real choice but to let Jantz go and engage Compton in a missile duel.

So Terrance Compton saved the man who had tried so hard to relieve him. Now he faced a missile fight with an enemy that outnumbered him three to one in both hulls and tonnage. It would be a tough fight, he knew that. But it wouldn't be his first.

Garret sat on the bridge of the AS Perryville. He didn't have a proper flagship. In fact, he didn't have much of a fleet either. He'd rallied what forces were available, but time had been of the essence, and there were only so many idle ships posted along his course to Eta Cassiopeiae. He had a few cruisers and a bunch of destroyers and attack ships, and that's all.

It had been quite a journey from that cell in Alliance Intelligence HQ. Cain's people had gotten him to the Martian embassy undetected, and Roderick Vance had smuggled him to Mars and then out of the Sol system entirely. When they filled him in, he knew he had to get to Columbia – he couldn't imagine the mess the imposter had created. He wanted to gather a large force, but Compton's Second Fleet was the only major concentration of naval strength in the sector. Most of the rest of the fleet was posted out on the rim. It would have taken months to assemble a large task force, and that was time Garret knew he didn't have.

The situation was desperate; there was no doubt of that. But it felt good to be doing something and not just sitting in that cell. Holm had been telling him for years what a gifted officer Cain was, and Garret himself had followed the young general's career with considerable interest and amusement. But now he owed him a personal debt, one he sincerely hoped he'd be able to repay one day. He was well aware of what Cain and his people had done, of the overwhelming odds they had faced. Augustus Garret was many things, but an ingrate wasn't one of them.

He was looking at the force deployment diagram, hoping he'd come up with some way to help Compton before it was too late. There was a word for the tactical situation in the system right now...clusterfuck. Compton had the largest force posted near Columbia. There was another squadron – the ships that had originally planned to sit out the fight – about 30 light minutes from the planet. Jantz' group was right next to the Directorate forces, while Garret's incoming command was still near the warp gate, several light hours from the action.

Garret had his ships set a course toward the Directorate fleet. He knew more than anyone what was behind this mysterious force, and he'd be damned if he was going to let Gavin Stark get away with it. He wanted to take command of the scattered navy forces, but they were too widely dispersed, too far apart. Any orders he issued could only confuse things, so he just kept broadcasting the affirmation of Compton's command authority as his ships strained their reactors to get into the fight. He'd have to count on his senior officers to make their own separate decisions. They were good officers, well trained and experienced. He had faith in them.

Compton felt like a house had fallen on him. Forty years of service in space and he still hadn't gotten completely used to the pressures of high g acceleration. He hated the bloated, lethargic feeling the pressure equalization drugs caused, but without them he'd be in worse shape…unconscious at least, and probably dead. Staying focused on the tactical situation while drugged and being crushed almost to death was one of the hardest things for naval officers to master.

He'd needed the acceleration, and now the deceleration. The incoming missile barrage would devastate his fleet if he stayed where he was. Even with full countermeasures, a lot of those warheads would get through. But he was facing a less experienced opponent…of that he was sure. The spread blasting toward his fleet was textbook, simple, unimaginative. Maybe, just maybe, with the right evasive maneuvers he could save his people.

His first thought was to hide behind Columbia, but he wasn't about to risk letting thousands of megatons of high-yield fusion bombs impact the planet or its atmosphere. The warheads that ships hurled at each other were massive – bigger even than the giant city-killers used during the Unification Wars. It takes a lot of energy output for a near miss to damage a ship in space.

Columbia's moon, however, was a different story, and the entire fleet was blasting full, trying to put the large rocky satellite between them and the incoming missiles. The weapons would attempt to change course to follow, but they were at a disadvantageous angle and a high velocity. The Directorate commander was impatient; he'd accelerated his missiles aggressively, burning a lot of fuel in the process. A lot of them would expend the last of their thrust capacity before they were able to completely change their trajectories to target his ships. At least that's what Compton was betting on.

His own missile spread was focused, targeting just two of the big Yorktown class ships. What a waste, he thought. These big, beautiful new ships. The cream of the navy. He had been confused when so many of the new ships had been taken off active service, but now he understood. Alliance Intelligence wanted them; they wanted to create their own navy, under their complete control. Now Compton had to destroy them…or they would do the same to him.

He felt a pinprick in his arm – Joker adjusting his pressure drug dosage. They were almost in position, and Compton didn't want the fleet at high acceleration/deceleration when the missiles hit. Damage control efforts would be far more effective in freefall or at low g forces. Half a minute later he felt the relief as the ship's engines began to disengage and the massive feeling of pressure was gone.

"Missiles incoming in five zero minutes." Commander Larrison was Bunker Hill's tactical officer. Compton was linked into his com, but he was just a bystander. The fleet was in position; now the captains would fight their ships.

"Very good, commander." Elizabeth's voice sounded as calm as if she were having a picnic on the beach instead of waiting for tens of thousands of megatons of warheads to close on her ship. "Full countermeasures, program Epsilon-7." Bunker Hill and her escorts put out a blizzard of small rockets and sprint missiles, each targeting an incoming warhead. The effectiveness of the long-range point defense was unpredictable, highly dependent on a number of factors, including the vectors and velocities of the incoming missiles with respect to the targeted ships.

The rockets split into hundreds of smaller projectiles, each aiming directly for an incoming warhead, like a bullet. The sprint missiles were single units, and they employed the same strategy as their larger targets...trying to get as close as possible before detonating. The combined effect of the two weapons systems was devastating – the salvo from the Directorate fleet was savaged, with fewer than a third of the missiles surviving.

"On my mark, execute countermeasures, protocol Epsilon-8." Arlington's voice was just as calm, though perhaps just a bit of satisfaction had crept in after the success of the initial point defense program.

"Acknowledged, captain." A brief pause. "Locked in and waiting for your order."

Sitting idle during a battle was still difficult for Compton. It had been one of the hardest things for him to get used to when he left his last ship command to assume Flag rank. A good admiral didn't second guess his captains...if they needed that, then he'd already failed. No amount of interference from the flag bridge could make up for a bad captain.

"Execute." Arlington had waited as long as she could to engage her close-range point defense. Lasers pulsed, picking off missiles that had closed almost to detonation range, and then the big shotguns fired. Magnetic cannon that launched clouds of heavy metal debris at the incoming missiles, the shotguns were the last line of defense.

Compton was watching his monitors, and he could see the defense grid had been to be highly effective. His evasive maneuver cut down the incoming missiles to roughly half the overall barrage – the rest running out of fuel before they were able to complete vector changes. The layered point defense intercepted most of the remaining warheads. Less than 3% of the missiles launched at the fleet detonated close enough to have an effect, but even this small remnant caused widespread damage.

The cruiser Dublin was destroyed outright, bracketed by three explosions within 2 kilometers. Two attack ships were also lost, and a number of other vessels suffered varying degrees of damage. Bunker Hill had some radiation penetration in outer compartments but was otherwise unscathed. All things considered, Compton thought, it could have been much, much worse.

His own volley proved to be substantially more effective. Precisely targeted and focused, a large percentage of the warheads penetrated the poorly deployed and coordinated countermeasures, savaging the primary targets…two Yorktown class capital ships. One vessel was virtually destroyed, dead in space with fires raging out of control in her inner compartments. The second was shattered, bleeding atmosphere and trying to pull out of the battleline.

He'd won the first round, but he knew the energy battle would be tougher. There were fewer tricks he could use, and the relative inexperience of the opposing crews would have less of an effect. The enemy's numbers would tell.

"Admiral, the enemy is decelerating." It was Joker's voice in Compton's earpiece. "I project an aspect change. Probability 74% they are turning to face Admiral Garret's incoming ships."

That was a hell of a projection considering Garret's squadron was too far away to show up on Compton's scanners. Once Garret passed the detection devices deployed near the warp gate, his ships entered a dead zone, disappearing as far as the fleet's detection capability was concerned. Joker, or any of the other AIs could only predict the likely vector and location of the admiral's ships. Garret was blasting full when he left range of the warp gate sensors, heading directly toward the Directorate fleet; that much they knew for certain. What they had done since could only be an educated guess.

"Joker, put me on the fleetcom command circuit."

"You are broadcasting, admiral." Joker's voice was matter-of-fact, as always. "All fleet captains online."

"All ships prepare for full thrust in five zero minutes." He could almost sense the groans throughout the fleet, though no one made any sounds he could hear on the fleetcom. "I know we just got out of the couches, but Admiral Garret is heading straight for the enemy, pulling them away from us." His voice got louder, sharper. "And we are not about to leave him hanging alone." He paused then added, "All vessels confirm readiness in four zero minutes. Compton out."

He leaned back on the couch, feeling the pinprick a few seconds later as Joker prepped him for the coming high g maneuvers. He could feel the nausea and the sickly bloated feeling the drugs caused, then another prick and some relief…the stimulants that partially counteracted the side effects of the pressurization injections.

"We're coming, Augustus." He was whispering, talking to himself. "Thank God you're finally here."

Chapter 29

Foothills of the Red Mountains
Northern Territories, Concordia
Arcadia – Wolf 359 III

Kara Sanders was exhausted, but she kept walking along with the rest of the army. What was left of it, at least. The retreat after the Second Battle of Sander's Dale had turned into a near-disaster. The loss of Will Thompson infuriated the army, and the troops went wild, throwing themselves at the federals in a mindless rage. Will's plan had been to hurt the enemy and withdraw, not to get sucked into a battle of annihilation his army couldn't win. He knew they didn't have the strength to defeat the federal powered infantry in a pitched battle...that they would have to wear it down gradually. But his enraged and devastated soldiers weren't working on logic; they were out to avenge their beloved leader.

Kyle Warren had been everywhere, vainly trying to disengage and retreat. He had to save the army – for the rebellion of course, but also for Will. He owed that much to his fallen friend and leader. He got more than half their strength off the battlefield that day, but a lot of those had since been lost on the retreat, expended in desperate delaying actions or melted away in the attrition of the grueling march.

Warren knew he couldn't defend Concordia anymore, and he resolved to move the army north, into the mountains where they had a chance to hold out, at least for a while. But before anything, there was something he had to do, a task that was his and his alone. Telling Kara about Will was the hardest thing he had ever done, and he would have rather faced any enemy on the battlefield than seen the expression on her face. He didn't even have to tell her; she knew the minute she saw him.

She didn't cry, at least not when anyone could see. She just calmly went about her responsibilities. Their cause was looking hopeless, but Kara wasn't about to give up...not now, not ever.

This was Will's army, and she would stay with it as long as it existed. That much she owed him.

They'd had to abandon her factory too, the place Will had convinced them all to build years before. She'd become the heart and soul of the facility, keeping the weapons and ammo flowing out long after the raw materials stopped coming in. Sometimes it seemed they were making guns out of nothing but her raw will, but she kept the supplies coming to the army no matter what.

She had watched, silent and impassive, as Will's soldiers placed the charges. They couldn't defend the facility anymore, but she'd be damned if she was going to let the enemy have it. Kyle had tried to get her to leave, not to watch. But she wouldn't move from the site, and she insisted on triggering the detonation herself. It was her factory, and if anyone was going to blow it to oblivion, it was her.

She was finding the marches more difficult every day...and it was only going to get worse. She hadn't told anyone yet, but it wouldn't be long before she couldn't hide it anymore. They already treated her with an eerie sort of reverence, as if protecting her was the last thing they could do for their beloved general. She understood, but it was wearing on her too. She had her own grief, which she hadn't even begun to deal with, and the constant attention from the army was only making it worse. What would they do when they found out she was carrying Will's child?

Maybe it didn't matter. Maybe nothing mattered. Kyle was doing everything he could, but sooner or later the Feds would hunt them down, even in these mountains. And that would be the end. Kara would have made sure not to survive the last battle, but that was a solace she would now be denied, her responsibility to her child trumping her own wish to join Will in death. What kind of world, she wondered, will you grow up in? We have failed you; we have failed all the generations to come.

Erik Cain listened to the locking bolt click securely into the frame of the lander and felt the familiar vibration of his armor as the reactor roared to life and fed power into the servomechanicals of his suit. It felt and sounded like home.

Cain had anticipated the struggle between the Alliance and its colonies for his entire adult life, and he'd watched it unfold for the last several years feeling very much like a bystander. Now he was finally going to do something. He was going to do what he did best. His shoulder still hurt like hell, but nothing was keeping him out of the lander. Not now.

After he rescued General Holm, they escaped the Centauri system in Vance's Torch and set a course for Armstrong. Cain had commanded the garrison there for almost two years, and he was confident they would rally to him. The Corps was in disarray, shaken to its very core by the treachery of General Samuels. Some Marines were still under Samuels orders, unaware that he had sold himself to Alliance Intelligence; others were declaring for Holm. Many supported the rebels on the various colony worlds, while others blamed separatist extremists for the destruction of the Academy, an act actually perpetrated by Alliance Intelligence to sow dissension and confusion in the Marine ranks. There were even rumors that Marine contingents were fighting each other on some of the Rim worlds, but Cain wouldn't believe it. Not unless undeniable proof forced him to.

When they arrived at Armstrong they found a battalion of Directorate troops there already, and the Marines under orders from General Samuels to disarm. Erik's old garrison had been reluctant to follow the unorthodox command and had delayed. They rallied instantly to his impassioned plea, and when the Directorate troops finally attacked, Erik's Marines were ready. The battle was short and bloody – there was no time for finesse. The Marines crushed the less experienced Directorate troops and secured control of Armstrong.

Now he was finally about to land on Arcadia, answering the request he'd received from Will Thompson so long before. He had a rump battalion with him, about 400 strong. It was all he could spare and still hold Armstrong, and it was all the transport capacity Garret could get him on short notice anyway. But he'd put 400 of his veterans up against any force in occupied space.

Erik had launched a spread of probes, giving him a snapshot

of the tactical situation on the planet. From what he could tell, the rebels were on the verge of defeat, pursued into the wilderness by the Directorate troops. The armored federal soldiers had been hunting down the exhausted and ill-equipped Arcadian forces. Things were about to change, though. Now they would have to face Erik Cain and his veteran Marines. Cain was outnumbered at least 4-1, but he'd match up one of his vets against any four Directorate hacks ever made.

It felt good to be back in his armor, back doing what he was trained to do. It was even a pleasure to have Hector nagging him again, though a couple years of inactivity had done nothing to improve the AI's eclectic personality.

"Cut the shit, Hector." Arguing with the virtual assistant felt just like old times. "I know we have very little information, but when we hit ground, I want you to work on connecting me with the rebel communications network."

"Of course, general." Hector's voice was the same as always, calm and professional. There was a slightly obnoxious element to it as well, or at least Cain always thought so. "That is an obvious mission parameter. I was merely trying to advise you that it will be extremely difficult since we have very little information to utilize in making the linkup."

The AIs were designed to develop personalities in response to those of the officers they served. In theory, this created a customized assistant compatible with the Marine, thereby reducing stress in the combat zone. In practice, there were occasionally unpredictable results.

Cain didn't see any point in continuing the conversation; Hector knew what he needed to do. His visor was down, but he could see the launch status on the shimmering display projected on the inside of his helmet. They'd just been pressure-coated with heat-resistant foam. In less than a minute, they'd be on the way down to the surface.

"Second line, forward now!" Cain barked out the orders, and 100 Marines jumped out of their makeshift cover and jogged forward, covered by heavy fire from the first line. "Advance two hundred meters and assume firing positions."

The Directorate troops were arrogant at first, anxious to take on Cain's newly arrived Marines, especially since they had a massive numerical advantage. But the maneuverability and precise fire control of Erik's people was proving to be too much for them. Now he had about a thousand of them trapped, bracketed against the mountains.

He had to be careful – the Feds he had trapped outnumbered his attacking troops almost 3-1. But in the last week he'd completely taken the initiative from the Directorate forces. They had considered themselves an elite unit, but now they were facing real combat veterans equipped as well as they were. In seven days, Cain and his Marines had completely shattered the morale of the federal forces.

The Marines had losses too, but they'd been fairly light. Erik had made maximum use of the training and experience of his troops, keeping constantly on the move, stinging the enemy and pulling away before they could hurt him. But now he'd maneuvered them where he wanted them. This would be the battle of annihilation.

"Second line, commence firing. First line, forward now!" He was leapfrogging forward, pushing the federals up against the rugged terrain to their rear. His troops were coming in from the center and right, forcing the enemy back and to the left. There was a hole there, or an apparent one. Cain had placed all his heavy weapons – SAWs, rocket launchers, mortar teams – in a depression just back from the opening in his line. He was baiting the enemy to pour through that breach…and right into the perfectly prepared fields of fire.

The Directorate troops had the numbers, but they'd been completely unnerved by a week of fighting Cain's Marines. The aggressiveness of the Marines' tactics was unlike anything they had ever seen. If they'd dug in and fought it out, their numbers might have carried the day, but their morale was broken. Unable to stand against the advance of the Marines, they poured right through the gap Cain had left for them…and they were massacred by the hidden heavy weapons. By nightfall the Directorate forces on Arcadia were crushed. There were small packets of troops holding out here and there, but as a fighting force they were finished.

"Kyle Warren." Cain had popped his helmet, and he wore a broad smile on his face. "I see my efforts to make something useful out of you were not entirely wasted." His smile morphed into a wicked grin.

Warren walked over to Cain. He was tired, his uniform torn and filthy. "General Cain." His exhausted expression gave way to his own smile. "It is good to see you, sir." He stood at attention, at least as much as his partially-treated wounds would allow, and he snapped off a textbook Marine salute.

"I'd give you a damned hug, Warren, if I didn't think I squash you like an overripe tomato." Both men laughed. Erik Cain wore his armor like a second skin, and they both knew it. He could have juggled peaches without bruising one.

"I don't mind telling you, sir, you got here just in time." Warren was thrilled to see Cain, but he had trouble keeping the bone-deep fatigue out of his voice.

"Not in time to save Will Thompson, I understand." Cain's smile faded, his voice turning wistful.

Kyle shook his head. "No, sir. I'm afraid not."

Cain sighed. "He's not the first friend I've lost, but it doesn't get any easier." He looked at Warren, and he could see how devastated the officer was about Thompson's loss. He'd seen the same thing in all the other Arcadians he'd spoken with. Not just grief, but a somber reverence as well. "Will and I went way back. He was a Marine, that's for sure." He paused, his mind wandering back twenty years, to battlefields far from Arcadia. "And a friend."

"That he was, sir." Warren forced a tiny smile to his lips. "That he was."

"I've gotten a partial history, Kyle." He looked at Warren respectfully. "You and Will and your people have done something remarkable here. I know how much you paid; I know it as well as anyone could." He took a short breath. "You should be proud. Of yourselves as well as Will."

"Thank you, sir." Warren's voice was cracking slightly. He wasn't prone to overly emotional responses, but Erik Cain was a hero to him, a legend. The praise meant more to him than Cain could ever know. "It means a lot to hear that, sir." He paused. "For Will too."

They stood silently for a moment, each drifting back to other places, other battles. Finally, Cain spoke up. "Well, General Warren, I believe we still have federal forces at large on Arcadia. Shall we discuss how to do something about that?"

Warren looked up at Cain, a big smile back on his face. "Yes, sir. It would be my pleasure."

The rebellion on Arcadia reached its conclusion, not in a massive battle, but in a dozen small actions and a protracted campaign of maneuver. The Alliance army units had suffered heavy casualties in their victory at the Second Battle of Sander's Dale, and they pulled back, waiting for the armored units to hunt down the last of the rebels. Merrick, assuming that the rebellion was all but defeated, had dispersed his strength to firm up his hold on the planetary population centers, preparatory to turning over control to Federal Police or some other permanent occupation force.

But then Cain's Marines arrived and tore the Directorate troops to shreds, changing the situation almost overnight. Kyle Warren rallied the battered rebel army and led it south, first to reclaim Concordia and then to Arcadia City. Spearheaded by Cain's armored veterans, they retook the city, raising the new Arcadian flag atop the shattered remains of the Assembly Hall for the first time since the early days of the rebellion.

Merrick reluctantly began to concentrate his forces to carry on the fight, but it quickly became hopeless. A naval squadron arrived, sent by Admiral Garret to support the Arcadians, and they landed large quantities of weapons and supplies. Across the planet morale soared, the beaten down populations rising up again. Arcadian flags were pulled from hiding places and flown from rooftops, and revolutionary rhetoric was again spoken in meeting places and at rallies.

Merrick engaged in a battle of maneuver with the resur-
gent rebels, but with his supplies and reinforcements cut off, he
lacked the strength to take decisive action. Kyle Warren's army
grew, swelled by new recruits flowing in from every direction.
When fresh Marine units arrived and joined Cain's forces, Merrick knew it was over. Somberly, reluctantly he sent a communication to Warren asking for terms.

They met in a small building, a shed really. Sixty kilometers
east of Arcadia, it was equidistant between the two largest troop
concentrations. Warren could have insisted Merrick come to
his camp, or he could have negotiated the entire thing by comlink, but in the end he decided the federal general had acted like
a professional soldier, and he would treat him like one. The
atrocities of the early war were never repeated, even when the
rebels themselves committed a few of their own.

Cain went along with Warren, though he made it clear he
was an observer, and the decisions were Kyle's. They took a
platoon of Cain's troops as an escort – Warren had decided to
treat Merrick with respect, but neither he nor Erik really trusted
the federals.

"Hello, General Merrick." Warren motioned toward the
table he'd had set up in the room. "Please have a seat."

Merrick stood stiffly, obviously uncomfortable with the
whole situation. "Thank you, General Warren." It grated on
him to accord the rebel commander the dignity of his claimed
rank, but there was nothing to be gained by petulance. "And
thank you for meeting me so promptly."

"Allow me to introduce General Erik Cain." Warren walked
toward the table as he spoke, pulling out a chair.

"It is my pleasure to meet you, General Cain." So this was
Erik Cain, Merrick thought with considerable surprise. No
wonder Gravis and his Directorate troops were beaten so badly.
An arrogant fool like Gravis had no chance against an officer of
Cain's ability.

Erik nodded to the federal commander. "The sentiment is
mutual, General Merrick." His voice was deadpan, non-com-

mittal. Cain was never good at pretending to respect people or to act like he cared when he didn't.

Merrick took his cue from Warren and walked over to the table himself. "General Warren, as you are aware, the strategic situation has become problematic for my forces." He waited until Warren took a seat, and then he sat down himself. "I am here to request a cessation of hostilities pending the evacuation of my forces from the planet."

Warren cleared his throat. "General Merrick, I agree that nothing can be gained by further combat." He stared over at the federal general. "However, I must insist that your forces surrender and agree to immediate disarmament." Warren's voice was firm, a little too hard-edged he thought, even as he was saying it. He quickly added, "I am prepared to guarantee the safety of your troops and to allow all federal forces to depart as soon as transport back to Earth can be arranged.

Merrick sat silently for a few seconds, thinking. He didn't like the idea of laying down his arms and waiting indefinitely for transport. But he hadn't really expected a better deal. If he kept fighting he could inflict casualties and cause damage, but he couldn't change anything. In the end, his forces would be defeated and destroyed. "I accept your terms, General Warren."

Cain stood in the corner of the room, silently watching the two men negotiate specifics. He was in his armor, and sitting would have been more trouble than it was worth...especially since there wasn't a chair in the building that could hold him and the two metric tons of high-density metal in his suit. He spoke to himself, so softly he was really just mouthing the words. "Well, Will old friend, I brought you the help you asked me for." There was a slight smile on his face as he thought about Thompson, about the battles they had fought together. More than anyone else, Will had been responsible for turning the young Erik Cain from a green recruit into a Marine. Between war and duty and the vast distances of space, it had been years since the two had seen each other, but that hadn't diminished the bond. When Will called, Erik Cain came, though his path ended up being far longer and less direct than he'd expected.

"Yes, I brought help to your world, Will. I'm just sorry I got here too late to save you." His eyes looked straight ahead, but he was seeing scenes from years before. "Forgive me, old friend. One day I will see you in Valhalla. I'll be the newb again, and you the old hand...just like before."

Chapter 30

City of Weston
Columbia - Eta Cassiopeiae II

The air was thick with acrid smoke. Weston was burning, the District a blazing nightmare. Jill's mob had descended on the city, like some nightmarish vision out of hell. They were filthy and enraged, broken souls now freed from their torment to exact a fearful vengeance.

Jill was at the front of the surging mass, holding a rifle taken from a dead guard and shouting. Her clothes were tattered rags, her hair a twisted, mud-caked mess. But her eyes burned with a crazed determination. It was as if she was possessed, the cheerful college student gone, utterly subsumed by an avenging spirit.

They stormed the checkpoints and guardposts, ignoring their own losses as they did. The guards gunned them down, but there were too many, and the federal soldiers were trampled under the surging sea of humanity. The bodies of the Alliance troops were mutilated and carried along by the raging mob as it swept through the streets of the city.

Jill led the screaming murderous crowd to Founder's Square, where her nightmare had begun that terrible day almost three years before. The place was now a federal supply dump, and her people surged over the barricades and broke into the weapons lockers. Now her people were armed.

They ran wild through the city, breaking into every building. They were here to deal with collaborators as well as the federals. Civilians, many guilty of nothing more than remaining quiet and escaping the notice of the federal authorities, were dragged out into the streets and branded as traitors. They were stripped and beaten...and finally murdered. The anger of the crowd defied rationality or mercy. To those who had endured the deprivation and indignity of the camp, there was no ambiguity. Anyone not fighting the federals was a traitor. And there was only one way to deal with traitors.

The federal troops were busy trying to consolidate their hold on Carlisle Island. The battle had raged for days, and finally the rebels had retired to a smaller island just off the northern coast, a place they called the Rock. It was well named, a granite bastion rising ominously from the sea, promising a heavy fight to any who assaulted its jagged shore.

An aggressive commander might have attacked immediately, seeking to finish the rebellion with one last confrontation. But the Alliance forces were in no condition to mount such an operation. The fight for Carlisle had been difficult, despite their numerical superiority. They had suffered massive casualties, and all across the newly occupied Carlisle Island, makeshift field hospitals were set up.

Any possibility of attacking the Rock was lost when a communication reached Governor Cooper from Weston. There had been a breakout from the detention camp, and thousands of inmates were rampaging through the city. Worse, they had broken into the storage facilities and armed themselves. By all accounts, the city of Weston was a smoldering ruin.

"I want them exterminated, General Strom." Cooper's anger had taken control of him. "Immediately. I don't care how tired your troops are."

Strom was just as outraged as Cooper. The thought of a bunch of mindless Cogs – and that is how he thought of the colonists – running wild and murdering his troops was an affront. But he was also the one faced with the reality of putting together a force powerful enough to wipe out the now-armed mob…and right now, just hours after the fighting ended on Carlisle, he didn't know where he was going to find troops in any condition to go immediately back into a fight. "Governor, I share your feelings, but it will take some time to assemble a large enough force and ship them back to Weston." Strom was going to leave it at that, but then he added, "By all accounts, the mob is now heavily armed."

Strom was a procrastinator and an officer of, at best, marginal ability, however this time his read on the situation was dead on. But Cooper was acting on pure anger now. "General, we do not have time. We must eradicate these rampaging animals, and we must do it at once."

Cooper wasn't being rational, but he wasn't wrong tactically either. There was no way to calculate or predict the damage an armed and enraged mob could do if it was allowed to remain unchecked. "Governor, I have already issued orders for our pickets south of Weston to cordon off the area and pin the mob down near Weston. But our forces there are minimal, and they lack the strength to attack without reinforcement. I wi…"

"Then send reinforcements. Now!" Cooper interrupted Strom, his body quivering with rage. "I want them dead. All of them. No prisoners, no mercy."

Strom bristled at Cooper's tone, but he could see the governor was unbalanced, and he controlled his own anger. They were on the verge of success on Columbia, and Strom wasn't going to get into a fight with the governor if he could avoid it. Not this close to the end. "I will see to it, Governor Cooper." His voice was reasonably controlled, though he had no doubt his own anger bled through. "I will dispatch forces as soon as it can be done." It was a non-committal answer, but it was the best he was going to offer.

"And the other camps are to be destroyed as well. Hampton, Southpoint. All inmates are to be terminated immediately." Cooper looked at Strom, and his eyes wide and crazy. "See to it at once, general."

The Gordon landers swooped down out of the dawn sky, fiery trails streaking behind as they bored through the thick atmosphere on their way to the surface. The landing was precisely plotted – Jax had transmitted detailed coordinates, and the incoming forces were coming down on Carlisle Island, right in the middle of the federal army.

The defenders were taken by surprise. Admirals Garret and Compton had knocked out all of the observation satellites that Cooper could access, effectively blinding him. The first warning his troops had was seeing the agile five-man landers angling in for a final approach.

The alarm was sounded in the federal camps, but by the time the troops were mustered, the first wave of Marines had landed. The attackers fanned out from their landing craft in perfect order, forming a perimeter to protect the incoming second wave.

One Marine in particular stepped out of one of the first wave Gordons, followed by a small cluster of aides. Elias Holm knew he shouldn't have been on one of the first landers. Indeed, it felt like he'd spent half his career lecturing Erik Cain about the responsibilities of the commander to avoid unnecessary risks. But it was different this time, or at least that's what he told himself.

He was leading Marines, as usual, but the circumstances were anything but normal. He'd rallied these Marines, in direct opposition to the orders of the sitting Commandant of the Corps. He was mutinous, technically at least, though how it would end depended heavily on the outcome of the current struggle. He had split the Corps, planting his flag and rallying to it all those who would come. Those who followed him put their careers - their very lives - at stake. If he was going to lead men and women in this situation, he was goddamned going to do it from the front line.

Holm knew what he had to do, but he was still conflicted. Samuels was a traitor, one who'd conspired to destroy the Corps he'd been entrusted to lead. But after forty years of loyal service, Holm still couldn't entirely reconcile with the actions he had to take. He'd do what had to be done, but he knew he'd have a reckoning with himself eventually. He'd have to make peace with what he'd done, and he had to be in this front line if he was going to have any chance of that.

There was a reinforced battalion on the ground, 600 fully armored Marines. They'd landed on an island with more than 40,000 Alliance army soldiers. They could have been more prudent, landing in an unoccupied area and forming up the entire force, but Holm had faith in his troopers and their capabilities. He had a full report from Jax, and he knew the federals were exhausted and disorganized after the battle for Carlisle Island.

Now was the time to hit them, before they could regroup and resupply.

Holm only had two and a half battalions anyway, and they were a little low on supplies themselves. That was all he could assemble quickly after sending Erik Cain and his troops to Arcadia. It was clear that the rest of the rebel forces – and Jax's people too – were pinned down and facing annihilation. Waiting wasn't an option, so Holm decided to land immediately.

The battle in space was still raging. Garret and Compton had control of the area around Columbia, and they'd had the best of the first round with the Directorate fleet. Garret's move against the rear of the federal task force saved Compton, drawing off the superior forces before they could close to energy range. The federals let themselves get bracketed by all the converging forces, and they took heavy damage. The survivors blasted into the outer system at full thrust, and Garret's and Compton's forces were too disorganized and out of position to catch them.

Garret pulled the scattered squadrons back to Columbia, reorganizing the forces and positioning them to defend the planet. He had every intention of hunting down the rogue naval units, but his first priority was assisting General Holm to secure the surface and minimize the suffering on the planet.

So now 600 Marines held the perimeter while another 600 landed, along with all the supplies they had available. It was going to be 1,200 veterans, fully armored and ready for action, against 40,000 federal soldiers. They knew they were outnumbered, but they also knew they were led by General Elias Holm. And they knew they were Marines.

"Captain Kahn, bring your company forward and take Hill 109." It had been a long time since Holm had commanded a force this small, and he was focusing on every detail. These men and women were here, arguably committing treason because he asked them to, and he took the added responsibility to heart. "I want to get our heavy ordnance up there."

"Yes, sir." Kahn's response was sharp and instantaneous. There was hardly a man or woman in this force with less than five years experience, and it showed. "We're on the way, sir."

The powered Marines had been slicing through the Alliance forces like a knife through butter so far, but the federals were trying to bring some of their heavy weaponry into play. If they could get armored vehicles and artillery into the battle, they could give the Marines one hell of a fight. Holm wasn't about to let them pull it off, not if there was anything he could do about it.

The Marines had landed in the middle of the island, splitting the federal forces. Garret threw up a defensive line in the south and drove north, pushing toward the coastline opposite the Rock. It was a vulnerable position, but Holm had his reasons. Marek and Jax had their forces ready to cross back to Carlisle and link up with him, but the federal artillery emplaced on the coast opposite the Rock made the passage impossible…at least until Holms' forces took out the gun batteries. And the hill was part of his plan to do just that.

"General Holm…Captain Kahn here." Kahn sounded a little harried. "We have occupied Hill 109, sir. The enemy appears to be regrouping for a counterattack."

Holm was walking toward the hill when he got Kahn's message. "Very good, captain. Casualty report?"

"Moderate losses, sir. It looks like six dead and eight wounded. They had heavy weapons positioned all along the crest." Kahn paused for a second then added, "I'll have a final report for you in a couple minutes."

"Very well, captain. Carry on." Holm made a face, though his helmet hid it from anyone's view. They were doing pretty well, but his troops were suffering greater losses than he'd expected. The Feds, even though they were unarmored, had good weapons. Their SAWs, in particular, were quite effective at penetrating the Marines' armor. But that wasn't it, and Holm knew it.

His troops were pushing too hard, charging up the center instead of taking the time for a flanking maneuver. It hadn't occurred to him earlier, but it was his presence in such close proximity. They were trying to excel for him, even more than they normally did…and they were getting themselves killed doing it.

"Monty, put me on the master comlink." It was time to put a stop to this.

"Yes, general." Holm's AI took two seconds, maybe three to establish the link. "You are addressing the entire expeditionary force, general."

"Attention all personnel. This is General Holm." He paused, realizing he wasn't sure exactly what he wanted to say. He didn't want to scold them for their élan; he just wanted them to exert more caution. "As always, you are acquitting yourselves with distinction. I have never been prouder of troops under my command." He was thinking as he spoke – how do I put this? "However, I want all of you to proceed with greater caution. We cannot expect reinforcements on this campaign…and after we are done here we face an uncertain future. We may be compelled to fight again immediately. It is your duty, each and every one of you, to avoid unnecessary risks. Stay alive, people. I need you all. Holm out."

He cut the line. Hopefully they'd take what he said to heart. He didn't need any more of his Marines charging into the teeth of a heavy weapons emplacement trying to impress him. He carried enough guilt already.

"Captain Norton, we've occupied Hill 109, but it looks like the enemy is going to counterattack." Holm was reviewing his mental checklist of available forces as he spoke. "I want you to send someone forward with all your SAW teams. I want that hill fortified, and I want it done immediately."

"Yes, sir." Norton's reply was so sharp and fast she actually interrupted Holm, who had paused for an instant but wasn't finished yet. "I will lead them forward myself."

"No, captain." He didn't get angry with Norton. She was a good officer, but young. He'd given her a field promotion from lieutenant just before they'd landed and put her in command of the 1st battalion's heavy weapons company. He could let a little over-eagerness slide. "I want you to bring up the rest of the heavies – the mortars and rocket launchers. Hill 109 has a field of fire to the northern beaches, and we're going to start pounding those federal batteries." He paused again, but this time Norton was silent. "But first we need to hold the place, so get those SAWs up there now."

"Yes, sir. I'm on it now."

"Very good, captain. Holm out." He looked up toward the hill, a commanding position that dominated the entire area. The lower slope was gentle, normally grassy, but now a torn up, muddy mess. The crest was rockier, with a few jagged outcroppings extending out, creating small cliffs. It was a hard position for regular troops to haul up heavy ordnance, but his armored Marines could carry the stuff up there on their backs.

"Captain Kahn, Holm here." He still hadn't gotten that casualty report yet. With an officer like Mike Kahn, that meant things were hot. "How's it going up there?"

"The federals are hitting us in force, sir." Kahn sounded a little harried, but still in control. "They're having a lot of trouble getting up the rocky band below the crest. We've inflicted heavy losses. Most of my people are in cover. We're in pretty good shape so far."

"Norton's sending you the battalion SAW teams." Holm knew damned well things were harder pressed than Kahn's report suggested. For one, he could see on his own display that at least six more of Kahn's troopers were offline. That didn't mean they were all dead, but their suits weren't transmitting their vitals anymore, and that wasn't a good thing. "Feed them in wherever you need them. They should give you plenty of extra firepower to hold the hill."

"Yes, sir. That will be a big help." He paused then added, "I can see the first couple teams now. They're just making their way up the lower slope."

"Keep me in the loop." Holm took a deep breath. "And captain...hold that hill. No matter what."

"Yes, sir. You can count on us." Kahn managed to sound convincing.

"Holm out." He looked around for a few seconds, and then he started walking toward Hill 109. His mind wandered back to a dozen times he'd scolded Cain about moving too far forward…but he kept on walking.

Jax stood on the front of the barge, looking out at the beach. What a mess, he thought. The federal artillery batteries were twisted wreckage, mangled chunks of blasted steel littering the rocky coastline.

Everyone expected it would be another day or two at least before Holm's people could get to the beach, but the general had seized the highest point on the northern end of the island and loaded it with mortars and heavy weapons. The Marines opened fire on the federal artillery positions, and their precision fire was like nothing the Alliance regulars had ever seen. Mortar rounds tore into the guns, tearing them apart, and heavy auto-cannons raked the area, gunning down the federal crews.

The Feds launched two counterattacks against the hill, but they were beaten back both times. A few hours after the last assault, the beaches were clear, the federal artillery completely silenced.

Jax and Marek had their people ready and waiting, and within thirty minutes, the first wave was moving toward the Carlisle coast. Now that Holm had secured the beaches, allowing Jax's people and the rebel army to cross the narrow strait, he'd diverted most of his forces back south to face a large federal counterattack. The remaining enemy forces on the northern half of the island were now the responsibility of Jax and Marek.

The rebels had only been on the Rock for a few days, and they were still exhausted and disorganized. But their morale was strong. The arrival of Holm and the Marines was a huge boost, and Marek's troops were straining to get back into the fight. The federals in the north had been roughly handled by the Marines, and they were disordered and scattered in separate groups. Jax and Marek immediately began launching search and destroy missions, trying to wipe out the federal pockets before they were able to reorganize and regroup.

The fighting was brutal, with few prisoners taken by either side, at least in the early stages. The federals had no line of retreat; they were cut off and forced to fight to the end. The attacking rebels were still low on supplies, but they were angry from their recent defeat, and they fell on the Feds anywhere they found them. It took a full day, and most of the next, but by nightfall on the second day the battle was over on the northern half of Carlisle, and every federal soldier had been killed or captured.

In the south, Holm's forces were slicing through the masses of federal troops, driving them steadily back. Losses were heavy, but finally the federals were pushed back onto invasion beaches. There was chaos as terrified soldiers threw down their arms and scrambled into whatever craft could carry them. Overloaded hovercraft attempted to lift off and head out over the sea, but many of them crashed into the roiling waves.

Finally, at dusk on the fifth day, the federal General Strom transmitted his unconditional surrender to Holm. Strom had deliberately bypassed Marek, preferring to deal with the Marine commander. But Holm refused, instructing the federal leader to treat with Marek. The Columbian forces had fought the whole war; this was their planet, and Holm respected what they had achieved. Strom had no choice – he surrendered the federal army to John Marek, and for the first time he was compelled to accord the rebel commander his Columbian rank of general.

"That fucking coward, Strom." Arlen Cooper had gotten himself on one of the escaping transports. He was packed in, surrounded by filthy, sweat-soaked Alliance soldiers. Command and control had broken down entirely. There were several thousand federal troops fleeing Carlisle for the mainland, but there was no authority, no discipline.

Most of the transports landed on the original embarkation beaches. They were overloaded, damaged, and low on fuel – very few of them could have gotten much farther. The mass of men and women on the beach was no longer an army. Most of them had thrown down their weapons when they ran for the loading hovercraft, and now they streamed inland, mindless, terrified, lost.

They didn't get far. Jill's refugees from the camp were everywhere, armed now and hunting down any federals they could find. They fell on the fleeing Alliance soldiers, most of whom tried futilely to surrender. But the mob had no mercy, no pity. They massacred every federal soldier they found...all save Cooper. The governor had the misfortune to be recognized, and he was taken to Weston in chains and dragged before Jill Winton. He was a pitiful, broken wreck, and he groveled and begged for his life.

Jill just stared down at him and laughed as he cried and screamed for mercy. Arlen Cooper had lived his entire life as a sadistic bully, and now he'd reached judgment day. Jill pulled her knife from the sheath on her belt and did the deed herself. Cooper's end was neither quick nor pleasant, and when she was done Jill sat in the middle of the bloodstained street and laughed hysterically.

Chapter 31

Confederation Hall
Ares Metroplex
Sol IV - Mars

There was a din in the air, the confused cacophony of a dozen separate conversations melding together. The meeting hall was vast, a magnificent testimonial to Martian engineering and wealth. The low gravity presented challenges to the health and day to day life of the Confederation's citizens, however it was nothing but a gift to its engineers and architects.

The talks between the Alliance and its rebellious colony worlds had been going on for weeks, and finally they were close to agreement. Both sides had entered with hardline positions. The Alliance refused to recognize any level of colonial independence, insisting that each world had to submit to any federal authority it elected to impose. That position wasn't supported by the military situation, but Alliance Gov had many ways to pressure its colonies beyond pure military force.

The colonies, so recently on the verge of total collapse, also entered with an aggressive position. Bolstered by the recent defeat of the federal forces on several of the major worlds, they insisted on total and immediate independence. Admiral Garret had rallied the navy, and after his experiences at the hands of Alliance Intelligence, he declared openly for the colonies. His forces hunted down and destroyed the well-equipped but inexperienced Directorate naval units, establishing total dominance over Alliance-occupied space.

Generals Holm and Cain had rallied the Marine units they were able to reach, leading them into action against the Alliance forces on Armstrong, Columbia, and Arcadia, winning total victories on each world. And the Directorate attacks on Marine garrisons were generally failures, the Marines emerging victorious in most of the encounters. With Garret's fleet and Holm's and Cain's Marines standing with them, the colonial representatives felt strong, and they made harsh demands of the Alliance diplomats…demands that just led to a bitter impasse.

That's where Vance and his diplomats came in, pointing out to both sides the enormous weaknesses they were overlooking. The Alliance faced disaster without its colonies; even from a protracted stalemate. Stripped of the flow of extraterrestrial resources, the already tottering economy would collapse utterly, with severe and unpredictable consequences. The death throes of a Superpower, especially one as large and powerful as the Alliance, could even destroy the Treaty of Paris and start war on Earth again, and that was something no one wanted.

The colonies had their own problems as well, which Vance's team pointed out in great detail. They had the Marines and the navy backing them; that much was true. But the Marine Corps was shattered, its widespread garrisons unsupplied and demoralized. It would take time – and considerable resources – to rebuild it back to its former capabilities. Those resources – the weapons, armor, and ammunition a modern fighting force required – could only come from Earth. The colonies lacked the manufacturing capability to produce such high-tech items in any quantity. A Marine Corps backing the colonies without Alliance support would quickly find itself starved of almost every material item it required to function.

The navy was no better off. Garret had been forced to hunt down and destroy the Directorate-controlled ships, suffering considerable losses in the process. The massive post-war surplus of ships was gone, and there were barely enough functional vessels to patrol and provide basic defense…if they were lucky. There were shipyards in the colonies, most notably in the Wolf 359 system, orbiting one of Arcadia's sister planets. But those shipyards were assembly areas, and they still required sophisticated weapons, computers, engines – systems that could only be built now in Earth factories.

The colonies and the military could become self-sufficient, but it would take years, probably decades. And that was time they wouldn't have. Already, the other Superpowers, especially the CAC and Caliphate, were ready to pounce on newly independent worlds...planets without the resources to mount a sustained defense. Without the strength of the Alliance behind them, the colony worlds would be picked apart by the other Powers. They would win freedom only to lose it again almost immediately.

The Confederation Agreement was Vance's brainchild, patterned loosely after the structure of the Martian Superpower's own founding documents. It was a solution that made almost no one happy, which he considered a good sign.

The Alliance's colonies were to be guaranteed immediate and permanent self-rule. The Alliance government would have no involvement whatsoever in the internal affairs of the colony worlds, provided the new planetary republics adhered to their obligations under the Agreement.

The colonies agreed to recognize the authority of Alliance Gov to negotiate with all foreign powers, and to be bound to such policies as it may establish. The colonies would be allowed limited trade with each other, but all other interplanetary commerce was regulated by the Alliance.

The Marine Corps and navy were to be reformed. The Marine Charter was reaffirmed and strengthened, explicitly setting forth the rights and obligations of the Corps in greater detail. The navy, which had not been governed by such a document, would henceforth have its own charter, clarifying its rights and obligations. The two services would no longer be part of the terrestrial Alliance Joint Chiefs of Staff. A civilian oversight panel would manage the two services. Initially, half of the members of the group would be named by Alliance Gov, the other half by the colonies. In ten years the ratio would shift to 2/3 named by the colonies. The top military command would be a new board, consisting of two senior officers from each branch. The first Chairman would be Augustus Garret, elected by unanimous vote of the senior officers in both the navy and the Corps.

The colonies were to elect a Confederation Council, which would manage all inter-colony affairs not governed by the Alliance under the Agreement. The individual planets would form their own local governments, subject to the terms of the Colonial Constitution, which was set to be negotiated on Armstrong as soon as the Confederation Agreement was signed. But before it could be signed there were days and days more ahead, filled mostly with useless prattle and arguments. Such is the way diplomacy grinds slowly forward.

Vance sat in his office and considered how things had worked out. The end result was, in no small part, the result of his machinations. The colonials would have lost if Mars hadn't intervened, of that much he was certain. Gavin Stark's plans were masterful, and if they'd been allowed to continue, he would have controlled the navy and destroyed the Marine Corps. The Alliance would have ruled its colony worlds with an iron fist, strengthening its position even further from the preeminent status it had achieved in the last war. All of the Superpowers would have been threatened by the disruption to the balance of power.

Now the Alliance was weakened, forced to constantly negotiate with its unruly and partially independent colonies. Its armed forces were severely degraded. Indeed, in a perverse twist of fate, its navy had been compelled to hunt down and destroy many of its newest ships. And the Marine Corps was shaken to its very foundations by the treachery of General Samuels... though Vance didn't doubt that General Holm and his able commanders would quickly restore the morale and effectiveness of the organization.

He was satisfied overall. A dangerous situation had worked itself out, at least temporarily, and some level of stability had been restored. It was all short term, of course. The Alliance Directorate was already taking steps to build its own interstellar military, which they would undoubtedly use to force a rematch with the colonies one day. And the colony worlds bristled at their continued ties to Alliance Gov, no matter how much they knew deep down they needed them. One day, they too would revisit the Confederation Agreement and look to assert true independence. But that was at least ten years away, and probably longer. Neither side had close to the resources and capabilities to defeat the other in the near term.

Perhaps the greatest master stroke was the seizure of Epsilon Eridani IV. The Martian forces took control and immediately invited all of the Superpowers to send a garrison and a scientific team. Vance could only imagine Gavin Stark's rage when he got the word. But there was nothing Stark could do. Mars had immediately opened the system up to all, and if the Alliance wanted to take back sole control they would find themselves facing the rest of the Powers, all unified. It was brilliantly handled, and even Vance had to give himself credit for the flawless execution.

He looked through the dome to the untamed Martian surface. They had been terraforming the planet for fifty years, but he would be dead and gone before men could leave the domes and walk on those reddish hills without breathers and pressure suits. Technology, he thought...we are so advanced in some ways, yet in other it feels as though we've so far to go. Where would Epsilon Eridani IV lead them? Stark had been promulgating the absurd idea that the massive facility was some type of religious shrine, but Vance knew that was propaganda nonsense.

His intelligence was clear. In all likelihood, the structure on Carson's World was an anti-matter production facility...a big one. Man could produce anti-matter too, but in miniscule quantities and at prohibitive cost. But by all accounts, the alien artifact had once produced massive amounts, harnessing the planet's seismic energy to do it. It was as far ahead of mankind as a mag rifle was from a sling.

Someone built that, Vance thought with equal amounts of wonder and trepidation. We need to harness that technology, and we need to do it for all mankind, not for Gavin Stark's power games. Someone built that, he thought again. "And we have no idea what else is out there." His words were softly spoken, just for himself. "No idea at all."

Chapter 32

Astria City
Armstrong - Gamma Pavonis III

Jack Winton walked out into the bright sunshine. It was spring on Armstrong, and the weather had been perfect. He'd never been to the massive Marine hospital before, and it had been a sight to see. As big as it already was, there was construction underway on a massive expansion. Armstrong had been chosen to host the combined military establishment of the new Alliance Colonial Confederation, and there was construction everywhere.

Jack was smiling, for the first time in a long time. Jill was responding to her treatments, finally. She had a long road to full recovery, but when he'd first seen her in Weston he had given up hope his daughter would ever come back from the psychotic break she'd suffered. He struggled whenever he thought of how she must have suffered in that camp, what horrendous deprivation and torment it must have taken to turn her into what she'd become.

The mobs had killed thousands – innocent Columbians as well as federals. They had branded any who lived under federal rule as collaborators, and hundreds of people, whose only offense was living quietly and staying unnoticed, were dragged into the streets and murdered.

When the rebel troops and Holm's Marines liberated Weston, they found the city a ghost town full of horrors. There were bodies everywhere, lying unattended where they'd been killed. The mob had started to come apart, people wandering around in a state of near shock. They were broken men and women, driven past the point of rationality by Cooper's brutality, and in their despair they had acted no better than the hated governor himself.

Jack found his daughter, sitting alone against a half-wrecked building. He ran to her, but she looked at him without emotion, without recognition. He kept calling her name, but she just stared at him, through him really. Finally, Sarah Linden and her people began tending to the refugees. They weren't trained in psychiatry, but they did the best they could until Admiral Garret was able to land specialists from the fleet.

There was no liberation for the camps in the other areas of Columbia. When the rebels reached the facilities in Hampton and Southpoint they found everyone dead. Cooper's orders had been carried out with ruthless efficiency. The camp guards were gone by then, but General Marek had issued a death sentence on all of them, and he dispatched a large portion of the rebel army to hunt them down. It would take months, years maybe, to get them all, but he vowed they would pay.

But Jack Winton wouldn't be there to see it. He felt he had to get away from Columbia...start new somewhere. And he couldn't imagine going back to operating a transport business, no matter how successful it was. Admiral Garret made him an offer to rejoin the reorganized navy at flag rank, as head of logistics and supply, and he accepted immediately. A massive new job was just what he needed, and he'd be posted on Armstrong, where he could be near Jill and help with her recovery.

The navy was restructuring in a number of ways, rebuilding, moving facilities. Things were likely to be very busy for a long time. Jack would have more work than he could handle, which meant less time to think about what had happened. And that was just the way he wanted it.

Armstrong's yellow primary had just about set, and the capital city was beginning its extended twilight – the three hours before the red secondary also slipped beneath the horizon and the real night began.

The great Marine hospital had long been the only major installation on the planet, but the war years had seen a massive development boom. Armstrong wasn't as big as Columbia or Arcadia, or even Atlantia. But it was on the verge of taking its place as one of the major worlds of the new Colonial Confederation. Its new role as home to the main Alliance/Colonial military headquarters would insure its continued progress into the top tier of worlds.

Its ranking just below the planets of the first order made it an ideal place for the Constitutional Convention that was set to convene the following month – large enough to host the delegations, but small enough to prevent rivalries between the major worlds.

The Hotel Armstrong had been about to open when revolution swept the planet, forcing commerce to a halt. Now the damage it had suffered during the street fighting had been repaired, and the Armstrong was ready for business; at least most of it was…there was still last minute work going on in one of the wings.

The dining room hadn't opened yet, though for one night a private suite had hastily been put into use. A group, mostly old friends and some new, were gathered together. Responsibilities and duty would soon call them off in different directions, but for tonight they were all in one place. They were there to celebrate the end of the fighting and to bid farewell to other friends, for this war, like those before it, had left its share of empty chairs at their table.

"I am glad you could all be here tonight." Elias Holm wore a brand new gray dress uniform, and on each collar was a cluster of five platinum stars, the rank insignia of the Commandant of the reconstituted Marine Corps. The uniform wasn't all that different from the old one, but the design had been tinkered with a little, as if the slight changes somehow announced that things were different now. "There is an old quote; I read it long ago at the Academy. I have always remembered it, and I think it serves particularly well now. I'd like to share it with all of you." He paused for an instant. "It is not tolerable, it is not possible, that from so much death, so much sacrifice and ruin, so much heroism, a greater and better humanity shall not emerge."

He looked around the table, a grim smile on his face. 'That passage always resonated with me. Not only because of the sentiments expressed, but also the context. The quote is three centuries old, and I think most of us would agree, a better humanity did not emerge. At least not on Earth." He paused briefly, allowing those present to consider what he had said.

"We have fought and struggled and bled together, but we are not the first to do so, nor shall we be the last." He looked around the room, at those assembled, all warriors in one way or another. "Let us remember as we go forward from this day that we must fight, not just here and now, but always...each and every day...so that a better humanity emerges at last. Let us never forget that words alone achieve nothing lasting, and only our ceaseless vigilance can safeguard the future we so earnestly long for."

Holm raised his glass. "To a new future."

"To a new future," they all repeated, holding glasses high.

Cain spoke next, his voice somber. "The chance for that future was purchased, as always for such things, by blood and sacrifice. Thousands died so that the colonies might have this chance at freedom. William Thompson, my first friend in the Corps." He glanced over at John Marek, who was sitting silently across the table. "Lucius Anton, one of the finest Marines...and men...I have ever known." His eyes moved further down, settling on Jax. The big Marine was wearing his own new uniform, just like Holms', but with a single platinum star on each collar. "Edward Sawyer, another hero of the Corps." He paused, his voice wavering slightly. "The cadets, faculty, and staff of the Academy." The room was silent. To die in battle was one thing, but the horrific attack on the Academy seemed so pointless, so wasteful, it had been especially difficult for them to accept. Cain raised his glass above his head. "To the honored dead...and to friends lost."

Everyone rose, holding glasses high and repeating Cain's words. "To the honored dead, and to friends lost." They were silent for a few minutes, each thinking of brothers and sisters now gone...in this war as well as others they had fought.

Augustus Garret finally broke the silence. "The greatest way we can honor the memory of those who were lost is to protect that which they fought so bravely for. Some of you saw this coming." His eyes fixed on Cain. "However, I did not. I have always considered myself to be aloof from politics, an attitude I now realize has been naïve."

He scanned the table as he spoke. "I have tended to think of enemies in military terms – fleets and armies to be defeated in battle. But I have seen my beloved navy nearly seized from within by the machinations of those who would be our puppet masters." Garret's mouth was slightly clenched. He was trying his best to stay calm, but the thought of Gavin Stark's scheme still enraged him. "As you, my friends, have seen your own Marine Corps nearly destroyed by treachery." His eyes moved across the table, pausing for an instant as he faced each of the Marines present. "Indeed, both forces have paid the cost, in suffering and in needless death."

Garret inhaled and let out a soft sigh. "Let us never forget that those responsible for much of what has happened are still alive…still in power and likely plotting even now. Gavin Stark is still the head of Alliance Intelligence, and Rafael Samuels is now openly a member of the Directorate." Garret was restraining his anger with very limited success. "The realities of the current situation do not afford us the chance to pursue justice or a meaningful resolution, at least not now. Though we are here to celebrate the peace, let us never forget that it is but a brief truce. Let us remain vigilant and ready, for our enemies shall strike us again one day." He stared out over the table, but his eyes were looking past all those present. "And, by God, we will be ready."

Terrance Compton stood up and put his hand on his friend's shoulder. "Your words are wise, Augustus, and I believe everyone here agrees completely." He swallowed hard, not anxious to say what he intended to say. "Perhaps the worst thing our enemies have done to us is to compel us to become more like them." Everyone was looking at Compton, unsure where he was going with his comments. "We must rebuild the navy and the Marine Corps, and when we do we must never forget that both organizations were infiltrated by our enemies."

Compton paused. "As we move forward we must purge our forces of anyone who is suspect." He could feel the reaction in the room. They didn't want to agree with him, but they all did.

"We need not fear the enemy who launches himself against our defended gates, but rather the one who would sneak in and poison our soup. We must never be so easily and totally infiltrated again."

Cain sat and listened. He agreed totally. He was unquestionably the most paranoid person in the room, though since his abduction, Admiral Garret was sounding an awful lot like Erik Cain when he spoke. Cain knew this was only a brief respite in a struggle that would never end. But it was a step forward, and if he...and those in this room...pushed boldly forward into the future, maybe that future would be a fit place to live. As long as they never let their guard down.

"You are right, Terrance." Garret spoke up. "We must be vigilant, now and always. Let us never forget. Let us never let each other forget." Garret paused for a moment and then let a smile creep onto his face. "But for now, my friends, drink with me to our new Colonial Confederation." He held his glass over the table and watched as his friends and comrades did the same. "We shall make it something we can be proud of."

They spoke as they had fought and struggled...as one. "To the Confederation."

It was deep into the Armstrong night, and two lovers were out for a stroll. The riverwalk through the center of Astria wasn't finished yet, but the parts that were open were very picturesque, perfect for romantic interludes.

Erik looked up at the night sky, the darkness mitigated by the glowing light of Armstrong's moons. "Three moons...what more could you want for a seduction scene. And they are all almost full. They must have some local name for that...when the moons are all full."

Sarah Linden stood next to Erik, her hands lightly grasping his arm. "You don't need any moons at all, you silly Marine. And you know that." She glanced up and gave him a smile before her eyes panned over the river, watching the ghostly white moonlight dancing slowly on the calm water.

Sarah had been distraught when Erik went to Earth, certain

she'd never see him again. She'd almost burst into tears when General Holm arrived on Columbia and told her he was just fine. She was disappointed he was on Arcadia, but thrilled he had made it off of Earth.

She'd almost had a stroke when she saw the state of his shoulder, which had never been properly treated between his rapid series of battles and adventures. She barely allowed time for a hug and a few kisses before she dragged him to the hospital and had him in surgery. Courtship rituals vary considerably, especially when you're dating the best trauma surgeon in the Marine Corps.

This was another of their brief moments, their time together between the wars and disasters that separated them, sometimes for years. They had a relationship few people could have endured, but they had only grown closer with the passing years.

"You know this isn't going to last forever." Erik put his hand to Sarah's head, stroking her long, blond hair as he spoke. "I was ready to leave the Corps before all of this happened." He hesitated, clearly having trouble with what he wanted to say. "Maybe we should resign now. We deserve some peace, some real time together."

She smiled, but she was silent for a moment, fighting the urge to agree with him. Nothing would make her happier than the two of them spending the rest of their lives walking the beaches and forests of Atlantia or some other pleasant world. But that wasn't their destiny, and they both knew it.

"You know we can't do that." There was sadness in her voice, but also contentment. She might have lived her life truly alone if a CAC nuke hadn't send a shattered Erik Cain to her hospital. She and Cain both carried deep scars, and they complimented each other perfectly. They healed each other's wounds when everyone else tore them open. Everything she hid from others she shared with him. "Could you be happy knowing we abandoned our friends when they needed us? That we stepped aside when we finally had the chance to build a better future?"

He looked at her and smiled. "No, you know I couldn't. No more than you could." He pulled her closer, hugging her tightly.

"But let's make sure we build a place for ourselves in that new future."

She tightened her arms, feeling his warmth against her. "That, my love, is a promise."

Chapter 33

Independence Square
Arcadia (City)
Arcadia – Wolf 359 III

Kara sat on the cool grass holding little William as she gazed at the statue. It was a beautiful day under Arcadia's red sun, and there was a calm and a joyfulness in the air that had been absent for far too long.

She felt the calm, but while she loved her son and was grateful to have him, she couldn't feel the joy. The loss was still too fresh, too raw, and she felt an emptiness she wasn't sure would ever go away.

The Assembly had declared it a day of Thanksgiving. Henceforth, this date would be the most solemn one on the Arcadian calendar. Not a rousing, celebratory event with fireworks and bands...the Arcadians had paid heavily for their freedom, and this day would henceforth be dedicated to remembering those whose sacrifices had made it possible.

She looked up at the statue. It was a remarkable likeness, even she had to admit. She wiped a tear from her cheek and wondered if she would ever be able to come here without crying. The dedication ceremony had been the hardest; she still didn't know how she'd gotten through it. Kyle Warren and the rest of the Marine vets gave a moving tribute to their fallen leader, one that tore away her veneer of strength and left her quietly sobbing as she sat and listened.

She watched William crawling around, laughing. My God, she thought, he is already starting to look just like Will. "Your father was a great man, little one. You never got to meet him; he never got to hold you in his arms. When he was your age he lived in a terrible place, and he gave all he had so you could grow up somewhere better." She sniffled, unsuccessfully fighting to hold back her tears. "He never even knew he was going to have a son." She could feel the wetness on her cheeks, the tears streaming down her face. "His name will be remembered, and people will come here for generations and sit by this statue and point up and say, 'there is the hero of the revolution.' But he was more than that, more than the Arcadians who come here and pay their respects will ever know."

She pulled William close to her, feeling the warmth of her son against her body. He was the only thing that eased her pain. It helped her to speak to him of his father, though he was too young to understand what she was saying. "Glory is a veneer that reflects the light only from a distance. Up close you can see through it, to bitter price paid in pain and death." She looked up, past the tufts of William's blond hair, to the statue. "You will have glory forever, my love, and thousands – millions – of people will have a future of hope because of what you did." Her throat was raw and her red eyes ached from crying. "You died alone, in the mud of the battlefield, without even my hand on your face for comfort. Forgive me...for not being there, for the years I wasted when we might have been together...for living and going on without you."

She stood up, scooping William into her arms. "I will come back here on this day...every day until I die. And I will make sure your son never forgets his father. Not just the hero all Arcadians will know, but the grape farmer, the man who wanted nothing more than to settle down and live his life in peace."

The Assembly had unanimously asked her to assume Will's seat, but she had said no. She just couldn't do it. She would come to the constitutional convention; she would be there to insure that all that Will had fought for was codified and enacted...that no new generation of politicians would ever be allowed to usurp the freedoms Will Thompson had fought to preserve. But then she swore she was done with government and politics and war. All she wanted to do was take her son back home to Concordia, to see that he grew up happy and healthy in the world his father had died to create.

Gregory Sanders walked across the grass, still limping along on his cane but otherwise recovered from his wounds. The federals had treated him well, and he'd been released immediately after the truce was signed. Greg had wanted to go to Mars himself as Arcadia's representative, but in the end he'd sent Kyle Warren instead. He was just too old to make the trip, as much as he tried to ignore the constraints of mortality. Besides, he wasn't about to leave Kara alone, not after all she'd been through.

He saw Kara sitting, holding little William, and he flashed her a warm smile. The new prime minister of Arcadia paused and looked up at the statue. He, too, felt Will's loss acutely. "Well, my friend, we did what we set out to do, more or less." The Confederation Agreement didn't provide for true colonial independence, but it did guarantee the rights of the colonies to manage their own internal affairs without interference. It was a good result, the best they realistically could have achieved now. "We couldn't have gotten here without you."

One day, Sanders thought, still staring up at Thompson's likeness, they will come again and try to take back what we have gained by blood and sacrifice. If they do, he swore to himself, they will pay a heavy price, at least on Arcadia. He prayed his people would never again live under an oppressive government, though in the back of his mind there were doubts. Would they be able to avoid the mistakes the people of Earth had made? They had their chance at freedom too, and they lost it – some would say they threw it away. Would Arcadians five or ten generations from now appreciate what they inherited? Or would they go down the same path to tyranny? Only the march of time would tell.

For now, Gregory Sanders put his arm around his granddaughter and his great-grandson, and they all turned and walked slowly across the field, leaving behind the great bronze statue and its simple inscription, stenciled in platinum: General William Thompson, Father of the Republic of Arcadia.

Chapter 34

Willard Hotel
Washbalt Core
Washbalt Metroplex, Earth

Gavin Stark sat on the edge of the bed, the satin sheets, moist with perspiration, clinging to his legs and lower back. His face was grim, his stare focused on nothing really, just an imaginary point in space. His thoughts were dark, blacker even than those that normally dwelt in the sociopathic recesses of his twisted mind. His waking dream was one of vengeance.

Alex Linden was lying partially under the sheet, the rumpled material arranged over her naked body in just the right places, a tool of seduction she employed almost unconsciously. She was silent, her head propped up on the pillow, watching Stark carefully. She reached toward his shoulder but pulled her hand back. He'd been jumpy since Dutton's death...less predictable, more brutal even than before. She'd never realized just how much he had relied on the old man, and she was worried. It seemed to her that Stark, always tightly wound, was on the verge of truly snapping. What that could mean - for her, for the others in Alliance Intelligence, for God knows who else - she could only guess.

"It is fortuitous that we delayed reuniting you with your long-lost sister. It will prove far more useful to our current needs." Stark's voice was calm, but it was different than before. Stark had always been ruthless, unrestrained by typical ethical and moral constraints, but not really sadistic. He didn't hesitate to use torture, but he didn't especially enjoy it either. He just wanted results, and he didn't care how he got them. Now, though, she could hear the rage, the darkness...the madness.

He looked at her, his face slightly contorted despite his efforts to hide his fiery anger. "General Cain will undoubtedly be among the inner circle of the reformed Marine Corps." She could see his hand, partially hidden by the sheet. It was balled into a tight fist, the veins in his lower arm protruding. "We can now arrange a reunion with your dear sister, putting you in a perfect position to gain intel on their activities."

Alex just looked at him attentively as he spoke. He was too unpredictable right now; she wasn't willing to chance offering any real input, not until she knew what he had in mind.

"They think this is over, these rebel vermin." He'd be damned if he was going to call them Confederates, despite the Confederation Agreement the President had signed. Been forced to sign. "But this is merely an interlude. They will pay, all of them…and those interfering Martians too." His voice was thick with hatred. "They will pay if I have to exterminate every one of them and repopulate those worlds."

Alex just listened, nodding slightly whenever Stark looked back over his shoulder at her. She didn't particularly disagree with what he was saying, though she couldn't imagine what options they would have…at least for a number of years. It would take a long time to build enough Directorate-controlled military force to take on and defeat the colonies, especially with the navy and the re-organized Marines protecting them. Meanwhile, they were just going to have to undermine the new Colonial Confederation however they could and bide their time.

"We know that your sister is Cain's lover. Reuniting you with her will give you access to him as well. I want you to use that… I want you to become an expert in their organization, deployments…everything. When the time is right we will be prepared."

His voice was becoming louder, more brittle. She didn't particularly relish the idea of spending what could be years among the earnest, and now partially independent, colonials, but she couldn't argue with the logic of the assignment. She would be well-positioned to get valuable intelligence, and she didn't doubt there would eventually be a rematch between Alliance Gov and its wayward colonies.

She had mixed feelings about seeing her sister again. Alex had been eight years old the last time she'd seen Sarah – the day the men had come to take her away. Her beautiful older sister had attracted the eye of a powerful politician, and her resistance to his advances brought ruin to the entire family. Alex hated her for what she had done, now as much as then. If Sarah had gone along, Alex thought, if she'd willingly agreed, the entire family would have benefited. Instead, their mother and father ended up dead, and Alex was left alone to survive in the urban wastelands. She still had nightmares of some of the things she'd had to do to survive back then. She got through it all and clawed her way to power and privilege...all the while thinking her hated older sister was dead. Until the day Gavin Stark told her otherwise.

"It is Cain and his cohorts who are the architects of our misfortune. Had we held control of the navy for six months more we would have crushed the rebellion." Stark's voice dripped with searing hatred when he mentioned Cain. "Now we will use him for information...information we will utilize to destroy his new Marine Corps, and the miserable dustball worlds it is so determined to defend." He paused for a long moment, glaring the entire time at the same imaginary spot.

Finally, he broke the silence. "I know you want the Second Seat." He twisted his torso so he was facing her. "I want you to complete this mission. And I want you to do one more thing for me before you are finished." He paused, just for a second. "If you do, I will name you Number Two."

She'd had her eyes on Dutton's Seat for as long as she could remember, wanting it, aching for the power and prestige. Alex was a master at controlling herself, but she couldn't suppress her reaction completely, not for this thing she had wanted for so long. Stark smiled; he knew he had her.

"What is it you want me to do?" Her voice was strong, firm. She wasn't going to let the Second Seat slip away...not when she'd waited so long for that detestable old fool to die. Not when it put her one very fragile heartbeat away from total power.

His eyes bored right into hers, and she could see the insanity behind them. "I want you to kill Erik Cain."

Crimson Worlds Series

www.crimsonworlds.com

Made in the USA
Lexington, KY
07 August 2014